Praise for Laur...
the Scandal at...

"The best in historical romance!"
—Julia Quinn, *New York Times* bestselling
author of the Bridgerton series

"Laura Lee Guhrke has a lively style that sizzles."
—Jane Feather, *New York Times* bestselling author

## *BOOKSHOP CINDERELLA*

"Packed with chemistry and fun, this is a fairy tale treat."
—*Publishers Weekly*, starred review

"It has been a while since Guhrke's last superbly written historical romance, but her latest artfully constructed
literary confection is well worth the wait. George Bernard
Shaw himself would appreciate Guhrke's clever riff on his
classic, *Pygmalion*, not to mention her sprightly prose and
sparkling, champagne-fizzy wit."
—*Booklist*, starred review

"A promising start to a cheery new Victorian romance
series."
—*Kirkus*

"A great mix of wit and attraction as opposites clash and
romance blooms."
—*Library Journal*

# Bookshop Cinderella

# ALSO BY LAURA LEE GUHRKE

**Scandal at the Savoy Series**

*Lady Scandal*

# Bookshop Cinderella

## LAURA LEE GUHRKE

FOREVER
New York   Boston

Forever
Hachette Book Group
1290 Avenue of the Americas, New York, NY 10104
read-forever.com
@readforeverpub

Originally published in trade paperback and ebook by Grand Central Publishing in June 2023
First mass market edition: May 2024

Forever is an imprint of Grand Central Publishing. The Forever name and logo are registered trademarks of Hachette Book Group, Inc.

The publisher is not responsible for websites (or their content) that are not owned by the publisher.

The Hachette Speakers Bureau provides a wide range of authors for speaking events. To find out more, go to hachettespeakersbureau.com or email HachetteSpeakers@hbgusa.com.

Forever books may be purchased in bulk for business, educational, or promotional use. For information, please contact your local bookseller or the Hachette Book Group Special Markets Department at special.markets@hbgusa.com.

ISBNs: 978-1-5387-6867-9 (mass market), 978-1-5387-2263-3 (ebook)

Printed in the United States of America

BVGM

10  9  8  7  6  5  4  3  2  1

*For the incomparable Sophie Jordan.*
*She knows why.*

# 1

*London, 1896*

"Darling Max, just the man I need!"

Maximillian Shaw didn't have to turn his head to recognize the owner of the feminine voice murmuring so persuasively in his ear. "Delia? What a delightful surprise."

He set aside the newspaper he'd been reading and turned, smiling into the piquant face of his favorite cousin. "Even though it's clear you're about to cage a favor."

Unrepentant, Delia bestowed a dazzling smile on him. "I've gotten myself into a terrible pickle, Max, and I need your help. I realize that asking favors of a duke is the height of impertinence—"

"As if that's ever stopped you before," he cut in wryly.

Still smiling, she leaned closer, the wide brim of her hat raking over the crown of his head and ruffling his dark hair. "It's nothing difficult," she promised and gave his cheek an affectionate pat, seemingly oblivious to the fact that they were in the foyer of the Savoy, London's most luxurious hotel. "A mere trifle."

Max knew well the dangers of participating in Delia's

so-called trifles. A year younger than him, she'd been embroiling him in her schemes almost from the moment she learned to walk. "The last time you said something like that," he said, standing up as she came around to the front of his chair, "I ended up with a bloody nose and a black eye."

She waved away his discomfort over the occasion in question with an airy gesture of her hand. "All part of our misspent youth. May I join you?" she added before he could reply, nodding to the empty chair to his right.

It would never have occurred to Max to object. Doing favors for Delia did tend to land a chap in trouble, but he liked a bit of trouble now and again; and besides, he'd never been able to turn his back on a beauty in distress.

"I'd be delighted to help, of course. Shall we have tea and talk about it?" he added, gesturing to the Savoy's famous dining room nearby. "Or would you prefer the American Bar? Frank is probably on duty by now. We could have him mix us some delectable new libations."

"Women aren't allowed in the American Bar," Delia reminded him, making a face that clearly conveyed her opinion of that particular rule.

"The bar isn't open yet, so Frank won't mind."

"Do stop tempting me with these delights. I've no time for cocktails or tea. Not today. I've only half an hour to get to Charing Cross station or I shall miss my train for Dover." Despite those words, she sank into the empty chair beside his. "I'm just waiting for my maid and the bellman to bring my luggage down," she went on, casting a glance past him down the length of the Savoy's opulent foyer. "Then I'm off to the Continent."

"The Continent, eh?" he echoed as he resumed his own seat. "Pleasure or business?"

"Both, of course. If work didn't amuse me, I'd never do it."

That, Max reflected, was undoubtedly true. After all, it wasn't as if Delia needed an income. Her third husband had left her an absolute packet when he died. No, she chose to work for her own amusement, though Max was rather at sea as to just what her job entailed. Something for the hotel, reporting to César Ritz himself, with duties that involved parties, shopping, and the exercise of considerable charm—a post tailor-made for his cousin, in other words. "So, what is this favor?" he asked. "And why can't you do it yourself, if it's so trifling?"

"But I've just told you! I haven't the time. César called me in an hour ago and ordered me at once to Rome—some sort of disaster at his new hotel there. Only César would think it a perfectly simple thing to manage four hotels in four countries simultaneously. Anyway, I warned him he was stretching himself too thin and offered to help with the other hotels as well as this one, and he's finally decided to give me a chance, so I'm off to Rome. But I was in such a flutter to pack that it was only as I was coming down in the lift that I remembered I'd also made a promise to help Auguste. It's a promise I've now no time to fulfill, and when I spied you sitting here in the lobby, it was like the answer to all my prayers."

"Auguste Escoffier?" Max shook his head, bewildered by the mention of the Savoy's famous head chef. "Delia, we both know I enjoy an excellent meal, but I know nothing about how such meals are prepared. In a pinch, I might be able to boil an egg," he offered dubiously. "Though I doubt anyone would want to eat it."

"You don't have to cook anything," she assured him, laughing. "Now, listen. Auguste has this banquet for the

Epicurean Club coming up in three weeks—enormous affair, over a hundred people—members, their wives, even the Prince of Wales."

"I know. I'm a member of that club, and I've already received my invitation."

"Yes, exactly." Delia beamed at him with all the delight of a child who'd just been handed a present. "Which is why you're the perfect person to aid Auguste in my stead. As you know, the Epicurean Club always presents an array of exciting new dishes at these affairs, which is why they hold them here at the Savoy. Auguste has been racking his brain about what to serve, but he's just as overworked as César these days, poor pet, and his ingenuity is sapped."

Not a surprising bit of news when one considered that the Savoy's dining room had become the most popular and fashionable restaurant for every aristocrat within a thousand miles, and the culinary brilliance of its head chef had been in continual high demand for over five years now. Still, if Escoffier was suffering a bout of creative drought, Max didn't see what he could do to assist in alleviating it. "The price of success for both of them, I fear."

"Just so. Auguste has asked for my help to create the menu. And he wants me to plan the decorations, order the flowers, that sort of thing. So, of course, I set Evie Harlow onto it at once."

This mention of someone entirely unfamiliar sparked Max's curiosity. "Evie who?"

"Evie Harlow. She owns a bookshop near here and does research for me when I'm planning one of these affairs. She's a marvel. Do you remember that banquet a few years ago for the Edelweiss Club? The one that was such a sensation because of the flowers?"

"Not really, since I'm not a member of that club. And I can't imagine how mere flowers could cause a sensation, but I'm sure you'll enlighten me."

"Not just any flowers," she corrected. "Edelweiss. It only grows in the highest mountain regions. I wanted it for the table decorations, and how on earth was I to find it, I ask you? Climb the Alps and pick it myself?"

The picture made him want to smile, for Delia's notions of athletic endeavor were limited to walking (in fashionable clothes along fashionable thoroughfares), driving (with a chauffeur), and waltzing (usually with the best-looking, richest men in the room). "That would be ridiculous," he agreed.

If Delia perceived the amusement beneath his grave reply, she didn't show it. "But Evie managed to procure some for me. How she did it, I still don't know."

"I begin to see why you have such a reputation as a canny shopper."

"Oh, dear, I've given myself away now, haven't I? But Evie really is a marvel. What I'd do without her, I can't imagine. Anyway, for the Epicurean Club, she and I have dreamed up a theme of the Far East, and she's promised to find me some exotic recipes from that part of the world. She mentioned a dish of chicken feet, if you can believe it."

Max stared, not certain he'd heard correctly. "Chicken feet?"

"We discussed various soups as well—one made from birds' nests and another from shark fins."

Max had always considered himself an adventurous sort of chap, always willing to try new things, which was why he was a member of the Epicurean Club, but the food she was describing might be a bridge too far, even for him. "How...ahem...exotic."

Delia smiled, showing the fetching dimples in her cheeks. "It's not to my taste, but Evie assures me these are prized delicacies in Peking."

Max wasn't sure he found that particularly reassuring.

"In addition to the recipes," Delia continued, "she's also promised me a list of merchants who can provide the ingredients, and ideas for the table decorations and flowers. But she's late with the information, which isn't at all like her, and I'm growing concerned. I had thought to pop by and see her this afternoon, but now that I'm off to Rome, I can't manage it. So, I'm hoping I can persuade you to call on her, pick up the information she's compiled, and take it to Auguste."

Max felt a bit let down. Delia's requests weren't usually so mundane. "I'm a duke, Delia, not a footman."

"A good thing, since a footman would be of no use at all. I don't need someone merely to fetch and carry. I need someone who can work with a great chef like Escoffier, who can take the information Evie's compiled and use it to help him craft the perfect menu. That requires someone with a vast knowledge and appreciation of fine cuisine, someone of taste and discernment—"

"Stop trying to butter me up, Cousin," he interrupted. "It never works."

"It always works," she corrected, laughing. "But in this case, I'm not buttering you up. You truly are the perfect person to act in my stead. You're a member of that club, and you've attended many affairs of this kind."

Despite his membership, Max didn't see how he was the least bit suited to judge the epicurean quality of chicken feet, birds' nests, and shark fins, but he had no chance to say so.

"César, darling!" Delia exclaimed, looking past him,

and when Max turned in his seat, he saw Ritz himself coming toward them.

A dapper little man with an enormous mustache, a receding hairline, and a bit of a limp due to his habit of wearing shoes a half size too small, Ritz also had deep lines of exhaustion in his face that bore out Delia's assessment. Running four large hotels in four different countries was clearly wearing the man to a nub.

"You've met my cousin, of course?" Delia went on as Ritz paused beside where they sat. "The Duke of Westbourne?"

"I have had that honor, yes." Ritz bowed. "Your Grace, we are delighted you have come to stay with us for the London season."

Max almost groaned aloud as this bit of information slipped from Ritz's lips. Given that Delia worked for the hotel, it was inevitable that she would learn of his plans, but he'd hoped to at least have the chance to unpack before she pounced on him with questions. Still, the damage was done, and as Ritz bid his farewells and departed, he faced the avid gleam of curiosity in his cousin's eyes with a resigned sigh.

"You're in town for the entire season?" she asked. "This isn't just a quick trip to vote on something important in the Lords, attend the banquet, and see a few old friends? Goodness," she added as he shook his head, "I believe the planets have just stilled in their courses."

"Really, Delia," he said with good-humored exasperation, "you needn't sound so shocked. I have been known to attend the season once or twice."

"Not since your youngest sister came out, and that was half a dozen years ago, at least. Still, it makes sense now, I suppose, since you just had a birthday. Your...thirty-second, isn't it?" She leaned closer, studying him with disconcerting thoroughness. "I do believe I see a tiny hint of gray in your hair."

Instinctively, Max touched a hand to the few—very few—silvery strands at his temple. "Oh, don't be ridiculous."

"A good thing, if it's made you see sense after so long," she said, blithely ignoring his reply. "But why stay at the Savoy? You've a splendid London residence. Why not reside there for the season?"

"Rattle around in that enormous house on my own? How absurd."

"Is it absurd, given why you're here?"

Though it was probably a futile exercise, Max donned an air of bewilderment. "I've no idea what you mean."

"Don't be coy. It's clear you've decided to remarry at last. The family will be relieved not to see the dukedom go back to the crown. And what better place than London in May to choose the perfect duchess?"

Max didn't tell her his choice had already been made. Instead, he attempted to dissemble. "You really do adore jumping to conclusions, dear Cousin."

If he'd hoped this tactic would veer Delia off the topic, he was disappointed. "Well, it's the same conclusion your sisters will jump to, if you stay more than a few weeks. And once they figure out what you're really up to, they'll be down like a shot."

His four sisters descending upon London to assist him with his matrimonial goals was a prospect he would prefer to avoid. And it wasn't necessary, in any case, since he had already found a young lady who perfectly fit his requirements. Still, he intended to keep mum about that for as long as possible.

Winning the hand of the beautiful and beguiling Lady Helen Maybridge would not be easy, even for a man of his position and wealth, and he didn't want to jinx his chances. Helen had taken London by storm during her debut last year, captivating every person who met her, and she was well on her way to repeating that honor again this year. Barely May, and she already had suitors lined up outside her door, including—if the rumors were true—Crown Prince Olaf of some obscure Balkan realm. As a mere duke, Max knew he'd have his work cut out for him, and the last thing he needed was the interference of four well-meaning but nosy sisters. He could just imagine them remarking to Helen at every turn how handsome their brother was and dropping hint after hint as to his intentions.

"That," he said with a shudder, "is exactly what I'm afraid of."

"So, you don't want your sisters to know anything about your plans?"

"Can you blame me?" he grumbled. "The last time I was here for the season, my sisters spent half their time searching for husbands—and enlisting my help to do it, much to the dismay and irritation of my unmarried friends. And when they weren't occupied with their own matrimonial ambitions, they were shoving their friends at me as suitable duchess prospects. All to make sure," he added with a slight touch of bitterness, "I didn't make the same mistake twice."

"They only want what's best for you and to see you happy."

"I'm aware of that, and I love them for it. Nonetheless, I prefer to make my marital arrangements without assistance. And," he added before she could reply, "this time around, I don't intend passion to be my guide."

She shook her head, eyeing him with sadness. "Max, we all know Rebecca wasn't right for you, but that doesn't mean—"

He cut off that line of reasoning with an exasperated groan. "Must we revisit the ghastly business of my first marriage? Yes, I fell in love with someone completely unsuitable when I was young and stupid, and we both paid the price. But when she left me and ran back to America, it all worked out splendidly, didn't it? How convenient for us all," he added, his voice hard, his chest suddenly tight, "that she stepped in front of a carriage a few days before my arrival in New York, saving me from the scandalous choice between using force to drag her home or using her desertion to gain a divorce."

"It wasn't your fault."

"Wasn't it? I was so mad with passion that I ignored my own judgment, her reluctance, and all warnings of my family and friends, and married a girl completely alien to our way of life, never once considering if she could handle the job. If I am not to blame, who is?"

"In cases such as this, I'm not sure blame is a particularly useful concept, darling. You and Rebecca fell in love. We can't always help who we fall in love with. It certainly doesn't mean you can't fall in love with the right girl this time around."

"If love happens after the wedding, all very well and I'll be grateful for it."

"And if it doesn't?"

He gave a shrug. "As long as we are well-suited, fond of each other, and aware of our duty, I hardly think it matters."

"What a sensible approach," she said so heartily that Max gave her a sharp, searching glance. "I cannot help but wonder, though...if love isn't part of your criteria, what is?"

"I intend that my wife shall be well prepared to assume her position as Duchess of Westbourne. She will be someone already born and bred for this life, with a full awareness of the responsibilities involved. And if I choose someone who has the same background I do, enjoys the same interests I do, and who possesses an outlook on life compatible with mine, I think our union will be most satisfactory."

"Well, then, everything is simple, isn't it?" she said with cheer. "So, why don't you just save yourself the trouble of a season, and let me arrange your marriage? I'd pick someone perfect for you, I promise."

He straightened in his chair, feeling a prick of alarm, and he feared he might have to tell her about Helen, but then she grinned, and he relaxed again.

"Darling Max," she said with affection, "I do love ragging you, and I hope by the time I return you'll have fallen madly in love with just the right girl. But as busy as you'll be, you will find the time to do that other little favor for me, won't you?"

"You know I will, though I don't see why this Harlow woman can't sort out which of these exotic Eastern recipes she's uncovered would be best and discuss them with Escoffier herself."

Delia was shaking her head before he'd even finished speaking. "That won't do, I'm afraid. Evie's a darling, and brainy, too—which is what makes her so wonderful at digging up information. But there's a language barrier, you see. Auguste doesn't speak English."

"And she doesn't speak French?" That surprised him, rather.

"I thought all girls were required to learn French," he said. "Isn't it mandatory to a girl's education?"

She frowned a little. "It's mandatory in our set, darling. Not in everyone's."

He held up his hands in a gesture of peace. "I didn't mean to sound like a snob. But you've told me nothing about her background except that she owns a bookshop, which, to me, implies a certain level of literary education. I took it for granted that knowing French would be part of that."

"Oh, Evie *knows* French well enough. Reading it, writing it...but speaking it?" Delia broke off, making a face. "Listening to her stumble her way through the menus for a French banquet we planned last year was absolutely painful to my ears. As to her background, it's quite respectable—upper-middle-class family once upon a time, but gone to seed during the last few generations. Her mother died when she was a child, and her father raised her alone in a dingy little flat over the shop, which seems to be the only asset left in the family. And he's passed on as well, leaving her nothing else. She's determined to keep the place going, though. I don't know whether to deem her foolish or admire her pluck."

"Not much profit in it, I gather?"

"Sadly, no. The building is a valuable piece of property, of course, for it's right here in the heart of London. If she sold it, she could gain a nice little dowry out of it, but the shop itself earns next to nothing. It's the sort of place that caters mostly to musty old men who want equally musty first editions no one else has ever heard of. Such a dreary life for a young woman; heaps of hard work, and no time for amusements."

"She has no family?"

"A cousin or two." Delia's brows drew together in an

effort of memory. "Her aunt's second husband is a baron—Lord Merrivale, if I've got it right. But there's some animosity there. He demanded she sell the shop and she refused, and he rather washed his hands of her—something like that. And Evie's proud as the devil, so I doubt she'd ask him for help even if she were destitute."

"Either way, she sounds like a capable enough young woman. You don't think she can manage Escoffier on her own, despite the language barrier?"

"Auguste? He wouldn't have the patience to hear her say *bonjour* before he tossed her out."

"My French isn't much better, I daresay."

"Ah, but it's different for you," she purred. "You're a duke. You're also a member of the Epicurean Club. And you know the prince and have dined with him countless times. Who better than you to help Auguste plan this party? Ah," she added, glancing past him, "there's my maid, at last. I must be off."

She stood up, and when he followed suit, she rose on her toes to kiss his cheek. "Thank you, Max. I should be back in about a month. In the meantime, do write to me in Rome and let me know how the banquet pans out. And if I read about your engagement in some Italian paper before you've told me, I shall be quite put out."

"But where do I find this Harlow woman?" he asked as Delia turned away and started across the foyer toward the dour-faced woman in black and the Savoy bellman who were waiting for her by the exit doors with a pile of trunks and suitcases. "Where am I to go?"

"Harlow's Bookshop," she called back over her shoulder without pausing. "Straight across the Strand and two blocks down Wellington Street. Tiny little place, but I expect you'll find it without too much trouble. Ta-ra."

Max stared after her in bemusement as she sauntered through the plate glass exit door held open for her by the liveried doorman, and he could only hope that doing this favor for Delia wouldn't have the same result as the last one. A bloody nose and a black eye were not a stellar way for any man to start the season, especially not when his goal was to win the most desired woman in London.

# 2

Anyone who knew Evangeline Harlow would probably have used the words *hardworking* and *sensible* to describe her. Evie, after all, had managed to pay off her father's many debts and keep the little bookshop she'd inherited from him out of the hands of creditors, something that no woman without a willingness to work and plenty of good sense could ever have accomplished.

Harlow's had never been much patronized, particularly by the smart set, but left with few options after her father's death, Evie had known it was her only way to earn a living, and she'd spent many hours working to gain it a favorable reputation among collectors. The financial rewards during the seven years of her stewardship had been meager—as Cousin Margery insisted upon reminding her at every opportunity—but Evie was proud of the fact that anyone who wanted an obscure title or a rare first edition knew Harlow's was the place they were most likely to find it.

Lately, however, Evie's innate good sense and staunch

work ethic had developed the unfortunate tendency to desert her, at least on certain very specific occasions.

"Evie," her young assistant, Clarence, whispered beside her. "You've already put heaps of sugar in that cup."

"Yes," Evie agreed absently as she dropped another crystalline chunk into the teacup before her. Setting aside the sugar tongs, she reached for a spoon and began to stir the tea as she leaned back from the counter to peer through the open doorway of the shop's pantry, a move that gave her a clear view of the young man perusing the bookshelves along the center aisle of the shop.

Rory Callahan. Who would have thought the gangly boy she'd known all her life would transform into such a devastatingly attractive man during his years abroad? Was there something magical in the waters of Europe?

Born a few months apart in side-by-side houses, she and Rory had become close friends in childhood. She'd loaned him books, and he'd shared with her the violet creams he pinched from his father's confectionery shop when the old man wasn't looking. Evie had helped him with his schoolwork, and in return, he had confided to her his secret dreams to change the world. They'd had affection and camaraderie, but despite the matchmaking efforts of their fathers, there had never been anything remotely romantic between them.

Both of them had gone away to school, and upon graduating, Evie had returned to assist her father in the bookshop, and Rory had gone to Munich to study politics at the university there. Upon his father's death two years later, he'd come home only long enough to sell the confectionery shop to Clarence's widowed mother before returning to Germany. He hadn't remained at university very long, however, before deciding it wasn't for him, and he'd taken off to see the world.

During the next seven years, they'd kept up a steady and affectionate correspondence, but though she'd thoroughly enjoyed his descriptions of Viennese palaces, Swiss mountains, and the villas of the French Riviera, if anyone had ever asked Evie to describe her feelings for Rory, she'd have said he was like a brother.

And then, two weeks ago, he'd come home.

The moment he'd walked into Harlow's for the first time in over a decade, carrying a box of violet creams under one arm and looking as handsome as a prince in a fairy tale, everything had changed, and during the half dozen visits he'd made to her shop since then, any notion that he was like a brother had vanished from her mind. His hair, nearly white when he was a youth, had darkened to a golden color that even in the mellow dimness of the shop seemed shot with sunlight. His eyes seemed bluer than she remembered—as blue as the summer sky—and for the first time since she was a young girl, Evie had begun to dream of romance and what it might be like to fall in love.

"But, Evie," Clarence said, his insistent whisper once again breaking into her thoughts, "you don't take sugar in your tea anymore. Too expensive, you said."

Evie made a face at the unpleasant reminder of her perpetually low bank balance. "That's because you put enough sugar in yours for both of us," she replied with a good-natured nudge in the boy's ribs. "I ought to have Anna give me free sugar from her stores in compensation."

"If you do, Mum will only make me work more hours in the confectionery to make up for it. Between her, you, and school, I've not a moment to call my own."

"Yes, your life is so hard." She leaned back, peering again through the doorway to find that Rory was still surveying the bookshelves. "And anyway," she added before he could reply, "this tea isn't for me. It's for Rory."

"Even worse, then, since you like him so much!"

Evie felt a pang of alarm at those words. Were her feelings really so obvious? She straightened with a jerk, a move that forced Rory out of her line of vision. "What nonsense you talk," she told Clarence. "Of course I like him. I've known him forever. And he likes sugar in his tea."

"I hope he does, for your sake."

Evie didn't know what the boy meant by that, and she didn't have time to find out. She poured a second cup of inky black tea for herself, but as she moved to add it to the tray she was assembling, Clarence—for some unaccountable reason—grabbed her arm. "Evie, wait," he implored, jostling the cup and causing the contents to slosh over the rim, splashing not only Evie's hand, but also her right cuff and the left side of her white blouse.

She groaned. "Now look what you've done."

"But, Evie, you've put seven lumps of—"

"Oh, do leave off, Clarence," she cut him short impatiently and nodded to the two remaining finger sandwiches and single slice of seedcake on the counter. "Have your tea. Then you can unpack that crate of books that came this morning."

The fifteen-year-old glanced down at the meager offerings without enthusiasm. "I don't know how you expect me to work so hard if you never feed me," he grumbled as he put the food on a plate and poured himself a cup of tea. "I shall tell Mum you're starving me to death. She'll believe me, too," he added as Evie laughed. "I am her son, after all."

"Which is exactly why she won't believe you. Anna can always tell when you're lying. And since she's one of my oldest friends, she knows that I don't tell lies. Now, off you go."

Clarence heaved a long-suffering sigh, grabbed his tea-cup in his free hand, and departed for the storage room. "If that man keeps coming in here, I'll never have a decent tea again."

"Oh, stop complaining," Evie called after him as she attempted to blot the stains on her blouse with a napkin. "I'll make you more later, I promise."

Her efforts to remove the unsightly stains from her shirt-front did little good, however, and Evie gave it up. Tossing the napkin aside, she refilled her cup with the dregs from the pot, and after unsuccessfully attempting to tuck some of the wayward strands of her brown hair back into the bun on top of her head, she picked up the laden tea tray and went in search of Rory.

He was no longer wandering amid the bookshelves but was now lounging by the counter at the register, as if waiting for her. As she hurried forward with the tray, the bell over the door jangled and another man entered the shop, moving to stand behind Rory near the register as Evie took her place behind the counter.

She gave the newcomer a nod of greeting, but her hurried glance took in only an expensive, well-cut morning coat and dark hair peeking beneath the brim of a gray homburg before Rory spoke and once more diverted her attention.

"Why, Evie, what's all this?" Rory glanced over the tray as she placed it on the counter between them. "Oh, dear, I hope I haven't interrupted your tea?" he asked, looking up, a frown of concern knitting his brows together.

"Oh, no, of course not. I thought...that is, I wondered... um..." She paused, seized by sudden shyness, and she had to swallow hard before she could go on. "I was making tea anyway," she managed at last.

"Perhaps, but nonetheless, I'm honored that you would think of me."

"Of course I think of you," she blurted out, then could have bitten her tongue off, but Rory only laughed.

"I think of you, too, Evie." He paused and leaned forward over the counter. "All the time."

Instinctively, she leaned closer, too, but then the stranger gave a cough, and she straightened with a little jerk and glanced at him. "I'll be with you in a few moments, sir."

"Dearest Evie," Rory murmured, once again diverting her attention, "you shouldn't have gone to so much trouble."

"As I tell you every time you come by, it's no trouble making tea for you. Besides, it's the least I can do after that box of violet creams you brought me."

"That's different. Eating violet creams with you is a tradition. But since you insist," he added, laughing as he reached for the cup in front of him, but when he took a hefty swallow of the tea, he immediately choked.

"Is something wrong?" she asked in dismay.

"No, no." He set the cup down, cleared his throat, and patted his chest. "I...um...I just swallowed wrong, that's all. But perhaps..." He paused, giving another cough and casting a hungry glance over the tray. "Perhaps one of those sandwiches might help?"

He helped himself, taking two, wolfing down the first one in two bites.

"Better?" she asked as he finished the second one and took a third.

"Yes, thank you. You've always been so good to me," he added, reaching for a fourth sandwich. "But I didn't come intending to cadge a meal."

The man behind him made a stifled sound of disbelief under his breath.

"Of course not, Rory," she said, giving the other man a frown of reproof. "I know you'd never do such a thing."

The stranger lifted one black eyebrow, clearly skeptical of her contention, and Evie decided it was best just to ignore him. Returning her attention to Rory, she asked, "Have you decided what you're going to do now that you're home? You'll take up a job, I suppose?"

"Me? Work in an office adding up figures or taking dictation for some wealthy magnate?" Rory laughed, shaking his head. "No, I've a soul above double-entry bookkeeping and typewriting machines."

"Of course you do," the stranger murmured, sarcasm in every syllable.

Thankfully, Rory ignored him. "Besides," he went on as he took another sandwich off the tray, "I have a university education, so I've decided it's time I put it to use."

"Doing what?" she asked.

"I have a plan, but before I tell you about it, there's a question I need to ask you."

Her heart gave a leap of excitement. Perhaps he wanted to take her to a music hall show? She hadn't had an outing like that since well before her father died. Or he might take her for a walk—an evening stroll on the Embankment. They could stop at Brown's and have ice cream. He might dare to touch her hand on the way back—

"I was wondering," he said, his voice interrupting these delightful contemplations, but then he paused to pop the last bite of sandwich into his mouth and reach for a slice of seedcake, leaving Evie in intolerable suspense. "I was wondering," he resumed at last, "about that storage room you've got."

She blinked, taken aback, blissful dreams of romance faltering. "The storage room?"

"Yes. Do you use it for anything?"

"Do we use it?" Realizing she was beginning to sound like someone's pet myna bird, Evie got hold of herself with an effort. "Well, we use it for storage, obviously. And it also functions as an office of sorts for me. Why?"

"I'm looking for a place to hold meetings." His slice of cake finished, he helped himself to another one. "To generate interest, raise funds, that sort of thing."

"Raise funds for what?"

"Me." He took a deep breath. "I've decided to go into politics."

Her astonishment must have shown on her face, for he laughed. "Is it such a surprise? You've always known I'm political."

She did know. It was one of the things she liked best about him. He cared about things that mattered, as she did. He wanted to improve the lot of ordinary people. "It's so good that you want to make the world a better place, but—"

"Making it happen won't be easy. We have to rid society of the flawed old way first. We have to tear it down—all of it. We have to shatter the outmoded institutions, destroy the privileged classes and everything they stand for—bring down the bankers, the aristocrats, even the monarchy—"

Evie frowned, feeling suddenly uneasy. She *liked* the Queen. "That's rather reckless, isn't it?"

"It has to be done, Evie. Only then, after we've rid ourselves of the decadent old world, can we build a new world, a better world. We can't rely on those doddering fools at Westminster to change anything—it will never happen. They'd rather just stay comfortable in their stodgy beds, fat and complacent and so damnably smug. No, if things are ever going to change, it's the working men who will bring it." He took another sandwich from the tray. "Men like me."

The man behind him made a sound of derision, and Evie cast a reproving look in his direction, but it was wasted, for he wasn't even looking at her. Instead, he was studying the books on the display table nearby, and she returned her attention to the man in front of her. "So, you want to run for office?"

"I do, but that takes money, so I need to raise funds."

"What about the money from the sale of your father's shop? Surely you still have some of that?"

"Of course," he replied at once, "but it's not nearly enough. Politics is an expensive game, Evie. It will take a lot of time and work, but I'll get there in the end, and when I do, the men who do the labor will finally have a true voice."

Evie's uneasiness deepened. "I hope..." She paused and cleared her throat, crossing her fingers beneath the counter. "I hope you will push for the ladies to have a voice and fight to gain us the vote? After all," she added, forcing a self-deprecating laugh, "we are workers, too."

She needn't have doubted Rory. "Absolutely!" he said at once, his voice firm with conviction. "I regard women as the most important workers of all."

"Of course you do," the man behind him muttered under his breath, turning the page of a book.

"I'm glad to know you support the women's vote, Rory," she hastened on, fearing he might take umbrage to the stranger's rude remark. "It's so important."

"Of course it is," Rory replied as he took another slice of cake. "About that storage room—I was hoping you might let me use it to hold meetings."

"I suppose that could be managed. Did you have a particular day in mind?"

"One night a week should be adequate. We can bring in a table, add some chairs—"

"Every week?" She stared, appreciating the difficulties of such an arrangement in a way Rory could not. Her storage room was small, and it contained not only the shop's excess inventory and stationery supplies, but also her desk, filing cabinets, and several more shelves of books. With a table and chairs shoved in as well, there would be no room to move back there. "You want to use it every week?"

"It would only be for a few hours," he said at once. "It's vital we have a place to meet, you see, and that storage room of yours would be perfect. It's for the workers, Evie," he added as she continued to hesitate, and once again, he leaned closer, giving her an intimate smile. "It's for us."

As she looked into those gorgeous blue eyes, how could she refuse? "All right, then," she said, laughing. "You've won me over. We'll make it work somehow."

He smiled back at her, popped the final bite of cake into his mouth, and straightened away from the counter. "Would Wednesdays suit you? Seven o'clock?"

Without waiting for an answer, he removed the last two sandwiches from the tray and turned to depart.

"See you tomorrow," she called after him, hating that this lovely interlude was ending so soon. "Good day, Rory."

He acknowledged her farewell with a wave of his hand, but he did not pause until he reached the door, where he turned to look at her. "Evie?"

She leaned forward, smiling, hopeful. "Yes?"

"Do you think we might have some of those delicious sandwiches and cakes of yours as refreshments?"

Those words were not quite what she'd been hoping

for, but Evie could feel the stranger's gaze on her, and she pasted on a smile. "I'd be happy to," she said, as if serving up sandwiches and cake to a roomful of people was something she could afford to do every day.

"Thank you, Evie," he said, smiling back at her as he opened the door. "You're an angel."

And then he was gone.

Evie leaned over the counter, craning her neck to watch him through the shop's plate glass windows as he walked away, but he didn't glance back as he started down the street.

*You're an angel.*

He vanished from view, disappearing beyond the frame of the window, and Evie sank back down onto her heels with a dreamy sigh.

He'd be coming to the shop even more often now. He believed in women's rights. He needed her help. He thought she was an *angel*.

"Ahem."

The sound forced Evie out of her blissful reverie, and she turned to face the man who had been making those impolite sounds of derision and expressing derogatory opinions about a conversation that was none of his business.

For some reason, he seemed as irritated by her as she was by him. His dark eyes told her nothing, but an unmistakable frown creased his brow beneath his hat, and his mouth was pressed into a tight line. His face was handsome enough, she supposed, but in its lean, chiseled contours was the undeniable arrogance of a man accustomed to being immediately obeyed. That, along with his disdainful remarks a few moments ago and the expensive cut of his clothes, forced Evie to conclude he was one of those spoiled rich toffs who didn't like being forced to wait his turn.

He gave a nod toward the door where Rory had just gone out. "Friend of yours, I take it?" he asked.

His voice was a well-bred drawl, but she caught the cutting edge beneath it, and her animosity shot up a notch. It wouldn't do to show it, however. "May I help you?" she asked with cool courtesy.

"I believe so, yes," he said, doffing his hat. "I'm—"

He was interrupted by the jangle of the bell, the opening of the door, and the raucous laughter of three young men who entered the shop.

"Ha! There you are, Westbourne!" one of them pronounced in a loud voice unmistakably slurred by drink. "We knew we'd lost you somewhere along here, but in looking for you, we passed right by this place twice. We never dreamed you'd be in a *bookshop*."

The other two men who'd entered with him laughed uproariously at that, though Evie couldn't for the life of her fathom what they found so entertaining.

"It's not my usual line of country, Freddie, I grant you," the man replied, giving Evie the heaven-sent opportunity to make a derisive sound of her own.

Sadly, he didn't seem to hear it. "I'm here," he continued, "on an errand for my cousin."

"You're filled to the brim with family feeling, and I do admire you for it," the man called Freddie replied. "But you won't be long, will you? Bookshops are so damnably dull. This one especially so," he added with a disapproving look around that made Evie bristle. Her shop might be small and not very posh, but when it came to the quality of the books, Harlow's defeated any of the fashionable bookshops frequented by the nobs.

"Not long," the man Westbourne replied. "Five minutes, at most."

His companions wandered off to explore, making no effort to modulate their voices or quiet their laughter, and as Westbourne returned his attention to her, Evie couldn't resist getting a bit of her own back. "Friends of yours, I take it?" she asked sweetly.

Having his own question tossed back in his face didn't discomfit him in the least. "I wouldn't precisely say that," he answered with a shrug. "To these young turks, I fear I'm far more like a tiresome older brother than friend."

The tiresome part, Evie could believe, but despite his words, he didn't look all that much older than his companions. His hair was thick and unruly and as black as ink, with just a few strands of gray at the temples. The only lines in his face were faint crow's-feet at the corners of his eyes and bracketing the edges of his mouth. In addition, there didn't seem to be an ounce of superfluous flesh on his tall, broad-shouldered frame. At a guess, Evie would have put him only a few years past her own age, and though being twenty-eight established her firmly as a spinster, it was not, by any stretch of the imagination, *old*.

"I am the Duke of Westbourne," he said with a bow. "I take it that you are Miss Harlow, the proprietress here?"

That he had a lofty title didn't surprise her, for he seemed to have the same air of entitlement most in his circle possessed, and his title only served to confirm her initial impression of his arrogance. But the fact that he knew who she was took her back a bit. Granted, most of her customers did come to her by word of mouth, but his conversation with his friends indicated he wasn't the sort to be interested in books. Far more likely, she thought with another glance over his body, that he spent his time engaged in athletic pursuits rather than literary ones. "I am Miss Harlow, yes."

"Pleased to make your acquaintance, Miss Harlow," he said, glancing around as he returned his homburg to his head. "I've been told you have a fine establishment here."

That, she supposed, was meant to be a compliment, but as he continued to study his surroundings, Evie wondered if he was noting the faded wallpaper, dim light, and chipped plaster ceiling and deeming it a contradiction to what he'd been led to expect. The thought that he might be judging her shop and finding it wanting based on superficialities made her feel both self-conscious and oddly defensive.

"Your companions don't seem to hold that opinion," she replied, wincing as the loud laughter of the younger men echoed through the shop. "At least not well enough to respect other patrons."

"How fortunate, then," he said smoothly as he returned his attention to her, "that there aren't any other patrons here at present."

Evie stiffened. "I wasn't aware that behaving like a gentleman required an audience."

If she hoped her tart reply would sting, she was disappointed. "It shouldn't do," he agreed at once. "But in defense of my companions, may I say that they are young and filled with high spirits. And they've been penned up at their family estates in the country all winter long."

She donned an expression of mock sympathy. "The poor little dears. How arduous for them."

His mouth twitched with amusement, but when he spoke, his voice was grave. "Just so. And now, having only just arrived in town, they are attempting to savor all the delights of the season in a single day. It's made them quite ebullient."

She watched as the one called Freddie, a foppish dandy with dark red curls peeking beneath his straw boater hat, pulled a book from the shelf, glanced at the title, and made a disparaging comment about silly lady novelists that sent his two companions into another fit of boisterous laughter.

"That's one way of calling a goose a swan," she countered dryly.

The duke had no chance to reply.

"Westbourne, do hurry," Freddie urged, "or we shall have no time for a drink before we're off to change for Lady Trent's card party. And if we're late, we'll both fall several notches in my dear sister's estimation."

"Me more than you, Freddie, I fear," Westbourne answered, turning a bit to look at the younger man.

"Only because Helen expects more from her suitors than from a mere brother," the younger man countered at once. "Either way, my point remains. If you continue to dawdle, we'll be late to Lady Trent's, and Helen will be furious. She hates being late."

Westbourne gave a shrug, as if the displeasure of his love interest didn't matter at all, a reaction that Evie supposed was natural under the circumstances. He was a duke, after all, and among his set, that consideration clearly outweighed the defect of overweening arrogance. In fact, the latter was probably a direct result of the former.

"In the game of courtship, dear Freddie," he drawled, "it's best for a man not to make himself too available."

Her estimation of his character now firmly validated, it was Evie's turn to make a sound of disdain, causing the duke to return his attention to her. "I take it you have a different opinion, Miss Harlow?"

"It's not for me to say."

"Perhaps not," he agreed with a chuckle, "but I'll wager you're itching to say it, just the same."

She pressed her lips together and didn't reply, reminding

herself that it was not wise for a woman in trade to antagonize a customer, especially a duke.

In the wake of her silence, he looked down at the empty tea tray between them. "No doubt," he murmured, tracing the rim of the tray with one gloved finger, "you believe one should put oneself at the absolute mercy of one's love interest."

His voice was light, but his meaning was plain, and Evie's usual prudence and common sense went to the wall.

"If, by that, you mean that I don't believe courtship is a game, Your Grace, then you would be right."

"Ah, but I must disagree with you there," he said, looking up. "Courtship is very much a game."

"And love?" she countered. "It that a game, too?"

"Love?" He laughed softly, but there was no humor in his eyes. They were dark, hard, and strangely opaque. "My dear Miss Harlow," he murmured, his voice too low for the others to hear, "what does love have to do with it?"

Freddie reentered the conversation before Evie could reply. "I daresay you're right, Westbourne. It is a game, and I applaud your strategy. Having at least one man in town who's not panting over her will do my sister a world of good. In fact," he added, tossing the gilt-edged, rather fragile first edition of Brontë's *Jane Eyre* to the floor with careless disregard, "she'll probably like you all the better for it."

This manhandling of the books was too much for Evie. "Please don't do that," she called sharply. "Books should be treated with respect."

"Uh-oh," one of the other men said with a laugh. "That's done it, Freddie. We shall all be swatted with a willow switch any moment now."

"And sent to bed without our supper," his other friend added.

"If she did such a thing," Westbourne told them before Evie could respond, "it would be no more than you three scapegraces deserve."

If he had intended his words to be a rebuke, the indulgent tone of his voice as he spoke quite spoiled the effect and did little to improve Evie's opinion of him; and when one of his companions bumped into a display table, tumbling several more of her books to the floor, she began to wish she really did possess a willow switch so she could shepherd the lot of them into the street before every book was upended.

"Now then, gentlemen," Westbourne went on, "since we've already caused Miss Harlow enough aggravation for one day, why don't you put all the books back where they belong and go on to the Savoy? I'll join you when I've finished here."

His friends seemed amenable to his suggestion, much to Evie's relief. With the unsurprising assurance that Westbourne would find them in the Savoy's American Bar, and after tossing the books, including Brontë, haphazardly back onto the display table, they started for the door.

"I fear the claret cups at Lady Hargrave's afternoon-at-home were stronger than they realized," Westbourne remarked as his friends departed. "Please allow me to apologize on their behalf. I hope you can forgive them?"

That smooth question seemed to take her forgiveness as a foregone conclusion. Sadly, it was a correct one. "Of course," she said, repressing a sigh as her usual common sense reasserted itself. "How can I help you, Your Grace?"

"I am here on behalf of my cousin, Lady Stratham. I understand you have some information for her, and she has asked me to fetch it."

She blinked, taken aback, for she would never have

imagined the delightfully charming Delia to be a relation of this man. "Lady Stratham is your cousin?"

"Yes. She's been called away to Rome, and in her absence, she has asked me to fetch the information you were to provide her for an upcoming dinner party. For the Epicurean Club?" he prompted when she didn't reply.

She'd forgotten all about it, she realized in dismay. Rory's return had filled her mind so completely that she'd given no thought to anything else, but now, the details of what she and Delia had planned came roaring back, spinning through her head like the flotsam of a tornado. Strange and exciting dishes of the Far East. Table decorations of pagodas and dragons. Big vases of lovely pink cherry blossoms.

"Ah, yes," she murmured, feeling oddly wistful as she imagined it. "The party."

Another big, elaborate affair for the smart set, where women wore beautiful gowns and men wore white tie, where glasses of champagne sparkled beneath the glittering light of crystal chandeliers. It was the sort of event she had often helped Delia plan, but not the sort she'd ever be able to attend.

Not for the first time, she wondered what it would be like to wear a silk evening dress and flowers in her hair, to drink fine wine and eat luxurious food, to talk of the Riviera and Rome and the events of the season beneath the crystal lights.

But such was not for the likes of her. Her days at Chaltonbury had made that fact brutally clear. No, her life was here—had always been here, in these three stories of crumbling brick and plaster fifteen feet wide.

With that thought, she felt a sudden, unexpected stirring of discontent and longing. Not longing for life among the nobs, of course, but something that wasn't only these rooms and the day's work, something beyond her little flat upstairs with its gas ring and tiny windows that looked straight into the brick walls next door, something even her beloved books could not provide. Something...more.

The Duke of Westbourne was looking at her, waiting, and Evie shoved aside such nonsense, reminding herself that there was no "something more." There was only this, and that was quite all right with her. "Yes...um...yes..." she stammered, working to recover her poise. "I believe Lady Stratham did ask me to procure some information for her."

"And?" he prompted when she fell silent. "May I have it?"

"No." Such an abrupt reply caused him to raise his black brows in surprise, but Evie wasn't about to confess her inexcusable lapse of memory. "It's not ready, I'm afraid. It's taking longer than...ahem...longer than I'd thought it would to find the information. I'm sorry."

"I understand." He glanced at the crumbs on the tea tray. "You've been busy, no doubt."

That flicked her on the raw, partly because it was the truth. Rory's entrance back into her life two weeks ago had turned her upside down, inclining her to bouts of day-dreaming rather than work, to silly longings for parties, entertainments, and romance, to discontent with the life she had.

Mortified by her own irresponsibility, angry with him, and thoroughly annoyed with herself, Evie had to take a deep breath before she could reply. "I should have Lady Stratham's information ready in another day or two," she said, her voice coolly polite even as heat rushed into her cheeks.

"I shall return on Thursday, then." He tipped his hat and turned away. "Good day, Miss Harlow."

Deprived by her own good sense of any chance to tell this man what she thought of his irritating remarks, his appalling views on romance, his presumptions about her friends, and the bad taste he had in choosing his own, Evie expressed her frustration in the only way open to her. She stuck her tongue out at his back as he walked away.

"I say, Miss Harlow?" He stopped abruptly by the door, forcing Evie to school her features into a more benign countenance as he turned around. "Been having problems with street thieves, have you?"

Evie's suppressed irritation faltered a bit at such an unexpected question. "I beg your pardon?"

He grinned, a flash of brilliant white teeth in his dark, lean face, as he lifted his hands to point at the two mirrors she'd positioned in the upper front corners of the shop. They were there to catch fingersmiths in the act, but Evie appreciated that she was the one who'd just been caught, and the blush in her cheeks deepened to what was surely a vivid shade of scarlet.

Still grinning, he reached for the door handle. "Until Thursday, Miss Harlow."

With that, he opened the door, gave a nod of farewell, and departed, leaving Evie staring after him in hot chagrin.

# 3

The American Bar was one of the Savoy's most popular features, and its creative head barkeep, Frank Wells, was one of the main reasons why. His intoxicating concoctions, made possible by the addition of ice, bitters, and various liqueurs to such mundane libations as whisky, gin, and rum, had brought the American cocktail to the posh and privileged palates of British high society.

After one hour and four rounds of something Frank called a "Manhattan," however, Max's head felt a bit foggy, his enthusiasm for American cocktails was waning, and he wondered how many more Manhattans it would take before he had fulfilled his promise to Helen.

*Please look out for Freddie until Papa returns from America*, she had pleaded earlier today at Lady Hargrave's afternoon-at-home. *My brother is so filled with high spirits, and Papa's had him on such a tight leash since he was sent down from Oxford. He's longing for the entertainments of the season, and Mama and I are finding it impossible to*

*manage him. With Papa away and no steadying masculine
influence, I fear he will fall into bad ways.*

Max had been tempted to point out that it was impossible
for the lad to fall into bad ways since he'd never fallen out
of them. But faced with Helen's tear-filled green eyes, he
hadn't had the heart to voice such an unfavorable opinion
of her dearly loved twin brother and had remained tactfully
silent. Moments later, however, when she had murmured
something about how handsome Olaf looked that afternoon
in his princely regalia, Max had imagined his own courtship
slipping decidedly into second place and had agreed to her
request without further demur. A decision, he appreciated
now, that showed his jaded words about courtship earlier in
the day to be nothing but empty rhetoric.

Worse, his promise to Helen meant that he was now
stuck, possibly for the entire season, playing nursery
governess to a spoiled brat.

Max lifted his gaze from his drink to the face of Helen's
brother, one that, despite its strong resemblance to that of
his lovely twin, wasn't nearly as good looking, for it was
already pudgy with alcoholic excess and marked by lines
of dissipation. Studying the younger man across the table,
Max feared it was far too late for any of his "steadying
influence," if indeed he possessed such a thing.

Making matters even more nauseating, Helen hadn't
told him he'd be required to watch over not only her insufferable sibling, but his best friends, too. Herding cats into
pens, Max reflected as he returned his gaze to the chilled
amber depths of his drink, would have been easier.

The Banforth brothers, born only ten months apart,
weren't really bad lads—or they wouldn't be, he amended,
in other circumstances. But in Freddie Maybridge's company, the pair became hellions, as the dons at Oxford had

already discovered, and a single afternoon of keeping this trio out of trouble had already worn Max to a nub. An entire season of it would surely do him in.

"We need some more of these, Frank," Freddie called out, his voice, slurred and far too loud, impelling Max to take another hefty swallow of his drink, and giving him cause to reconsider the goal of making Helen his duchess.

But only a moment of pondering the subject banished his doubts.

Helen, like her mythological namesake, was a breathtaking beauty—graceful, accomplished, and refined, with a melodic voice, lustrous auburn hair, and a face fully capable of launching a thousand ships. Her beauty was of such renown, in fact, that it had brought Prince Olaf to London from his remote Balkan realm, and had, if rumors were true, made her the recipient of six marriage proposals since her debut the previous year. The daughter of England's wealthiest marquess, Helen was the perfect choice of bride for a duke. She, unlike the previous Duchess of Westbourne, understood the responsibilities that came with high positions and knew they could not be discarded like last season's hat.

Thinking of Rebecca no longer brought him pain. Eight years had passed since her defection and death. Now he could look back on the entire debacle with little more than a sense of bewilderment at how he could have made such an awful mistake, and a determination not to make it again. He would never feel about Helen the way he had felt about Rebecca, and what a blessing that was.

Helen would never abandon her duty and run away. She would never shame his family, appall his friends, or cause a scandal. And she would never, ever break his heart.

"Frank, are you deaf?" Freddie shouted, breaking into

Max's musings about the past and reminding him that Helen's brother had none of her intelligence, charm, or regard for duty. Freddie Maybridge was a scandal in the making. As if to prove it, the young man's voice rang out again, even louder than before. "We need another round!"

Max took a breath, downed the last swallow of his drink, and told himself for the tenth time today that he would be marrying Helen, not her family.

"Careful, Freddie," he said, working to inject a good-natured heartiness into his voice as he set his glass back down. "Best to moderate your voice a bit, or Frank will toss us out."

"A duke and a marquess's son?" Freddie laughed. "He wouldn't dare."

That, Max thought sadly, was probably true.

"Deuce take it, Westbourne, I never thought you could be such a stickler for the proprieties," the younger man went on, proving Max's attempt to sound like a well-meaning friend, instead of a scold, had fallen flat.

"Indeed," Thomas Banforth added. "He sounds almost as prim and disapproving as Little Miss Bookshop. Did you see how she glared at me for knocking over her books? I felt as if I were back in the nursery with my nanny."

Max thought back to his own nanny, and he couldn't say that he saw any resemblance there to Miss Harlow. His nanny had been built like a rugby player, as ugly as a mud fence with the savage temperament of a badger. The willow-slim Miss Harlow, prim though she might be, was a cream puff by comparison.

An image of her face came into his mind, a thin, gamine face of hazel eyes and straight dark brows, with a deter-mined jaw, a pointed chin, and a turned-up nose spattered with freckles. It wasn't a pretty face, he supposed, at least not by the conventions of the day. But it was an arresting face, with a quirky, unexpectedly charming smile. What a pity that smile only chose to show itself for a cad who'd been too busy gobbling up her sandwiches to notice it.

No, as far as looks went, the only defects Max could recall were the overly pale hue of her skin that told of too little time outside in the fresh air and the dark circles under those fine hazel eyes. She was, he appreciated, just as Delia had described her—a girl who worked too hard and worried too much.

A shame, for Miss Harlow was clearly an intelligent young woman, with a quick wit and a saucy tongue, far too good for the young swain who'd held her captivated this afternoon.

Why, he wondered, not for the first time, was love so damnably blind? Couldn't she see that the young man she'd set her sights on was a worthless waste of space and air? And a blatant hypocrite to boot, droning on and on about a political party for workers. Worker? Him? Not bloody likely. Given his obvious aversion to employment and the blatant way he took advantage of Miss Harlow's hospitality, Max suspected that work of any kind held little appeal for him. And all his talk of women's rights? What a hum *that* was.

*Women are the most important workers of all.*

No surprise he'd view women in that light—after all, how could he sponge off women, eating their food and taking advantage of them, if they didn't work?

"Who's she to be putting on airs, I ask you?" Freddie said, forcing Max to put aside his speculations about Miss Harlow's taste in men. "Lording it over us, ordering us about that shop like some sort of army general. Who's she think she is?"

"The owner?" Max countered, tact impelling him to phrase his point as a mere suggestion rather than an inconvenient statement of fact.

Freddie gave a snort, clearly not impressed. "Being the proprietress of a second-rate bookshop is hardly notable enough to justify rudeness toward those of a superior class. Maybe if she were pretty, she might get by with it. But the girl's plain as a currant bun. What chap would accede to her demands?"

Max opened his mouth to reply, but he was given no chance.

"Did you observe her appearance?" Timothy Banforth gave a laugh. "Tea stains on her shirtfront, and ink stains on her cuff. Wisps of hair falling out of that bun on top of her head. And that necktie. Ugh. Perhaps she's one of those suffragists. She looks like one."

Max, having overheard her question about women's rights, knew there was no *perhaps* about it, but he didn't say so. And having once had a very passionate and rewarding interlude with a widowed suffragist, he could also have pointed out the charming advantages of being in the company of women who regarded men as equals instead of superiors. But with these three, it would be a waste of breath. Besides, a gentleman couldn't give chapter and verse on things like that. It simply wasn't done.

"I say you're right, Timmy," Freddie went on. "That vinegar-tongued, freckled thing who looks as if some brute's given her two black eyes? No gentleman would look at her twice, much less comply with her demands."

Perhaps it was all the strong cocktails he'd consumed. Or his innate sense of fair play. Or perhaps he just had a weakness for defending those who were not available to defend themselves. But whatever the reason, Max found himself unable to stand by as these scathing criticisms of the absent Miss Harlow were bandied about.

"I fear I must disagree with you, gentlemen," he said.

"Miss Harlow strikes me as a young woman with a great deal of potential. All she needs," he added as the other three burst into disbelieving laughter, "is some new clothes, an awareness of her own attractions, and some sleep."

"She has attractions?" Freddie asked. "I didn't notice."

"Get the poor girl some rest," Max persisted, "find a maid to dress her hair and massage away those dark circles, a modiste to put her in a fetching ball gown, and a jeweler to hang some glittering baubles around her neck, and you three would soon sit up and take notice."

"You're mad, Westbourne." Timothy Banforth shook his head, staring at Max with pity.

Max gave a shrug. "Laugh if you like, but I think the girl has the potential to be an incomparable beauty. And I daresay there's plenty of men who'd agree with me. Launch her into society, introduce her about, and she'd have suitors lined up outside her door within a month."

"He's raving," Thomas agreed at once. "What do you think, Freddie?"

"That girl, a beauty?" Freddie laughed. "She's about the plainest, most unremarkable girl I've ever seen. The duke would have his work cut out to change her into a beauty. I say," he added, slapping one hand down on the table with enough force to rattle the empty glasses, "that's an idea. Westbourne thinks Little Miss Bookshop is some sort of Cinderella? All right, then; he needs to prove it. A wager is clearly called for."

Max laughed. "What are you saying? That you want me to play Fairy Godmother—Godfather, in this case— and transform Miss Harlow into the sort of girl who could captivate the handsome prince?"

"If you can." Freddie gave him a smirk. "A hundred pounds says you can't."

He was tempted, by God, if for no other reason than to put this man-child in his place. And it would probably do the girl a world of good to have some fun for a change.

Delia's words came back to him, something about how the men she met were usually musty old duffers, and after seeing her shop, he could well believe it. Young men might read, but their literary choices didn't often include an original *Malleus Maleficarum* or a pristine edition of *The Pilgrim's Progress* printed in the time of Queen Anne. No, eligible young men would most likely be found at Hatchards, perusing copies of *The Prisoner of Zenda* in the hope of impressing any young ladies who might stroll by.

Given her situation and lack of desirable suitors, Max supposed her attraction to that odious Rory fellow was understandable, but he was still irked by it. She was far too good for him.

Ah, but get a few good men clamoring for her attention, asking for dances, treating her with the consideration and respect she deserved, and she'd soon see she could do much better for herself than a lout on the make whose primary interest in women was what he could get out of them. What a lark it would be, Max thought, to watch her make that particular discovery.

"What's wrong, Westbourne?" Timothy asked, interrupting his contemplations. "Losing your nerve now that there's money on the line?"

Max's current bank balance could have supported a bet a thousand times greater than this one, but he didn't say so. "On the contrary," he replied as he set down his empty glass. "You've challenged me, and I adore a challenge. Just how long," he added recklessly, "would I have to effect the transformation of Miss Harlow?"

"Oh, we'll give you plenty of time before you have

to pay up," Freddie assured him with a breezy confidence Max found irritating as hell. "You're sponsoring a charity ball in the middle of June, aren't you? London hospitals, army widows, or some such?"

"Orphanages."

"There you are, then. Arrange for her to be at the ball, and if she dances every dance, then you win. That gives you six weeks to get her ready."

"That's enough time, I grant you, but..." He paused, frowning, trying to think past the exhilarating fog of too much rye and vermouth. "There are difficulties."

"Oh, listen to him, gentlemen," Freddie said, laughing. "He's trying to back out already."

"You misunderstand me. The girl doesn't move in society. She's unknown."

"Which is why your charity ball is perfect. You don't need to worry that inviting a nobody like her will raise eyebrows, since all she has to do to attend is buy a voucher."

He suppressed the impulse to roll his eyes. A voucher for his charity ball cost far more than a woman of Miss Harlow's station in life could afford. So like Freddie to be oblivious to facts like that. "I'm not worried about how to get her into the ball, Freddie. That's easily managed. It's my ball, after all. But the girl can hardly go alone. She'll need a chaperone."

"Nothing could be simpler. Get one of your sisters to take her."

That, Max knew, was an untenable option. Even if one of his sisters could be prevailed upon to chaperone a girl she didn't know, he had no intention of putting his own matrimonial plans in the sight of his interfering sisters to make it happen.

"They're not coming for the season," he said, crossing

his fingers that keeping the house closed would be enough to deter them until his engagement to Helen was a *fait accompli*. "But perhaps..." He paused, considering. "Perhaps my cousin Delia could be prevailed upon. She returns from Rome in about a month, and she already knows the girl and likes her."

"Then we're on," Freddie countered triumphantly. "But you must agree to play fair. No dancing with the girl yourself at the ball, and no persuading or bribing friends in your own circle to fill her dance card."

The implication that he would even think about cheating only served to heighten Max's determination to prove Freddie wrong about the girl. "You have my word not to stack the deck in my own favor," he said dryly. "But if this wager is to proceed, I must insist upon certain conditions."

Freddie laughed. "Lobbying for a bigger prize, eh?"

"Sod the money," Max said. "One hundred pounds, or two, or five, it makes no difference to me."

"Then what are these conditions you speak of?"

"As I said, the girl's unknown. Even the most beautiful woman in the world couldn't fill her dance card for an entire ball if no one knows who she is."

"Fair enough," Freddie replied and considered a moment. "Your cousin Delia knows everyone. In the fortnight leading up to the ball, have her take the girl to a few parties and introduce her about."

He considered the sort of men suitable for Miss Harlow. No peers, of course, but he and Delia between them could surely scrounge up plenty of well-off, respectable men to introduce to her. Many bankers, barristers, army officers, and young MPs would happily purchase a ball voucher for the chance to meet an attractive girl with connections to a duke's family.

"A couple weeks should do the trick," Freddie said, breaking into his speculations. "As long as your cousin agrees, like you, not to bribe anyone to dance with the girl, I don't see a problem. She just has to dance every dance."

Satisfied, Max moved on to his second, equally important consideration. "It must be understood that discretion is called for. No discussing this wager with your friends, now or at any point in the future. I won't have Miss Harlow embarrassed or her good name tarnished by gossip. And since we've talked of stacking the deck, I want it made clear that none of you are allowed to do that either. No trying to turn anyone against her by negative comments or gossip. I want your word of honor on that point, gentlemen."

"We'd never do that," Thomas said with dignity.

"Of course we wouldn't," Timothy agreed.

"We all promise to play fair, and mum's the word," Freddie assured him and glanced around. "Are we agreed, then?"

"Steady on," Thomas interjected before Max could reply. "There is still one problem none of you seem to have thought of. Timothy, Freddie, and I are stone broke at present. After we got sent down from Oxford, our fathers reduced our quarterly incomes to a pittance. How would we pay the duke his winnings if we lose?"

"We won't lose," Freddie said.

"I'm not sure I want to risk it. I'm in enough debt as it is."

"As am I," his brother added. "As are you, Freddie."

Exhilarated by the idea of transforming Miss Harlow into a beauty that would stop these three in their tracks and save her from a worthless swine who was clearly unworthy of her, Max was not about to let them back out now. "I shall be content to take a note for my winnings," he said. "You can pay it back whenever opportunity allows, however long that takes."

"Which, speaking for Tommy and myself, might be forever," Timothy grumbled. "Our father is of no mind to soften."

"Nor mine," Freddie added, looking suddenly gloomy. "It's a devil of a mess. But," he added, brightening, "there is a way to resolve that tiresome little problem, if Westbourne agrees."

Max braced himself. "I'm listening."

"You're a duke. You have a great deal of influence, especially with the admissions board at Oxford. If you wrote them a letter, asking them to reverse our expulsion—"

"We'd be back in our fathers' good graces!" Timothy cried. "With our full allowances reinstated. Freddie, old chap, you're a genius."

Max could imagine where this was going. He could see them, money back in their pockets, gambling, drinking, being indiscreet, endangering not only Miss Harlow's reputation, which was unthinkable enough, but also making his promise to Helen all the more difficult to fulfill. At once, he tried to dissuade them. "Oh, I doubt the admissions board would listen to me."

"Oxford named a college after you," Thomas reminded him.

"Exactly," Freddie added. "They could hardly deny such a simple request to the man who endows Westbourne College."

Max considered, trying to think clearly enough to walk the fine line he found himself on. "Very well," he said at last, "I can't guarantee the results, of course, but I am happy to write a letter to Oxford and urge the admissions board to reconsider your expulsion. If," he added as the other three gave whoops of joy, "you three promise to behave yourselves until the season is out."

Their joy faded away into uncomprehending silence, making it clear that circumspection and self-awareness were traits these pups did not yet possess.

It was Freddie who finally broke the silence. "My dear Duke, what on earth do you mean?"

"I mean exactly what I say. Until the season is over, your behavior is to be beyond reproach. If you can do that, thereby demonstrating that you are worthy of Oxford's reconsideration, I will write the letter asking for your reinstatement."

"But—" Freddie broke off, frowning with obvious displeasure. "What do you care how we behave?"

Max decided honesty was the best course. "Because, dear Freddie, with the season on and your father in America, I promised your sister I'd look out for you and keep you in line. And," he added as the younger man muttered an oath, "I'd like my efforts in that regard to be minimal."

"But I don't see why Timothy and I have to be included in that," Thomas put in. "Helen's not our sister."

"No, but the two of you are every bit as notorious in your conduct as Freddie here and could easily lead him further astray if you're not subject to the same rules."

An immediate wave of protest greeted this accusation, but Max ignored it.

"My condition applies to all of you," he said. "For me to write that letter, you must earn it. Come now, gentlemen," he added as they continued to hesitate. "It's not as if you've got the blunt for heavy-stakes gambling, cancan dancers, and East End drinking bouts just now anyway. And," he added as the other three gave gloomy sighs of acknowledgment, "if you behave, you won't incur any additional debt, much to your families' joy and relief. And with a clear conscience, I will be able to inform the good gentlemen at Oxford of your exemplary conduct when I write that letter."

He waited as the other three considered this new development, but when the waiter placed another round of Manhattan cocktails on the table, he lifted his glass and pressed for an answer. "Well, gentlemen, are we agreed?"

Thomas was the first to speak. "I'm in," he said and picked up his own glass.

His brother did the same. "Me too. What about you, Freddie?"

"I think I can manage to be a good boy for a couple of months." Freddie laughed, reaching for his cocktail. "And once we're safely reinstated at Oxford, I will thoroughly enjoy spending my share of the hundred quid Westbourne will be paying us."

"Hear, hear," his companions replied in unison.

"After all," Freddie added, laughing as he lounged back in his chair with his drink after the toast was complete, "even a duke can't make a silk purse out of a sow's ear."

Max's temper flared suddenly, putting the cocktail glass in his hand at serious risk. With an effort, he relaxed his grip so as not to snap the stem, tamped down his anger, and reminded himself that winning would be the best way to put Freddie in his place.

And he would win, by God. He raised his gaze to the laughing face of the young man opposite, set his jaw, and lifted his glass for a second toast, a silent one.

No matter what he had to do, no matter what it took or what price he had to pay, he would transform Bookshop Cinderella into the belle of the ball.

With that vow, Max downed the rest of his drink, and as he set his glass on the table, he grinned, his good temper restored. This was going to be fun.

# 4

Twenty-eight finger sandwiches. Four plum cakes. Seven pots of tea. Eleven dashes up and down the stairs to her flat, five trips to the costermonger on the corner, and zero chances to put her feet up.

Evie stared at the wreckage that had been imposed upon her once neat and tidy storage room—the crates of books shoved carelessly aside, the scattered chairs, the empty plates and cups, the tea-stained floor, and the crumbs on the table—and she wondered how only five men could have eaten so much food and made such a mess in only a few short hours. Too exhausted last night to tidy things up, she'd decided to leave it until the morning, telling herself it would be easier to face in the light of day.

It wasn't.

Still, the mess wouldn't clean itself, so she unbuttoned her cuffs, rolled up her sleeves, and donned her apron, but she'd barely taken the first tray of dirty dishes up to her flat and returned for the second when she heard the unmistakable sound of tapping on the window at the front of the shop.

Puzzled, she glanced down at the watch pinned to her lapel. Confirming that there was still half an hour before she was required to open, she resumed her task, but then the tapping came again—more insistent this time—and Evie gave up trying to ignore it.

She expected to find an impatient customer waiting, but when she paused in the pantry and took a peek into the shop beyond, she discovered she'd been mistaken. Rory stood by the front door, his hands cupped to the plate glass as he tried to see into the shop's unlit interior, and she came forward to unlock the door.

"Hullo, Rory," she said, pulling the door wide. "What are you doing here so early?"

He smiled, a smile that could have melted stone, and Evie forgave the mess in her storage room and how all those plum cakes and sandwiches had nearly emptied her cash register.

"I wanted to express my thanks for your generosity yesterday," he said. "And to give you something in return."

"Oh, Rory, you don't have to give me anything," she protested, even as she felt her flagging spirits lifting a notch. "I was glad to help."

"Nonetheless, I wanted to show my appreciation." He pulled a slim package wrapped in brown paper from his breast pocket. "For all your hard work."

He held it out to her, and even before she took it from him, she knew what it was.

A book.

Resisting the temptation to glance at the overflowing shelves all around her, she took the package from Rory's outstretched hand and hoped for the best as she untied the string and tore off the paper. Maybe it was a novel, something new and exciting she hadn't already read.

"*A Contribution to the Critique of Political Economy,*" she read aloud, and hope of literary excitement fizzled and died. "How...ahem...delightful," she added, reminding herself that it was the thought that counted.

"It's one of my favorite political tracts, Evie. It's brilliant. I know you'll find it as fascinating as I do."

"I'm sure I will," she lied, even as she feared there was no way to avoid reading it without hurting his feelings. "Thank you."

The door opened, tinkling the bell, and Evie glanced past Rory, to watch a stunning blonde woman in a fashionably tailored blue walking suit come floating into the shop.

"Margery," she greeted her cousin, suppressing a sigh as her cousin approached the counter. "This is a surprise. What brings you down from Hampstead Heath?"

"Evie, darling, it's so delightful to see you. It's been far too long." Margery squeezed Evie's hands as she leaned over the counter and planted a perfunctory kiss an inch from each of her cheeks in the French fashion, just as they'd been taught in finishing school. "I hope you're well?"

"Well enough," she began, a partial answer that seemed satisfactory to her cousin.

"I'm so happy to hear it." Letting go of Evie's hands, she straightened away from the counter. "What have you been up to? You must give me all the details."

"I'd be happy to, but—"

"Did I tell you Randolph is off at school now? Winchester. I'm so pleased. It's a very exclusive school, you know. Most boys who apply don't get in. But of course, Randolph is so keen, so intelligent, we never doubted."

"Of course you didn't."

Margery, thankfully, didn't notice the dry note of her voice. "But the twins are at home still," she chirped on happily. "They wanted to go with their brother, naturally, but they are much too young yet. Though they are very advanced for their age. Why, they're learning Latin already. Oh, and Susan is learning French! Can you believe it? She's such a clever little thing—she'll attend Chaltonbury, of course, just as we did. And enjoy it just as much."

"No doubt," Evie murmured.

"We did have fun, didn't we?" Margery went on, taking no notice of Rory's presence. "Remember the dances by the river?"

*You mean the ones where no one wanted to dance with me?* The words hovered on the tip of her tongue, but Rory's presence kept her silent. With a handsome young man in the room, what self-respecting girl wanted to admit to being a wallflower?

"The setting sun on the water," Margery went on, her voice dreamy, "the paper lanterns strung over the dance floor, the refreshment tables laden with fruit and cheese. And the boys coming over from Eton, looking so grand and yet so awkward in their white tie and tails." She gave a wistful sigh. "Oh, those were such halcyon days."

"Oh, yes," Evie agreed, her hands curling into fists behind the counter. "Halcyon."

"Susan's dance card will be full for every one of those cotillions when her time comes, I'm sure."

"Of course." Her hands were aching now, and she forced herself to unclench them, reminding herself she was past all that. The wellborn girls looking down their noses at her inferior pedigree, the relentless teasing about her unimpressive bosom and her abysmal French accent, the dismay on the faces of the Eton boys who'd had to be forced by well-meaning matrons and tutors to partner with her—none of it mattered now. She was just tired and out of sorts, her spirits low, making her cousin's glowing descriptions of their life at Chaltonbury seem particularly trying today.

Rory gave a cough, and she seized on his presence like a lifeline. "Margery, you remember Rory, of course?"

Her cousin turned, her big blue eyes narrowing as she gave Rory the same sort of look a conscientious housekeeper might give a scurrying black beetle. "Oh, yes," she said in a voice reeking of disapproval. "The confectioner's boy."

Her opinion was plain, not only to Evie, but also to Rory, who muttered at once that he really must be off. Tipping his bowler hat, he beat a hasty retreat.

Evie sighed as she watched him go, her spirits sinking even further at what she could not help but feel was a craven defection.

"Oh, Evie," Margery wailed as the door closed behind him, "why is that awful young man hanging about?"

"You only think he's awful because you don't approve of his station in life."

"And what station is that, pray?"

She thought of Margery's prosperous banker husband and titled stepfather, and she decided not to mention Rory's political ambition to bring down the bankers and the aristocrats. "The same station we came from, Cousin," she said instead.

Margery sniffed at this reminder of their middle-class roots. "Mama elevated me above that when she married Harold."

"How fortunate for you."

The sarcasm behind that lightly uttered remark penetrated Margery's armor. "And for you," she said with asperity. "My stepfather paid for both of us to attend one of the finest finishing schools in England. It was a great gift. Had you taken advantage of the opportunity, as I did, you could have become acquainted with a much higher social sphere and found someone desirable to marry, but instead you chose—"

She broke off, but Evie was in no frame of mind to let her slip the hook. "So, I chose to be a social failure, is that what you're saying?"

Margery might be thoughtless, but she didn't mean to be cruel. "Oh, Evie," she said, looking stricken. "Darling, let's not quarrel. I didn't come for that."

Evie didn't want to quarrel either. What would be the point of it? Margery was incapable of seeing what she didn't want to see, and she had been blissfully blind to her cousin's torment, torment she had not suffered herself because she was pretty and charming and had a natural ability to use both traits to her advantage. And it hadn't hurt, of course, that her stepfather was a baron while Evie's father was in trade. In the rarified atmosphere of Chaltonbury and its rich, pampered girls, Margery had flourished and blossomed like a hothouse orchid, while Evie had spent two years feeling like a scrawny, bloomless twig.

Evie relented. "About Rory," she said, reverting to their former topic, "you needn't fear that his situation has limited him. He's very political and ambitious. He intends to stand for parliament."

"Does he, indeed?" Margery did not seem impressed. "What could possibly make him qualified for such a role?"

"He did attend university."

"In Munich. And he didn't finish. You told me he abandoned his studies and went off to see the world, or some such nonsense."

Evie cursed the day she'd mentioned that little tidbit. It had been ages ago—eight or nine years at least—but, unlike the torment Evie had endured during their school days, that trivial piece of information about Rory was something her cousin had clearly felt it important to remember.

"Dearest Evie, I hope you're not encouraging him? I realize your matrimonial prospects are limited now, but—"

"Did you have a particular reason for coming down today?" Evie cut in, looking past her cousin, praying for a customer, any customer, to walk in.

"I thought I'd make calls on several acquaintances, so Wilfred brought me to town in the carriage on his way to the bank. But it's a bit early yet, so I thought I'd drop in for a nice visit with you."

Perhaps she could explain that she was working, that this was not a good time. "Margery," she began, but the other woman forestalled her.

"And while we're on the subject of paying calls, that man should not be calling on you at this time of day. For a gentleman to call on a young lady before three o'clock in the afternoon is unthinkable, even if he is an old acquaintance. And to do it when you are unchaperoned is not just bad form, it's reprehensible. Oh, Evie, don't roll your eyes. I have your best interests at heart, you know."

Margery, Evie reflected, probably believed that. The problem was that Margery's idea of what was in Evie's best interests always seemed to coincide with her own convenience. But again, there was no point in saying so. "It's just that I'm unchaperoned all the time, you know," she said instead.

"I do know, and it's tragic. I really don't understand this insistence upon earning your own living when it really isn't necessary. If you sold the shop, that would give you a nice, tidy sum to put by for your old age. Five thousand pounds, at least. And Wilfred would be happy to invest it for you."

"Oh, I'm sure," Evie agreed, an acerbic note in her voice Margery quite failed to notice.

"Better still, you could pack all this in and come live with us."

"You're very kind," she said, trying not to shudder at the prospect, "but I should go mad without an occupation of some sort."

"You could look after the children. You've always wanted children."

Silently, Evie began counting to ten. "It's not quite the same thing, Margery."

"No, no, of course not, but it would surely be better than this."

Evie thought of Margery's children and was doubtful.

"As I said, Randolph's off to school, but it's at least three years before the other two boys go, and even after that, little Susan would still be at home. Being a nanny is a most respectable occupation for a spin—for an unmarried woman," she amended, perceiving the slight narrowing of Evie's eyes. "And the children do adore you. You're so, so good with them. Why, I think being a nanny is perfectly suited to your talents and temperament."

The door opened before Evie could reply to that backhanded compliment, and she looked up, grateful her prayers were at last being answered, but her gratitude to the Almighty dimmed a bit as the Duke of Westbourne entered the shop. Him again?

Still, as distractions went, even he was better than nothing.

"Well, hullo," she said with forced enthusiasm, bustling around the counter to greet him. "What a great pleasure to see you again so soon."

The duke's brows lifted at such effusive sentiments, but thankfully, he didn't express his doubts aloud. "Indeed?"

he murmured, doffing his hat. "I'm delighted to hear you say so. Nonetheless, your words indicate that you were not expecting me."

"Expecting you?"

"It's Thursday."

Evie stared at him, realizing in astonishment that she'd once again forgotten Delia's request. "Of course," she answered, improvising quickly, wondering what had happened to her brains. "It's just that we're not even open for business yet."

"Which means," Margery put in as she eased between Evie and the duke, "it's far too early for a gentleman to be paying a call on a young lady."

"Forgive me, madam," the duke said at once. "I saw you through the window conversing with Miss Harlow, and I concluded the shop was open." He turned to Evie. "I can return later, if you prefer?"

"Oh, no," Evie said at once. "I wouldn't dream of asking a duke to do such a thing."

The moment those words were out of her mouth, she cursed her mistake.

"Duke?" Margery echoed, her lovely, vapid face lighting with curiosity, an unmistakable gleam coming into her doll-like eyes, reminding Evie that her cousin's self-absorption was only exceeded by her social ambition. Still, the damage was done, and she had little choice but to perform introductions.

"Your Grace, may I present my cousin, Mrs. Symmington? Margery, His Grace, the Duke of Westbourne. As for your concern for the proprieties, dear Cousin, you need have none. The duke is here on a matter of business."

"I am," Westbourne confirmed at once, turning to Margery. "Please allow me to assure you, Mrs. Symmington, that I would never pay a social call upon a young lady when she is unchaperoned. I am here merely as a customer."

"And I really must assist him," Evie put in briskly. "Before other customers begin arriving."

A frown marred Margery's forehead at having this golden opportunity to converse with a duke cut short. "But, Evie," she protested, "we've had barely any time for our visit."

"I know," Evie said, donning her best expression of heartfelt regret. "Such a shame."

The duke, however, almost ruined all her efforts. "As I said, I can return later. It would be no trouble. Or," he added, gesturing to the two wing chairs in the bay window near the front of the shop, "I'd be happy to select a book and wait my turn."

Evie watched in dismay as he picked up the book Rory had given her earlier, bowed, and started to turn away as if abandoning her to her cousin.

Margery, however, didn't like that possibility any more than she did. "Oh, no, Your Grace," she protested, laughing. "I can't allow you to go sit alone in the corner. Please do join us. Evie might even make us some tea?"

"Sorry, Cousin," she was quick to reply before the duke could agree to such an awful prospect. "I've no tea to offer. I ran out last night. And besides, the duke did come on a matter of business." She shot a pointed glance at him. "*Urgent* business."

His mouth quirked, showing that though he might be as irritating as a burr under a saddle, he was also quick on the uptake. "Very urgent, I confess it."

"You see?" Evie turned, tucked her arm through Margery's, and began propelling her toward the door. "It's just as I feared. We shall have to leave our little visit for another day."

"Oh, very well, but you must promise to think about my offer. I mean it sincerely. When you're ready to give all this up, we have a nice little room in the attic all ready and waiting for you. It has a window overlooking the kitchen garden. And there's a servant's staircase straight down to the nursery, which will be most convenient for you."

"I'm sure it's lovely." She opened the door and nudged Margery across the threshold. "And I'm so very grateful. Your kindness and generosity know no bounds, dear Cousin."

Behind her, the duke gave a chuckle, making her fear she'd overdone it, but when she glanced over her shoulder, she found that his attention had been diverted. He was lounging against the counter, the book Rory had given her open in his hands, a grin on his face.

She couldn't imagine what he found amusing to read in a political tract, but she didn't have time to speculate on it. "Good day, dearest," she said, turning to Margery and moving to close the door. "Do come again next time you're down from Hampstead."

Amid a flurry of farewells, Evie closed the door and watched, waiting until the other woman had safely turned the corner before she leaned forward to press her forehead against the glass with a heartfelt sigh of relief.

"My arrival seems to have been most opportune," Westbourne commented behind her, causing Evie to straighten away from the window with a jerk, and when she turned around, she found to her dismay that he had set aside the book, but he was still smiling. It was a knowing smile, making her realize that despite the book, his attention had never been diverted at all.

"Impeccable timing on your part," she was forced to

agree. "At least for me. Not for you, though, I'm sorry to say. I've not progressed much further on that information I promised Delia."

To his credit, the duke didn't seem put out by this admission. And thankfully, he made no references to Rory being the reason for her distraction. "I see. Might I at least review what you do have? Monsieur Escoffier needs to begin making preparations, and I'd like to discuss with him at least some of the ideas you've been working on."

"Of course." She began walking toward the back of the shop, beckoning him to follow her. "Let's go into my office."

She led him through the pantry and past the stairs to the storage room. Averting her gaze from the dirty dishes still waiting to be taken up to her flat, Evie picked her way through the maze of scattered chairs to her desk, which Rory had pushed into the very back corner facing the wall.

"Forgive the mess," she muttered, well aware he knew the reason for the chaos. But there was nothing she could do about it, so she sank into the swivel chair of her battered oak desk, shoved aside stacks of account books and unpaid bills, and pulled out the file containing her notes for Delia's party arrangements.

"No need to apologize. May I?" He gestured to the closest chair, and when she nodded, he drew it forward, positioning it beside her own. "You look tired, Miss Harlow," he remarked as he sat down and set aside his hat.

Evie sat up straighter in her chair at once. "I'm perfectly well," she lied. "Just very busy these days."

Turning, he faced her, propping one elbow on the back of his chair. His eyes, she realized, were not black, but blue—the blue of midnight, and as they scanned her face, she feared they saw far more than they ought. "You work too hard, if I may say so."

"Only until I jaunt off to the Riviera on holiday," she countered, trying to make light of it.

His lips twitched in appreciation of the joke. "Well, I should advise against making the trip anytime soon. The Riviera is beastly hot in summer. Far more pleasant to be here in London at this time of year, enjoying the season."

She gave him a wry look as she opened the file on her desk. "As if the London season were any more likely a prospect for me than the Riviera."

"Would you like it to be?"

Evie frowned, puzzled by the offhand question. "I'm not sure what you mean."

"Precisely what I said. Would you enjoy the season if you had the chance to participate?"

She looked down at her notes about exotic foods she'd never eat at the sort of party she'd never attend. "Your inclination to tease me is not amusing, Your Grace," she said, her voice low.

"Please don't go all prickly on me, Miss Harlow. I was not teasing, and I meant no offense. I was merely curious."

"I can't imagine why."

"My curiosity stems from a conversation I had with the three young men who accompanied me the other day. A conversation about you."

Evie turned her head, eyeing him askance. "Me?"

"Yes."

He said nothing more, and though Evie knew it was probably folly to probe further, she couldn't help it. After all, who could hear something like that about oneself and not follow it up? "What was said?"

He opened his mouth to reply, but then he hesitated as if suddenly uncomfortable with the question. "You won't like it, I daresay," he said at last.

"Given you and your friends, that's not surprising."

Her tart reply caused a rueful smile to curve his lips. "You seem to adore putting our lot in our place, don't you? That very quality, in fact, is one of the things we were discussing. You see, the lads rather took offense to you ordering them about and being so prim and disapproving."

Evie laughed, genuinely amused. "Did they, indeed?"

"They felt it was damned impertinent of you, scolding them as if you were their nanny."

Evie's amusement faded, her cousin's words from earlier in the day echoing through her mind.

*Being a nanny is perfectly suited to your talents and temperament...a most respectable occupation for a spinster.*

She swallowed hard. "My, my, how devastating," she said, striving to keep her voice carelessly offhand. "Having heard that, I just don't know how I'll sleep tonight. No doubt," she added as he chuckled, "you agreed with them."

He sobered at once. "On the contrary, I disputed their contentions, and thereby launched a spirited debate on the subject."

That his friends had disparaged her wasn't particularly astonishing, but the idea that this man did not share their view and had felt the need to speak in her defense was such a surprise, she didn't know how to respond.

"I can't imagine how my so-called impertinence could evoke such strong reactions," she replied after a moment. "There must have been more to the conversation than that."

"Your instincts do you credit, Miss Harlow. I—" He

broke off and gave a short laugh. "I confess, my intro-duction of this topic was deliberate and for a specific purpose, but now that I have launched it, I am finding it far more difficult than I had anticipated, and I am realizing—belatedly—that in discussing it I will very likely offend you, something I do not wish nor ever intended to do."

Evie was of no frame of mind to let it go now. "It's a bit late for regrets, isn't it? I think you need to tell me what this is really about."

"Very well. My reason for informing you of this discus-sion is that a wager was laid as a result."

"A wager?" She stiffened. "You and your friends made a wager about *me*?"

He grimaced. "Yes."

"Of all the cheek!" Highly indignant, Evie knew the right thing to do was toss him out on his ear, but much to her chagrin, she realized that her indignation was not as strong as her curiosity. "What sort of wager?"

He gave a cough. "Yes, well, as I said, it all began with their view of you."

"That I was prim and disapproving and reminded them of their nanny?"

"That, yes, and..."

"And?" she prompted when he paused.

"It wasn't...ahem..." He stirred in his chair, obviously uncomfortable. "It wasn't a flattering portrait, I'm sorry to say."

"So I'm discovering. Go on."

"What they said doesn't matter, and I'd rather not get into the weeds with irrelevant details. The point is—"

"It clearly does matter, since you brought it up," she said, becoming impatient. "And the more you prevaricate, the more determined I am to hear what was said about me."

He sighed, raked a hand through his hair, and sat back, eyeing her unhappily.

"Very well." He drew a breath and let it out. "They deemed you rather plain and unremarkable."

That stung, though she knew it shouldn't. The proper thing to do, of course, was to tell him what she thought of him and his friends and their thoughtless discussions about young women they didn't even know. But some imp inside her that was clearly a glutton for punishment drove her on, seeming not to care about the proper thing.

"Goodness," she said, forcing a lightness into her voice that she feared didn't fool him for a second. "And what did you say?"

"I disagreed."

"You did?"

"I did." A smile crinkled the corners of his eyes. "How do you think the wager came about?"

A strange warmth pooled in Evie's stomach, as if she'd just downed a swallow of brandy, and she suddenly found it hard to breathe, or even think. "I don't think I understand."

"I contended that they were all blind as bats, that you were far more attractive than they gave you credit for, and that, if given half a chance, you could be regarded as an incomparable beauty."

"What?" She gave a disbelieving laugh that she feared sounded more like an inelegant snort. "Me? Now I know you really are teasing. Or you're the one who's blind as a bat."

He didn't reply at once. Instead, his gaze lowered, then lifted in a slow, thorough perusal that made the warmth inside her deepen and spread.

"On the contrary," he murmured, meeting her eyes again,

"I have many defects, Miss Harlow, but let me assure you there is nothing wrong with my eyesight."

Something new stirred inside of Evie, something nebulous that flickered to life and began rising up from the very depths of her: the yearning to believe him.

It baffled her, and it made her afraid, though what she feared, she could not have said.

Unable to endure the onslaught of so many powerful emotions at once, she jumped to her feet. "I told you before," she said, her voice cold, "I don't appreciate being teased."

He rose, facing her. "I know that this entire conversation has offended you—quite rightly—but please let me say that I was not teasing, not in the least."

The fear inside her grew stronger. "I see no reason to believe you. And I don't appreciate being discussed in bars by gentlemen who ought to know better. And I really don't appreciate being the subject of their wagers!"

"I'm sure," he conceded. "But at the time, I was far too irritated with their idiotic point of view to consider the sensibilities. And," he added as she made a sound of skepticism, "I also felt that you would enjoy participating."

"Participating in what?" she asked crossly, offended and out of patience with him and this entire conversation. "You want me to place a bet, too?"

For some reason, the question made him chuckle. "I'd be happy to allow that if the lads would agree, but it isn't what I meant."

"Then what did you mean?"

"For the bet to proceed, your cooperation—indeed, your full and active participation would be needed. You see, when I said you could be regarded as an incomparable beauty, they called on me to prove it, and bet me a hundred pounds I couldn't make it happen. Well, I wasn't about to let a challenge like that pass, so I agreed to arrange your launch into society, and here we are."

Evie frowned, utterly lost at sea. "And where is 'here,' Your Grace? Just *what* are you suggesting?"

"A holiday, Miss Harlow. I am suggesting that you take a holiday."

# 5

*A* holiday? The prospect was so ludicrous, so impossible, and so typical of what a member of his class would suggest, that Evie could only laugh.

"At least I've succeeded in amusing you," he said, "and I'm glad, even though it's at my expense."

"Can I be blamed for that?"

"No," he conceded, "but after you stop laughing and before you send me packing, let me make my case."

"Case for what? Helping you win a hundred pounds?"

"For you to take a holiday," he reminded. "Delia told me how hard you work, so I suspect you're in need of one."

"How sweet of you to think of what I need," she murmured.

He grinned, not seeming the least put out. "If you agree to this, there would be other benefits for you."

"Ah, yes." She gave a sigh of mock rapture. "I always knew I could be a beauty if only some man would come along and show me how."

His grin faded, but a suspicious curve still lingered at

the edges of his mouth, showing that her attempts to needle him were a waste of breath. "I don't intend to show you anything," he said. "Revealing your very best self to the world will be your responsibility, not mine."

"I do all the work, and you win a hundred pounds. What girl could resist such an offer?"

"Does a fashionable new wardrobe tempt you? If you're going into society, you'll need one."

Sadly, she couldn't argue with him about her clothes. They were...

*Unremarkable.*

"I'll arrange for you to see a modiste who will help you to assemble a wardrobe appropriate to the season. For the next six weeks, I propose you stay at the Savoy and have a maid attend you. You can sleep as late as you like, have breakfast in bed—"

"But I can't afford—"

"Will you stop interrupting?" he chided.

She made an expansive gesture, though she knew he was wasting his time. "Do go on."

"I can arrange for you to attend the theater, the opera, whatever you'd like. In a few weeks, when Delia returns from Rome, she can chaperone you, and with a bit of help from me, she'll introduce you into the appropriate circles. You'll meet new people, make new friends, and enjoy all the pleasures the London season has to offer. You will have fun, I promise you, and fun is something I sense you don't often allow yourself."

The indulgences he was describing were beyond her experience and even her imagination, and she couldn't see why anyone would be inclined to launch her into society merely to win a bet or how any of it would transform her into something she wasn't.

She could, however, appreciate the practical difficulties. "But what about my shop?"

"I propose that for the next six weeks, you close your shop."

"What?" She stared at him, aghast. "I can't do that."

"Why not? It is your shop, isn't it?"

"I realize running a business seems incredibly mundane to someone of your position, but for someone like me, it's a bit different. And I can't afford to do without an income, not even for a week, much less six."

"Very well. Leave your shop open. We'll hire someone from an employment agency to run things while you're away."

"Which still costs money."

"But not that much."

"And besides," she went on as if he hadn't spoken, "I have other duties that can't so easily be handed off to a subordinate. I have clients—authors—who need me to do research for their books. What about them? Am I to turn them away?"

"Yes," he answered uncompromisingly. "That's why it's called a holiday, Miss Harlow. It's a time away from one's work for the purpose of rest and relaxation. Believe it or not," he added as she made a sound of impatience, "people do it all the time."

Oddly, the more he refuted her arguments, the more arguments she felt inclined to make. "But what about my customers? What if someone is searching for a rare book? A temporary help hired from an agency wouldn't know where to look for such things. And how could I trust a person I don't know to run things in my stead? And what about Delia's party? And what about my friend who holds his political meetings here?"

"Friend?" he echoed with obvious disdain. "You mean that scoundrel who was eating all your sandwiches and tea cakes the other day?" He glanced at the table, noting the plates and cups still there from last night. "Raided your larder again, I see. I hope he left you more than crumbs this time?"

Evie scowled at him. "That is a most obnoxious thing to say."

"Is it? When it's clear he takes blatant advantage of you?"

"Oh, he does not."

He shrugged. "Well, you know him better than I."

This sudden acquiescence only made him more irritating. "Are all peers as opinionated, interfering, and insulting as you?"

"Some are worse," he answered with cheer.

"I can well believe it, if you and your fellow blue bloods from the other day are anything to go by."

"Never fear. Delia and I will ensure that you meet many worthy young men of your own class."

"My own class?" she echoed, bristling even though she was the one who'd underscored the class difference.

He didn't seem to notice. "You'll surely meet one or two that take your fancy, and who would suit you. You might even find one to marry."

"But not a peer," she reminded. "Why the distinction? Is it that I'm not good enough to marry a peer, in your view?"

"Do you want to marry a peer?" he countered, looking surprised.

"Of course not!" Evie was now angry enough to spit nails. Not that it would do any good. She doubted even the sharpest nails could penetrate his arrogant sense of superiority. "I wouldn't have one of your lot on a plate."

"Well, there we are, then. But don't worry," he added as she made a sound of utter exasperation. "Any men to whom you are introduced by Delia or me will be men of good family with excellent prospects, men far more deserving of your attentions than your so-called friend."

"I doubt it."

"I don't. Hell, if I have my way, you'll have suitors bringing you flowers, penning you sonnets, and giving you books you might actually want to read. You won't miss that blackguard's attentions in the least."

"What I will miss is something you are not qualified to judge," she shot back. "And I don't need flowers or sonnets or suitors lined up at my door. One suitor is good enough for me."

"Even if he is unworthy of you?"

"He's as worthy as they come. There are many women," she added as he gave a shout of laughter, "who would find Rory quite a catch, I'll have you know. He's very handsome."

"Yes, he is," the duke unexpectedly agreed. "And he knows it."

"He and I have been friends since childhood."

"One might just as well be friends with a pigeon."

"What are you saying? That Rory is like a pigeon?"

"Isn't he? He serves no useful purpose, gobbles up all the food in sight, makes messes everywhere, and struts about like he's the cock of the walk."

A brutal assessment. But one, she realized, her anger faltering, that had a ring of truth, confirming the secret suspicion hovering around in the back of her mind during the past several days, a suspicion she had refused to acknowledge.

No wonder her spirits were low. The best chance for romance she'd ever had, and after only two weeks' reacquaintance, he was already proving a disappointment.

She'd have died, however, before admitting any of that to this man. "So, he's a bit like your friends, then?" she said instead.

"Very similar, I agree, but as I told you the other day, those young men are not my friends. They are mere acquaintances, and rather tiresome ones at that. Ones I'd dearly love to see set down a notch or two."

If he thought that would disarm her, he was mistaken. "One point we can agree on!"

"Just so. Which is the best reason of all why you should agree to take this on and help me win the bet."

"I don't see how any of what you describe helps you do that. The whole thing's ridiculous."

"But deuced good fun. Come now," he added before she could argue the point, "wouldn't you love to prove to Freddie Maybridge and his friends that they were utterly wrong in their assessment of you? Wouldn't you like to see them eat humble pie?"

Evie thought of them, swaggering about, knocking over her books and demeaning her shop—demeaning her, too, from the sound of it. The chance to show them up was almost irresistible. She bit her lip, wavering a little.

To wear a beautiful gown and jewels, to watch their jaws drop as they realized just who they were looking at, to have them dancing attendance and clamoring for her attentions after the things they'd said about her...what a sweet, sweet pleasure that would be.

As if it would ever happen.

Evie brought herself firmly back down to earth. "As I said, it's ridiculous. And even if it weren't, it's not possible. I can't close my shop. And I haven't a fraction of the blunt to buy a new wardrobe, or stay at the Savoy, or—"

"I'll stand all the expenses, of course."

Evie was shocked. "I couldn't possibly allow a man to buy clothes for me or pay for my hotel room. It would be most improper."

For some reason, that amused him. "Well, the whole thing's a bit improper, really," he said, laughing. He leaned closer, so close she caught the scent of bay rum on his cheek, and it was so luscious, she inhaled a deep, appreciative breath before she could stop herself. "But no one ever has to find out."

"That's not..." She paused and swallowed hard, trying to gather her scattered wits. "That's not the point," she whispered.

"Perhaps not," he agreed, smiling faintly. He leaned even closer, and for no reason Evie could fathom, her toes curled inside her shoes. "But it'll be our little secret."

He made it sound so...deliciously naughty.

Desperate, Evie took a step back. "What about your friends? They would never keep such a secret."

"Don't worry about them. They won't tell, I promise you. If they do, they'll never get back into Oxford. Even worse, they'll remain stone broke for years."

She had no idea what he meant by that, but it didn't really matter. "I don't see how mere clothes could transform me into something I'm not. And, anyway, I see no reason to allow myself to be dressed up like a doll and paraded in front of your friends for amusement."

"It wouldn't be like that."

The very gentleness of his voice, as if he could read her mind, as if he could sense, somehow, the secret fears that lurked inside of her, was more than she could bear. It made her feel raw, exposed, so very vulnerable.

Who was this man to see inside her? she thought, her

anger reasserting itself like a protective wall. She didn't need him to defend her to his awful friends or protect her from their stupid opinions. And who were they to pass judgment on anything about her anyway? She could imagine them, huddled together over glasses of port, dissecting her looks and her character, and making wagers over whether she could be made over to suit their notions of beauty and behavior. "I won't be a toy in your silly, aristocratic games. My answer is no."

He didn't reply. Instead, he studied her for a long moment, so long, in fact, that she had to fight the impulse to wriggle under that piercing blue-black stare.

"I can see why it might seem that way," he said at last. "But, somehow, I don't think that's the real reason why you're refusing. You want to know what I think?"

She set her jaw. "Not particularly."

"I think the real reason you're turning down my proposition is that you're afraid."

"Afraid? That is absurd!"

"On the contrary, it's perfectly understandable. After all, if you change things, you move into unknown territory. If you dream, your dreams might be crushed. If you aspire to more than you have, you might fail. If you hold your standards too high, you might never find romance. So instead, you try to reconcile yourself to the hand you've been dealt and tell yourself it's good enough. You settle for less than you deserve, including the attentions of a man who is unworthy of you."

"How dare you say such things?" she cried, her anger flaring higher. "You don't even know me."

"Neither do you. You can't see yourself as you truly are or explore what you could become. Don't you want to find out? Don't you want to at least peek out of your safe little nest to see what exciting, wonderful possibilities might be out there for you?"

"That's torn it. I've heard enough." Turning, she picked up the file from her desk. "Here," she said, jabbing the edge of the folder into his abdomen. "This is all the information I have for Delia's party at the moment. Take it, along with your wager and your insufferable presumptions, and go."

He didn't move, adding to her anger, and as they stared at each other in hostile silence, Evie feared she might have to grab a chair and drive him out like a lion tamer might do with beasts in the circus ring. But thankfully, Westbourne capitulated at last.

"Very well," he said as he pulled the file from her fingers. "I often speak my mind, Miss Harlow, sometimes far more bluntly than I should, and I have certainly done so in this case. Please accept my apologies."

He turned and reached for his hat. "When you have the rest of Delia's information ready, send word to me at the Savoy, and I will have my valet come and fetch it. Good day. I doubt we shall meet again." He met her gaze as he donned his hat. "Much to my regret."

He bowed and walked away, and after a moment, the bell jangled, the door closed, and she knew he had left the shop. His departure, however, gave Evie no sense of relief, for in the silence that followed, his words echoed through her mind.

*Their view of you wasn't a flattering portrait...rather plain...unremarkable...*

With a muttered oath, Evie stalked out of the storage room, reminding herself that she had better things to do than contemplate what he or anyone else in the smart set thought of her.

*I contended that they were all blind as bats, that you*

*were far more attractive than they gave you credit for, and that, if given half a chance, you could be regarded as an incomparable beauty.*

Incomparable beauty. And pigs might fly, too.

But as she passed through the pantry, she caught a glint of light in the tiny mirror above the counter, and almost against her will, she stopped to stare at it, wondering what could have inspired such an opinion.

She leaned forward, peering at her reflection in the rather wavy glass, but it offered no answers.

All she could see was a pointy chin, a tired mouth, dark circles, and too many freckles.

Evie turned impatiently away from the mirror and continued on with her work. As she turned the placard in her window from Closed to Open, as she rearranged books, dusted shelves, and filled the cash register, she tried to forget the entire appalling episode. But that, she soon discovered, was easier said than done.

*You will have fun, I promise you, and fun is something I sense you don't often allow yourself...You'll meet new people, make new friends...*

Evie gave a snort of derision. Not his circle, of course, for he'd made it very clear she wasn't good enough for that. Not that she wanted to be anywhere near his circle. At least they had agreed on that much.

*Wouldn't you like to see them eat humble pie?*

No, she wouldn't. She'd be mad to seek for the second time the good opinion of people who would talk about her behind her back and ridicule her because of things like physical appearance and background.

*It wouldn't be like that.*

Ah, but it would. Evie stilled, her hands resting on the drawer of the cash register. It would be just like that.

*You can't see yourself as you truly are or explore what you could become. Don't you want to find out? Don't you want to at least peek out of your safe little nest to see what exciting, wonderful possibilities might be out there for you?*

Evie looked up, staring at her surroundings. The shop, the flat, the books—this was her safe little nest, she realized with a grimace. It was familiar and predictable. And she had always been happy here.

Until now.

Evie slammed the cash register closed. She'd been glad to come back here, happy to help her father in the shop, relieved to be back in a world that accepted her for just what she was, a world she knew and understood. And after Papa's death, she'd welcomed the distraction of running things on her own. Making it solvent again had been a challenge, one that in her grief, she had badly needed and had eventually come to enjoy. And with each debt paid off, there had been a sense of triumph and satisfaction.

But now, there was no debt. There was no challenge. Only the mundane daily routine. And lately, hadn't she felt a faint discontent stirring in the air? During the past year or two, there had been mornings when getting out of bed and going downstairs had seemed like a pointless journey, endless days when even her beloved books weren't enough to hold her interest, nights when she'd lain in bed, staring at the ceiling, bone tired yet unable to sleep. She'd wondered, more often than she liked to admit, if perhaps it might be best to let it all go, do something else.

But one thing had always hushed her questions and silenced her doubts before they could ever take hold: What else was there for a woman like her?

*Better still, you could pack all this in and come live with us.*

Margery's offer felt like the last straw, the period punctuating the end of a decade of hard work, work that had once been exciting and enjoyable, but that now seemed stale, joyless, and dull.

And then Rory had come home, bringing with him the possibility of romance, love, perhaps even marriage. Was that what she really wanted—to marry Rory?

*A man who is unworthy of you.*

Her gaze slid to the book still sitting on the counter beside her, and as she stared at it, she remembered the duke with the book open in his hands, entertained by something he'd read within its pages. On impulse, she snatched up the slim little volume, wondering if she could determine what that man had found so amusing in a political tract.

The moment she opened it, however, the words scrawled across the flyleaf in Rory's nearly illegible handwriting caused her to regret her curiosity and curse the duke's painfully shrewd perceptions all over again.

*To my favorite worker.*

Evie stared at the words and felt a sudden, absurd impulse to cry.

"Hell," she muttered, tossed aside the book, and sagged wearily against the counter.

No, she would not be marrying Rory. She supposed that wasn't a loss to be mourned, but it felt shattering just the same, because with it came the acknowledgment that there might not be another chance.

She was twenty-eight, every bit the spinster Margery had almost called her. How could she ever hope to be anything else? She never went anywhere, and she never seemed to meet any eligible men, at least none under sixty. She supported herself—barely—with a business that had once been a challenge but had somehow become a chore.

She had just been presented with the chance for a holiday, a way to alleviate the tedium, but as she'd told the duke, it was impossible.

But what if it weren't?

Evie found herself wavering. Yes, it was a sting to her pride that men were debating her attractiveness and placing wagers on it. Yes, the duke's proposition was absurd. Yes, it had risks.

But maybe it was time to be a bit absurd and take a few risks?

That tiny little surge she'd felt earlier welled up again, the longing for something else, something more, something that would lift her out of a rut she hadn't even realized she'd fallen into.

*You're afraid.*

The duke had been right. She was afraid. What a ghastly thing to admit. And yet, she wasn't a naïve girl in finishing school anymore. She was different now, wasn't she? Older, wiser, stronger, braver.

She didn't feel brave. But wasn't that what came of playing too safe?

"This is ridiculous!" she cried aloud, exasperated with herself for even considering it. "It would be insane to agree to this—set myself up to be humiliated by people who think they're better than me? Let some bored duke and his friends amuse themselves at my expense? Why should I?"

She looked up, staring in resentment at the ceiling overhead, imagining she could see beyond it to the heavens above, demanding an answer to her question from the highest authority possible. "Why the hell should I?"

Suddenly, an explosive bang rang out from above, a sound so loud it rattled the plate glass windows and caused the very walls of the building to shudder. In its wake, Evie could hear a strange, gushing sound that was somehow even more ominous than the bang had been.

With a cry of alarm, she raced for the stairs at the back of the shop, the duke's proposition, her agonizing doubts, and her questions to the Almighty all forgotten.

She started up the staircase, but on the landing, she stopped, her hand clenching around the cap of the newel post as she stared in horror at the flood of water that was tumbling down the steps toward her.

It washed over her feet in a warm wave, and as it continued on toward the shop below, Evie realized with a sick sense of dismay that the ancient boiler must have exploded, sending its three hundred gallons of water spreading throughout the attic and down into her flat. Soon, it would completely flood the shop.

She looked up from her soaking wet shoes and scowled venomously at the ceiling overhead, appreciating that her defiant question had just been answered.

God, she decided, had a wretched sense of humor.

# 6

If Max had to make a list of lessons learned in life, the first one would have been to never marry out of your class. Prominent placement would also have been allotted to never giving cheek to Oxford dons and never kissing a girl while in church. But after his most recent encounter with Miss Harlow, Max was prepared to add another to his list: never make a bet if you're drunk.

He had been decidedly in his cups the other night at the Savoy, granted, but even the following day, he'd still regarded the wager as little more than a lark. It wasn't until he'd begun laying out the circumstances to Miss Harlow that he appreciated how insulting it all might sound to her ears.

A serious mistake on his part.

Sitting down with her face-to-face, stumbling his way through explanations of how the bet had come about, he'd felt as embarrassed as an unprepared schoolboy reciting an essay. In consequence, he'd behaved boorishly, abandoned any shred of tact, and been deservedly booted out of her shop. Now, walking back to the Savoy with her scathing words still ringing in his ears, Max was forced to acknowledge that he'd made a mess of the whole business.

There was nothing for it but to forfeit the wager. A shame, really. He was more certain than ever Evie Harlow was in serious need of fun. He also remained convinced there were many young blades about town who'd be happy to oblige her in that regard, men far more deserving of her attentions than the one she'd set her sights on. Sadly, making her appreciate all that seemed as likely as the Prince of Wales playing the fiddle in Leicester Square. And if all that wasn't enough to make Max gloomy as an undertaker, he'd have to admit defeat to that impudent pup Freddie Maybridge. What a nauseating prospect.

It wasn't long, however, before Max discovered his pessimism might have been premature. Among the letters delivered with his breakfast the following morning was one from Miss Harlow inquiring if he might pay a call on her at the bookshop that afternoon to further elucidate the terms of what they had discussed.

Scarcely able to believe it, Max read the neatly penned lines of script a second time, but before he'd gotten halfway through, he was laughing with astonishment and relief. "Well, I'll be damned."

"Happy news, Your Grace?" Stowell inquired as he paused beside Max's chair to pour coffee.

"Indeed, it is. News so happy that it might result in my winning a sweet hundred quid."

Stowell, who had the face of a church warden and the temperament to match, and who had valeted him since he was twelve years old, merely raised an eyebrow. "Wagers,"

he said with disapproval, "often have the opposite consequence, Your Grace."

"Not this time, Stowell," he replied with glee. "Not if I
can help it."

Though Miss Harlow's note gave him reason to hope, he
knew it was nothing more at this point than the opportunity
to try again. Max, never one to make the same mistake
twice, took the precaution of preparing far more for his
next conversation with her than he had the previous one.
By the time he reached the bookshop that afternoon, he
had at least a dozen reasons why she ought to accept his
proposition, reasons that had nothing to do with her looks,
her undesirable suitor, or her current station in life.

When he arrived, however, he found that she was not
equally prepared to receive him. A placard on the door
declared the shop to be closed.

Despite the sign, however, she was on the premises.
Peering through the plate glass window, he could see her
plainly, hands on her hips, conversing with a bearded
fellow in a checked suit and bowler hat. Not a customer,
he judged, if her battle-ready stance and the frown rippling
her brow were any indication.

Max tried the door, and it opened, jangling the bell as
he entered, but she did not even glance in his direction, and
when he put his foot over the threshold, he immediately
appreciated the reason why.

The floor was covered by at least an inch of water,
enough to slosh over the toes of his boots and soak the hem
of his trousers, enough that the floorboards were cupping
and the books on the lowest shelves were precariously
close to ruin. The problem seemed to have come from
above—if the water stains marking the ceiling plaster and
streaking the wallpaper were any indication.

Max, glad of his ankle boots, paused by the door to wait, and soon found that his guess had been correct. He also discovered the cause of Miss Harlow's displeasure.

"You must understand," the man was saying, "a boiler only explodes when it is old and the owner has not taken the proper steps to maintain it."

"But I have properly maintained it, as I have been trying to explain. I can show you—"

"The Metropolitan Insurance Company," he interrupted coldly, "cannot be expected to merely take your word. We have to judge the situation based on what we see, and having examined the boiler, I can find no such efforts on your part, nor any reason for us to pay for your obvious negligence."

"My negligence?" Her frown deepened and her lips pressed into a tight line, giving her face an implacable expression that Max immediately recognized.

"There was no negligence on my part, Mr. Walpole, I can assure you," she said. "The boiler is old, I admit, but as I have already said—"

"Just so," the insurance agent cut in again, "and a boiler as ancient as yours requires far more diligent care than you have been willing to exercise. The fact is obvious."

Her shoulders went back, her chin went up, and he knew she was about to do something she'd regret.

Max gave a loud cough. "Ahem."

Both of them glanced his way, and he jumped into the breach before either of them could speak. "If I may," he said, sloshing toward them through the standing water, "insurance companies always make property assessments before issuing a policy." He paused beside the insurance agent and his customer, glancing back and forth between them as if puzzled. "Surely Metropolitan did a thorough inspection before offering Miss Harlow insurance and must have been aware of the boiler's age and condition. When was the policy issued?"

The agent did not seem pleased by this intrusion into the conversation. "I am not at liberty to reveal such information to a random stranger, sir."

"Your discretion does you credit," Max replied, assuming as chastened an expression as he could manage in the face of this rebuke and trying not to spoil it by laughing. "And I'm sure Miss Harlow appreciates that, but in this case, an exception can surely be made."

"Metropolitan," Walpole said with withering scorn, "does not make exceptions."

"Even if your customer has no objection?"

He glanced at Miss Harlow, who played up beautifully.

"The policy was issued ten years ago," she told him. "No concerns about the boiler were noted by Metropolitan at that time."

"Ah." Gratified, Max returned his attention to the agent. "Now, as a—"

"And as I have already told Miss Harlow," Mr. Walpole interrupted, making no effort to conceal his growing impatience, "in those ten years, the boiler has been allowed to deteriorate to an appalling condition."

Beside him, Miss Harlow stirred, making a smothered sound of outrage, and he gave her foot a gentle, cautionary nudge with his own.

"As a Metropolitan customer myself," Max continued as if the other man had not spoken, "I am astonished that your company seems so unwilling to fulfill your obligations in this case. The vast holdings of my dukedom have sometimes required insurance claims upon Metropolitan, and in those distressing situations, I have always found your company to be most cooperative and helpful." He paused, frowning. "Until now, that is."

"Dukedom?" Mr. Walpole echoed, staring at him in astonishment. "Vast holdings?"

"Oh, did I not introduce myself? Forgive me." Max removed his hat and bowed, by now thoroughly enjoying his role. "I am the Duke of Westbourne. Also, Marquess of Denby, Earl of Rievaulx, and Viscount Marbury, of course."

One didn't usually rattle away all one's titles, but Max felt that Mr. Walpole needed to hear them all. When the insurance agent failed to reply, however, Max decided he may have overdone it, and his permission to speak would clearly be needed. "And you are...?" he prompted.

"Walpole, Your Grace," the insurance agent muttered, looking a bit green and wilted, and reminding Max of a boiled lettuce. "Mr. Edgar Walpole, at your service."

"Are you indeed at my service, Mr. Walpole? I'm gratified to hear it, for Miss Harlow's establishment is my favorite bookshop in London, and the unreasonable stance you have taken on her claim makes me inclined to doubt your assurances. Further," he went on, overriding the other man's feeble attempts to reply, "this intransigence on your part might force her to close Harlow's permanently, which would cause me a great deal of inconvenience. I'm sure you don't wish me to be inconvenienced, do you?"

"Oh, no, Your Grace," Walpole whispered, now ashen white.

"Excellent." He condescended to bestow a hint of a smile on the other man. "You will, I trust, expedite Miss Harlow's insurance claim and schedule all the necessary restorations to begin immediately? Be sure they are careful in packing up the books for storage. Most are rare and precious volumes in need of delicate handling."

"Yes, Your Grace." Walpole's head bobbed up and down. "It will be done."

"And," Max went on, taking full advantage of the other man's newfound cooperation, "if you could have the contractors send their bills to you directly, it would make this stressful time so much easier for Miss Harlow. That is possible, I'm sure?"

"Yes, yes, of course," Walpole said, so desperately eager to please that Max was sure ordering him to jump off the roof would send the poor fellow scurrying for the stairs.

He suppressed the impulse to test this mischievous theory. "I knew I could count on Metropolitan to do the right thing," he said instead. "I am most grateful, Mr. Walpole. I look forward to seeing workmen here first thing tomorrow."

Amid stammering expressions of regret for ever having given offense, hopeful queries that his superiors would not be told of his error in judgment today, and reassurances that the work on the bookshop would begin tomorrow as requested, Mr. Walpole took his departure.

"Now that," Max said, laughing as the door closed behind the agent, "must rank as one of the most gratifying uses of ducal privilege I've ever exercised."

Beside him, Miss Harlow made a smothered sound, and when he glanced at her, he was struck by something extraordinary. "Why, Miss Harlow," he murmured, turning toward her and leaning closer to study her face, "is that a smile I see? Directed at me? I am all astonishment. Can this mean I am forgiven for my conduct yesterday?"

Her expression turned rueful. "Given you may have just saved my shop from permanent closure, I can hardly do otherwise, especially since I was getting nowhere with that awful man."

"Perhaps not. But if I may offer a word of advice, it never does to lose one's temper with pettifogging clerks who have power, such as insurance agents."

"I kept trying not to, but after nearly an hour of discussion that made me feel as if I were banging my head into a stone wall, I was finding it hard to hold on to my temper."

He glanced over her face, noting the same signs of hardship and worry that had struck him upon their first meeting, reminding him how close to the bone she lived. She had not only been frustrated earlier, he realized, but also frightened.

"An understandable reaction," he said gently, "when one's entire livelihood is on the line."

"Yes." She stirred, as if she could sense what he was thinking and it made her uncomfortable. "Which means you could not have arrived at a better time. Are your holdings really insured with Metropolitan?"

"One." He paused, considering. "I think," he amended.

"You're not sure?"

"Well, it's a bit hard to keep track, if you must know. My land agents usually handle that sort of thing. It hardly matters anyway. Shall Mr. Walpole ignore the wishes of a duke?"

"I suppose not. Either way..." She paused and cleared her throat. "Thank you. I'm very grateful."

"No gratitude is necessary, truly. I can't recall the last time I enjoyed myself so much. And besides, what are friends for?"

"Friends?" She sniffed, though he suspected she wasn't really displeased by the presumption. "Are we, indeed?"

"Well, I live in hope. Especially given that you sent me an olive branch this morning." He reached into the breast pocket of his morning coat and pulled out her note. "I take it you may be reconsidering my proposition?"

She sighed, gesturing to their surroundings. "I have little choice. Until repairs are made, my flat is uninhabitable, the shop will have to be closed, and with the season on, there isn't a decent room available anywhere in London that I can afford. I stayed with my friend Anna and her son last night. She owns the confectionery shop next door, so it's convenient, but I can't stop on there too long. The renovations could take weeks, and the flat above their shop is tiny."

Unable to resist teasing her, he said, "I'm surprised you didn't take up residence with your cousin. She offered you a room in the attic, if I recall. It even has a window."

She pressed her lips together to hide her smile. "I'd rather not."

"Prefer the Savoy, do you?"

"That was part of your proposition, if I remember correctly?"

"It was," he assured as he tucked the note back into his pocket. "A suite and all the room service you like. Just give me a few hours to make the arrangements, then I shall send a cab around to fetch you and your things. I shouldn't advise bringing too much luggage, since you will be visiting a modiste straightaway. You'll want some amusements while we wait for Delia to return, of course—the theater, ballet, the opera, and such. Simply inform me of any performance you might wish to see, and I will arrange for tickets. Remember, since Delia's not here, and I can't escort you anywhere, you'll need someone to go with you."

"Not Cousin Margery, please."

He grinned. "No, not Margery. Not if you don't wish it. Do you have a married friend or two who can accompany you?"

She considered for a moment. "I suppose Anna could come with me. She's a widow."

"She'll do nicely, then. If you want any other friends, feel free to include them."

She bit her lip, eyeing him with doubt. "This all sounds terribly expensive."

"I already told you, I shall stand every penny of the expense. But if that doesn't suit you," he added as she started to protest, "we will use the winnings to pay the expenses. A hundred pounds will be more than enough."

"And if we lose?"

"We won't lose, but if we do, I will simply expect impeccable service when I need to acquire any additional rare books for my library."

"You have a library?"

"Does that surprise you?"

"Well, yes, actually. The other day, I heard you admit to your friends that a bookshop isn't where you could usually be found."

"I do wish you'd stop calling them my friends. They are mere acquaintances. But they were right to say that I don't frequent bookstores as a rule. If I want a book, I simply order it and have a footman pick it up."

"Ducal privilege?"

"No, I simply detest shopping."

She laughed. "Then I shall be happy to assist you with your literary requirements. Still, to return to the point, it would be absurd to think of that as repayment for all this."

"Miss Harlow, please stop. This is a sporting wager. Repayment is not necessary."

She shook her head, laughing a little. "You aristocrats astonish me. It seems madly extravagant to spend so much just for a wager of one hundred pounds. Even if you win, you won't profit much by it."

"Monetarily, no, but there are other compensations."

"Such as?"

Unbidden, an image came into his head of Miss Harlow, her hair piled up high on her head, candlelight shining on the mink-brown strands, dark circles and worry lines soothed away from her face, her slim figure in a provocatively low-cut gown, jewels nestled in the cleft between small, perfect breasts—

"Your Grace?"

Appreciating the unexpectedly erotic direction his thoughts had taken, Max blinked, dissolving the picture. "Sorry, I...ahem..." He paused, pushing carnal masculine imaginings out of his mind. "I consider it money well spent. I appreciate your pride, and it does you credit, but please do not allow that, or any sense of propriety, to deprive me of the enjoyment I shall feel at watching Freddie taken down a notch or two. In addition, he'll be forced to behave himself, which will be good for him and will please his sister, Helen, who is a charming girl, and a friend of mine—"

"Friend?"

The question made him laugh. "You needn't sound so surprised. I do have friends, you know. Including you, I might add."

"I would not call you a friend yet," she couldn't resist pointing out. "I hardly know you. And to be honest, I'm not sure I even like you."

"Evie, that's not fair. I put that wretched Mr. Walpole in his place for you, didn't I? Come now, that's the start of a friendship, surely?"

"Perhaps," she conceded. "But," she added before he could rest on his laurels there, "I didn't give you leave to call me Evie. The cheek!"

"I'm a duke," he said, giving her a look of mock apology.

"We're often cheeky. And I'm willing to reciprocate and let you call me Max. There, that's friendship for you."

She laughed, and he began to feel he was making progress. "Don't you like your name?"

"Maximillian?" He made a face. "Would you?"

"It sounds quite ducal."

"Even so, I don't allow most people to call me by my Christian name, I assure you. So, you see? We have to be friends now."

"Oh, very well," she capitulated, "for though it's not proper, I am coming to realize propriety makes no impression on you. As for Freddie's sister," she added, reverting to their previous topic, "I received the impression she was more than a friend?"

"Well, that's my hope, at any rate. And when she expressed concern that her brother was becoming too wild, what else could I do but offer my help?"

"You seem to do that often."

"In this case it's self-preservation, since Freddie will become my brother-in-law if my hopes come to fruition. Besides, I've a soft spot for damsels in distress. What can I say?"

"Yes, you're such a hero."

He grinned at the barb. "Helen thinks so, since I agreed to watch over her wretched brother and keep him out of trouble until his father returns from America. Not the most agreeable favor I've ever done for a lady, I confess," he added, his grin becoming a grimace, "but as a gentleman, I could hardly refuse to help keep the boy out of trouble."

"I suspect you'll have your work cut out for you there."

"You have no idea," he agreed with a sigh. "But now, thanks to the bet, he'll be forced to behave himself."

She frowned, understandably bewildered. "How do you make that out?"

"Simple," he replied and proceeded to explain.

"So, that's what you meant about them not being allowed to return to Oxford," she said at the end of his narrative. "And having no money to spend."

"Precisely. Now I have his promise and that of his friends to not only be discreet about our little arrangement, but also to stay on the straight and narrow path in their conduct until July, at which point they will once again become Oxford's headache and cease to be mine. And since that will put them back in their fathers' good graces, they will easily be able to pay our winnings when they lose."

"And you will have fulfilled your promise to Freddie's oh-so-charming sister without having to watch over him yourself."

"Yes. A delightful outcome all around, wouldn't you say?"

She studied him for a moment, a searching glance that made him wonder what she was thinking. "You do like arranging things to suit you, don't you?" she asked at last.

"Doesn't everyone?"

"Most of us don't have the luxury," she told him wryly. "Unlike your lot."

He tilted his head, and it was his turn to study her. "You really don't think much of us," he said after a moment. "Aristocrats, I mean. Is that because of Freddie and his friends?"

"Well, that didn't help, but no."

"Then I can only conclude I'm the reason for your poor opinion of us."

He waited, curious what she would say. Most women would be spurred into speech, either to demur out of politeness—not a likely possibility—or to explain and justify their feelings. But Miss Harlow, he was coming to realize, wasn't like most women. She could speak her mind, as he was already well aware, but she could also refrain. She chose the latter course now, and after several moments, he was forced to admit himself beaten.

"I can see you're of no mind to soothe my pride by disagreeing," he said with a grin as he donned his hat, "so I won't press you. But I do hope the next two months will serve to change your opinion—at least of me."

She gave him that funny, quirky smile. "Don't make any bets on that, Your Grace."

# 7

For Evie, feeling like a fish out of water was not an unfamiliar sensation. Shy as a child, tall and awkward as an adolescent, neither athletic enough for games nor lively enough to garner attention, she'd always preferred to retreat behind the refuge of a book.

But now, as the cab rolled into the courtyard of the Savoy and Evie eyed the splashing fountain, potted trees, and elegantly liveried footmen standing by the entrance doors, she appreciated that here there would be no book to hide behind, and she was seized by an unreasoning jolt of panic. Staying with Margery, she suddenly felt, would be a much better option.

But then the cab came to a stop, and Evie was forced to shove trepidations aside as two of the footmen rushed forward, one to open the carriage door and one to remove her suitcase and hatbox from the back. If they noticed the paucity of her luggage or the decidedly middle-class cut of her clothes, they did not let on.

Evie turned toward the plate glass entrance doors and

took a deep breath. "Here I go," she muttered and started forward. "Straight into the lion's den."

She passed through the door held open for her by a third footman and stepped into the entrance hall, a wide expanse of Corinthian columns, black-and-white marble floors, and plush crimson carpets. Ahead of her, arched doorways framed in polished mahogany led into a dining room crowded with guests. Some of them, she noted in amazement, were women.

Nearby where she stood were more ladies, clustered around small tables and sipping cups of early tea as they engaged in conversation. Gentlemen in morning coats and cravats lounged in wingback chairs reading the papers. A woman swathed in sable strolled past where Evie stood, a Baedeker in her hand and a leashed Afghan hound by her side.

To Evie's eyes, it was a scene of contrasts. The din of hundreds of voices poured from the dining room's open doors, bellboys rushed to and fro with clattering luggage carts, and waiters scurried about, handing out newspapers and serving tea, but despite all the hustle and bustle, there was an air of infinite leisure about the place, giving her the distinct impression of a duck sailing smoothly across a pond with its webbed feet paddling hell-for-leather beneath the surface. It was exciting, and stylish, and terribly modern, and Evie felt more like a fish out of water than ever.

"Checking in, miss?"

Evie turned to find that the footman who'd taken her things down from the cab had vanished, and in his place was a bellboy, holding her suitcase and hatbox.

"Front desk is to your right," he told her. "By the palm trees."

"Ah." Evie started to reach for her luggage, but the

bellboy stepped back at once. "I'll see to your things, shall I, miss?"

"Oh, of course," Evie mumbled, quite self-conscious as she appreciated the fact that the Savoy wasn't the sort of place where you did anything for yourself. "Yes, thank you."

He didn't depart, but waited, staring at her expectantly. "Yes?" she prompted.

"Your name, miss?"

As a fish out of water, she feared she was now flapping helplessly on the sand. "Harlow. Miss Evangeline Harlow."

With a nod, the boy turned away and walked off with her things, and Evie made her way to the carved and gilded opulence of the front desk.

Having never stayed in a hotel in her life, she wasn't certain how one handled the business of "checking in," but she needn't have worried. Upon learning her name, the clerk located her reservation in the opened volume before him. "Ah, yes, here we are," he said, looking up. "You are staying with Lady Delia Stratham, I understand?"

Evie frowned, puzzled. She already knew, of course, that Delia lived at the Savoy, but the duke had mentioned the other woman had gone to Rome. Either way, it was clear the clerk's question was a perfunctory one, for he turned to retrieve a key from the bank of cubicles behind him without waiting for an answer, and Evie put her bewilderment aside. Perhaps Delia had changed her mind.

"Number fifty-seven," he informed her as he faced her again and handed over the key. "Fifth floor, of course."

She nodded, doing her best to seem worldly and ho-hum. "Of course."

"I shall send the bellboy up with your luggage. Would

you care to go straight up, or would you like to take tea and refreshments in the restaurant after your journey?"

The question made Evie want to smile. A two-block cab ride that had taken barely five minutes was hardly a journey, but she didn't say so. "No tea just now, thank you," she said instead. "Which way do I go?"

"The electric lift is through there," he said, gesturing to a doorway at the other end of the long gallery.

"Lift?" Evie's voice squeaked as her heart gave a leap of exhilaration. She'd always wanted to ride in one of those things.

"If you prefer the stairs," he began, seeming to take her excitement for fear.

"No, no," she reassured him at once, laughing a little. "The lift is perfect. How do I operate it?"

The clerk smiled, making it clear that question was one he'd heard many times before. "There is a lift attendant. He will operate it for you."

Perfectly understandable, she supposed, but a few minutes later, as she watched a boy of no more than twelve select the desired floor with the turn of a dial and send the lift carriage into motion with the pull of a lever, she couldn't see why an attendant was needed at all. Why, operating the cash register in her shop was more complicated!

Aristocrats, she could only conclude as the boy pulled back the iron gates to let her out at the fifth floor, must need assistance with everything.

Number fifty-seven proved to be a suite three times the size of her flat, with a sitting room, two bedrooms, two dressing rooms, and a splendid view of the Thames. Between the bedrooms was a luxurious bath with a tiled floor, enormous tub, and taps for both hot and cold.

There were three marble fireplaces, thick pile carpets, electric lights, and a speaking tube to receive room service, proving that the accommodations at the Savoy were every bit as luxurious as the newspaper accounts and advertisements claimed.

The larger of the two bedrooms was evidently where Delia slept, for the armoire and chest of drawers were filled with clothes. Evie hung her coat in the empty armoire of the smaller bedroom, but she'd barely removed her hat before there was a knock at the sitting room door.

She was expecting the bellboy, but when she opened the door, she found the duke standing in the corridor.

"I was downstairs and saw you arrive," he explained, noting her surprise, "so I thought to pop by and have a word. I won't be long, since it's most improper for a man to be caught standing outside a lady's hotel room."

"More improper to be caught inside it, I should think."

He chuckled. "Quite right. Either way, I shall be quick. I've arranged an appointment for you at Vivienne in New Bond Street for half past two this afternoon. Vivienne is the London modiste for all my sisters, and Delia as well, and she will meet with you personally to help you choose what you'll need."

"What did you tell this dressmaker about me?"

He shrugged. "That you're a friend of Delia's, your house was flooded, and the damage has required you to obtain a new wardrobe. Order what you like, of course, but I should advise not purchasing too vast a wardrobe until Delia returns, for she will be bringing you out, and she will have a much better idea of what you'll need than you or I would. And I've arranged for the Savoy to have one of their maids attend you while you're here. What?" he added, noting her doubtful expression.

"I've been dressing myself my entire life, you know. I hardly need a maid to help me."

"You will need a maid once those new clothes arrive," he assured her. "Trust me. The gowns Vivienne is sure to make for you will be far too complicated for you to manage on your own."

"And how do you know so much about women's clothes?"

The question was barely out of her mouth before his amused chuckle made her regret it. "Best not to ask," he advised, "or I shall have to stop being a gentleman and explain how I acquired my vast knowledge on the topic."

Evie blushed to the roots of her hair, but thankfully, he didn't seem to notice. "Whenever you need your maid's assistance," he said, "ring the bell beside your bed, and she'll come straightaway." He nodded to the suite behind her. "I hope you find your rooms comfortable?"

"I do," she answered, relieved to veer the conversation away from how she would be getting dressed, "but I understand this is Delia's suite."

"It is. The hotel is packed to the rafters, I'm afraid, so I told Ritz to put you in here. You'll have it all to yourself for now and share it with her when she returns."

"Does Delia know any of this?"

"I'll write to her in Rome and tell her. She won't mind," he added at once. "Delia's a brick."

With that note of praise for his cousin, he paused, reaching inside his jacket to pull out a slim, folded newspaper.

"The latest edition of *Talk of the Town*," he explained as he handed it to her. "It will have listings of the latest plays, operas, gallery openings, and such. Choose whatever you'd like to see, and I will arrange it. Just be sure to take your friend—Anna, is it?—with you."

"I do know how chaperones work," she told him. "I

know how to curtsy, too. I can even do watercolors and embroider cushions."

He grinned at the acerbic reply. "Sorry. Was I talking down?"

"Very much so." She gave him a frown of mock severity. "I went to finishing school, I'll have you know. I'm not a complete noodle."

"I shall keep that in mind," he said, replacing his grin with a chastened expression that didn't fool her for a moment. "If there is anything you wish to see or do this evening, send me a note as soon as you can."

"I think..." She paused, considering, then shook her head. "Tonight, I think I will stay in and just...relax. Read a book I want to read for a change, instead of one I have to read for the shop. And I shall sleep on in the morning," she added dreamily, savoring the prospect. "With no alarm clock to wake me."

His eyes creased at the edges, smiling approval. "Excellent plan. A few days of that," he added, lifting a hand to lightly trace a half moon across each of her cheeks with the tip of his finger, "and you'll be rid of those."

The contact was brief, his hand falling away before she could fully realize he'd touched her, so brief that she might have thought she'd imagined it, except that the skin beneath her eyes felt oddly warm, almost tingly.

She forced herself to speak. "What about food?"

"When you wish to dine, it's a simple matter to order room service. Just speak into the speaking tube and give your order, or you can request an attendant to come wait on you. Or, if you prefer, you can eat in the restaurant."

"I can't believe women dine there! I saw them when I arrived, and I was shocked." She shook her head. "Women in restaurants? That doesn't happen in my part of town."

"Your part of town?" he echoed, laughing. "Woman, you live just down the street."

"But it's a whole different world."

"Yes," he agreed, sobering, his expression becoming thoughtful. "Yes, I suppose it is."

"A woman in my neighborhood might go to a tea shop in the afternoon or stop in at a milk bar for a penny sandwich, but that's all. Eating a full luncheon or dinner in a restaurant? And without a husband or father along?" She shook her head. "It's so...daring. Not to mention outrageously extravagant."

"Welcome to the Savoy. Daring and extravagant might sum up the entire experience. And while it's true that you don't need a male escort to dine here, you can't go alone. At least one other woman must accompany you. And remember in the evening, they require formal dress. And for God's sake, don't wear a hat in the restaurant, whatever you do."

"What?" That sounded so absurd, she laughed. "Why not?"

"It's not allowed. César Ritz discovered that certain women of—ahem—doubtful virtue were dining there, and forbidding hats is how he put a stop to it. I hope I haven't shocked you?"

She supposed she ought to be shocked, having had a staunchly respectable, middle-class upbringing, but she wasn't. She was, however, a little confused and terribly curious.

"Courtesans always wear hats?" she asked, earning herself a shout of laughter from him.

He quickly smothered it, pressing a fist to his mouth as he cast a quick glance at the empty corridor behind him.

"The lower-class ones do, evidently," he answered after a moment, lowering his hand to his side. "Extravagant hats and vast quantities of cosmetics. Ritz doesn't mind a few glamorous, beautiful courtesans sprinkled about the place, but these women were not in that class, and in consequence, they were hurting the hotel's reputation. So, he forbid ladies to wear hats in the restaurant, thereby solving the problem."

Evie shook her head. "Your set is very odd," she commented. "You divide everyone into classes, even the courtesans."

"Of course. How else can we keep ourselves convinced of our innate superiority? Now, one more thing before I go. I've looked over the notes you gave me for that dinner party, and though I haven't presented your ideas to Escoffier yet, I can already see that what you've given me isn't going to be enough."

"I know. I told you it was incomplete. Sorry."

"Please don't apologize. You've had your own troubles. But once I've discussed what you've given me with Escoffier, you and I will need to meet. The problem is that there is nowhere in the hotel we can do so without raising eyebrows, so perhaps your shop will do?"

She nodded. "Tomorrow? Eleven o'clock? I shall be there anyway, supervising the packing of the books. I don't trust the workmen to do it properly."

"Very wise of you." He started to turn away, then stopped and reached into his trouser pocket. "I almost forgot. Here." He pulled out a sixpence and handed it to her. "To tip the bellboy when he brings your luggage," he added when she looked at him in bewilderment. With a wink, he turned and walked away.

Vivienne's establishment proved to be a fantastical, wholly feminine enclave of black, white, pale pink, and gold, where ladies lounged on satin sofas, sipping iced lemonade as sylphlike living mannequins paraded before them in the modiste's latest creations.

Archways on either side of the main showroom led into high-ceilinged rooms that displayed bolts of fabric, rolls of trim, and shelves of notions, while above, a mezzanine ringed the main showroom where she stood. Reached by a curving staircase of wrought iron and warm brass, the mezzanine seemed to be where the fitting rooms were located, if the vast quantity of doors along each side were any indication.

Macarons in all the colors of the rainbow reposed in crystal trays on glass-topped tables for any patrons needing refreshment. In a far corner, a string trio of female musicians played a soft, pretty melody. A marble sculpture by the front entrance was, Evie realized upon closer inspection, a whimsical depiction of a pile of shoes, impossibly shaped shoes stacked to a dizzying height.

It was unlike any dressmaking establishment Evie had ever seen.

"May I help you, madam?"

Evie tore her gaze from the shoe sculpture to face an efficient-looking shop attendant in a dark blue dress and bibbed cambric apron. "Yes, my name is Evangeline Harlow. I have an appointment for half past two."

"Ah, yes, Miss Harlow, Vivienne is expecting you, and she will be with you momentarily. You may wait here," she added, gesturing to a nearby settee. "Or you may wish to look over some of our most recently acquired fabrics and trims. The fabric room is to your right, trims and notions to your left."

Evie chose to explore the fabric room, but she had wandered amid the bolts of velvet, cashmere, and silk for less than a minute before she wished she had chosen the trimmings room instead.

"Evie? Evie Harlow?"

She looked up from the exquisite China silks she had been admiring, expecting to meet the famous Vivienne for the first time. But instead of London's most fashionable modiste, she found herself facing someone she already knew, someone she'd hoped to never see again.

"Goodness, it is you!" Arlena Henderson came closer, her big brown eyes wide with shock, one gloved hand pressed to the side of her face, a face that even after eleven years was still stunningly beautiful. Her hair was still that enviable shade of honey-blonde, and her figure was still an hourglass of perfect proportions. Naturally.

"Evie Harlow, as I live!"

Before she could recover enough to reply, Arlena turned away, but if Evie thought this awful encounter would be over as quickly as that, she found her hopes dashed at once.

"Lenore?" Arlena called, beckoning to a petite brunette standing nearby. "Come look who I found skulking amid the silks!"

The sight of Lenore Peyton-Price coming to join Arlena impelled Evie to cast a longing glance at the door, but then, Lenore spoke, reminding Evie it was too late for escape.

"Evie? Why, what an extraordinary coincidence! We never thought to see you here."

Evie pasted on a smile, a polite, perfunctory curve of the lips. "It's my first visit."

Arlena glanced over Evie's plain white blouse and un-fashionable gray walking suit. "Yes," she agreed smoothly, "it must be."

Beside Arlena, Lenore gave a soft, smothered laugh, and Evie felt the earth shift beneath her feet, fracturing time and space, hurtling her backward.

Suddenly, she was seventeen again, standing on a field at

Chaltonbury, waiting with all the other girls as Arlena and Lenore, field hockey captains, picked their teams, listening as names were called one by one, watching as girl after girl was chosen to join, until she was the only one left.

Evie felt sick to her stomach.

"Evangeline Harlow?"

She turned, bracing herself to encounter more ghosts of school days past, but to her relief, she found someone beside her who was not the least bit familiar—a tall, slender redhead she knew at once must be the famous Vivienne, for her clothes gave her away.

Unlike her simply dressed showroom assistants, Vivienne was wearing a tea gown, a smashing silk confection in teal blue and mustard yellow, two colors that shouldn't have looked amazing together but absolutely did. Evie had never taken much interest in clothes before, but now, as she studied the modiste's exquisite dress with admiration and a touch of pure feminine envy, she appreciated for the first time the power of beautiful clothes.

Across from her, she heard another of Lenore's stifled giggles, a reminder that she was staring, and with an effort she came to her senses. "I am Miss Harlow, yes," she confirmed.

"Oh, Evie," sighed Arlena, "still not married? What a pity."

Evie's smile now felt so tight she feared her face would crack, but when she spoke, her voice was careless and light. "Is it? I fear I've been having too much fun to notice."

She returned her attention to the modiste and found the other woman smiling at her.

"I know just what you mean," Vivienne said, leaning forward as if to impart a secret. "The married ladies," she added in a whisper Evie sensed was designed to carry, "just don't understand, do they?"

She gave Evie a conspiratorial wink, and everything shifted back into proper perspective. Evie returned Vivienne's smile, and Arlena and Lenore's catty remarks were forgotten. "Thank you for seeing me on such short notice."

Vivienne laughed. "Not at all. I am always happy to help a friend of the duke's family. Especially when she has such a lovely figure."

Evie almost cast a doubtful look down at herself, but well aware of Arlena and Lenore's avid scrutiny, she checked the impulse just in time and allowed herself to take Vivienne's word on the matter.

"Evie, friends with a duke's family?" Arlena interjected, laughing. "But that's absurd."

"The duke told me what happened to all your clothes," Vivienne went on as if Arlena had not spoken. "A flood, I understand? How terrible."

"It was, rather," Evie agreed, following her lead and ignoring the other two completely. "And now, I've nothing at all for the season," she added with an exaggerated sigh. "I hope you can help?"

"I have dozens of ideas already." Vivienne turned, tucking her arm through Evie's. "Come with me, my dear, and let me show you what I have in mind for you."

The modiste led her away, but Evie couldn't resist a glance over her shoulder, and at the sight of Arlena and Lenore staring after her, their mouths open in stupefaction, the duke's words came echoing back:

*You will have fun, I promise you.*

"Lovely to see you both again," she called, feeling a sweet, wicked glee as she gave Arlena and Lenore a wide smile—genuine this time—and offered them a cheerful wave of farewell.

In the beginning, she'd been doubtful of the duke's promise that she'd have fun in society, but now, as she followed Vivienne across the opulent showroom, she realized in surprise that he might turn out to be right.

For the next three hours, Evie found herself immersed in the world of women's haute couture. After being measured by a shop assistant, she sat side by side with Vivienne, sipping lemonade, nibbling macarons, and discussing which of the sumptuous fashions modeled for her by the mannequins would suit her figure and her tastes.

She learned more about fabric and design than she'd ever dreamed possible, and she was astonished to discover that bold hues she'd never have dared to pick for herself were the best choices for her complexion and coloring. Emerald? Amethyst? Sapphire? Never would she have dreamed she could wear such colors, but when swathes of fabric in these jewel tones were draped around her, the gold glints in her hazel eyes seemed to sparkle, and her skin took on a vibrant glow that made her appreciate just why Vivienne was London's most famous modiste. The woman knew her business.

Evie tried to take the duke's advice, content to order only a minimal wardrobe, but she soon found that Vivienne's idea of what defined minimal involved a bewildering array of garments, undergarments, shoes, and hats, and she was forced to trust that the dressmaker's laughing assurance that she was purchasing the bare minimum for a fashionable woman was not an exaggeration.

She concluded her shopping by selecting two ready-made ensembles—a walking suit of deep blue serge and an evening gown of plum velvet with a matching cape—so that she was assured of being appropriately dressed for any occasion during the fortnight while her other clothes were being constructed.

After offering instructions for all her purchases to be delivered to the Savoy, making an appointment five days hence for her first fitting, and treating herself to one last macaron, Evie departed the showroom, exhausted and yet strangely exhilarated, too exhilarated to go straight back to her hotel. Instead, she walked up New Bond Street, where she stopped in at a perfumery. Perfume, of course, was much too dear for a woman of her means, but she was able to afford a toilet set of bergamot-scented soaps, talc, and hand cream.

On the way back to the Savoy, she instructed the cabdriver to stop at Hatchards in Piccadilly, where she purchased what the clerk assured her was the newest, most sensational romantic novel the store possessed. She then went next door to Fortnum & Mason, where she treated herself to a box of chocolates and a tin of scandalously expensive Darjeeling tea. She then returned to the hotel, where she ordered dinner from the prix-fixe menu what was proclaimed to be a "simple" meal: filet of sole, roasted ptarmigan, potatoes Anna, salade Niçoise, and baba au rhum.

She fell into bed, too full to do anything else, and just before she drifted off to sleep, it occurred to her that if she continued to eat so much rich food, Vivienne would need to provide her with a much stouter corset.

# 8

*H*arlow's Bookshop was alive with activity when
Max arrived there the following morning. Workmen flitted about like industrious bees, moving crates of
books, empty bookcases, and display tables to one side of
the long room. Other workmen stood on ladders against the
opposite wall, peeling and scraping at the water-damaged
wallpaper. Overhead, the sound of booted feet and pounding hammers could be heard.

He found Evie near the back of the shop, lodged between
two tall bookcases. Occupied with her task of packing
books into a crate, she didn't notice his approach.

As he came toward her, he opened his mouth to inform
her of his presence, but then she hiked up her skirt, moving
to mount the stepladder in front of her, and at the glimpse
of a delicate foot, shapely calf, and scarlet-red satin garter,
he came to a dead stop, and any sort of coherent thought
vanished from his mind.

Evie Harlow wore red satin garters? At this heretofore
hidden bit of knowledge, Max grinned in pure masculine
appreciation. How deliciously shocking.

Far too soon, her white petticoat and dark blue skirt settled back into place, once again hiding her lower leg and naughty garter from view, but that did little to stop Max's imagination. His gaze traveled upward, and as his mind envisioned the legs beneath those skirts, his grin faded, and his body began to burn. Miles long, those legs, he decided. Long enough to—

She stirred, moving to descend the ladder again, and though courtesy dictated that a gentleman rush forward to assist, Max's second tantalizing peek of garter, calf, and ankle prevented any such noble idea from entering his head. Her feet hit the floor, her skirts fell again, and she turned, bending down to put the book in the crate. As she straightened, she spied him standing there.

"Your Grace," she greeted, then she immediately frowned, as if puzzled. "Is something wrong?"

The erotic images conjured by his imagination were still so vivid in his mind that it took Max a moment to realize he was staring at her and looking—no doubt—like a prize idiot.

"Sorry," he said at once, shaking his head and shoving aside any speculations regarding Evie Harlow's legs. "I was...ahem...woolgathering."

Feeling as ridiculously embarrassed as a boy in short pants, he glanced around, striving for something, anything, to say. "Work's begun, I see. I'm glad Metropolitan Insurance took my expectations to heart."

"Mr. Walpole would be terrified to do otherwise. You put the fear of God in him, I think."

"I really did, didn't I?" The notion made him grin. "Poor fellow."

She laughed, pulling off the dust scarf wrapped around her hair, sending loose strands tumbling around her face in charming disarray with a shake of her head. "He may never recover."

"Yes, well, if it makes him a bit more lenient with his claimants, I will consider my ducal duty done."

Her laughter faded. "You consider acts of kindness to be a ducal duty?" she asked, seeming surprised by the notion.

"You needn't sound so skeptical," he said, laughing. "I have been known to be kind on occasion."

"I didn't mean it that way. It's just that you're the first duke I've ever met. I don't even know, really, what a duke's duties are."

Before he could reply, they were interrupted. "Miss Harlow?" called a workman from the other side of the room. "These crates of books are stacking up. Where do you want us t'put 'em?"

"By the door, Mr. Thornton. A lorry will be fetching them for storage this afternoon."

"Very good, miss." He resumed his work, and she returned her attention to Max.

"Did you meet with Escoffier?" she asked.

"I did." He sighed, hoping to prepare her for the bad news. "I gave him your list of suggested dishes for the party, but he was not—"

"Pardon, guv'nor." A workman carrying a ladder edged between them, and they both stepped back to make room.

"Yes?" she prompted once the workman and his ladder had passed between them and continued on. "I take it he wasn't enthusiastic?"

"I wouldn't say that," he began, only to be interrupted again, this time by the loud, rapid pounding of a hammer. "Perhaps we should adjourn to your office to discuss it?" he suggested.

"All right," she said, shoving her scarf into her skirt pocket. "Let me just finish examining these books."

She suited the action to the word, then after instructing the workmen that these volumes had no dampness and could be packed in a crate and stacked with the others by the door, she led him to her office in the back.

"First," he said, doffing his hat and tossing it on the table as they sat down, side by side, at her desk, "let me say that when Delia first told me you'd come up with a soup made of birds' nests, I was skeptical."

That made her laugh. "It does sound awfully unsanitary, I know."

"Exactly, but once I'd read your notes—the swallows they use, and what the nests are made of, and how they dissolve into the broth, I became intrigued. And let me add that it would be a fitting dish to serve the Epicurean Club."

"But?" she prompted when he paused.

"But when I discussed the prospect with Escoffier, I'm afraid he didn't agree."

She grimaced. "His chef's palate was revolted, I suppose?"

"On the contrary. He loved the idea. Loved it so much, he already did it."

She groaned, falling back in her chair. "Delia never told me that."

"I daresay she didn't know. The birds' nest soup was several years ago, probably before she began working for the hotel."

She considered. "Does a banquet like this require more than one soup?"

"Two is customary, but no. One would be all right. But if you're thinking of the shark fins, he's done that one, too."

She sighed. "Oh, dear. And I thought I was being so innovative."

"You were. I daresay most members of the Epicurean Club would never have heard of these offerings. Escoffier has made thousands of exotic dishes during his years at the Savoy, so the fact that he has already prepared a few of your suggestions isn't surprising. However, some members of the Epicurean Club have already tasted these dishes, and Escoffier feels it would be a letdown if he served them again."

"So, what happens now? Do you want me to find other dishes from China?"

"I suggested that. But while he liked the eels in rice wine and the panfried snake, some of the other dishes—pigeon eggs and goat sweetbreads, for instance—he's prepared in other ways, so he wasn't all that interested."

"Hmm..." She fell silent, thinking. "Perhaps," she said after a moment, "we ought to consider an entirely different theme."

"Start again? That would entail a great deal of work, wouldn't it?"

"I don't mind. It's what Delia pays me for."

He gave her a look of reproof. "Perhaps, but you are supposed to be on holiday, remember?"

"Let me pull out my notes for other ideas Delia and I have discussed in the past. Using ideas I've already researched would eliminate a large part of the work. Most of them were not implemented because the client didn't like them, or because the party was called off, but there might be something that strikes your fancy."

She rose and walked around his chair to a tall filing cabinet, opened it, and pulled out a fat manila folder. "The rejects," she said lightly.

Sitting back down, she opened the folder and began flipping pages, reading aloud as she went. "German Oktoberfest, Fairyland, Arabian Nights—"

"Wait," he interrupted, stopping her. "Arabian Nights? What a splendid idea."

She looked up, eyeing him with doubt. "It wasn't for a banquet. It was for a bachelor's stag party."

"Was it?" He laughed. "How fitting. Turkish pipes, scantily clad dancing girls flitting about...I'm sure the bachelor in question approved."

Her cheeks flushed pink. "I didn't suggest smoking or dancing girls!"

"This presents you to me in a whole new light, I must say," he murmured, ignoring her protest. "I never would have guessed you capable of conjuring such delightfully decadent ideas."

The blush in her cheeks deepened and she ducked her head, but when he leaned down to look in her face, he saw her lips pressed together to hide a smile.

Sensing his scrutiny, she slid her gaze sideways, meeting his, and her smile turned rueful. "The bride didn't share your opinion, I fear. The party was canceled, and so was the wedding."

"The groom's loss is our gain, then. I take it Escoffier and Ritz already approved this idea? Then it's settled," he added as she gave a nod. "Arabian Nights it is."

He picked up the sheet of notes on the desk and glanced over it. "Since this will be a full banquet, we'll need to give Escoffier a few more suggestions than what you have here. For one thing, we need a soup. And a fish course."

She reached for pen and paper, dipped the pen in the inkwell, and began taking notes. "Anything else?"

"Perhaps a dessert, since I think we need something

more than fruit, cheese, and Turkish delight. And two sorbets."

She laughed, causing him to look up. "Sorbet is amusing?" he asked.

"Rather. I doubt they eat much sorbet in the desert."

"Fair point," he conceded, laughing with her. "But in my defense, allow me to point out that not all of the Middle East is desert."

"Well, that's true enough. I'll do some research on it and see what I can find."

"Would you stop volunteering to take on more work?" he chided in good-natured exasperation. "We are trying to make this as easy as possible, since you are on holiday. Are there any native flavorings you can think of that would be good for sorbet?"

"Peaches would do for that, wouldn't they? Or rosewater. Or orange water. Or," she added as he began to laugh, "there's a mint tea that could work—why are you laughing?"

"We only need two sorbets, Evie. Peach will do nicely, and perhaps the mint. What about dessert?"

"Hmm..." She paused to consider. "I wonder if Escoffier has ever made knafeh?"

"Nothing would surprise me, given that he's made birds' nest soup, but we can try. What is this knafeh?"

"A flaky pastry stuffed with soft cheese and syrup and covered with pistachio nuts. Or, if Escoffier doesn't like that, we could suggest baklava. Or perhaps atayef."

"I don't think I've ever met anyone before who possesses such a vast knowledge of Middle Eastern desserts." He tilted his head, studying her. "Or is this knowledge due to research for another of Delia's party plans?"

"No, I just read a lot."

"I thought I was a pretty fair reader myself, but if someone had ever asked me to name a dessert of that region beyond Turkish delight, I'd have had to admit immediate defeat. And I'm a member of the Epicurean Club, too. I feel so ashamed, they might have to rescind my membership. Yet here you are, rattling off knafeh and balaklava, and all sorts of whatnot."

"Baklava," she corrected, laughing. "It's a pastry, layered with nuts and honey."

"I shall take your word for it." He shook his head in admiration. "Really, Evie, you're a marvel."

She shifted in her chair, clearly unaccustomed to compliments. "Well, I do own a bookstore," she said, laughing a little. "I'm one of the few people who actually reads a Baedeker without being a tourist."

"Don't do that," he said, a fierceness in his voice that surprised even him. "Don't hide your light under a bushel."

"I don't..." She paused, staring at him, clearly nonplussed. "I don't know what you mean."

"There's nothing wrong with being a well-read woman. Don't downplay your accomplishments or feel you have to explain them away. Oh, I know women are raised to be all maidenly modesty, but as a man, I find that one of the most infuriating things about your sex."

In the wake of this little speech, they stared at each other as if neither knew what to say next. For his part, he supposed he'd said quite enough.

"Heavens," she said after a moment. "You do speak your mind, don't you?"

"One of my many faults, as we both know." Still irritated and oddly off-balance, he took a deep breath and forced himself to veer off this topic. "Either way," he said, striving for a nonchalant air, "you must remind me to enlist your help the next time I want to have an extravagant party at Idyll Hour."

"Idyll Hour? What's that?"

"My ducal estate. It's in the Cotswolds."

"The Cotswolds?" she cried. "I should love to see the Cotswolds. I've heard it's lovely."

"You've never been?"

She shook her head. "I've seldom been out of London. School, of course, but that was only to Windsor, so it hardly counts. And my step-uncle has a country house in Sussex. I've been there for holidays a few times."

"Nowhere else? Ah," he added when she shook her head, "that explains it, then."

"Explains what?"

"Your passion for Baedeker."

"Yes." Her expression grew pensive. "I am quite the armchair traveler, I suppose."

"Well, if you ever have the opportunity to change that, as a loyal resident of Gloucestershire, I must advise you come to my part of the world first. Or better still," he added on impulse, "have Delia bring you when she comes up for Whitsuntide. I'll be in residence."

"I thought you were in London for the season?"

"I am, but I'm always home for Whitsuntide. We usually have some sort of house party, and I'm sure Delia would be delighted to bring you along with her. You'd be more than welcome."

She smiled a little. "Trying to hire me to plan the house party, are you?"

"I doubt I'll have to. Knowing your obsession with working all the time, you'll probably volunteer."

She grinned at that. "Well, then," she countered, taking

up the remaining notes on Arabian Nights, "since I've been accused of working too hard, and since I am currently on holiday..." she paused and held out the sheets of paper, "you can decide the decorations on your own."

"Dancing girls it is, then," he said at once, grinning back at her.

Her smile became a wry twist of the lips. "Are you sure that's wise? Your friend Helen might not like it."

He blinked, startled to realize that what Helen would think of the matter had never even occurred to him.

Still, it wouldn't do to say so. "True," he said instead, his voice light, "but in the game of love, one must never allow one's quarry to be too sure of one's affections."

"Is it love?" she asked, then flushed. "Forgive me. That was a very impertinent question."

"You seem quite happy being impertinent where I'm concerned," he countered dryly, "but since you're asking, no, it's not love."

She frowned. "You don't love her, but you seriously intend to marry her anyway?"

He met the disapproval in her gaze head on. "That surprises you?"

She sighed. "I suppose not. I long ago ceased to be surprised by the things your set does."

"If it soothes your sense of middle-class morality," he countered, feeling oddly defensive, "let me assure you Helen is not any more in love with me than I am with her. But we are fond of each other, and I would venture to say that both of us understand that fondness and affection can lead to love and make for a happy union."

"How inspiring you make it sound."

The dryness of her reply did not escape him. "In my position, a marriage has to be based on suitability, not love."

"All the more reason why I'd never marry a peer."

He decided it was best to leave it at that. "Speaking of Helen, I really must be off. I'm meeting her and her mother for luncheon."

"Before you go," she said as he reached for his hat, "there is something I need to ask you. I intended to ask you this yesterday, but it slipped my mind. All the stress of yesterday's events, I suppose."

"Something about the party?"

"No, about the bet. How do you know if you've won? You and your friends must have established some sort of criteria to determine the winner?"

"Oh, that." He laughed, touching a hand to his forehead in acknowledgment of his own absentmindedness. "Didn't I explain that part? Don't worry," he added as she shook her head. "It's perfectly straightforward."

"I don't see how that's possible. If the bet is about transforming me into society's idea of a beauty, who decides? And what are the criteria? Beauty is so subjective."

"It's much simpler than you think. Every year, I sponsor a charity ball to raise money for London orphanages. You will attend, accompanied by Delia, of course, and if you dance every dance, we win. You see? Easy as winking."

"A ball?" She straightened in her chair, staring at him, her hazel eyes wide with unmistakable horror. "I'm to attend a ball?"

"Oh, don't worry," he said, noting her obvious dismay. "It's not fancy dress, or some elaborate theme where everyone talks riddles, or speaks only in French, or wears a silly hat during the supper. Nothing like that. I always think affairs of that kind are so tedious—"

"You never mentioned there would be a ball." Her voice rose on the last word, sounding almost like...panic.

He tried to fathom what about a ball could evoke this sort of reaction but failed utterly. In his experience, women adored balls. "Sorry," he murmured after a moment. "I suppose I ought to have mentioned it sooner; but like you, I was distracted and forgot. My dear girl," he added as she groaned, "whatever's the matter?"

"A ball." She rubbed a hand over her forehead and began to laugh, but it was obvious she wasn't the least bit amused. "It would have to be a ball, of all the crazy things."

He'd been married, he reminded himself. He'd lived in intimacy with a woman for nearly two tumultuous years, and during his eight years as a widower, he'd had several mistresses. In addition, he was possessed of four sisters and countless female relations and servants. By this point, Max would have thought he'd developed a pretty fair understanding of the opposite sex; but as he studied Evie's face, he realized that women, heaven bless them, still had the power to confound him.

She laughed again, breaking into his thoughts. "If a ball is the criteria, I'm afraid we've lost this bet even before we've begun."

"May I ask why you say that?"

She grimaced. "I can't dance."

"What?" He laughed in sheer surprise, but appreciating her distress, he stifled it at once. "Sorry," he apologized. "It's just that I don't think I've ever met a girl who couldn't dance."

"Well, you have now. I'm terrible."

"I doubt that—unless you never learned?"

"My mother taught me the waltz, as well as a few reels and quadrilles when I was a little girl, but she died when I was ten."

"But you know how?"

"After a fashion."

He ignored that rather dampening reply. "Then this is an easy problem to solve. Just tell me which reels and quadrilles your mother taught you, and I'll make certain the ball committee only chooses those. And I'll have them put in plenty of waltzes. Everyone always wants more waltzes at a ball anyway."

"I've never been to a ball, so I wouldn't know."

"Never? Not a dance of any kind?" Max was appalled. What sort of upbringing had this girl had, in heaven's name? And what about her step-uncle, the baron? Hadn't he ever bothered to invite her to such entertainments?

He had no time to ponder these questions, however, before she spoke again. "They had these dances at school. The matrons would arrange them with the tutors at Eton for the end of each term. The boys would come over, and there would be games, dancing, and supper afterward."

He made a face. "I remember those affairs."

"You went to Eton?"

"No, Harrow, but these events are all pretty much the same, I expect. Deuced awkward."

"To say the least." She paused, rubbing a hand over her forehead. "Look, you might as well know that I was a hopeless wallflower at those affairs. I only danced," she added, lifting her chin, "when well-meaning matrons shoved unwilling boys in my face."

Max studied her, noting the proud tilt of her head and the rigid set of her shoulders, and he had no idea what to say. Pity was something that she would not welcome, nor would it do her any good. "If it helps," he said at last, "most people find those school dances to be a nightmare. As for being a wallflower," he added gently, "I doubt the boys were unwilling for any reason other than a fear of getting their toes smashed."

"Even so, does it matter?"

"Hell, yes, it matters. Any girl can waltz if her partner can lead. Boys of that age," he added as she gave a sound of disbelief, "aren't always very good at it."

She smiled a little. "I doubt that had anything to do with turning the wrong way during a reel or quadrille and messing up the whole show."

"But didn't you practice your dancing at school?"

"We had dance classes, of course, but..." She paused, and she was silent so long, he thought she wouldn't finish. "None of the other girls wanted to practice with me," she said at last. "I was an outsider, you see. An interloper, not their sort. And my dancing ability gave them plenty of ammunition to prove their point. They'd jeer and laugh, and the more..."

She paused again, but he knew what she hadn't said.

"The more they laughed, the worse you got," he finished for her.

"Yes."

"And your tutor didn't intervene?"

"No. She didn't see the point. Girls like me...well...why should we need to dance well?"

Max sucked in a breath. "I see."

"I don't think you do." Her voice was hard, uncompromising. "I went to finishing school because my cousin wanted me to go with her. She didn't want to go alone. So her stepfather asked my father to let me go with her. He even offered to pay all my expenses. Sounds familiar, doesn't it, Your Grace?"

He grimaced, but he did not reply, and his silence seemed to goad her on.

"My father didn't want to agree, but I persuaded him. I wanted to go. What girl wouldn't want the chance for a better education, a wider circle of friends and acquaintances, a chance to improve her station in life? Little did I know that daring to—How did you put it?—peek outside my nest was an unforgivable presumption, one that earned me nothing but contempt and ridicule."

The gold lights in her eyes seemed to glitter, proud, defiant, daring him to laugh, too.

His mind flashed back to a house party at Westbourne House—a lifetime ago, and yet, he could recall every moment of the four-day ordeal as if it were yesterday. The awkward introductions of Rebecca to the county families, the awkward silences at dinner, the frozen faces of the guests trying to hide their scorn, Rebecca sensing it and already looking to crumple, his own eyes in the mirror over the fireplace, filled with the same proud defiance he saw in Evie Harlow's eyes now.

He felt anger roll over him like a thick, smothering wave, anger at the breathtaking cruelty people could display, cruelty that had driven Rebecca to a despair he couldn't resolve. Anger at the absurd, stultifying class differences that had smothered his late wife, class differences that even he, a duke, had been unable to break for her.

To him, this bet had started as a lark, a game; but now, as he looked into Evie Harlow's eyes, he realized that this was not a game—for either of them.

He took a breath and forced himself to ask the obvious question. "Do you want to back out? If so, I understand."

"I'm not sure you understand at all," she countered with a shaky laugh. "I can't imagine you ever being the subject of ridicule."

"Can't you?" No one had dared such a thing during

that first house party so long ago, that was true. No, his humiliation had come later, after Rebecca had run home to New York, leaving him amidst the pieces of the wreckage and feeling like an utter fool for daring to kick against the pricks. He gave a short laugh. "You'd be surprised."

A perplexed frown rippled her forehead, but thankfully, she didn't pursue the subject. "The point is," she said instead, "I stopped going to those school dances, and I was allowed to stop attending dance classes. I gave up dancing altogether. I haven't done it since I was seventeen."

He caught something in her voice, a nuance of what might have been sorrow, or regret.

"Tell me something," he said, leaning forward in his chair. "You initially rejected taking this on, and now, after what you've told me, I fully appreciate your reasons. But there's one thing I don't understand. Why did you change your mind?"

She stared at him, surprised by the question. "You know why. I didn't have a choice."

"You could have gone to stay with your cousin," he reminded. "So, why didn't you?"

"You've met my cousin," she pointed out. "I'm sure you can see why I thought a paid holiday at the Savoy was the better choice."

Max didn't reply for a long moment. Instead, he studied her face, remembering the elusive wistfulness he'd seen there as they'd talked about the upcoming party and the spark of interest in her eyes when he'd asked if she wouldn't love to see Freddie eat humble pie, and the regret in her voice a moment ago over giving up dancing, and every instinct he possessed told him her flooded shop had less to do with her reasons than she wanted to admit.

"So," he said at last, "if I told you that you could back

out of the bet right now, keep the clothes, and still stay at the Savoy at my expense until your shop reopens, would you do it?"

"I—" She broke off, staring at him. "I couldn't continue to take advantage of your hospitality in such a way. It would be wrong."

"A very moral stance that allows you to neatly sidestep my question."

Her tongue darted out to lick her lips. "I don't know what you mean."

"Yes, you do. I asked you the other day if you would like the chance to prove Freddie and his friends were wrong about you, and I'm going to ask you again. Do you still want that chance?"

"For heaven's sake!" she cried and stood up so abruptly that her chair tipped over and hit the floor behind her. "What does it matter? I've already told you we're doomed to lose."

"Again, you sidestep the question. I asked what you *want*. Do you want to back out? Do you?" he pressed when she didn't answer.

"No!" she cried, pushed beyond endurance. "I just don't want to be laughed at! I don't want history to repeat itself."

Satisfied, he gave a nod. "Then let's make sure that doesn't happen."

"How?" She lifted her hands in a gesture of despair and let them fall. "If I go to this ball, I'll make a hash of the very first dance, and no one will ask me for another. You'll lose the bet, and I'll be the same wallflower I was at those school dances years ago."

"Why? Because you haven't been practicing your dance steps? Nonsense. I don't believe it for a minute."

She made a rueful face, her freckled nose wrinkling up. "Says the man who has never seen me dance."

"That is a very good point." On impulse, he turned to her desk and tore a corner off the top sheet of her blotter, then he plucked a pencil out of the glass jar on top of her desk and scribbled on the torn scrap of paper. "Here," he said when he'd finished, holding the slip of paper out to her.

"What's this?" she asked, taking it from his hand.

"I'm calling your bluff."

She looked down at what he'd written and frowned in puzzlement. "An address in Park Lane?" She looked up again. "I don't understand."

"My London residence," he supplied as he tossed the pencil onto her desk. "It has an enormous ballroom, and I know there's a gramophone because I bought it myself less than a year ago. Come there tomorrow night, and you can show me how horrible a dancer you are."

"What?" She stared at him, looking appalled. "I can't come to your house."

"Why not? Because it's not proper?"

"Well, it isn't!"

"Who's going to find out? There's no one staying there at present. No one to see you make a mistake," he added gently. "No one to laugh. As for propriety..." He paused, his mind veering toward red satin garters and firmly back again, "I give you my word of honor as a gentleman to behave myself."

She blinked, showing that the possibility he might misbehave if he were alone with her hadn't even entered her head, demonstrating just how unaccustomed to male attention she truly was. For his own part, he could surely keep his baser needs under control, although it would probably be for the best if he didn't do any more thinking about her ripping long legs in red satin garters.

"Come at eight." He picked up her notes on Arabian Nights and reached for his hat. "And use the servant's entrance on Green Street. It's less noticeable that way."

"And if a constable catches me slipping into a duke's closed-up house after dark?"

"Don't worry," he whispered, leaning closer to her. "I won't let him arrest you."

"That's comforting," she answered dryly, "but I don't know what purpose you think any of this is going to serve."

"To show which of us is right, of course. You think you're a terrible dancer, but I'll wager you aren't nearly as bad at it as you think."

She sighed. "Is making wagers a compulsion with you?"

He gave her an unapologetic grin. "I suppose I am a bit of a gambler at heart. Besides, this will be good for both of us. I haven't danced in ages, and I daresay I could do with a bit of practice myself."

She frowned, looking uncertain, but after a moment, she capitulated. "Oh, all right," she said, tucking the note into her skirt pocket, "but you'll regret this when your toes are black and blue."

"That won't happen," he said lightly and turned to go. "I'm very quick on my feet."

# 9

Only rarely had Evie's life given her cause to visit the West End. A delivery for a customer when Clarence was unavailable, or an occasional Sunday afternoon in Hyde Park when the fickle English weather allowed it, was the extent of her familiarity with Mayfair, and even then, she'd never paid much attention to the luxurious mansions that lined Park Lane.

Nonetheless, she found Westbourne House easily enough. Located between North Row and Green Street, the duke's residence proved to be a massive four-story structure of Carrara marble and black granite, with French windows, full-length balconies, and a magnificent view of the park.

The front entrance was closed off from the street by ornate iron gates and guarded by a pair of stone griffins taller than Evie. Beyond the gates, Evie could see a courtyard ringed with flowering trees, and their scent wafted to her on the cool spring breeze, mingling with the Corsican mint that grew between the flagstone pavements. The courtyard made an agreeable picture, a patch of serenity and ease amidst the hustle and bustle of London, but when she looked up, she found a pair of granite-faced gargoyles frowning down upon her from the pillars of the courtyard gate with haughty disdain, as if wondering what on earth she was doing there.

They were not the only ones to wonder. Evie had been pondering the very same question all day, her apprehensions growing stronger with every hour. She wanted to dance well, she did, and yet that reminder seemed less and less of an incentive with every block the cab had traveled bringing her here.

Sadly, however, it was too late to back out. The duke was expecting her, and Evie continued along Park Lane to Green Street, trying to convince herself that this was just one of many exciting new adventures in her life. It didn't help, and by the time she turned the corner onto Green Street, she was as jumpy as a cat on hot bricks.

Westbourne House, she soon discovered, was posh enough to boast not one, but two servant's entrances. Evie paused again, eyeing the pair of identical oak doors before her in some uncertainty, but after a moment, she shrugged and started toward the one closest to where she stood. If it was locked, she would know she'd guessed wrong.

Despite the duke's assurance, she cast a quick glance up and down the street to be sure there was no constable bearing down upon her, then she grasped the ornate door handle and pressed the lever at the top with her thumb. The door opened, proving she'd guessed right, and as she pushed it wide, light from the lit gas jets on the walls revealed a long passageway flanked on either side by a bewildering number of doors. The duke, however, was nowhere in sight.

"Hullo?" she called as she slipped inside and closed the door behind her. "Your Grace?"

"I'm in the kitchens," he called back. His head appeared, emerging from a door about halfway down the passage. "Back here," he added, beckoning her to join him, then he vanished again.

Evie walked down the passage and through the open doorway into a kitchen that was at least twice the size of her shop. Along the back, white sheets covered a long line of what were undoubtedly storage cupboards, and to her left, two enormous cast-iron cooking ranges took up the entire wall. To her right was the second door leading out to Green Street, flanked by wooden counters set with copper sinks and brass taps.

In the center of it all, Westbourne stood between the kitchen's two long worktables, a loaf of bread and various jars spread out before him. His jacket was off, his cuffs were rolled back, and yet, despite this deshabille, his clothes were far more elegant than his prosaic surroundings would suggest.

Within the confines of a cream-colored satin waistcoat, his pristine white shirt fit his wide shoulders and tapering torso to perfection. His high collar displayed the unmistakable white tie of formal dress, and in the center of his bibbed shirtfront was a single stud of black jet and polished gold. A pair of matching cufflinks lay on the table, and his evening jacket, hanging on one of the hooks beside the door, displayed a crisp white carnation boutonniere. Out of one jacket pocket peeked a pair of white gloves.

In contrast, his hair seemed determined to rebel against the expectations of formal dress, for the thick strands were already curling in defiance of the pomade that was making them gleam like black silk, and as he bent his head to open one of the jars before him, one stubborn lock fell forward over his brow.

He shook it back, to no avail, for it immediately fell forward again, reminding her of the small boys in church whose mothers tried in vain to keep their hair slicked back and their bow ties knotted. The duke's unruly hair, she suspected, was his valet's despair.

When he turned his head to the side to reach for another jar, however, she appreciated that there was nothing boyish about his profile, for it was lean and strong, with a straight Roman nose and a determined jawline.

He was, she realized suddenly, a very handsome man.

She'd known that all along, of course, but until this moment, she'd never really thought about it, perhaps because the first time Max had walked into the shop, she'd dismissed him as nothing more than another arrogant aristocrat and any attractions he possessed had seemed unimportant. Or perhaps she'd just been too enamored with Rory at the time to notice any other man. Either way, it was extraordinary how only five days could completely change one's point of view.

"Is something wrong?"

His voice brought her out of her contemplations with a start, and she realized he was watching her, a quizzical little frown between his black brows. Evie forced herself to say something. "I don't know what you mean."

"You haven't said a word since you came in," he told her as he flipped up the bail of the jar in his hands. "Instead, you're just standing there, staring at me as if dumbstruck."

"Am I?" She realized in dismay that staring at him was exactly what she'd been doing. Because he was *handsome*. How mortifying.

Heat rushed into her cheeks, and she turned away before his perceptive eyes could see. "Sorry," she said, striving to think up a reason for her woolgathering as she took off her hat and hung it beside his black silk top hat. "It's just that...um...you're wearing white tie. Compared to you," she added as she began to unbutton her cloak, "I'm terribly underdressed."

"Are you? I can't tell. Show me."

Evie's heart gave a lurch; her fingers fumbled and froze.

"Evie? Are you certain you're all right?"

She simply must get hold of herself. She could not keep standing here as if she were a gauche schoolgirl mooning over the handsome new drawing master.

"Yes, of course." She took a deep breath and resumed undoing buttons, striving for an explanation to offer. "I thought we were only practicing for a ball," she said as she slid her cloak off her shoulders and hung it between her hat and his tailcoat. "I didn't realize we were going to one."

Squaring her shoulders as he laughed, she turned around. "You see?" she said, spreading her arms wide, trying to seem perfectly at ease when she felt as skittish as a colt.

His lashes lowered, his gaze sliding down over her plain shirtwaist and skirt in a slow perusal that did nothing to decrease her nervousness. "You seem fully dressed to me," he murmured, meeting her gaze again, his eyes crinkling at the corners as he smiled. "How disappointing."

He was flirting with her. At that realization, Evie's heart gave another nervous lurch, slamming into her ribs with enough force to rob the breath from her lungs. Thankfully, he didn't seem to notice.

"As for my attire," he said, "formal dress is *de rigueur* for anyone out and about in London at this time of year. And I'm joining friends at the opera after we finish here. Have you ever been?"

"To the opera?" Grateful for the neutral subject, she

shook her head as she moved to stand opposite him across the table. "Never. Just penny operas at music halls."

"True opera's a bit different." He picked up a spoon. "Would you like to go?" he asked as he began removing the hard wax that sealed the top of the pickle jar. "Delia has a box at Covent Garden, and she has not reserved it for any of her friends next Saturday. If you and your friend Anna or any of your other acquaintances wish to go, just let me know and I'll reserve it for you. If Saturday doesn't suit, I can see what other nights the box might be free. I can get you ordinary tickets, too, of course, but a box is much more fun."

"Thank you. It sounds lovely. I'll ask Anna and let you know."

He nodded, set aside the spoon, and reached for the long baguette of bread. "Did you have any trouble finding the house?"

"How could I miss it?" she countered flippantly. "It takes up the entire block."

"Not quite," he corrected as he began tearing bread into chunks. "There's a mews as well."

"Which doesn't really count, since your carriages probably take up most of it. Either way, your house is terribly grand, isn't it? Grand enough to need two entrances to accommodate all the servants. I had to toss a coin to decide which door to use."

He grinned at that. "Only the one you came through is for servants. The other," he added, nodding to the door to his left, "is the tradesman's entrance."

"Oh, of course, the tradesman's entrance," she drawled, waving one hand as if fanning herself. "Well, my word and la-di-da."

"I can see you are of a mind to tease me tonight," he

replied, "but since we are friends now, I suppose you have the right." He gestured to the viands on the table. "I've made something to eat before we dance. I hope you don't mind, but I didn't have time to dine before I came, and I'm absolutely famished. So, I bought a few things on my way here and raided the rest from my cook's store cupboard. Care to join me?"

"I already ate in my room."

"And how are you enjoying room service?"

"It's heavenly, although they give you far too much food for one person to eat. But I am enjoying the respite from cooking over a gas ring in my flat."

"I'm sure. Although, again, we come from such opposite experiences. Doing for myself is proving to be a nice change of pace. I'm enjoying this."

She watched as he reached beneath the table, opened a drawer, and extracted a knife with an easy familiarity that surprised her. "You've never prepared your own food?" she asked, puzzled. "But you seem quite at home here."

He chuckled, shutting the drawer with his hip. "Well, this is my house."

"I meant *here*, in the kitchens," she said, laughing with him.

"I spent many hours down here as a boy, perfecting my ability to steal tarts or cakes from under the cook's nose without getting caught, so I know where everything is." He opened another jar and scooped out some of the contents, then picked up a hunk of the bread. "You've already dined, but nonetheless, I'm happy to share. Care for a bite?"

She leaned closer, eyeing the pinkish brown paste he was spreading on the bread with doubt. "What is it? Fish paste?"

"Pâté."

"Liver?" Her opinion of that must have been obvious, for he laughed.

"Not liver," he corrected, placing a gherkin from the pickle jar atop his creation. "Pâté. It's completely different."

"But still liver," she pointed out.

"You're far too literal," he chided, holding the canapé out to her. "Here. Try it."

She pulled off her gloves, set them aside, and took the offered snack. Still skeptical, she hesitated, but when he gave her an encouraging nod, she took a bite.

"It's delicious," she exclaimed around the mouthful of food in her mouth, too surprised to be polite.

"Of course it is. I'm a member of the Epicurean Club, you know," he reminded, preparing another canapé for himself. "We don't eat anything that isn't delicious."

She savored the combination of creamy pâté, soft bread, and crunchy pickle a moment longer, then swallowed it and said, "It's not at all what I expected. As a little girl, I remember our cook serving me fried liver with onions for supper." She shivered at the memory. "It was nothing like this."

"I imagine not. Fried liver sounds ghastly." He took a bite of his own canapé, chewed, and swallowed. "So, your family had a cook?"

She nodded. "And a housekeeper. In those days, we owned the entire building. The shop took up half, and our home was in the other half. After I went away to school, Papa let both servants go. He said it was silly, having servants for just one person, that he'd never had servants growing up, and that he was accustomed to doing for himself. He even said he preferred it. I didn't really believe him, but there wasn't much I could do. When I graduated and returned home, however, he was forced to admit that his reason had really been the expense, warning me that we would have to practice strict economies from then on, since we had very little money. I didn't know just how little until—"

She broke off, looking away as memories rose up, memories of pain and grief, the anguish and fear of being utterly alone and nearly destitute.

"Until?" he prompted in the wake of her silence, sliding a canapé into her line of vision.

She took the offered snack, but she didn't look up. Instead, she kept her gaze on the table. "Until he died," she finished. "That's when I found out that though I'd inherited everything, there was really nothing much to inherit."

"Your father had no savings? No investments?"

She shook her head. "The shop had been losing money for years. Even before I was born, my parents were in debt, and every year it had gotten worse."

"But you did inherit the building?"

"Yes, but there were two mortgages on it, one on the house and one on the shop. The cash from that didn't solve anything, though, because Papa speculated with the money, hoping to recoup his losses. He didn't succeed, of course. My father," she added, smiling a little as she traced the swirls and cathedrals in the oak table with her fingertips, "was not a good man of business."

She paused and ate her canapé before going on. "Two days after the funeral, creditors informed me they were calling both his mortgages."

"That must have been terrifying for you."

His voice was grave, but when she looked up, she was glad to see no pity in his face. In fact, he wasn't looking at her at all. Instead, his attention seemed wholly fixed on making canapés, for there were now a dozen on the table between them. But if she thought that meant he hadn't been giving her story his full attention, she was mistaken. "So, what did you do?" he asked. "Obviously, you were able to keep the shop."

"Yes. I managed to convince the creditors to only take the house and leave the loan on the shop in place."

"They agreed, obviously." He rose to his feet and circled the second worktable to the back wall. "Although," he went on as he pulled off one of the sheets and extracted a plate from the shelf behind it, "I can't imagine how you managed to persuade them."

"It wasn't easy. I presented them with dozens of reference letters, assuring them I was fully capable of taking over in my father's stead—one from my cousin's stepfather, who is a baron, and some from Papa's customers—university professors, prominent book collectors, even a bishop. I suppose that did the trick, because in the end, they allowed me to assume the loan on the shop, but only at a higher interest rate, and only if I paid half the principal immediately, made monthly payments, agreed to a prepayment penalty, and paid the entire mortgage off at the end of eight years."

"And you agreed?" he asked as he returned to the table, plate in hand.

"What else could I do? I cut the shop in half and turned the first floor into a flat. Then I sold all the excess inventory, all our furniture, my mother's jewelry, and anything else of value we had left. In the end, I managed to scrape up just enough to meet their demands. But the income from the bookshop alone is meager, and I knew I wouldn't be able to save enough to pay off the mortgage at the end of the term, so I started taking on extra work."

"From Delia, for example?"

"Delia, and a few others. I type manuscripts for authors, do research for them—that sort of thing."

"And did you pay the mortgage in time?"

"I did," she said proudly. "Eight weeks ago. The bankers were dumbfounded."

"And chagrined, I daresay," he said as he began filling the plate with canapés. "Being that you are a woman, they probably thought you'd mismanage everything and that you'd end up having to default at the end, and they'd get the other half of the building anyway—a very valuable piece of London property—after already recouping half their original investment, while making a tidy sum off the interest payments in the meantime."

She grinned. "I enjoyed defying their expectations."

"No doubt. But what about now?"

Evie froze, her canapé halfway to her mouth. "I'm not sure what you mean."

He ate a bite of his canapé before he answered. "I'm curious if you still enjoy managing your shop."

"Of course I do!" She saw his eyebrow lift in obvious skepticism of such an emphatic answer, and she set her bread and pâté down with a sigh. "Sometimes," she qualified. "As a little girl, I loved being in the shop because I loved books. I was shy as a child, and books were like a window opening into other worlds, where I could slay dragons and dance with princes and conquer the Huns. And being away at school, I was so homesick that coming back afterward was a relief, and working with my father was a pleasure. But lately..." She paused, curiously reluctant to go on.

He wasn't about to let her off the hook, however. "But lately?" he prompted in the wake of her silence.

"When I first took over the shop after Papa died,

everything was uncertain and chaotic, and I was terrified, but I loved the challenge of it. Now things are much more stable. I'm not prosperous, exactly, but I do all right, if I'm careful with my money. And yet..." She paused again, took a deep breath, and said it—the truth that had been weighing her down for weeks. "Now that the mortgage is paid off, I've started to feel as if the shop is more of a burden than a joy. I don't know why."

"Even our greatest joys can become burdens," he said gently. "Especially when we no longer have something to prove. Then things can seem anticlimactic, stale, even pointless."

"Even if that's true, it's not as if I have much of a choice. The shop provides my best means of earning a living."

"Perhaps," he conceded, sounding doubtful, but before she could even think about debating the point, he went on, "Either way, everything you've said proves one thing that I find immensely gratifying."

"What's that?"

"That I was right."

"Right?" she echoed, laughing. "About what?"

"You were definitely in need of a holiday."

She wrinkled her nose at him. "I suppose I have to give you that one. Although I never would have agreed to any of this, if I'd known there would be dancing."

"You dreamed of dancing with princes once upon a time," he reminded her. "I'm not a prince, I know, so practicing with me will be a bit of a comedown for you, but nonetheless..."

His voice trailed away. He straightened away from the worktable with purposeful intent, and as she watched him circle around it, she realized the moment she'd been dreading was at hand. "I doubt we have time for much of a lesson now," she murmured. "You haven't even finished eating, and—"

"Oh, no, no," he said, cutting off her pathetic attempt to evade the inevitable. "This equivocation will not do, Evie. We must practice our dance steps."

"But what about the food?" It was a feeble excuse, and she knew it.

He knew it, too. "We can dine between dances," he told her, picking up the plate. "C'mon."

Plate of canapés in hand, he started for the door, and she knew she could stall no longer. She followed him to the end of the corridor, up a flight of stairs, through a green baize door, and along another corridor. They finally emerged into a large foyer at the top of what seemed to be the house's main staircase. Evie couldn't see much, for the duke had lit only enough gas jets to guide their way, but in the dim light, she could make out inset panels painted with landscapes, ancient but luxurious Turkish rugs, and an enormous crystal chandelier, unlit, over her head.

The white plasterwork and sheet-covered furnishings lent a mysterious, ghostly appearance to the place, but despite that, she could easily imagine London's most fashionable and influential people—the men in elegant white tie like the duke, the ladies in some of the luscious creations she'd seen at Vivienne the day before—coming up the elaborate wrought iron staircase to attend a party or ball. For herself, however, it was harder to form the picture. The people in her mind's eye had been born into this environment. Like the duke, they belonged here, while she, in her plain white blouse, dark skirt, and necktie, was firmly entrenched in the genteel poverty of Wellington Street.

In agreeing to this holiday, she'd known she would be entering an entirely different world, but even as she'd checked into the opulent Savoy Hotel, even as she had eaten the rich cuisine of the famous Escoffier and chosen beautiful frocks from the fashionable Vivienne, Evie hadn't appreciated just how alien her holiday world would prove to be.

Now, however, as the duke led her into an enormous ballroom of gold and white, with an intricate parquet floor, dozens of gilt-framed mirrors, and a domed ceiling at least thirty feet high, the contrast between her life and that of her companion could not have been more stark, and she was more convinced than ever that when the time came for the duke's ball, when all of those fashionable people in her imagination became real, when they were staring at her with the same disdain as the gargoyles on the gate outside, she was going to make an utter fool of herself and justify all their expectations. Her fantasy to triumph over Freddie Maybridge and his friends, her need to face the past and put it behind her, her wish to have a more fulfilling, interesting life in the future—it all seemed ridiculous now.

Westbourne was watching her, smiling a little, and she forced herself to say something. "Goodness," she muttered with another glance around before returning her attention to him, "I didn't realize aristocrats were so vain."

"Vain?" His smile gave way to a puzzled look. "I'm not sure I follow."

"All these mirrors. What are they for? To admire yourselves or each other?"

He chuckled. "Sound logic either way, but that's not the reason."

"No?"

"They're to reflect light and make the room seem brighter, a holdover from the days of candles." He gestured to a magnificent Berliner gramophone nearby. "Are you ready?"

The sight of it, and the stack of gramophone records on a narrow, sheet-covered table beside it, caused all of Evie's apprehensions to return. "I should be asking you that," she quipped shakily.

"Have some faith in me, Evie. I told you before, I'm quick on my feet." He turned, setting the plate of canapés beside the stack of records, then he pulled the top record off the stack and slid the disk from its paper jacket.

Intrigued despite her nervous jitters, she moved to stand beside him. "Aren't gramophone records made of glass?" she asked, studying the disk he was holding carefully between his palms. "This one is black."

"The newest ones are made of shellac," he explained, placing the record on the gramophone's turntable. "A bit less likely to break, I'm told."

"What—" She broke off and took a deep breath. "What are we dancing to?"

"I thought we'd try a waltz first." He turned the crank on the side of the machine and pushed the switch to set the turntable in motion. "A waltz doesn't require you to remember specific figures or steps. And besides," he went on as he placed the stylus needle on the edge of the now-spinning disk, "you're already familiar with the music, no doubt."

Unlike him, Evie had every doubt, but the first notes that floated from the gramophone's enormous tortoiseshell horn proved him right. "The Blue Danube," she said. "I think one would have to have lived their entire life in a cave not to recognize that melody."

"All right, then," he said, turning toward her, "let's see what else you know. May I have this dance?"

She stared at his outstretched hand for a moment—the long, strong fingers, the casually rolled-back cuff, the mature, sinewy muscles of his forearm, and it was such a contrast to the reluctant boys shoved at her in her school days that she felt oddly reassured. Until she took his hand.

The contact of his bare skin against hers was startling, for she hadn't held hands with anyone—not bare hands, anyway—since she was a small girl, when she and Rory would walk hand in hand to Brown's Ice Cream Parlor for a penny lick.

This, she appreciated as the warmth of the duke's touch penetrated her skin, rippled up her arm, and spread through her remaining limbs, was completely different.

He led her to the center of the vast ballroom, and though she hadn't danced in over a decade, her body moved automatically into the proper position, facing him the correct distance apart, her free hand coming to rest on his right shoulder, just as she'd been taught. "This part is easy to remember," she said, laughing to cover her nervousness as he put his free hand against her back.

He didn't seem to agree with her memory, however, for he shook his head. "You're too far away."

"Am I?" Surprised, Evie glanced down at the space between them. "But this is the distance I danced at school."

"Real life," he told her, his fingers pressing into her shoulder blade, "is different."

As he drew her closer, the scents of bay rum and sandalwood invaded her senses, an earthy, masculine scent. *Crikey*, she thought, instinctively leaning into his neck, breathing deep, *he smells good*.

"That's a bit too close," he said, his laughter soft against her ear. Evie jerked back, cursing whatever luscious soap, aftershave, or pomade was making him smell like that.

"Now, that's a bit of all right," he told her, and before

she could reply, he was swaying on his feet, rocking her with him as he counted. "One and two and three."

And then, off he went, pulling her along, but she was only able to move with him for about a dozen steps before her body lost the rhythm and she stumbled, stepping squarely on his toe and bringing them both to a halt.

"Sorry." She pulled, but he wasn't about to let her get away so easily, and his fingers tightened, keeping her body in the proper pose. Trapped, she gave a little shrug of her tense shoulder muscles and tried to make light of it. "But I did warn you."

"So you did, and there's nothing to be sorry about, so don't apologize. As for your waltzing, I think I perceive the problem."

"You do? Already?"

For some reason, that made him smile. "Well, it's fairly obvious. You weren't letting me lead."

"Yes, I was." Even as she made that protest, she knew it was a lie. "At least I thought I was," she amended, cursing herself for ever agreeing to this.

"What you were doing was fighting me for control. Not that I usually object to that sort of thing from women," he added, still smiling faintly. "But in this case, it's best if my body gives the orders."

With his body so close to hers and the scent of him filling her nostrils, Evie wasn't at all sure she liked the idea of him being in charge.

As if he sensed what she was thinking, his smile faded to a serious expression. "Don't worry, Evie. I won't take you anywhere you don't want to go. I promise."

"I'm not sure I find that very reassuring," she muttered.

"I can tell." He wriggled their wrists experimentally back and forth. "You're stiff as a board. You need to relax."

"That," she choked, "is easier said than done."

"Just remember, there's no one watching. No one here but us."

Strangely, that did not make her feel any better, but she nodded, took another deep breath, and worked to shove aside her apprehensions as he counted off. Once again, however, her uneasiness proved justified, and this time, they were only able to take half as many steps before she stumbled over his feet again and they were forced to stop.

"We are making progress," he told her before she could speak.

"We are?" Exasperated, she pulled out of his hold and rubbed her hands across her face. "I hadn't noticed."

"I am serious, Evie. We're making progress because I've discovered something else that is hindering you."

"Aside from my natural grace and noble tendency to take charge?" she joked.

He grinned. "You keep looking down."

"Well, of course I do! How else can I avoid stepping on you?"

"And how is this method of dancing working out for you?"

That earned him her fiercest scowl.

It made no difference, of course. "Think what happens when you carry a cup of water up or down a flight of stairs," he told her. "If you stare at the cup, trying not to spill the water, you invariably do spill it. But if you don't look at it, you're less likely to spill."

Evie didn't argue with him. Why bother? "Come on," she said instead, holding up her right hand and beckoning with her left. "Let's go again."

They did, and she tried not to look down, and she tried not to lead, but doing both of those while also trying to relax seemed impossible, and after less than one turn around the ballroom, she stumbled again.

Desperate to avoid treading on his feet for the third time, she overcompensated, pitching sideways with enough force to pull her hand from his grasp.

She would have fallen, but his arm came fully around her back, encircling her waist and catching her up, hauling her body hard against his.

Time seemed to stop. Her toes barely touching the floor, her torso pressed to his, Evie felt suspended in space. His eyes seemed to darken as she looked into them, turning from blue to black, making the pupils indiscernible. His arm was like a steel band across her back, she had no air in her lungs, and she wondered wildly if he was going to let her go or hold her imprisoned like this forever.

His lashes lowered, as if he were wondering the same, and she felt a jolt of panic that had nothing to do with dancing. Along with that panic, however, Evie also felt a faint, unmistakable thrill.

But then, he eased her down, and relief washed over her—relief and something else, something vague and hard to define. It might have been...disappointment.

Feeling two such contradictory emotions simultaneously made no sense, and she was impelled to break the silence.

"Well, at least I didn't step on your toes this time," she said, trying to sound flippant, but her words came out in a breathless rush, quite spoiling the effect.

Thankfully, he didn't seem to notice. "I think perhaps we need a different approach." Letting her go, he stepped back, tilting his head as he looked at her. "I just wish I knew what it was."

"I told you I was terrible," she reminded him with a sigh. "You just didn't believe me."

"Stuff," he contradicted at once. "None of that. By the night of the ball, you'll be flying around the ballroom as if your feet have wings. But until we get there," he added as she made a sound of disbelief, "I think we need some additional help."

"Help? You mean more people?" Feeling more awkward and self-conscious than ever, she tried to smile. "I thought you wanted me to relax."

"I do. And I might have an idea to help that along." Abruptly, he turned and started for the doors leading out of the ballroom. "Wait here. I'll be right back."

Evie watched him walk away, and the craven thought crossed her mind that during his absence she might have time to make her escape. Out the way she'd come, up Green Street and onto Park Lane, she could be halfway to the cab stand by the Marble Arch before—

"And no running off while I'm gone," he added over his shoulder as if reading her mind. "You're going to see this through."

"Oh, very well," she said crossly, her hopes dashed. "But I shan't feel any pangs of conscience when you are icing your feet tomorrow and cursing my name."

He merely laughed, the wretch, and vanished out the door.

Evie couldn't imagine what sort of help he had in mind, but when he returned a few minutes later, her apprehension gave way to an exclamation of happy surprise. "Is that champagne?"

"It is. A Clicquot '88. A pity it's not iced," he went on as he set the glasses on the table by the gramophone and began to open the bottle, "but it's cold enough from the cellars to be drinkable."

"Far be it from me to argue with a duke about the quality of his champagne," she said as she came to his side, "but I'm not sure how getting drunk will help my dancing ability. I would think the opposite to be true."

"You won't be drinking enough to get drunk," he assured as he popped the cork and began to pour. "I shan't allow it. But one glass will relax you and improve your dancing."

She leaned closer, watching as the sparkling wine foamed up to the rim of each glass, then receded. "I shall have to take you at your word, since I've never had champagne in my life."

That seemed to take him aback, for he stopped pouring. "Never?" he asked, turning his head to give her a doubtful look. "Evie, you have been deprived of one of life's greatest joys."

He set aside the bottle, handed her a filled glass, and took up his own. "To your first pâté, your first champagne, and the much better dancing that is sure to follow."

She clinked her glass against his, then took a tentative sip, not sure what to expect, but as the wine bubbled and danced on her tongue, she laughed with delight.

"Like it, I gather?" he asked, laughing with her.

"It's lovely!" she cried and lifted her glass for a second toast. "To making up for lost time," she declared and took another hefty swallow.

"Whoa, there, tigress," he cautioned, his free hand closing over her glass to stop her. "I told you I was not going to let you get drunk. Don't prove me a liar."

Letting go of her hand, he reached behind him and plucked another canapé off the plate. "Here," he said, handing it to her. "Eat that and at least one more while you sip that champagne. Then we'll try again."

She obeyed, though she still didn't see how any of this was going to help. When she had finished, he took away her glass, restarted the music, and grasped her hand.

"Ready?" Without waiting for an answer, without escorting her to the center of the room, and without even counting off, he started, pulling her with him so fast, she had no time to think.

"Look at me, not the floor," he reminded before she had the chance to do exactly that. "And let your body move with mine."

She did her best to follow those instructions, and though she still felt terribly awkward, she managed not to stumble through several full turns around the ballroom floor. By the fourth turn, she was even beginning to enjoy herself.

And then, on a crescendo of lilting violins and horns, the music came to an end. "You see?" he said as they swirled to a halt. "Not a single stumble."

"You're right," she said, laughing in astonished pleasure. "I stopped worrying about making a mistake."

He smiled. "It's amazing how much better life is when that happens."

Suddenly, something flickered in his eyes and his smile faded. His hand tightened at her waist, his fingertips pressing at her back, pulling her closer even than before. His lashes, thick and blunt and black as coffee, lowered as he looked down, and when she realized what had captured his attention, her breath caught in her throat.

Her lips, the focus of his stare, began to tingle, and she wondered wildly if he was going to kiss her. Her heartbeat, already rapid from the exertion of dancing, quickened even more, thudding in her chest so hard that she was sure he could hear it, even over the rasping, rhythmic hiss of the gramophone.

He stirred, leaning even closer, so close that the heady, delicious scent of him filled her nostrils, and his breathing, warm and quick, fanned her cheek.

Her first kiss, she thought with a dreamy sigh as she closed her eyes and tilted her head back.

"We should go."

The words had barely penetrated her senses before he was stepping away, widening the distance between them and crushing any hope that a kiss was in the offing.

He turned to gather the empty glasses, half-empty plate, and nearly full bottle of champagne, while Evie could only stare at his broad back, her senses in tumult, her wits in shambles, her heart twisting with a crushing disappointment.

Still, what could she have expected? He was practically engaged to a girl already, a lady. And he was every inch a gentleman. She could hardly blame him for acting like it.

"I want you to do something for me," he said over his shoulder, breaking the silence.

Evie took a deep, shaky breath and got hold of herself. "What's that?"

"Remember this night, at least until we dance again." He turned to look at her, smiling so casually it was as if the magical moment of his mouth so close to hers had never happened. "If only to spare my feet. Shall we?"

He nodded toward the door and began moving in that direction. Evie followed, her body still tingling everywhere he had touched her, her heart still thudding like a trip-hammer, and she knew she'd have no trouble doing what he asked. She'd remember this night, not only for their next dance, but for the rest of her life.

# 10

His intentions tonight had been laudable, his conduct gentlemanly, and his fortitude quite commendable, considering the circumstances.

His thoughts, on the other hand, had been decidedly reprobate. The moment she'd talked about being underdressed, he'd begun to think of red satin garters and long, slim legs. When they'd eaten bread and pâté, fantasies of feeding her food while both of them were naked had insisted on invading his mind. When they danced, he'd used some stupid excuse—what, he couldn't even remember now—to pull her closer than was proper, close enough to make dancing with her a delicious, agonizing hell.

She smelled like powder and flowers and virginal innocence, which ought to have been a deterrent, but instead, it had been a siren, harkening to deep, dark desires inside him. He'd swirled her around the room while he'd imagined taking her down to the floor and kissing every freckle on her face and every inch of her talcum-scented body.

And then, when the music stopped, he'd almost given in to these carnal imaginings. She'd looked up at him with those eyes full of gold and amber lights, and then she'd laughed, showing him that adorable smile, and everything in his world had tilted, skidding sideways, sending him tumbling to the brink of oblivion, making him almost forget he'd been on this particular precipice before and the heavy price he'd paid for falling over the edge.

How he'd pulled himself away, he still didn't know, but even now, two hours later, his body was in the painful agony of unrequited lust, cursing him for his caution, his common sense, and his gentlemanly notions of honor.

For God's sake, he thought in aggravation, did he want history to repeat itself? Hadn't Rebecca taught him to stay away from women like this, women who were not born in his world and not bred for his life, women who knew nothing of what it meant to be a duchess and had no experience with the duties inherent to such a role? And it wasn't as if his own bitter experience was the only example he had to go by. The peerage at present was filled with unhappy marriages between British lords and dollar princesses from the States who had married into the aristocracy with no clue what they were taking on. The results had been universally disastrous, a misery for nearly all concerned.

On the heels of all these reminders came another, one that was far more unsavory.

*You don't have to marry her.*

As if in reply, the soprano on the stage below hit the high C. Properly rebuked, he leaned forward in his seat, forcing himself to pay attention to the performance. It was *La Traviata*, an irony if ever there was one, but if he hoped this cautionary tale about an innocent woman seduced and ruined by a man would quell the lust raging in him, he was disappointed. His body remained fully aroused, impervious to the dictates of his conscience or the rules of society.

Evie's life had given her very little in the way of romance, and he'd started this whole adventure partly to help her along in that regard. This, he reflected, shifting painfully in his seat, was not the sort of help he'd been envisioning. Worse, she was a thorough innocent, and if he were responsible for taking her down the road to ruin, he'd never forgive himself, nor should he.

The music ended, and in sheer self-preservation, Max pulled off his evening coat, throwing it onto his lap as the lights came up. All around him, people began rising from their seats, preparing to mingle, obtain refreshments, or stretch their legs. Max, however, did not dare move. His body was still in a most vulnerable state, and if he stood up, the entire world would know it.

Beside him, Helen's voice came to him as if from a far distance. "Duke, shall we take a stroll?"

"Hmm? What?" Still lost in thought, Max looked up to find Helen had risen from her seat and her eyes were staring down at him, eyes lauded by all in society for their beauty, eyes of pure emerald green with no murky, intriguing glimmers of amber and gold in their depths.

"Duke?" she prompted in the wake of his silent stare, and Max jerked to his feet, an automatic gesture born of a lifetime of good manners, and he could only thank God for the protection of his evening coat.

Vaguely, he thought she would excuse herself, enabling him to sit back down and get hold of himself, but instead, she stood there, waiting, looking at him in expectation.

He tried in desperation to muster a reply—an impossible feat, since he had no clue what she'd said.

In the wake of his silence, she laughed a little, smiling—

a smile of dimpled cheeks and perfect teeth that did absolutely nothing to send him skidding sideways.

And that, he reminded himself, was a very good thing.

"Or perhaps you would prefer to sit?"

He blinked at the sound of her voice, still uncomprehending. "Oh, yes," he said, falling back on the age-old masculine notion that in circumstances such as these, agreeing with a woman was always the safest bet. "Absolutely."

He thought she'd excuse herself at that point, but instead, she continued to just stand there, staring at him, her smile faltering, then vanishing altogether.

"My dear Duke," she murmured, looking at him with obvious bewilderment, "are you unwell?"

"Not at all," he lied, pasting on a smile as he forced down the arousal in his body by sheer force of will. "I'm right as rain."

This reply, emphatic as it was, didn't seem to convince her, but thankfully, a distraction appeared in the edge of his vision that gave him a moment of breathing space.

He turned his head, watching as Colonel Anstruther and his wife entered his box with their son—their *unmarried* son—right behind them, and as he looked at them, everything in Max's world suddenly shifted back into proper perspective.

"Or at least," he amended to Helen, "I soon will be. If you will excuse me, my dear?"

A look of hurt crossed her face, but Max couldn't take the time just now to rectify that. "I shall see you again shortly," he said instead, the best he could do.

He bowed and turned away, moving past the rows of seats in his box to greet the new arrivals, and he could only hope that no pretty little debutante of the season had already stolen Ronald Anstruther's heart.

During the week that followed, Evie saw nothing of Westbourne, and she heard from him only once. After explaining the bet and how it had come about to a very surprised Anna, and after the other woman's assurance that she'd love attending the opera, Evie sent the duke a note confirming Saturday night, and his reply instructed her to call for their tickets at the Will Call box when she and her friend arrived for the performance.

Other than that brief correspondence, she heard nothing from him, but that, she discovered to her chagrin, didn't stop her from thinking about him. As busy as she was with renovations to the bookshop, trips to art galleries and museums she'd never had time to visit in the past, and dress fittings at Vivienne, enticing memories of dancing with the duke would steal into her thoughts at unexpected moments, filling her with an exhilarating, breath-robbing euphoria unlike anything she'd ever felt before.

Every time it came, she tamped it down, reminding herself that all of this was a holiday, a mere interlude sandwiched between the ordinary days of an ordinary life, but it didn't stop a shivering little thrill from running up her spine whenever she remembered how it felt to be in his arms.

*Remember this night*, he'd said, but days later, she was still wondering how he'd think she'd ever forget it.

Nonetheless, there was one much less agreeable piece of the duke's advice also nagging at her mind, one she found far easier to shove aside, and it wasn't until the night of the opera when she was trying to put on the plum velvet evening gown that had arrived from Vivienne that afternoon that that particular piece of advice came back to her.

*You'll need a maid. The gowns Vivienne is sure to make*

*for you will be far too complicated for you to manage on your own.*

She'd dismissed the idea as absurd. Maids were a silly extravagance of the idle rich, and an intimacy she wasn't the least bit comfortable with. She could dress herself, thank you very much. She didn't need a maid—a perfect stranger, at that—to help her. It was only a dress, after all, with all its buttons in the front and a few hooks and eyes under each arm. How hard could it be to put it on by herself?

An hour later, she was red-faced, out of breath, and thoroughly exasperated, wearing nothing but her undergarments, shoes, and the absurd little fascinator Vivienne had sent over for her to put in her hair.

Evie stared at the pieces that comprised her new gown in utter vexation. When the fitters at Vivienne had put the pieces of the gown on her at the showroom to make alterations, it had never occurred to her that they wouldn't be sewing the pieces together, and as she stared at them scattered hither and yon across her bed, she wondered what the hell she was going to do now.

Just then, there was a knock on the door, and Evie dashed to the front door and opened it a crack. "Anna!" She pulled the door wide, hauled her friend into the suite, and shut the door again. "Thank God you're here."

Anna, whose honey-blonde hair, angelic face, and calm, serene manner always reminded Evie of a Bellini Madonna, actually burst out laughing. "I didn't know fashionable gowns these days had their corset covers and petticoats on the outside," she joked.

"This isn't funny. You've got to help me get dressed."

"Doesn't this little holiday at the Savoy include a maid?" Anna asked as Evie propelled her across the sitting room and into her bedroom.

"I thought I could just dress myself."

Anna paused by the bed, staring at her with pity. "Silly girl," she chided as she removed her coat. "I could have told you any gown from Vivienne would make dressing yourself impossible."

"Yes, well, I know that now," Evie muttered, picking up the plum velvet skirt and shoving it at her friend. "Here. Show me how to put this thing on."

Half an hour later, the pieces of Evie's gown were satisfactorily assembled on her person, all the buttons and hooks had been fastened, and Anna was burrowing underneath the hem to tie the tapes that would keep the goldenrod silk underskirt securely fastened to the plum velvet overskirt.

"It's a good thing for you I once worked in a dressmaker's showroom," Anna told her, her voice muffled beneath layers of silk and velvet. "Or we'd never make it to the opera in time. It's a beautiful gown, though, Evie," she added, emerging from beneath the hem to smooth the panels into place and adjust the elaborate velvet bows, tucks, and flounces that cascaded down each side of the exposed underskirt. "And very expensive."

There was a nuance in her voice, something thoughtful and grave, but Evie didn't have the time or inclination to speculate on it. "It's something Vivienne already had on hand, a reject from another client. I'm just glad they were able to alter it for me."

"It does fit you like a glove." Anna rose, moved to her side, and turned her toward the mirror. "See for yourself."

Evie stared at her reflection, hardly able to recognize herself. The velvet fit her figure to perfection, and although she wore no padding, the elaborate gown and its accompanying undergarments somehow made her body look different. Shaped by the Vivienne-designed corset and framed by the low neckline, her breasts seemed fuller. Beneath the velvet bows and swags, her hips seemed more rounded. She looked almost...voluptuous.

This was not the same woman who had stared into the wavy mirror above her shop sink, wondering what the duke had seen in her that she could not see in herself. It was a superficial change, perhaps—an illusion or a mirage or a trick of cut and color—but even to her own eyes, she did not seem plain or unremarkable. She no longer felt bored or boring.

*If given half a chance, you could be regarded as an incomparable beauty.*

That day in her shop, she'd laughed at the duke's assessment, but she wasn't laughing now. She might not be a beauty, but at this moment, in this gown, she began to feel like one.

"Goodness," she breathed. "All this for the opera."

"You look splendid. I feel quite plain beside you in my made-over silk."

"You?" Evie shot a disbelieving glance at her friend, who was far too beautiful to ever be considered plain by anyone with eyes, and who had succeeded in making a cast-off emerald-and-sapphire silk gown from her dressmaking days into something both fashionable and lovely. "Don't be silly," she said as she slid on her elbow-length gloves. "I'm not a patch on you, Anna Banks, and you know it."

Anna smiled. "Darling Evie. There isn't a catty bone in your body, is there? It's one of your finest qualities, did you know that?"

"I'm a peach," she agreed, picking up her plum velvet cape and her gold silk reticule. "Now that we've established that, we must go, or we'll be late."

"Well, we can't have that," Anna agreed, reaching for

her own gloves, cloak, and handbag. "I've never been to the opera before, and I don't want to miss a thing. So generous of Lady Stratham to let you borrow her box."

They started out of the room, but as Evie followed her friend through the doorway, she couldn't resist one last glance over her shoulder at her reflection, and for the first time, she wondered if perhaps Freddie Maybridge and his friends might have to eat their words after all.

# 11

The interior of the Royal Opera House, or Covent Garden as most Londoners called it, was an opulent display of crimson, ivory, and gold. Sandwiched between two floors of ordinary seats, three floors of boxes ringed the stage, and it was to one of these boxes that Evie and Anna were shown by an usher.

"Goodness," Evie murmured as they took places in the first of three rows of empty seats overlooking stage left. "Seems very grand for just the two of us. I could have invited half the neighborhood."

As impressive as the setting was, Evie wasn't so sure about the opera itself. She'd been expecting something a bit like Gilbert and Sullivan. Wagner's *Lohengrin*, she decided, wasn't her cup of tea, and she was rather glad she hadn't invited half the neighborhood. Most of the people on Wellington Street probably wouldn't think Wagner their cup of tea either.

Intermission, however, proved to be delightful, for the curtain had barely rung down before a waiter arrived, pushing a cart laden with luxurious food.

"Heavens," Anna murmured as the waiter began placing loaves of bread and plates of canapés, ham, cheese, and fruit on a cloth-covered table behind the rows of seats. "Evie, I thought you were treating me to salmon sandwiches downstairs. What's all this?"

"Courtesy of His Grace, the Duke of Westbourne," the servant explained as the two women removed their gloves, rose from their seats, and came to have a look.

"Oh, Anna, look!" Evie cried, eyeing the food with delight. "He ordered us pâté. I love pâté. And champagne—a Clicquot '88, too," she added as the waiter placed an ice bucket containing a bottle of the same champagne she and the duke had shared on the table. "Isn't it lovely?"

"Yes, lovely," Anna agreed as the waiter poured champagne for them, but something in her voice caught Evie's attention, and when she looked up, she found Anna studying her with a thoughtful expression. "It sounds as if you've eaten pâté and drunk champagne before."

Evie reminded herself that there were some things even her best friend didn't need to know, and private picnics and dance lessons with a duke were definitely two of those things. "Well, I am staying at the Savoy," she reminded, giving the waiter a nod of dismissal. "It's given me the chance to try many new things."

"Yes, I can see that." Anna's voice was dry. "And all at the duke's expense. Such wanton extravagance seems odd just to win a bet."

Evie shrugged and took a sip of champagne. "It seems odd to me, too, so don't ask me to explain it. Still, you know how unaccountable aristocrats are."

"Actually, I don't," Anna said bluntly. "I've never met one in my life, and neither had you, until a week ago."

Evie felt inexplicably defensive. "That's not true. You

know full well my step-uncle is a baron, and that I've known the duke's cousin for several years. And," she added, impelled for reasons she couldn't quite identify to embellish her list of titled acquaintances, "I met the daughters of several peers when I was at finishing school."

"And have any of these acquaintances ever provided you with pâté and champagne?"

Evie, thankfully, was given no chance to reply.

"Is this a private party? Or can anyone join?"

Relieved, she turned her head, but when she saw the object of their conversation standing in the doorway, looking as handsome and debonair as ever in his white tie and tails, her heart skipped a beat, and her relief at the interruption vanished as quickly as it had come.

Still, she couldn't just sit here, staring at him, even if he was a treat to look at. "Duke," she greeted, setting down her glass and rising to her feet. "I didn't know you were coming this evening, too," she added, moving toward where he stood, Anna in tow.

"I didn't want to waste my tickets," he told her. "Like Delia, I have a box."

"Of course you do," she replied, laughing as she touched a hand to her forehead. "What was I thinking?"

Turning, she gestured to Anna, who had halted beside her. "Duke, may I present my friend, Mrs. Banks, to you? Anna, the Duke of Westbourne."

"Your Grace." Anna gave a deep curtsy, but Evie didn't miss the look her friend shot in her direction as the duke bowed to her in return, a meaningful look of raised eyebrows more eloquent than any words.

"A pleasure to meet you, Mrs. Banks." He straightened and nodded to the table behind them. "Your refreshments arrived, I'm glad to see."

"It was very kind of you to send them," Evie replied. "Thank you."

"Not at all. The tiny salmon sandwiches they serve in the intervals here are never enough to stave off hunger pangs, and since this is Wagner, an opera supper is hours away yet. Besides, I heard a rumor you are very fond of pâté." He paused, a glint of humor appearing in his eyes, creasing the corners. "Even though it's liver."

"But it's not liver," she corrected, smiling back at him. "It's pâté."

He chuckled and bowed his head in concession. "I stand corrected. And you, Mrs. Banks?" he added, transferring his attention to Anna. "Are you fond of pâté?"

"I don't know, Your Grace," she replied. "I haven't yet had the chance to find out." She glanced from the duke to Evie, a tiny frown knitting her brow. "But since both of you seem to love it so much, it's clear I must try it. If you will excuse me?"

With another short curtsy, she picked up one of the canapés and returned to her seat, turning her face discreetly away from them to study the stage below.

Evie frowned, watching her, sensing that something was bothering her friend, though she was given no time to ponder the topic.

"New dress?" the duke asked, regaining her attention, and when she nodded, he leaned back to study her, tilting his head to one side. As his gaze traveled over her in a slow perusal, all the newfound poise the gown had brought her disintegrated, her throat went dry, and by the time he looked up again, her heart was thudding in her chest like a mad thing.

"Well?" she asked lightly, forcing a laugh. "Do I pass ducal approval?"

"Freddie and his friends shall be eating their words."

Those words were a compliment, and yet, the light, careless tone of his voice as he said them hurt somehow. She ducked her head at once, hiding it. "Yes, well," she mumbled, smoothing her hand over the plush velvet of her skirt, "that dressmaker you sent me to is a marvel."

"I'm glad you like her. All my sisters adore her, too— that is, if the amount they spent on clothes while living in my household was any indication." His gaze lifted to her hair. "I like the hat, too, by the way."

The only thing a self-respecting girl could do was return raillery with raillery. "It's not a hat, Duke. It's a fascinator." She touched a hand to the silk and feather confection tucked into the crown of her hair, giving him a frown of mock severity. "I thought you said you knew all about women's clothes."

The moment those words were out of her mouth, she remembered his implied reasons for such knowledge and wanted to bite her tongue off, especially when he laughed and murmured, "Only from the neck down, Evie."

Her heart skipped a beat, but she'd have died rather than show it. "Yes, well, I wish I had your vast knowledge on the topic," she joked. "That way, this dress might not have been so tricky to get into."

"Tricky?" He frowned at the word, clearly puzzled. "Why should it have been? Didn't you ring for your maid?"

She shifted her weight, hating to admit she'd been too shy to call on a complete stranger to help her dress. It would sound so gauche to someone like him. "There wasn't...um...enough time," she muttered, tugging at her ear, aware of how lame an excuse that was. "So...um...I just thought I'd do it myself."

"Evie, you're hopeless. Have you not enlisted the

services of your maid at all? Not even once? Have you even met the girl yet?" he added as she shook her head.

"No," she admitted and rushed on, "The truth is, I don't think having a maid help me dress suits my temperament. It seems so odd. So alien."

"I wouldn't know," he replied with a shrug. "I've never been required to dress myself."

"Never?" Diverted from her own embarrassment, she couldn't help a grin. "What?" she teased. "Don't you know how?"

"Of course I know how," he said, sounding defensive enough to make her doubt the veracity of his assurance, especially when he jerked his chin. "I've just never had occasion to do it, that's all. I've always had a valet."

"Of course," she said gravely, pressing her lips together.

"Let's return to the subject, shall we? You need your maid, as the tricky dress you're wearing clearly demonstrated to you already. Best to become familiar with her now," he added as she made another protest. "That way, if you don't like her, you have time to find another before Delia's got you in the teeth of the season's whirlwind. And Delia will tolerate no missishness about maids if it makes the pair of you late for an engagement."

"Oh, very well," she replied, heaving an aggrieved sigh as she gave in to the inevitable. "But I'm only agreeing to the maid because if Anna hadn't arrived when she had, I'd still be trying to do up all the tapes and tabs and buttons on this thing. I mean it, Max," she added as he laughed. "It was like wrestling with an octopus!"

"I can't imagine any octopus getting the better of you, Evie," he replied, still grinning.

"Heavens, Westbourne," a feminine voice broke in, "what am I hearing?"

Both of them turned as a striking, silver-haired woman paused in the doorway of the box, one young male companion and one older one behind her. "Did you really just compare this sweet-looking girl to an octopus?"

"Only in the most favorable way, Alicia," he assured, bending down for the woman to kiss his cheeks in the French fashion, then moving aside so she could enter the box.

"I hope so," she replied. "Otherwise, I should begin to think you were losing your touch with the ladies. If I were you, my dear," she added to Evie as she moved to stand beside her, "I should not believe a word he says."

"I don't," Evie countered at once. "Since most of what he says is utter tosh."

Everyone laughed at that, including Max. "She adores me, really," Max assured, shifting sideways so that Alicia's two companions could join them. "Allow me to perform introductions. Miss Harlow, this is Mrs. Anstruther, her husband, Colonel Anstruther, and their son, Ronald. This is Miss Harlow. And," he added as Anna rejoined them, "Mrs. Banks."

Somehow, in the mutual bows and curtsies that followed this introduction, Ronald Anstruther ended up by Evie's side. "How are you enjoying the opera, Miss Harlow?" he asked her.

She hesitated, and her opinion must have shown on her face, much to everyone's amusement.

"Not much, then, it seems," Mrs. Anstruther said and turned to Anna. "And what about you, Mrs. Banks?" she asked as Ronald Anstruther leaned closer to Evie.

"I don't like opera either," he confided to her in a whisper. "Caterwauling cats are more pleasant to the ear."

"Maybe they sing like that on purpose," Evie answered, considering.

"On purpose?"

"Yes. If they're anything like the alley cats outside my flat, their singing will ensure no one falls asleep."

He threw back his head and laughed. "I think you might have something there, Miss Harlow. We all come to the opera, but most of us don't like it much. Not that it matters, anyway, since we're all far too busy staring at the people in the other boxes to care about the performance. My mother, for instance, was staring at you most intently earlier this evening."

"What on earth for?"

"Oh, the duke had mentioned you to us not long ago, saying you were a dear friend of his cousin, Lady Delia Stratham, and quite a pretty girl, and that made my mother curious." He grimaced. "I expect she's considering the possibility of matching us up. Just thought I'd warn you," he added, reddening, "because my mother is determined in her efforts to marry me off, and it could prove embarrassing for you."

Evie laughed. "I understand, believe me, and I won't hold it against you. Before my father died, he often tried to throw me together with the boy next door. Parents ought to be intelligent enough to know that forcing these things never works, but alas, they never seem to."

"Mine certainly don't," he agreed with a long-suffering sigh. "Not that I mind," he hastened on. "In your case, I mean. I'm sorry. That sounded rude."

"It's all right," Evie assured him, laughing. "I take no offense."

"Good, because I truly didn't mean any. Because I like you," he added, to her surprise, "and I wouldn't mind at all seeing you about town." As if embarrassed by this sudden admission, he gave a cough and changed the subject. "I'm sorry about your father. Did he die recently?"

"Oh, no, it's a decade ago, now."

"And do you really live in a flat?" he asked, sounding oddly impressed. "All on your own?"

"I do, yes. What about you?"

"Me?" He blinked, startled. "God, no. My father would never allow that."

"What won't I allow?" Colonel Anstruther broke in, joining them.

"I was just telling Miss Harlow that I'd never be allowed to lease a flat of my own. You'd cut off my allowance in a heartbeat if I ever tried."

Ronald's voice was careless, but Evie thought she detected a hint of resentment beneath the easy reply.

If there was any, Colonel Anstruther didn't seem to notice it. "Quite right," he said staunchly. "It might be a necessity for Miss Harlow, here, though I'm not sure why old Merrivale hasn't put a stop to it, my dear," he added to her, "and brought you under his roof."

Evie forced a smile. "I haven't given him the choice," she said lightly. "I own a bookstore, Colonel Anstruther, and it enables me to support myself."

"Yourself?" He frowned a little, not seeming to like that answer. "Well, well," he said heartily as the other three joined them, "living in a flat with a latchkey wouldn't do for a daughter of mine, but I suppose old Merrivale's got his reasons for giving you your head, letting you be a gadabout and one of these New Women."

"But, Papa," Ronald said, "all the New Women seem to wear Turkish trousers and ride bicycles. Miss Harlow here, by contrast, is very clearly wearing a dress."

"Don't be impudent, Ronald," Mrs. Anstruther chided her son. "I'm sure Miss Harlow wouldn't dream of wearing trousers."

"Well," Evie clarified, "not to the theater anyway."

"And the bicycle?" asked the duke as everyone laughed. "Would you ride one?"

"I'd adore it, if I knew how," she answered at once. "But what I would really love to do is learn to drive a motorcar."

"A motorcar?" Colonel Anstruther's voice was incredulous. "Impossible, Miss Harlow. You are a young lady."

"Really, George, you are so old-fashioned," his wife put in. Turning to Evie, she went on, "My husband thinks for a lady to drive anything but a pony trap along a country lane is shocking beyond belief. Don't pay him any mind, my dear."

A gong sounded before either her husband or Evie could reply, and Mrs. Anstruther gave a vexed exclamation. "Heavens, is intermission over already? We must return to our seats. Miss Harlow, Mrs. Banks, we're adjourning to supper at the Savoy afterward, and though Westbourne has another engagement, perhaps the two of you would care to join us? We'd be happy to take you in our carriage."

Evie looked at Anna, who gave a nod, then she said, "We'd be delighted to come. Thank you."

"That's settled, then. We'll come fetch you once the curtain comes down, and now, we simply must toddle."

The Anstruthers duly toddled, and Westbourne turned to Evie and Anna. "I must go as well, I'm afraid, or my companions will wonder what on earth's become of me." He bowed. "Mrs. Banks, Miss Harlow. I hope you enjoy the remainder of your evening. Good night."

He departed, following the Anstruthers out the door, leaving Evie and Anna alone again.

"You've been holding out on me, Evie," her friend murmured as they resumed their seats.

"About what?" Evie asked, reaching for her opera glasses.

"You never mentioned how good looking he is."

Evie froze, her hand tightening around the glasses as the memory of the moment when she'd made that rather shattering discovery flashed through her mind, a moment of shared intimacy she'd been unable to voice aloud, even to her best friend. "How could I?" she countered, unfolding the glasses and turning her attention to the boxes around them and the stage below. "I met Ronald Anstruther at the same time you did."

Her reward for this transparent prevarication was a gentle sideways kick. "I'm not talking about him, and you know it, so don't be coy."

"Oh." Evie perched the glasses on her nose. "You mean the duke."

"Who else would I mean but the duke?" she confirmed. "Yes, the tall, dark, absolutely gorgeous duke whose smile could charm the ink off paper."

Evie felt Anna's assessing gaze on her, but she didn't turn her head. "He's handsome enough, I suppose," she said, working to don an air of supreme indifference. "But considering the fact that he decided I'm in need of sprucing up in order to become attractive, I'm not so sure about his charm."

"Tell it to the marines!" Anna scoffed. "They might believe you, but I don't. You told me he stood up for you to his friends. He wouldn't have done that," she added as Evie made a sound of aggravation, "if he didn't find you attractive himself."

At those words, Evie felt a faint, answering thrill, but when she spoke, she kept any hint of it out of her voice. "Either way, why does it matter how good looking he is?"

"It doesn't, not to me. But it might to you. The bet

was a joke, you said this afternoon when you invited me out. A lark to put it over on some nobs. But it seems a very expensive joke to me, not to mention a bit improper. And now that I've met him, I'm wondering if there's more to this than meets the eye. Evie..." Anna paused, reaching out to lay a hand on her arm, forcing her to leave off her fascination with the view beyond the box. "As your friend, I must speak plainly. Has it even occurred to you that the duke might have designs on you?"

"Me?" Evie shook her head, laughing at that ridiculous possibility. "Heavens, no. He's courting a girl already."

"I'm not talking about courting. The hotel," she went on as Evie opened her mouth to protest, "the clothes, all this..." She paused again, gesturing to their elegant surroundings. "Those are just the things a man might give his mistress."

That sparked Evie's temper. "A fine opinion you have of me, that you think I'm immoral enough to engage in that sort of arrangement with a man."

"I'm not saying that—"

"What, then?" she demanded, growing angrier and more defensive by the moment. "Perhaps you think I'm so weak I'll fall into his lap like a ripe little plum because of some champagne and clothes? Give me a bit of credit, Anna. I'm not a fool."

"I'm not saying you're weak or immoral or a fool, so don't put words in my mouth. But it wouldn't be hard for any woman to fall for a man like him and to deceive herself into thinking he loved her."

"Love? What nonsense. I'm not sure I even *like* the man. As for him, he's been a perfect gentleman every single moment. And even if that was a trick, even if he was as two-faced and nefarious as you seem to think, I'm sure he could find himself a far more enticing woman to make his mistress than me. And," she added as Anna tried to speak, "he would hardly be introducing me to other men and their mothers at the opera or putting me in the hands of his cousin—a woman I know, like, and trust, by the way—if his intentions were so dishonorable."

Anna lifted her hands in a gesture of defeat. "All right, all right. Forgive my suspicious mind. As your friend, I felt it needed to be said. And if I might be allowed to give you one more piece of advice, it might be wise to keep in mind that he's not part of your world, and you're not part of his."

"I'm well aware of that," she said with a sigh, her temper cooling, her earlier enjoyment of the evening now completely gone because she knew, deep down, Anna was right to caution her. Any girl could fall for a man like him, easy as winking, and end up shattered and ruined. "And I have no intention of forgetting it."

"For your sake, my dear friend," Anna murmured gently, "I hope so."

The lights went down and the music started, saving her from any reply, but she made one anyway, a whispered confession in the dark, smothered by the lurid notes of Wagner. "I hope so, too."

Seven years spent working the Riviera and the resorts of Biarritz had taught Rory Callahan all about luxury hotels. The Savoy, as he well knew, was not the sort of place where anyone could just come in and lounge about. That sort of largesse was only offered to the hotel's patrons, and though he didn't have the funds to be one of those, he knew he could get past the doormen by looking the part.

Rory straightened away from the mirror above the washstand to study his reflection in the dim lamplight. He brushed a speck of lint from the satin lapel of his dinner jacket and tweaked his white tie, then he smoothed his pomaded hair back from his temples, donned his top hat, and took another look. Satisfied by what he saw, he gave his reflection a wink, turned away, and picked up his gloves, pulling them on as he left his lodging house in Queen Street and started toward the Savoy.

As he walked, he thought about the astonishing things he'd learned from Clarence this afternoon. Evie staying at the Savoy? Where had she gotten the money for that? When he'd asked how she could afford it, the boy had merely shrugged, saying she must have come into a legacy or won the sweeps, or something, because not only was she staying at the Savoy for the next six weeks, she'd also bought herself a slew of new clothes from a very posh dressmaker and she was taking his mum to the opera tonight as a special treat.

Rory paused at the corner, and as he waited for the traffic to clear so he could cross the Strand, he considered his next move. He'd stroll into the hotel like any gent coming back from the theater, park himself in a reading chair, and pretend to read the paper as he watched the entrance for Evie's return from the opera. That way, he could easily intercept her before she went upstairs. But what then?

Playing the part of concerned friend was his best bet, he decided as he crossed the Strand. He'd tell her he'd come to find her because he was worried about her. That made sense, considering he'd heard from her only once—a letter to his lodging house ten days ago, telling him about the boiler explosion and the closing of the shop for repairs. He'd confirm getting that note, then he'd play on her conscience, gently chiding her for not telling him where she would be staying, pointing out that he shouldn't have to learn such things from Clarence. Then, he'd invite her to have supper with him in the restaurant, and there, he'd ply her with wine and worm out of her just how much money she really had.

He knew she had the shop, of course, and that the mortgage was paid off. Selling the place, along with all its musty, crumbling old books, would bring in a pretty sum— five thousand pounds, at least. And if she could afford expensive clothes and a holiday at the Savoy, she had cash, too. But to get his hands on all that, he'd probably have to marry her.

A week ago, settling for plain little Evie hadn't been his plan, of course. No, he'd had other fish to fry. But now?

Resentment flared in him as he thought of the fish in question, a voluptuous, decidedly pretty British fish named Gladys Otterbourne, a fish he'd been sure was on the hook after the splash he'd made for her and her wealthy father in Nice. He'd spent the last of the Zurich swindle following them from the Côte d'Azur to Paris to England, and by time he'd arrived in London, he'd only a few shillings in his pocket, a suitcase of expensive suits, and Gladys's well-primed passion. Never had he dreamed her father would set private detectives on his track or that Gladys's passion would cool upon learning the truth about him. Women, Rory knew from experience, usually loved a bad lot. Just his luck that Gladys was more hardheaded and practical than most. She and her father had sent him off with a flea in his ear a week ago, destroying all his plans.

Now he was nearly broke again. The few quid he'd made the other night by milking chaps in his old neighborhood for donations to fund nonexistent political ambitions would soon be gone. And he doubted he could keep up the politics trick for long before everyone got wise. No, he needed a new source of funds, and since Gladys and her fat dowry had gone sailing into the wind, Evie had become his best option.

She wasn't as pretty as Gladys, of course, but that only meant she'd be a much easier conquest. Just ten days ago, she'd practically been eating out of his hand, and at that point, he hadn't even been trying to impress her. A few weeks of seduction, and she'd be panting to marry him.

Just outside the Savoy, Rory stopped at a flower stall to buy a fresh carnation for his buttonhole. At the newsstand beside it, he purchased an evening paper, then he entered the hotel courtyard, circled the fountain, and made his way to the entrance doors. As he'd anticipated, the doorman didn't blink an eye at the sight of him, but instead opened the door wide, giving Rory a respectful nod as he passed into the foyer.

Once inside, he made for the cluster of reading chairs to his left. He selected one with a clear view of the entrance doors, settled in, and opened the paper to wait for Evie's return from the opera, but he didn't have to wait long. He'd only been there about fifteen minutes before the number of people returning to the hotel rose significantly, telling him the theaters had let out. Covent Garden would not be far behind.

Over the top of his paper, he watched the nobs as they strolled by in their finery, and he was so occupied with calculating the value of their jewels, tiepins, and gold-topped walking sticks that he almost missed his quarry.

Not that he could be blamed for it. In a gown and matching cape of plum-colored velvet, a feathery falderal in her hair, she didn't look anything like the gawky, freckle-faced girl he'd always known. Scrawny as ever, of course, but the velvet seemed to pad her a bit in all the right places. She walked differently, too, moving in her elegant finery with a newfound assurance and grace that made her seem quite different.

As she paused by the cloak room, he noticed her friend Anna with her. He hadn't counted on that. He'd have thought Anna would have gone straight home from Covent Garden. Even more surprising, Anna was not her only companion. She was also accompanied by several other people, none of whom he'd ever seen before. Who were these people?

She and her companions started across the foyer in his direction, and he tensed in his seat, his mind striving to come up with something to say now that inviting her to dine with him was out the window. But he soon discovered that he needn't have bothered. She walked right by him without even glancing in his direction. Too elegant in her velvets and too preoccupied with her toplofty new friends, he thought sourly, to even see him anymore.

He turned his head, watching as she continued on toward the restaurant with her companions. What was she on about, gallivanting around London, making new friends, spending money like water? Now that she had some money to spend, was she trying to move up the social ladder? She did have an uncle who was a baron—perhaps that was the older gentleman? If she was trying to ingratiate herself with her titled relations and she succeeded, Rory knew he didn't stand a chance.

His eyes narrowed, his gaze boring resentfully into her slender back. He'd taken a lot of trouble with her over the years, writing all those tiresome letters, carefully keeping her in reserve in case nothing better turned up, and he wasn't about to let all those efforts go to waste—not now, when the tree he'd tended so carefully was about to bear some much-needed fruit.

Rory's eyes narrowed on the doorway as Evie stepped inside the Savoy's elegant restaurant, and even before she had vanished from view, he began planning how to get her away from these people.

# 12

$\mathcal{B}$etween renovations for the shop, some last-minute research for the upcoming Epicurean Club banquet, more dress fittings, and bookstore reconnaissance to survey her competition, Evie kept busy, trying not to dwell on the duke or Anna's words of caution about him during the week following their evening at Covent Garden. When the two women took Clarence to the Adelphi to see George Bernard Shaw's *Arms and the Man*, Anna made no mention of the duke at all, for which she was grateful.

Much to her surprise, a note arrived from Mrs. Anstruther, inviting her to an upcoming afternoon-at-home. Evie had never attended such an event, but she knew it was akin to a large afternoon tea, and she accepted the invitation with pleasure.

She also heard from Delia, a short note dashed off in the other woman's usual chaotic style, informing her she'd be arriving home within a week, expressing delight at the prospect of bringing Evie out for the season, and offering advice not to trust her cousin Max's opinions about anything because men, it must be said, were maddeningly obtuse on any subject of consequence.

Evie, however, was finding the duke maddening for reasons that had nothing to do with supposed masculine obtuseness. She knew Anna had been right to warn her. A man like him usually only wanted one thing from a girl like her, and though she didn't really think him to be that sort, she couldn't ignore the possibility. Tales of innocent women used and ruined by men of the aristocracy were the stuff of countless newspaper stories and penny dreadfuls, and every time she found herself remembering those magical moments in the duke's ballroom, she ruthlessly reminded herself of harsh realities.

Whenever she thought of his midnight-blue eyes staring at her mouth, she forced herself to open a scandal sheet and read the gossip about him and the lovely Helen Maybridge, and each word complimenting Lady Helen's extraordinary beauty, grace, and impeccable breeding helped Evie to banish any romantic notions about him from her mind.

There were some moments, however, when the idea that his intentions toward her might be honorably romantic flashed through her mind, but those were easily quashed. For one thing, it was ridiculous to think he could have any interest in a spinster with freckles and an overbite when he had in his sights the most beautiful debutante in London. And besides, as lovely as it was to live like an aristocrat, to treat herself to the rich foods, beautiful clothes, and luxurious accommodations they enjoyed, Evie was cleareyed enough to know that she fit into the aristocracy about as well as square pegs fit into round holes.

No, it was far better to dream of the sort of man with whom she could make a happy life, a man like Ronald Anstruther, for instance. A colonel's son was a perfectly suitable match for a girl like her, and as she sat across from him sipping tea during his mother's afternoon-at-home, she told herself it didn't matter that the idea of kissing him seemed as exciting as kissing a doorjamb.

Still, all her mental discipline paid off. By her second dancing practice with the duke, Evie had regained her composure. Romantic daydreams of the duke's eyes no longer invaded her mind, and thoughts of being in his arms while they danced no longer brought a tingling anticipation. The sight of his bold, dashing hand on a letter delivered with her breakfast tray brought no quickening of her pulse, and the suggestion it contained that she share a picnic dinner with him instead of ordering her usual room service evoked simple pleasure but no euphoric thrill. Evie set the letter aside, happy to conclude that she was back to being her former sensible, middle-class self.

But late that afternoon, when she returned from her shop to the Savoy, she found that her new wardrobe from Vivienne had been delivered, and all her efforts to remember caution and good sense went to the wall. The moment she opened the first box and saw the exquisite dinner gown of peacock-blue taffeta the dressmaker had made for her, Evie tossed aside her boring old blouse and skirt, sent her new gown to be pressed, and bathed with her new, lusciously scented soap. She also shoved aside her usual reticence and summoned the maid Westbourne had arranged for her to have.

In less than ten minutes, the maid arrived, a round-cheeked, dark-haired girl named Liza Moore. Perhaps it was because Evie's new gown was so irresistibly lovely, or perhaps it was because the maid seemed more awed by dressing her than she was about being dressed, but either way, Evie found that having a maid wasn't nearly as awkward as she'd thought it would be. In fact, by the time the last buttons had been fastened, she was wondering what had made her so reluctant in the first place. Not having to use the assistance of a door-knob to lace her corset or having to do up the many buttons of her shoes herself made dressing so much easier. And what a delightful indulgence it was to sit at her dressing table while someone else put up her hair.

Moore tentatively suggested she might like to try the newest hair fashion from America, assuring her that it would look a treat on her, and Evie happily acquiesced. After all, she thought, her glance sliding to the coroneted letter on her dressing table, it wasn't every day a girl danced with a duke.

Max was usually pleased when people took his advice. But the moment Evie walked into the kitchens at Westbourne House, dressed to the nines in a low-necked evening gown with her soft brown hair piled atop her head in a fashion that looked ready to tumble down any moment, he cursed himself for his well-meant admonishments to employ the services of her maid.

For God's sake, he thought as he slid his gaze over the slender column of her throat to the pale golden freckles scattered over her bosom, didn't the girl have any sense of self-preservation? A buttoned-up blouse, necktie, and scratchy wool skirt would have been so much safer—for both of them. A nefarious thought, he knew, and most unworthy of him, and yet, as she turned to hang up her cloak of ivory silk, he couldn't resist a study of her slim waist and the gentle outward curve of her hips, and at once, arousal stirred within him. By the time she turned again, his gaze was already halfway down those mile-long legs, and as she approached the table, he inhaled the spicy-sweet bergamot scent of her skin and realized to his chagrin it wouldn't have mattered if she'd been wearing a sack.

"I see you iced the champagne this time," she said and leaned over the table, peering into the opened picnic basket. "What did you bring to eat? More pâté, I hope?"

"I'm afraid not."

She looked so let down, he couldn't help a laugh, and the sound of it succeeded in hauling his hopeless masculine imagination away from scented skin, shapely thighs, and naughty red garters.

"I brought something even better," he assured her as he began pulling things from the basket, latching gladly on to the safe, neutral subject of food. "The Epicurean banquet was last night, if you recall. I thought you might like to try some of the dishes Escoffier concocted from your ideas."

He was rewarded for his trouble with one of her smiles.

"What a splendid idea! All the parties and banquets I've helped Delia plan, and I've never had the chance to sample a single thing. I always wonder," she went on as she removed her gloves, "if any of it ever tastes as exciting and exotic as it seems when I'm reading about it."

"Now's your chance to find out. I had one of Escoffier's assistants set some of last night's leftovers aside. You won't get to sample everything, I'm sorry to say," he went on as he began unwrapping bundles, opening jars, and spooning food onto two plates. "None of the lamb, for it's much too fatty to eat cold, and when I sampled the chilled lentil soup and fish shakshuka this afternoon, they weren't particularly appetizing either. So, for tonight's menu, we have skewers of roasted beef with yogurt sauce, cucumber and chickpea salad, and pilaf soufflé."

"Pilaf soufflé?" She frowned, looking doubtfully at the concoction on her plate. "That's not something I suggested. In fact, I'm not sure it's even a true recipe of the Middle East, is it?"

"I have no idea, but a great chef is allowed to take creative culinary liberties like that. Escoffier," he added, pouring yogurt sauce over their beef, "isn't as concerned with the accuracy of these things as you are."

"Had I known that," she grumbled good-naturedly as she accepted her filled plate, "I wouldn't have spent so much time finding truly authentic recipes for all the themed parties."

"The Epicurean Club appreciated your efforts, though," he assured her, reaching for the champagne. "Using your notes, I had a calligrapher do up the menus with a brief historical word about each dish."

"Even the pilaf soufflé?" she teased.

"You're not the only one who can do research," he said as he poured champagne. "I spent an entire afternoon at the London Library, I'll have you know, composing a report about pilaf."

"I'm impressed. Keep doing that and Delia won't need me anymore. She'll just hire you."

"If she does, you'll be far too busy to care. Once she returns from Rome, you'll be inundated with invitations, and I shall probably not even see you."

The way he felt right now, that prospect seemed heavenly and hellish in equal measure.

"It's not as if you don't have plenty of distractions of your own," she said and took a bite of the soufflé. "This is delicious!" she cried around a mouthful of pilaf.

He grinned. "You needn't sound so surprised. If Escoffier heard you, he'd be insulted by your lack of faith in his abilities."

"It's only that rice is usually so boring. But this isn't at all." She took another bite, savoring the combination of rice, dried fruits, and seasonings with such pleasure that Max's grin faded and arousal awakened inside him.

He looked away, forcing his attention to his own plate, and as they ate, his mind searched desperately for a new topic, something safely neutral that would keep him on the straight and narrow.

"How are the renovations to your shop coming along?" he asked at last.

"The weather has been fine, so everything finally dried out. They painted the flat, and next week, they'll paint the shop. The week after that, the floors will be sanded and waxed and the wallpaper put up. The book restorers tell me they will be finished around the same time, so I can start moving back in."

"Just remember you're on holiday. By the way, you haven't asked me to procure any more tickets for you. Please tell me you're taking some time to enjoy yourself?"

"Anna has been very busy. We're now in the midst of the season, so she's had many confectionery orders to fulfill and hasn't been able to come out with me. But I am enjoying myself, I promise you. I've been to the opening of the Royal Exhibition, the British Museum, and Madame Tussauds. I've even done a bit of shopping."

Max had been keeping his gaze firmly fixed on his food, but he couldn't resist a glance at her from beneath his lashes, and when his attention caught on the shadowy cleft between her breasts, his throat went dry, and his body began to burn. "Shopping, eh?" he managed, reaching for his wine. "What did you buy?"

"Some novels at Hatchards. And Delia's suite has an enormous bathtub, so I bought some lovely bergamot soaps at Fortnum & Mason. I had a lovely soak before I came tonight."

Max choked on his wine.

*So much for safe, neutral topics*, he thought as the arousal he'd been trying to suppress began spreading through his body. Desperate, he turned away and flipped open the picnic basket. "I'd better serve you some dessert, or we'll have no time left tonight to do any dancing."

He pulled a paperboard box from the basket, cut a generous square of baklava for her, garnished her plate with a few dates and figs, added a fork, and slid the plate across to her, resolved that by the time she finished dessert, he'd have snuffed out the desire flaming in his body.

She picked up her fork and took the first bite. "Oh, my God, that's so good," she groaned, closing her eyes in such an ecstasy of pleasure that Max's resolve fell completely to pieces and all he wanted was to come around that table, haul her into his arms, and kiss her senseless.

"Glad you like it," he said, telling himself firmly to stay on his side of the table. "Have a sweet tooth, do you?"

She nodded, taking another bite of baklava. "I'm terrible. If you put a tea tray in front of me, I will always choose the sweetest, most decadent tea cakes on it." She paused and took a sip of champagne, ate a date, and nibbled on another piece of baklava. "One of the greatest trials of my life is that I don't put sugar in my tea anymore."

That puzzled him—a petty distraction, but he'd take it. "If you like sugar in your tea, why not have it?"

"Sugar's so expensive, I don't use it anymore."

The reminder of how close to the bone she lived while he was surrounded by more wealth than he could spend in a lifetime might have given his conscience a smack were it not for the arousal in his body. He appreciated grimly that if this sort of hedonistic pleasure was her usual response to sweets, she'd have Ronald Anstruther and every other young man in London clamoring to take tea and cake with her every day of the week.

She savored each bite of her dessert with maddening slowness. At last, she set down her fork and pushed back her plate, but any relief he might have felt was quashed when her tongue darted out to lick the sticky vestiges of honey from her lips.

Max jerked upright, smothering an oath.

The sound made her pause, and she suddenly noticed that he hadn't served any baklava for himself. "Don't you want any dessert?"

*Not that kind*, a devil inside him whispered.

Max shook his head. "I don't care much for sweet things."

"Really?" She shook her head, clearly confounded. "I've never encountered a sweet I didn't like."

"I prefer savories," he said firmly, tearing his gaze from her honeyed lips. "Scotch eggs, you know, or caviar."

She gave him a skeptical look, as if he were an escapee from Bedlam, and despite the precarious state he was in, he couldn't help a grin.

"I take it you've never had caviar?" he asked.

"No, and I don't think I want to. Who would ever look at fish eggs and think it would be something good to eat? Ugh."

He watched her nose wrinkle up in distaste, and he decided ragging her was his safest option—and hers. "You didn't like liver either, remember?" he reminded. "I think I'll bring caviar next time so you can try it. In the mean-time," he added to console her as she shivered, "you can have my share of the baklava."

"Thank you, but I don't think I could eat a second piece.

I'm far too full." She ate the last bite, set down her fork, and pushed back her plate with a contented sigh. "That was lovely, thank you."

He lifted his glass of champagne and bowed his head. "My pleasure."

She looked down at the remains of their meal. "It was very thoughtful of you to bring the food from the banquet for me to try," she said softly, and looked at him again. "I never would have thought it when we first met, but you're a very kind person, did you know that?"

*Kind*? His gaze slid irresistibly downward, his mind in the gutter. *If she only knew.*

He was fully aware that being deemed kind when his thoughts were absolutely carnal proved him the worst of hypocrites. "Yes, well," he muttered, "I'm just sorry you couldn't sample all the dishes that were served last night. But," he added, rummaging in the basket, "you'll be happy to know I did bring you some of the peach sorbet."

"Sorbet?" She stared at him dubiously as he pulled out a stoneware crock and placed it on the table. "But you brought it from the Savoy, didn't you? It must surely be melted by now?"

"No doubt, but when one is on a picnic, one must sometimes improvise." He flipped open the bail on the crock and reached for her champagne glass. "And sorbet," he went on as he added a dollop of the syrupy liquid to her half-empty glass, "is sometimes served in champagne."

She sampled the concoction and when she smiled, he was glad he'd insisted to Escoffier that yes, he wanted some of the sorbet, too. Within a minute, she'd downed the last swallow.

"That was luscious," she said, peering into her glass with a sorrowful expression. "But it's all gone."

Never in his life had Max contemplated plying a woman with alcohol to take advantage of her, but he would not have been a man of flesh and blood if an image of Evie, naked in his bed upstairs with a tipsy smile on her lips, had not crossed his mind.

He'd feed her dates and figs and honey-infused baklava, tasting each one on her mouth as he kissed her. He'd kiss her freckles, too, he decided. Every last one of them, from the tip of her nose to her small, sweet breasts, to her—

"Can I have more?"

The sound of her voice hauled him firmly back. "No," he said and plucked the glass from her hand, ignoring her cry of vexation. "We have to practice."

Setting aside her glass, he picked up her gloves, circled the table, slapped the gloves into her palm, and began propelling her toward the door. "Come on."

Knowing he needed all the self-protection he could muster, he paused by the door long enough to don his evening coat and pull on his gloves. Fully and properly dressed, he felt once more the master of himself, and by the time they had made the journey to the ballroom, he was reasonably sure he could make it through the remainder of the evening without ravishing her.

His certainty about that lasted for half a waltz. His hand on her back, the scent of her hair, the warmth of her body so tantalizingly close to his all chipped away at his resolve, and he found himself wishing she would stumble so that he had an excuse to pull her fully into his embrace.

She proved aggravatingly unwilling to cooperate with that idea, however, and they reached the end of Strauss's "Voices of Spring" without a single misstep.

"I did it! Max, I did it!" She laughed, showing that rum, off-kilter smile of hers, pushing him closer to oblivion, and he knew his body could not endure the agony of another waltz with her.

"You might have been waltzing since your cradle," he said and let her go. "Let's see how you do with a polka." He stepped back, working to regain his balance. "You know how?"

She made a rueful face. "I suppose there's only one way to find out."

He walked to the gramophone, putting some much-needed distance between them, and placed the liveliest polka he could find on the turntable. He closed his eyes for a second, praying for fortitude, then put the needle on the disk and returned to where she stood in the center of the dance floor.

"Remember, it's a bit like a waltz," he told her, taking her hand in his and spreading his other hand across her back as the strains of an accordion filled the room, "only livelier. Just follow my lead and don't look down."

She nodded, he counted off, and they began, swirling around the room in four-four time, and though they stumbled once or twice, he kept her moving quickly across the floor, ignoring her laughing protests, certain that if they stopped moving, he'd do something he'd regret.

But they couldn't dance forever, and when the music ended, he proved to be an excellent judge of his own character, for as they came to a halt, he couldn't bear to let her go. Instead, he slid his palm down her back, and as he did, he felt himself sinking. Down, down he went, into that place where his body did all the thinking and very bad decisions were made.

Evie, still laughing from their wild, crazy dancing, didn't seem to notice the change in him. "Oh, that was so much fun!" she cried, panting.

"Ripping," he agreed, spreading his hand across her tailbone, just above the curve of her buttocks.

"As fast as we were going, I only stumbled twice." She laughed again, shaking her head in disbelief as she looked up at him, smiling that smile of hers. "Can you believe that?"

"I never doubted you for a second."

"I was only able to do it because you didn't give me any time to think."

"Thinking," he said, pressing his fingers against the small of her back to bring her closer, "is overrated."

She came, following his lead, bless her sweet, trusting soul. "In dancing, I suppose it is," she said, still laughing, but when he slid his arm fully around her waist, her laugher faded, her smile vanished, and a sudden hint of feminine self-preservation snuffed out the gold glints in her eyes. "Max?"

He tightened his arm around her waist, embracing her fully. The feel of her body against his own was so exquisite, it almost drove him to his knees, and even her shocked little gasp couldn't deter him. He pulled his hand from hers, cupped her face, and pressed his thumb beneath her chin to lift it.

"I don't think this is a good idea," she whispered, her breath warm and soft against his mouth.

"That's your problem right there," he muttered. "You think too much."

Before she could reply, he gave up the fight with his conscience completely, bent his head, and kissed her.

# 13

Having spent so much of her life among books, Evie had read plenty of novels. Some had merely hinted at romance, while others—those her father would have been appalled by had he ever caught her with them—had been much more lurid. She'd also read enough scientific texts to have a pretty fair knowledge of the biological aspects of male-female relations. And if all that wasn't enough to make her feel reasonably well-informed on the subject, she'd also gone to boarding school, where kisses and more had been much discussed among the other girls, usually in speculative whispers and hushed giggles in the dormitories after the lights were out.

Nonetheless, despite all this knowledge, nothing in Evie's experience could have prepared her for the reality.

The moment Max touched her lips with his, she felt a pleasure so exhilarating, so dizzying, it was as if she were soaring high in the sky like a bird in flight. Her heart lifted, her blood sang through her veins, and when she closed her eyes, any conscious thought went spinning into oblivion.

She could not think, she could not reason, she could only feel, and it was glorious.

He overwhelmed her senses—the masculine, earthy scent of him, the warmth of his palm where his hand cupped her cheek, the strength of his arm around her waist, and the hard thud of his heartbeat beneath her fingertips. Every cell in her body seemed to open and bloom like primroses in the spring sunlight.

She slid her hands upward over the slick satin of his waistcoat and the finely textured linen of his shirt, and she could feel the strength of his muscles beneath his clothes.

When she wrapped her arms around his neck and pressed closer, the move seemed to spark something inside him. Making a rough sound against her mouth, he tightened his hold, lifting her onto her toes, pulling her body fully against his own. His free hand slid to the back of her neck and his tongue touched the seam of her closed lips as if urging her to part them, and when she did, his tongue entered her mouth.

Shocked, she gave a gasp, but then, his tongue touched hers and the pleasure of it was so great that her gasp ended in a groan and her knees wobbled beneath her. If he hadn't been holding her so tightly, she'd have melted into a puddle right there on the ballroom floor.

She was pressed fully against his body, and yet that didn't seem close enough. She stirred, her hips moving against his, and the sensation was so sharp, so exquisite, she gasped, her hands raking through his hair, her tongue tasting his with an abandonment that shocked her.

It must have shocked him, too, for suddenly, he tore his mouth from hers. "Good God, what am I doing?"

The hoarse sound of his voice opened her eyes as his arm loosened its tight grip around her waist. Her body slid down, her feet hit the floor, and then he was gripping her arms, pushing her back. His breathing was harsh and rapid, and so was hers as they stared at each other in the glittering light of the ballroom.

His eyes were as murky and dark as a starless sky.

"I never learn," he muttered, letting her go and stepping back, shaking his head as if appalled. "I never, ever learn."

Evie blinked, her euphoric haze dissipating as she tried to assimilate his words, but he gave her no chance.

"We must go." He turned abruptly away and started for the door. "I'll fetch a cab to take you home. Wait ten minutes, then go out the way you came. A hansom will be waiting for you."

He vanished, his footsteps echoing back to her from the corridor, then fading away into silence.

Finally, she thought in amazement, pressing her fingers to her still-tingling lips. Long after the silly hopes of girlhood had given way to spinsterhood and romance was nothing more than a forgotten dream, she finally knew what it was to be kissed.

She ought to be angry with Max, she knew, and ashamed of herself. He was practically engaged to someone else, and though he'd already acknowledged it wasn't a love match, that did not absolve either of them for what had just happened.

Besides, it wasn't as if love had been the inspiration leading them both to abandon their good sense and their moral scruples. And even if love had played some part, between a man like him and a woman like her, nothing could come of love like that. Nothing honorable, anyway.

Anna had warned her that perhaps the duke wanted more from her than to win a bet, something unsavory, but she hadn't taken that warning seriously. Even now, she found it hard to credit him with such licentious intent, but with his searing kiss still burning her mouth, she'd be a fool to deny the possibility.

And yet, despite all that, she could not bring herself to regret that kiss. It was the most glorious, romantic, delicious thing that had ever happened to her, and though it might have been terribly wrong, Evie wouldn't have traded those wild, heavenly moments in his arms for anything in the world.

As Max left the ballroom, raw physical need pulsed through his body, and only one coherent thought pounded through his brain.

He was an idiot.

For the second time in his life, he was in the throes of an uncontrollable passion for a woman who was completely wrong for him.

He thought he'd learned his lesson. Arrogantly, he'd presumed that his longing for Rebecca had been a singular happening, a ghastly mistake born of young lust and foolish romantic ideals that would never happen again, but Evie Harlow had just shredded those presumptions and proved to him that he'd learned nothing at all.

A galling thing for a man to admit.

What the hell was wrong with him? he wondered in exasperation as he left the house and strode up Green Street toward the nearest cab stand. Even a child learned after being burned on a hot stove not to touch it again. What flaw inside him, what stupid perversity, impelled him to desire women who did not belong in his world and had no reverence for the life he lived?

The lines of a letter came back to him, a letter he'd received from his mother while he was in New York preparing for his wedding, a letter that had begged him not to do something he would regret. He'd read the epistle only once, then he'd angrily torn it in half and tossed it into the nearest wastepaper basket. Yet, despite the fact that it had been written over a decade ago, he could recall one line of that letter as if he'd first read it only yesterday.

*A fish and a bird can fall in love. But they can never make a home together.*

He and Rebecca had tried to prove her wrong, and they had failed. Though his mother had died before seeing the results of his intransigence, those results had been tragic for all concerned.

There was a hansom by the Marble Arch, and the driver straightened up on the box as he approached. "Where to, guv'nor?" he asked, gathering the reins in his fists.

"It's not for me." Max jerked a thumb over his shoulder. "Turn onto Green Street and wait there by the first doorway. A woman will be coming out, and when she does, I want you to take her to the Savoy Hotel."

He handed over the shilling required for the fare, the driver snapped the reins, and the cab jerked into motion, rolling away down Park Lane.

Max turned to follow the vehicle, retracing his steps slowly, for he did not want to see Evie again, not with this insatiable need for her still thrumming through his body. Even now, even as he reproached himself for his conduct and berated his obvious stupidity, he wasn't entirely sure he could refrain from jumping into the hansom beside her and kissing her senseless all the way back to the hotel.

Damn it all, he had a plan for his life. He had already

chosen the perfect girl, a girl who would embrace the role of duchess, who would shoulder all its responsibilities willingly. Helen would never be intimidated by dancing with the Prince of Wales or hosting a house party for fifty guests. Helen would never seat the wrong people together at dinner or blurt out blunt derisions of the aristocracy to the prime minister over dessert. Helen would never have to endure the pain of being shunned and ridiculed, and he would never have to endure the pain of watching it happen with no way to stop it.

Evie wasn't raised for any of that, and expecting it of her would have been like expecting a bird to live underwater. Like Rebecca, she'd be suffocated by the rigid rules of the ton. Like Rebecca, she thought those rules were pointless and silly, and given that, how could she ever successfully play the game?

Wanting her could only end in tragedy, not only for him, but also for her. She had moved in his world, however briefly, once before, and the results had been disastrous, inflicting wounds that still hurt her to this day. He could not be responsible for giving her more of the same pain.

He turned the corner onto Green Street and came to an abrupt halt, for the cab was still there, waiting for Evie. She came out before he had time to step out of sight, but fortunately, she crossed the pavement to the hansom without even glancing in his direction.

Max watched, riveted, his fingers curling tight around the granite cornerstone of his home to keep him where he was as she stepped carefully into the cab, arranged the skirts of her gown around her, and pulled the hansom's wooden doors down over her lap.

The cab once again jerked into motion, and as it rolled away, Max relaxed his grip and let his hand fall, but even after the hansom had turned safely onto South Audley Street, he felt no relief.

Stepping back onto Park Lane, he stared up at the elegant facade of Westbourne House, and Evie's words of a week ago came back to him.

*Your house is terribly grand, isn't it? I had to toss a coin to decide which door to use.*

To him, it had never been grand. It was merely his home, just as Idyll Hour was his home, and if Evie thought Westbourne House so grand, he couldn't imagine what she'd make of the hundreds of rooms and thousands of acres of his ducal seat.

To Rebecca, raised in the mining towns of Colorado, it had never been home. Could it be any different for a girl raised in a tiny flat above a bookshop?

Max thought of Evie, of the way she'd been snubbed and mistreated by the upper classes as a girl, and he knew the answer to that was probably not.

He had a duty to be the best duke he could be, for the sake of his family and his tenants and the hundreds of people whose lives and livelihoods depended on him. He had to marry someone who could help him fulfill the many duties of that position. He could not afford to give in to a passion he wasn't sure could deepen into love for a girl who had no desire to share the life he led and who might very well be relentlessly mocked if she dared to try. He was not willing to take a chance like that, not again.

Max reentered Westbourne House and set about removing any signs that Evie Harlow had ever been there. He put away the gramophone records, packed up the remains of their picnic, and tidied the kitchen, trying to ignore the heavy weight inside his chest as he accepted the fact that he would never dance with her again.

Through sheer force of will, Max managed to drive any lustful thoughts about Evie out of his mind, put his priorities back in order, and regain his equilibrium, but he knew his feelings on the matter were not the only ones to consider.

In kissing her, he had taken an unpardonable liberty and broken his word that she was safe in his company. Making matters worse, Evie's unrestrained response to his kiss had clearly been one of inexperience, and she might be thinking love, not lust, had inspired his action. She might even be falling in love with him. If any of that was true, he owed it to her to extinguish such romantic notions before they could deepen and cause her to be hurt.

It took him three days to compose what he felt was a proper apology, complete with a vow that it would never happen again, a gentle letdown in case she was harboring false hopes, and the reassurance that with Delia arriving any day now, she'd soon have plenty more suitable men dancing attendance and she'd surely forget all about him.

He then sent her a note requesting an appointment, and her rather alarming reply made him glad he'd taken such pains with his speech. She felt it would be best if they talked privately and suggested that he come to the bookshop that evening. The only reason he could think of for such a request threatened to reignite all the fire he'd spent three days putting out, and worse, it seemed to justify his worry that her feelings for him were deepening. Being such an innocent, she'd have no idea that her request was like lighting matches in a room full of gunpowder.

Still, it would have been cowardly to refuse. If he couldn't refrain from hauling her into his arms at this point, he might as well jump off a cliff and save himself from any future torment. But just in case his carefully crafted speech wouldn't be enough to let her down gently and soothe away any injured feminine feelings, he ordered a bouquet that afternoon from the Savoy's florist, carefully choosing those blooms most appropriate for conveying what he needed to say: white orchids for apology, irises for affection, and yellow roses for friendship. Of course, his most honest feelings would have been most accurately portrayed by flaming orange lilies, but wisely, he didn't include any of those.

With his bouquet in hand and his speech engrained in his memory, he stepped out of the cab in front of Harlow's Bookshop that evening, and though he felt reasonably in control of the situation, he nonetheless paused with his hand on the doorknob and took a deep breath before opening the door.

"Evie?" he called as the bell over his head jangled.

She emerged from the back almost at once, but she hadn't taken more than two steps into the main room before she came to an abrupt halt.

"Oh, no!" she cried, staring in obvious dismay at the tissue-wrapped bouquet in his hand. "You brought me flowers?"

Since she couldn't see the blooms themselves, she couldn't possibly have discerned the friendly message they were meant to convey, and he launched into speech before she could make any romantic assumptions. "It's nothing much," he said, removing his hat as she crossed the room to stand opposite him. "Just a posy to show my regard for our—"

"I can't accept them." She looked up at him, frowning. "You're practically engaged."

Since he'd met this girl, there were times when his plans for his future did seem to go straight out of his head, but he felt it necessary to clarify the matter. "Helen would be stunned to hear it, since I've declared no such intention. Nor even hinted it, really, for it would be far too soon for such things. And I certainly haven't kissed her," he added wildly, and the moment those words were out of his mouth, he appreciated that this meeting was not starting out as he'd planned. Taking firm hold of his wits, he tried again. "Still, I do appreciate your point, and you have every right to think ill of me, but I brought you flowers because after what happened the other night—"

She groaned, interrupting this rather incoherent jumble of words. "I'm beginning to think Anna was right, after all."

Max had no idea how to respond to such a singular remark. "I beg your pardon?"

"She warned me, but I didn't listen. I didn't believe it was possible, but I don't think I can really be blamed for that. I mean...you and me?" She paused and gave a laugh, though he sensed she was not the least bit amused. "You could have any woman you wanted. It seemed ludicrous you'd ever pick me."

"Well, I wouldn't quite say that, Evie," he said, impelled to correct such self-disparagement. "You're a very attractive woman, as my...ahem...attentions the other night demonstrated—"

"Oh, Max, stop," she cried, cutting him off again. "I fear you have developed an entirely wrong impression about me. Though after the other night," she went on, her cheeks flushing pink, "I suppose you have some reason for expectation."

"Expectation?" he echoed, now thoroughly at sea.

"And I realize that asking to meet privately like this might have served to fuel that expectation, but I couldn't bear the idea of having this conversation in a hotel corridor or in whispers among a roomful of people, and after the other night, I felt it vital to set things straight between us as soon as possible. I should not want you to think...I wouldn't have you believe...that is—" She broke off, sucked in a deep, shuddering breath, and burst out, "I can't possibly become your mistress!"

With that astonishing declaration, every word of Max's carefully crafted speech went straight out the window. "Good God, is that what you think? That I intend to make you my mistress?"

"I didn't think that, not at first. Anna did warn me that it was a possibility, but I dismissed her concerns. After all, you are courting someone!"

"Quite so," he muttered, not sure what else to say.

"And I should hate to think that you would ever behave dishonorably toward her or me. But you did say it's not a love match, and men of your class do seem to acquire mistresses as a matter of course, no matter who they might be intending to marry. Why, many of you even have mistresses after you're married—"

"Evie," he cut in, to no avail.

"And you are paying for my stay at the Savoy, and you did insist on buying me those clothes, and I let you, which in hindsight I realize I never should have done. And the two of us were meeting in secret, after all, and dancing, and...and—" She broke off amid this rambling tangle of words, and the pink in her cheeks deepened to scarlet. "And you did kiss me."

As she spoke, it began to sink into his brain just how all his actions would seem if one put them in the worst possible light. Worse, his thoughts, as well as his actions, had proved there was a grain of truth in her words, and he felt more dismayed by his actions than ever. "Evie—"

"And I kissed you back, and now, you're bringing me flowers, which seems to confirm that my actions encouraged you to believe I'm the sort of girl who would fall into unsavory liaisons. I hate to think that's your goal, because I do like you. I didn't at first, of course. I thought you cynical and rude and snobbish and most high-handed. But then, I began to believe my initial impression was a bit harsh—"

"A bit?"

She didn't seem to notice the wry note of his voice. "And later, when you said we ought to be friends, you were so affable and charming about it all, that I did start to like you."

Max slid his gaze irresistibly to her lips. "I like you, too," he murmured.

"But if you have come to propose an illicit arrangement," she went on as if she hadn't heard, "it would certainly ruin our friendship, since I could never have a friend who would be so duplicitous—"

"Evie, please stop." Unable to bear it any longer, he dropped the flowers to the floor beside him and reached out, cupping her cheek and pressing his thumb to her mouth, an unthinking gesture meant only to enable him to get a word in, but her lips were so warm and her cheek so velvety soft that his resolve faltered, proving he was still far too vulnerable where she was concerned, and he jerked his hand back.

"Please allow me to reassure you," he said, and his hat joined the flowers on the floor as he clasped his hands safely together behind his back. "I appreciate your blunt honesty and your justifiable apprehensions, but it was never my intent to impugn your virtue or your honor. I am fully aware you are not the sort of girl to willingly allow a man to take the liberties I took the other night."

She gave a little laugh. "After the wanton way I kissed you back, I can't think why."

"There is nothing wrong in what you felt, Evie, or the way you responded." His throat went dry at the memory of just how sweet her response had been, and he had to swallow hard before he could go on. "You have nothing to reproach yourself with. Which brings me to what I came to say, if you'll allow me." He paused just long enough to suck in a deep breath, then he said, "Any of the blame in this is wholly mine. I promised that you were safe in my company, and it never occurred to me that you would not be. It's just that, when you smile that adorable crooked smile you've got, it makes me rather lose my head."

Her eyes widened in astonishment. Her lips parted as if to reply, but afraid that he'd never say what he came to say if he let her, he continued desperately, "But despite my conduct the other night, please believe me when I say that I have never at any point intended to make you my mistress. I would never dishonor you in such a way. I admit that carnal thoughts of you have crossed my mind, because I am a man, Evie, God knows, as weak as any other—"

He broke off, appreciating too late that these confessions of his vulnerability where she was concerned were sending him onto very thin ice, and if her wide eyes and scarlet cheeks were anything to go by, he'd already fallen through to the chilling depths of eternal condemnation. "The point is," he said, hoping to hurl himself back onto the much safer ground of friendship, "you are a young lady, far too virtuous and good for any course but an honorable one, and after the other night—"

"Good heavens, Max!" she burst out, staring at him in what could only be described as horrified shock, "you're not here to propose marriage to me because of what happened, are you?"

He blinked, aghast, feeling every bit as shocked as she looked, but for the life of him, he could think of nothing to say. His carefully prepared apologies and explanations had long since sailed off into the wind, what he had been saying was proving dismally incoherent, and now, he could only shake his head helplessly in reply to her question.

"Oh, thank heaven," she breathed, pressing a hand to her chest with a laugh of obvious relief. "But you denied wanting to make me your mistress with such vehemence, and with the flowers, and the compliments, and the...ahem...feelings you describe, it did suddenly occur to me that you might be leading up to a much more honorable proposition than I'd originally thought, and if you were, that would be so awkward."

This entire conversation was awkward. He was glad, of course, that she wasn't harboring any false hopes that he'd have to quash, but really, did she have to be so relieved about the fact that he wasn't offering matrimony? After that searing kiss, most women of his acquaintance would have been crushed to learn a proposal of marriage was not in the offing, especially one from a duke.

But then, he'd known all along the expectations associated with his rank and his privileged world did not impress Evie. Perverse bastard that he was, he found that very quality of hers to be both beguiling and aggravating, in equal measure.

"I realize that in these circumstances, some women

might feel that a man has an obligation to propose," she said, almost as if reading his mind, "since kissing a woman when you're not engaged to her isn't the sort of thing a gentleman like you is supposed to do. But really, Max, it was just a kiss."

"Just a kiss?" he echoed, insulted when he ought to be relieved.

She seemed to sense his chagrin. "I don't mean to say it wasn't wonderful," she rushed on, "because it was. Truly. Not that I'm much of a judge about such things because I'd never been kissed before in my life."

"Yes," he managed to say. "I gathered that."

"You did? How?"

Despite everything—the warmth of her cheek still lingering on his palm, the temptations that still danced on the edge of his mind, the damnable awkwardness of this moment—he almost wanted to smile. She was so charmingly unaware. But it wasn't as if he could explain. Talking about her passionate, astonished, obviously inexperienced reaction to his kiss would only start him back down a road it had taken him three days to veer from. "A man can often sense these things," he said.

"Oh," she murmured, looking suitably impressed. "Still, as wonderful as it was, a kiss is hardly sufficient reason to contemplate marriage. And we both know we would be completely unsuited as marriage partners." She laughed again. "Me, marry you? Why, it would be a mad idea."

As much as he might agree with the gist of that sentiment, it irritated him that she found the idea of his hand in marriage something to laugh about.

"Very mad, indeed," he agreed stiffly.

"Even if it is the honorable thing to do after what happened between us, I could never marry you. I could only marry a man I was in love with. I realize it's not the same for you. You have other considerations, but even so, I'm sure the girl you've chosen is perfect for you."

"Oh, yes, perfect," he agreed, having no idea what else to say.

"She's beautiful, of course."

"Stunning." He tried to summon some degree of enthusiasm about Helen's well-known beauty, but his brains were so scrambled just now that he was finding it hard to even remember what she looked like.

"She's accomplished, too, I'll wager, and charming, and of course, she's a lady."

"Naturally," he said and wondered why this list of Helen's many admirable qualities was making him feel so depressed.

"She'll be a wonderful duchess. I, of course, would make a hash of the whole beastly business."

"Oh, yes, no doubt," he agreed automatically, not realizing how insulting that sounded until the words had spilled out. "Sorry, I didn't mean—"

"No, no, Max, please don't be sorry. It's true. Me, a duchess? What a dreadful prospect."

She was shaking her head and smiling, but for his own part, Max was finding no humor whatsoever in this conversation.

Evie seemed to sense at least something of what he was thinking, for her smile faded. "Max?" she said in some uncertainty. "I haven't offended you, have I?"

"No, no." Not unless deservedly cutting a man down to size without even realizing it was offensive.

"And we can agree that...that it's best if we just put what happened the other night behind us and go back to being friends?"

"Absolutely," he said with all the conviction he could muster, even as he feared such a thing might not be possible. Relaxing his right hand's death grip on his left wrist, he bent down to retrieve the flowers.

"Here," he said, straightening and holding the bouquet out to her. "Please accept them," he added as she hesitated, "for they were never meant as a step toward seduction or a marriage proposal. They were meant as an apology. See?" he added, pulling back the tissue-paper wrapping. "White orchids mean apology."

He looked up, putting on a smile. "I hope you are now reassured that I have no nefarious thoughts about you."

Lightning ought to strike a man dead, he thought, for a lie like that.

Still, Evie seemed willing to take him at his word, for she nodded. "And...we are friends again?"

"Absolutely." He pointed to the bouquet. "Yellow roses for friendship."

"Thank you, then," she said and took the bouquet from his hand. "I will accept them."

They both looked up, but they said nothing. Instead, they stared silently at each other, as if neither of them quite knew how to end the conversation.

"Shall I call a cab for you?" he asked at last.

"No, thank you. I still have some work to do here."

He nodded. "Don't work too late."

"I won't. Half an hour, no more."

"Good. As I keep reminding you, you're still on holiday. And since it's night and you'll be here alone, lock the door behind me."

Bending down again, he retrieved his hat. "I will send a cab from the Savoy to fetch you in thirty minutes' time."

"Oh, no. It's only two blocks."

"A young woman shouldn't walk alone after dark, so don't argue."

"Thank you. You're very kind."

He didn't feel the least bit kind, and he knew he'd better leave now, before he said or did anything to spoil the friendly truce they'd forged. "Good night, Evie," he said and donned his hat, then he bowed and departed.

Everything had been resolved in the best possible way, and yet, as Max closed the door of the shop behind him, he felt dissatisfied, off-balance, and thoroughly unsettled, and he didn't have any idea why.

Sometimes, he thought in exasperation as he started down the street, Evie really was the most unaccountable girl.

During the past five days, Rory had discovered that getting Evie back wasn't going to be as easy he'd thought. The shop was still closed, Anna and Clarence, busy at the confectionery shop, had hardly seen her, and though she was still staying at the Savoy, whenever he inquired there, she always seemed to be out. He'd left a letter for her there, expressing his concern, asking if he could help, and suggesting that perhaps she might come out and have a cup of tea with him, but it was a full three days before she replied, and that reply only served to deepen his frustration, turning it to outrage.

As he read the lines penned in Evie's neat copperplate script, apologetic lines that explained she was terribly busy just now and suggesting perhaps it would be best to postpone tea together until after the shop reopened in a month or so, he could hardly believe it.

*Too busy*? he thought in baffled fury. *Busy with what*?

But even as he asked himself that question, he knew the answer.

No doubt it was her newfound friends who were keeping her so occupied, and if he didn't take some sort of action straightaway, she could slip from his grasp altogether, and that blond dandy would be the one selling her shop and pocketing the money. As if a toff like that even needed it.

Rory slapped down her note, donned his hat, and left his lodging house, determined to find out what was going on before the evening was out.

He decided to try talking to Anna first. Even if she didn't know where Evie was tonight, she could at least tell him something about Evie's new friends, for she'd been at that opera supper, too. But when he arrived at Wellington Street, his plan to pump Anna proved unnecessary, for as he passed the bookshop, he saw that the lights were on, and when he peeked into the inch-wide gap between the door frame and the window shade, he spied the very person he was trying to track down.

The problem was that she wasn't alone. There was a man with her, and though this one was not the blond dandy he'd seen with her the other night, this one was similarly dressed in a top hat, white tie, and tails, and in his hand was a bouquet of flowers.

Flowers? *Bloody hell*, he thought, his outrage and fear deepening as he watched them through the window from the darkened street. How many rich toffs did Evie know nowadays? And what was this one doing here?

Suddenly, the man dropped the flowers and reached out to touch Evie's face, bold as brass, and Rory had the answer to his question. A man like that wouldn't touch her in such an intimate way if he wasn't paying for the privilege.

*Well, well*, Rory thought in amazement as he watched them, *little Evie's got a fancy man.*

It was ridiculous to think a wealthy chap like this would pay for access to Evie's bed, but if he were a true suitor with honorable intentions, he'd never be here, alone with her at night with the window shades down, touching her face. And if Evie was this man's mistress, it explained everything—the money, the clothes, the hotel.

The contact between the pair lasted only a couple of seconds before the man pulled his hand back and clasped both his hands behind his back. They continued to talk, and as he watched, Rory realized that though this wasn't the same man who had escorted Evie into supper at the Savoy the other night, he had seen this chap before. This, he realized, was the man who'd been in the bookshop the day he'd persuaded Evie to allow him the use of her storeroom for political meetings, the same one who'd been making cutting remarks under his breath. At the time, Rory had thought him merely a customer, but he was evidently far more than that.

Rory waited, continuing to observe the couple on the other side of the glass, but though they talked for perhaps another ten minutes, the man made no move to touch her again. At last, he bowed, retrieved his hat from the floor, and turned to go, and Rory quickly moved to the darkened doorway of the confectionery, pressing himself as far back into the shadows as possible, ducking his head, and pulling his cap down low over his eyes.

These precautions proved unnecessary, however, for the man didn't even glance in Rory's direction as he passed by. Rory was torn between going in to see Evie immediately or following the man, but after a few moments of indecision, he decided on the latter course and stepped out from the shadows. To get Evie back, he'd have to convince her he was a better choice than the wealthy man keeping her, but the honorable intentions he needed to convey would not be demonstrated by cornering her in the bookshop alone at night. Besides, it was best if he knew as much about Evie's protector as possible, and it wasn't as if he could tackle her on the subject. Keeping a discreet distance, he followed the other man down Wellington Street and onto the Strand. It was no surprise to Rory when the man entered the Savoy courtyard. After all, when a man was keeping his mistress at his own hotel, it would be an easy matter slipping in and out of her bed.

Rory continued to follow, but when the toff stopped by the door to converse with the doorman, he stopped as well. Pretending to be lost in admiration for the Savoy's splendid fountain, he waited, watching out of the corner of his eye, and when his quarry finally entered the hotel and disappeared, he started forward again to take his turn for a bit of conversation with the doorman.

"That gentleman who just went in looks familiar to me," he commented, nodding to the doorway beyond, "but I can't place him. Do you know his name?"

The doorman looked him over and frowned, clearly doubtful of any possible connection between him and the man who'd just preceded him, and Rory, well aware that he wasn't dressed in the formal evening attire required at the Savoy, hastened again into speech.

"Worked for him once," he went on. "It was a long time ago, but I'm hoping he might have some work for me again."

The doorman's frown gave way to a condescending, vinegary smile. "I doubt it. That gentleman is the Duke of Westbourne."

Evie's fancy man was a *duke*? Rory blinked, not certain he'd heard correctly. "Duke of Westbourne? Well," he murmured as the other man nodded. "Fancy that. Looks just like my former employer."

"Will there be anything else?" the doorman asked coldly.

"As a matter of fact, yes." Improvising quickly, he patted his breast pocket. "I've got a message for one of the guests. It's urgent, and my employer asked me to bring it straightaway. Who do I see about that?"

The doorman's stiff demeanor relaxed slightly now that Rory had placed himself in the class of secretary, a class that made sense. "Messages for guests can be left at the front desk."

Rory nodded and turned to enter the hotel, pausing expectantly. With reluctance he couldn't quite hide, the doorman opened the door, and for the second time in his life, Rory passed into the luxurious confines of the Savoy Hotel.

"I'm sorry, sir," the clerk said in response to his inquiry at the front desk. "Miss Harlow is not in at present."

"I say, that's unfortunate. I've a message for her. From my employer."

To add credibility to his hastily invented role as secretary, he pulled an envelope out of his pocket and waved it in the air, careful not to let the other man see the name and direction written on it.

"I see." The clerk held out his hand. "I would be happy to have it delivered to Miss Harlow."

Rory shook his head, giving the man a look of apology as he shoved the letter to a friend of his in Germany back into his breast pocket. "Sorry, but I was told to put it into the lady's hand myself. It's urgent, you see. Would you have any idea where I might find Miss Harlow?"

"No, but perhaps her maid would know. Would you care to speak with her?"

Rory blinked in surprise. A fancy hotel, clothes, opera tickets, and a servant, too? That duke was certainly spending a lot on little Evie. What did she have going, he wondered, that made her worth all that? Well, whatever it was, Rory would enjoy discovering it for himself once he got the duke out of the picture.

"Ahem."

The concierge's cough brought him back to the matter at hand, and he put aside speculations about Evie's heretofore unimagined talents in the boudoir. "Yes, I would," he answered. "Perhaps she can tell me where to find Miss Harlow."

A bellboy was summoned to fetch the maid, and while he waited, Rory could only hope the servant wasn't some dried-up old hag who'd take one look at him and send him packing.

He need not have worried. When the bellboy returned ten minutes later and presented Evie's maid to him, Rory took one glance over the girl's plump figure and eager face, and he knew finding out everything there was to know about Evie's lover would be easy as winking.

# 14

When Max returned to the Savoy, he'd barely entered his room and poured himself a whisky before a knock sounded on the door and a whirling hurricane of ecru traveling linen, black hair, and expensive French perfume swept into his suite.

"Delia?"

He had no chance to say more before he was enveloped in one of his cousin's affectionate hugs. "Darling Max! I'm back at last."

"So I see," he replied, his voice slightly muffled by a mouthful of ostrich plumes. "When did you arrive?"

"Not five minutes ago," she replied as she pulled back. "The bellboys haven't even brought my luggage yet."

"Knowing the way you travel, that Herculean task will take at least ten minutes, so we have time for a visit." Ducking the playful smack she aimed at his head, he held up his glass and gestured to the liquor cabinet. "Care for a drink?"

"I'd adore one. Whisky, please," she added before he

could even ask. Sinking down in one of his suite's comfortable wingback chairs, she plucked out her hatpin and removed her enormous hat of straw, ribbons, and feathers. "I need something strong after the Channel."

"Crossing that bad?" he asked with sympathy.

"Isn't it always?"

Unable to contradict the legendary tumult of the English Channel, he handed her a glass containing a generous two fingers of whisky, then he sank down in the chair opposite hers. "How was Rome?"

"Beastly hot already, and it's only May. But enough about my trip," she added, tossing aside her hat. "You simply must tell me everything that's happened while I've been away."

"The Epicurean Club banquet was a huge success. Escoffier—"

"I don't mean the banquet," she cut in impatiently. "You can tell me all about that later. What I want to know right now is what on earth this business with Evie is about."

His hand tightened around his glass. "What do you mean? I explained in my letter—"

"Yes, yes, the girl's working herself to death, could do with a holiday and a bit of fun, so you want me to show her the delights of the season and introduce her to some suitable young men."

"Well, there you are, then." He leaned back with a shrug. "I'm not sure what you expect me to add."

"Max! Stop being such an oyster. From your description, the fellow who was courting her does sound dreadful, and I agree that Evie deserves far better than the likes of him, but nonetheless, it's not at all like you to play matchmaker."

"I'm not," he corrected at once, pasting on a little smile. "You are."

"I'm happy to do so, as I already told you in my letter, and I agree that she needs a bit of fun after the life she's had, but you really have to tell me what inspired all this. Why such interest in dear Evie?"

"I explained that. That scoundrel hoping to take advantage of her put my back up. And then, the poor girl's flat was flooded—"

"Yes, darling, I know you've a soft spot for a beauty in distress, but there must be more to it than that, and I insist on knowing everything before we go any further."

He sighed. "I suppose I have to tell you how the whole thing came about, but be warned: you won't approve."

That conclusion was confirmed a few minutes later when Delia interrupted his narrative at the point of the Oxford letter to ask, "Have you gone absolutely mad?"

That was perfectly possible, but he didn't say so. "Not at all," he replied, assuming an air of dignity. "I may have been a bit drunk at the time, I admit, but that's neither here nor there—"

"A bet? You're playing with Evie's life and future to win a bet, and you don't call that mad?"

"I know it seems unorthodox, but—"

"Unorthodox? Of all the...I am...I can't imagine what you..."

He took quick advantage of his cousin's inarticulate spluttering. "I don't see how you can fault me here. Really, Delia, if you had heard the way Freddie and his friends were denigrating her, and for the shallowest, most puerile of reasons, you'd have been as angry as I was, and you'd applaud my actions."

Delia heaved an aggravated sigh. "It must have been galling," she conceded, "for Evie's an absolute angel, and to hear such things would have gotten my back up, too."

If Max thought he was out of the woods with that concession, her next words showed him he was mistaken. "But what does the expulsion of Freddie and his friends from Oxford have to do with it? Why should you care if they behave themselves during the season?"

He took a hefty swallow of whisky before he replied. "Because I promised Helen I'd look after the lad."

"Helen? Which Helen? Not Freddie Maybridge's sister?"

"The very same." He took another gulp of whisky. "I saw her at Lady Hargrave's afternoon-at-home, and she asked for my help."

She groaned. "Really, Max, you simply must curb this inclination to help every young lady you meet."

"Don't exaggerate. And," he added with studied indifference, "Helen is not just any young lady."

His cousin's eyes widened in astonishment. "She's the reason you're in town? Are you thinking of pursuing Helen Maybridge?"

On that question, he drained his glass and decided that if Delia's expression was anything to go by, he was going to need another. "Yes," he answered as he rose to his feet and crossed to the liquor cabinet. "I don't see why you should be surprised. Helen is—"

He broke off, Evie's words echoing in his head.

*Beautiful. Charming. Perfect for you.*

"I am surprised, I admit. I didn't realize you even knew the girl."

Delia's remark hauled him back to the moment at hand. "We met last year when I was in town for the Lords. We were introduced at Ascot. We've seen each other several times since then."

"Several times? And that's enough to decide you want to pursue her?"

He turned. Lifting his glass, he leaned back against the liquor cabinet and smiled. "I am a rather impulsive man, as everyone in the family knows."

"Impulsive, my foot. I think you made a very deliberate decision here. If you were to pick the one girl on earth who is the complete opposite of Rebecca in every way possible—except perhaps in beauty—you couldn't choose better than Helen Maybridge. Have you invited her family to the house party?"

"Helen's family has their own plans for that weekend. But I intend to see a great deal more of her when I return to town."

"Why? To be sure she'll make a good duchess?"

His smile vanished. "I'm already sure of her abilities on that score," he said coolly. "I expect she'll be excellent at the job."

"Oh, Max."

Delia's disappointment was evident, but he had no intention of asking the reason for it. "Let's leave off discussion of my matrimonial prospects, shall we, and return to the matter of Evie Harlow's. You have just over three weeks until the ball. Do you think you can introduce her to enough young men beforehand to fill her dance card?"

"Your hundred pounds is safe, don't worry."

That acerbic comment ignited his temper. "Sod the hundred pounds," he shot back, his voice hard. "I want the girl to have fun, damn it. Do you know she's never been to a ball in her life?"

Delia's appalled reaction to that was all he could have hoped for. "Never?"

"Never. And given that's the case, you might see that she has a few lessons with a dancing master. She's a bit out of practice since finishing school, I daresay. And I want you to see that she has the most stunning ball gown Vivienne has ever made. Spare no expense. Is that understood?"

Delia nodded, her eyes wide, though he wasn't sure if her surprise stemmed from Evie's woeful lack of society and amusements in the past or his outburst of temper. Taking a deep breath, he went on, "Bet or not, I want her to have plenty of partners, Delia. You know enough suitable young men for that?"

"Heaps of 'em," she answered, and began counting off on her fingers. "There's Desmond Hunt, Earl of Ashvale. He's still single. So is Earl Hayward, the Marquess of Wetherford's son. And Baron Holbrook. And there's Lord Longford's son, Viscount—"

"No," he interrupted, shaking his head. "None of those men will do. They're all peers."

"Of course." Delia stared. "Why shouldn't I introduce her to peers?"

"You know the girl. Isn't it obvious?"

"Not to me," she said, setting aside her drink, folding her arms, and giving him a pointed stare.

"Delia, be honest. Can you really imagine Evie would be content as the wife of a peer?"

"What I'm imagining right now," she said with asperity, rising to her feet, "is slapping your face. If you weren't a duke, I'd do it, too. Max, really! Do you hear how you sound?"

"I'm not being snobbish," he shot back, appreciating that was exactly how he'd sounded and how Evie had once thought of him, and he knew he was now decidedly on the defensive. "I'm not."

"No? If not snobbery, then the only possible explanation is that your judgment is so badly skewed from your own tragic experience that you can't see beyond it!"

"That has nothing to do with this," he said, and it crossed his mind that if a man's place in hell was determined by the number of lies he told in a day, he had surely been condemned to Dante's seventh circle by now. "Answer my question. Do you really think Evie would be happy as the wife of a peer? You said yourself," he went on before she could answer, "the girl wouldn't be able to hold her own with Escoffier over the plans for a dinner party."

"If young men of the aristocracy eliminated from consideration all the young ladies who could not communicate effectively with Escoffier, a third of those young men would never marry, and they'd be hypocrites, to boot. Quite a few people we know speak abysmal French, including you!"

That lame argument justifiably shredded, Max tried another one, the one that mattered, the one he ought to have offered in the first place: "Either way, you're missing the vital point."

"Which is?"

"Evie wouldn't welcome your notions to elevate her. She's completely unimpressed with the aristocracy. She wants no part of it."

"How do you know that?"

"She told me so herself. She said straight out she has no interest in marrying a peer."

"Only because she's never met any! Well, except for you, and given your recent behavior, you're hardly a shining example."

That, he reflected with a grimace, was undeniably true, and in ways Delia could hardly imagine.

"Just who," she went on, since he said nothing, "did you intend me to introduce to her, then, if not members of the peerage?"

"Men of her own sphere, of course. Bankers, solicitors,

sons of miliary officers—men like Ronald Anstruther, for instance."

"Ronald Anstruther?"

That scornful retort had Max wishing he could jaunt off to Rome and leave Delia with this mess, since she was the one who had gotten him into it by sending him to Harlow's Bookshop in the first place. "Ronald Anstruther is a gentleman, and a thoroughly nice chap. The perfect sort of fellow for the step-niece of a baron."

"Except that he's dense as packed sand! He'd drive a brainy girl like Evie mad in less than a week."

"She seemed to like him well enough at the opera the other night."

"They met at the opera?"

"I introduced them at intermission. They got on quite well at supper afterward, from what I gather. His mother was very pleased about it. She sent me a note afterward, singing the girl's praises."

"I daresay, since a colonel's wife would find Evie's friendship with a duke's family a very agreeable connection."

"Not because Evie's a delightful girl in her own right?" he countered in an effort to get a bit of his own back.

"She *is* a delightful girl, one who could do better than the likes of Ronald Anstruther, if she ever received some useful help."

That stung. "And you think it's helpful to attempt to elevate her to a place she isn't prepared for and doesn't want?"

Delia retrieved her hat and put it on. "Not all men share your bitter and cynical view about marrying out of one's class. First thing tomorrow," she went on before he could remind her again of Evie's preferences, "I shall write to your sister Idina."

"Idina?" he echoed, diverted by the alarming introduction of his most meddlesome sister. "Whatever for? Delia?" he added, following her as she started for the door. "What are you scheming?"

"Idina always plans the Whitsuntide house party, doesn't she?"

"Not this year, since she won't be there. She'll be in Paris with her husband. Some diplomatic conference he's attending. Nan's helping me with the house party this year. And I've already invited Evie to come, if that's what you're thinking. There are several young bucks in the county I thought might suit her."

"Indeed?" She pulled open the door and paused, glancing at him over her shoulder. "Well, I shall be asking Nan to add a few very handsome, charming, eligible *peers* to the guest list as well."

The door slammed in his face before he had any chance to reply, leaving him with no choice but to consider how his cousin's plan would play out.

It wasn't hard to imagine. He could see it all—Evie close and untouchable, Delia and his sisters shoving peer after peer at her, himself playing the genial host to it all—and he realized a man didn't have to be dead to enter Dante's Inferno. He was headed there in less than a fortnight.

The moment Evie entered the suite, she knew Delia had arrived, for there was a pile of trunks and suitcases in the sitting room and the delicate scent of Delia's distinctive perfume was in the air.

"Delia?" she called.

"In here, Evie."

She followed the sound into Delia's bedroom, where more luggage lay scattered about, clothing and hats were strewn across the bed, and bottles and jars cluttered the dressing table. Amid this chaos, Delia, clad in an exquisite kimono of orange, gold, and black, was bent over an open trunk, rooting through piles of filmy lingerie and lacy undergarments, as a stout, middle-aged maid attempted to clean up the mess her mistress was making.

"It must be in the alligator suitcase," Delia was muttering as Evie paused in the doorway. "I wonder if they've found the blasted thing yet?" Straightening up, she spied Evie in the doorway. "Ah, Evie, darling. Come in, come in."

Beckoning her forward, Delia turned to the maid. "Chapman, go down and see if they've found that other case, will you? If so, have them send it up. And take the blue velvet with you so the laundry can press it. Then go into the restaurant and make a reservation for Miss Harlow and me. Then you can come back and help me dress." She broke off, turning to Evie. "You haven't dined yet, have you? Excellent," she added as Evie shook her head. "We can have a nice long visit over dinner and make some plans."

She waved Chapman out of the room, and as the maid glided away with a blue velvet gown draped over her arm, Delia turned to give Evie a kiss on each cheek.

"Dearest Evie," she said with affection, "I wish I had been the one to force you to take a holiday, and I'm slapping myself for not having thought of it ages ago. But come," she added, sitting down in front of her dressing table and gesturing for Evie to take the closest nearby chair. "Sit with me while I fix my face, and you can tell me all the ways my wretched cousin has been wreaking havoc in your life while I've been away."

Evie complied, though she was careful to leave out

the one truly havoc-inducing thing Max had done. A kiss, after all, wasn't the sort of thing you could tell just anyone about.

In a way, Evie wished she and Delia were close enough for such intimate confidences, for that kiss and all the bewildering sensations it evoked were still vivid in her mind. She'd lain awake all last night, reliving it with shock, wonder, and a delicious, shivering pleasure that was not at all appropriate under the circumstances. And even now, after she and Max had agreed it was a moment of madness that was best forgotten, she knew there was no forgetting it, ever. Not for her.

Talking with a friend about the episode and all the bewildering emotions it had evoked, especially one with a wider knowledge of men than she possessed, would have been such a relief. And she couldn't very well discuss it with Anna, not after dismissing her friend's cautions on the subject.

Still, though she regarded Delia as a friend, they were not close enough for secrets like that.

"Men are such children," Delia declared, her voice bringing Evie back to the topic at hand. "To think that a bet over a woman's attractiveness would be amusing. Honestly, I could wring all their necks."

"The thought of doing that did cross my mind at the time," Evie confessed.

"I'll bet it did," Delia muttered, opening one of the jars before her and scooping out some sort of cream with two fingers. "And I applaud your restraint. You mustn't take what Freddie and his friends said to heart. Idiots, all three of them—trust me."

"I didn't care what they thought of me," Evie assured her. "At least, not too much," she added.

"Good, because they haven't the sense God gave a rabbit. Max has his faults," she added as she began dabbing cream on her face, "but at least he knows an attractive woman when he sees one."

*When you smile that adorable crooked smile you've got, it makes me rather lose my head.*

As she remembered his words from a short time ago, a warm little glow started in Evie's midsection. Her smile was crooked, no doubt about it—one side tipped up higher than the other, abolishing any notions of symmetry, and she had both an overbite and a tiny little gap between her two front teeth—and even now, she didn't see how a smile like that could have impelled a man to kiss her. Quite the opposite, she'd have thought.

*I admit that carnal thoughts of you have crossed my mind, because I am a man, Evie, God knows, as weak as any other...*

How could she ever have inspired him to such thoughts? she wondered, and with that question, the pleasurable glow inside her deepened and spread, making her blush with both delight and embarrassment. Delia, thankfully, was too occupied with dabbing cream on her face to notice.

"Still, their silly game did accomplish one good thing," the other woman said as she capped the jar and turned in her chair. "It gives me the chance to bring you into society, which someone ought to have done ages ago."

"My cousin wanted her stepfather to do it when she came out after we finished school. We're the same age, and she's fond of me, in her way. But I had no interest in giving up the shop to become a debutante, especially since if I didn't marry, it meant I'd have no means of providing for myself and I'd be dependent on Merrivale. As for him, he hates that I am in trade, and he bristles with disapproval about it every Christmas when he's obliged to invite me to dinner. He's never much cared for his wife's middle-class background, in any case."

"Believe it or not, I understand, in a very small way, how that sort of disapproval feels. I am fortunate enough not to have to earn my living, but I enjoy my work for the hotel, even though it has earned me disapproval from some within my family. Fortunately, though, the ones I love the most have been surprisingly tolerant."

"Perhaps because they consider it an amusement rather than a job?"

Delia laughed. "You may have something there," she agreed. "But nonetheless, Evie, as you move in society, you may find that while many will feel as your step-uncle does, not everyone will share that opinion."

Evie considered, but it was a hard thing to believe. Disapproval of her birthplace, background, and career by those higher on the social ladder was an ingrained part of her life experience and not easy to dismiss. "I'm not so sure," she said. "Colonel Anstruther didn't think much of it."

"Yes, Max mentioned you had met the Anstruthers. But don't worry about the colonel. He's a stuffy old bird. What did you think of Ronald?"

Evie hesitated, striving for a tactful reply. "Well..." she said at last, the long, drawn-out word making Delia laugh. "He's very nice."

"But a bit dull?" Delia said, as if reading her mind. "Let me assure you, Evie, that you can do better than Ronald Anstruther."

"Please don't think I'm looking to gain a husband out of all this," Evie hastened to say. "This is just a holiday, after all, and I know I will soon be going back to my old life. I'm not expecting anything more from it than to enjoy myself."

Delia cocked an eyebrow, giving her such a searching glance that Evie had to resist the urge to squirm. "Is your old life what you want, Evie?"

"I—" She broke off, laughing a little. "I'm not sure anymore what I want, to be honest. I never thought much about it. But lately, especially since all this has happened, I've wondered if there might be...more out in the world than what I've had."

"There is plenty more, believe me, but it's much easier to enjoy those things if a woman is married. Do you want to marry, Evie? Most women do, of course, but there's nothing wrong with it if you don't. If you do, I am happy to introduce you to every eligible man I know. But if you don't, I should hate to think that Max and I were encouraging something for you that you don't want for yourself."

Evie considered her words carefully before she spoke. "I won't pretend it wouldn't be nice to find someone to marry, but as I told your cousin, I would never marry for any reason but love—"

Delia's astonished laugh interrupted her. "You told Max that?"

"Yes. Why?"

"My cousin doesn't have a high opinion of love as a guide to matrimony," she said dryly.

"Yes, so I understand. But I do. Either way, there's no point in trying to find me a husband, Delia. The ball is in three weeks, and that isn't nearly enough time to fall in love with anyone."

Delia laughed. "My dear, you're not Cinderella. No clock is going to strike at the end of Max's ball and force you back into obscurity. If you want to continue to move in society after that, I am happy to help you do so. And I'm sure Max feels the same. You are our friend."

Evie appreciated the kindness of that offer, but she knew it wasn't realistic. Even if she were suited for a life of society, balls, and parties—which she wasn't—and even if she wanted that superficial sort of life—which she didn't—she could never afford it. And she couldn't allow anyone, not Delia or Max or anyone else, to assume the expense of providing it to her until some wealthy chap came along, married her, and took her off their hands. This was a holiday, and nothing more.

"Why don't we just find ways for me to have fun during the next few weeks instead of worrying about my entire future?" she suggested, smiling.

"Excellent plan," Delia approved. "Now, since it's nearly nine o'clock, we'd best dress and go down to dinner. Then it's off to bed for both of us. You need your rest, my dear friend, because I shall be providing you with as much fun and as many handsome princes as you can handle."

# 15

⚜

*D*elia's boast, as Evie soon discovered, was not an idle one. During the two weeks that followed, she met no princes, but she did meet barons, viscounts, and earls, and she soon discovered, much to her surprise, that Delia had been right. If any of them disapproved of a woman in trade, none were so tactless as to express it to her. Of course, the fact that Delia prefaced every introduction with a mention of Evie's step-uncle Lord Merrivale was probably the reason for their forbearance on the topic. What they said behind her back might well be a whole other story, but Evie refused to dwell on it. She'd done enough agonizing of that sort when she was a girl, and she refused to ruin her holiday by doing it now.

She attended more teas, afternoons-at-home, plays, and card parties in that fortnight than she'd attended in the entire twenty-eight years of her life prior. She went back to Vivienne to be fitted for a ball gown, and she was absurdly pleased with herself when Delia and the dressmaker both endorsed her choice of jade-green silk.

Mentioning that she might want a bit of practice before Max's ball, Delia suggested a few sessions with a dancing master, and Evie was happily relieved to discover that as long as she took Max's advice not to look down and not to think too much, she wasn't nearly as bad a dancer as she'd thought herself to be. With this newfound jot of confidence, she even dared to dance when Delia's friends rolled back the carpet after a dinner party, and when Lord Ashvale commented that she "waltzed divinely," it was all she could do to keep a straight face and murmur a dulcet, ladylike thank-you.

As the days passed, she found herself putting Max's principle to the test in ways other than dancing. In navigating the dizzying whirl of activity Delia pulled her into, she tried not to think too much. Anytime she made a social faux pas—and she made several during that week—she strove not to berate herself. If she couldn't remember which spoon to use or was uncertain how to operate a pair of escargot tongs, she learned to observe others at dinner before making any attempts. She joked with her partners whenever she turned the wrong way during a reel or took the wrong position during a quadrille, and she found them much more understanding than the boys from school days had been. Whenever waiters grimaced at her woeful attempts to order dishes in French, she found herself taking a mischievous pleasure in ignoring their discomfiture.

She didn't run across either Arlena Henderson or Lenore Peyton-Price, but she did encounter several other schoolfellows from her Chaltonbury days, and she found that this time, there was no sinking feeling of dread in her stomach and no desperate longing to bolt for the door.

A month ago, Max had promised her his proposition meant she'd have fun, but she had no chance to tell him that promise was now coming true, for she never saw him. After ten days with no glimpse of him anywhere, she made a carefully indifferent inquiry of Delia on the topic and learned he wasn't even in town. The day after bringing her flowers, he'd gone to Idyll Hour to make preparations for the Whitsuntide house party.

His absence, however, didn't stop him from being ever present in her thoughts. How could she not think about him, now that she knew he'd had carnal thoughts about her? She tried to tell herself that in light of his intent to marry Helen Maybridge, such feelings were hardly a testament to his character or hers, but sadly, reminders like that didn't stop the pleasurable thrill that came whenever she remembered his kiss or his astonishing confession afterward. No man, she was sure, had ever had carnal thoughts about her before, and no man probably ever would again, and if it was wrong to be thrilled about that, well, she'd atone for it once this fairy tale was over and she was back amid her books, living a life of no sugar, no pâté, and terminal spinsterhood. In the meantime, she was determined to enjoy every moment of her holiday among the nobs.

She'd never been to a formal house party, but when she and Delia journeyed to Max's home in the Cotswolds, Evie thought she knew what to expect. Granted, the only country house she'd ever visited in her life was Uncle Edward's for a day at Christmas, but she had also been to Max's London residence, and she'd seen pictures of Chatsworth and Blenheim, and by the time they reached the train station at Stow-on-the-Wold, the picture in her mind was the grandest amalgamation of these that her imagination could conjure.

When the carriage Max had sent to fetch them at the station rolled into the graveled drive of Idyll Hour, however, Evie saw at once that her imagination had proved woefully inadequate.

The place was massive, a three-story Italianate structure capped by a dome and flanked by two-story wings that seemed to sprawl endlessly in both directions.

"Good heavens," she muttered, "does one use a motorcar to get from one end to the other?"

Delia laughed. "There are times when that would be very helpful. One year, during a party for the prime minister, my first husband and I stayed in the Parisian Room, which is at the far end of the left wing, and I was late to dinner— which would have been a fate worse than death as far as the late duke was concerned. I remember tearing down the corridor, cursing the damned architect for building such a monstrosity, and wishing I could gallop to the dining room on a horse."

"That would be a spectacle for the prime minister, I expect," Evie said, laughing as the carriage rolled to a stop before a wide set of stone steps, where a young woman in a soft green tea gown with a retinue of servants stood waiting to greet them.

"Nan, my sweet!" Delia cried, jumping out of the carriage and taking the steps two at a time as Evie followed at a slower pace. "It's been ages."

"Last August at Henley, I think."

"That long? Heavens, time flies. Nan, do allow me to present my friend Miss Harlow. Evie, my cousin Lady Moseley."

Lady Moseley, a dark-haired beauty who bore a decided resemblance to Max, held out her hand to Evie with a friendly smile. "How do you do, Miss Harlow? Welcome to Idyll Hour. My apologies that my brother is not here to greet you personally, but my husband insisted upon a drive in the duke's motorcar this afternoon, and they had a puncture, ended up in a ditch, and came back looking like a pair of farmers who'd been in the pigs. They went straight up to change for dinner."

Turning, she gestured to the tall, dignified man and rotund, beaming little woman who stood slightly behind her. "This is Wells, Miss Harlow, the butler at Idyll Hour, and Mrs. Norocott, the housekeeper. They can assist you with anything you need during your stay. Do come in, please."

Lady Moseley led them into a dazzling entrance hall of creamy limestone and golden Siena marble. To the left and right, staircases with ornate wrought iron railings curved upward, leading to the second floor of each wing. High overhead, blue sky could be seen through the many glass panes of the domed ceiling.

"Would you like tea, Miss Harlow?" Lady Moseley asked as they paused between the staircases. "Or would you prefer to go straight up to bathe and change?"

"I'd like to bathe and change, please, if you don't mind. The train journey was a bit hot."

"I'll do the same," Delia said. "I'd like to lie down for a bit and have a rest. Send my maid up, will you, Mrs. Norocott, as soon as the footmen have brought in the luggage? And I hope you can spare a housemaid to do for Miss Harlow? Her maid was obliged to remain in London."

"Of course. I'll send Josie up with Miss Chapman."

The housekeeper bustled off and the butler returned outside to supervise the footmen as Delia returned her attention to her cousin. "I'm sure you've got heaps of things to do, Nan, and other guests to see to, so I can take Evie up. Where are we?"

"Venice and Athens." Lady Moseley turned to Evie.

"Dinner is at eight. We usually begin gathering in the drawing room about half an hour beforehand. I shall see you both at dinner."

The Venice Room, Evie was glad to note, wasn't so far away that a horse might be needed. It was about halfway down the wing and lived up to its name by being decorated with some truly beautiful pieces of Venetian glass. Paintings by Italian masters hung on the wall, and a jar of Italian *pesche dolci* biscuits stood on the mantel.

Evie walked to the window, which overlooked an enormous knot garden, and as she studied the intricate pattern of perfectly cut boxwood, she appreciated once again how vastly different her life was from that of her host. Royals, prime ministers, and titled nobility from all over England had strolled those gardens. Some, no doubt, had slept in this room. And here she was, an ordinary middle-class girl, with only seventeen shillings in her bank account. What was she doing here? Turning away, she leaned against the window, staring at the luxurious draperies of pink and gold that surrounded her bed, trying to imagine living one's whole life like this. What would it be like, she wondered, to be a duchess?

It wouldn't be all beer and skittles, she knew. Not even for the people who had been born to it. As for her, well, she knew she'd be in way over her head. Straightening, she pushed away pointless speculations and reached for the bellpull to summon her maid.

An hour later, bathed and dressed in a dinner gown of blue ciselé silk, Evie left her room and went downstairs. A footman directed her to the drawing room, but the journey there took her through a wide gallery at least forty feet long where family portraits were displayed. It took several minutes to find Max's portrait, for the serious young man staring down at her looked far too dignified to be the passionate man with unruly hair who had held her in his arms and kissed her and confessed carnal thoughts.

*I am a man, Evie, God knows, as weak as any other...*

"Admiring my handsome countenance, are you?"

Evie jumped at the softly murmured question, and she glanced sideways to find the man who'd been dominating her thoughts for days standing right beside her.

She ought to be accustomed by now to how devastatingly handsome he looked in white tie, but she wasn't, for as she turned to face him, her breath caught in her throat, and her heart started thudding hard in her chest. She sucked in a shuddering breath, and as the luscious scent of him filled her nostrils, she was suddenly as skittish as a colt.

"Heavens," she breathed, laughing a little to cover her nervousness, pressing a gloved hand to her chest. "How you startled me."

"Sorry." He grinned, giving a nod to the portrait on the wall. "What do you think?"

Seizing on the distraction, she turned toward the painting. "It's very...ducal."

He gave a shout of laughter. "Well, I should hope so," he said. "I'd hate to look earlish. And to look baronish would be a fate worse than death."

She laughed, too. "I only meant that it looks a bit haughty."

"Haughty? You think so?"

"Yes. And not much like you."

He studied his portrait for a moment, considering. "Perhaps you're right. It looks far too much like my father, really."

Evie looked to the portrait he indicated of a far haughtier man with Max's dark blue eyes, a stern face, and an ermine-trimmed robe around his shoulders. "It sounds," she said, looking at him again, "as if you didn't get on with your father."

"He was a hard man, uncompromising, determined to have his way. He wasn't cruel, but nonetheless, we had many, many battles, for I was both wild and reckless when I was young, with all his stubbornness, to boot. He died when I was nineteen. That," he added, pointing to a painting of an equally haughty-looking woman with auburn hair and a long, very English nose, "is my mother."

"Goodness, why does your portrait painter insist on making all of you look so out of sorts?"

"It's meant to show our superiority over the lesser mortals."

"Or to show that all of you suffer from indigestion."

He chuckled. "Possibly."

She glanced at the painting of an angelic, golden-haired beauty beside Max's portrait. "And who's this? Not Lady Moseley. Another sister, perhaps?"

"No. That is Rebecca." He paused a fraction of a second. "My wife."

"You were married?" Startled, Evie glanced at him, but he wasn't looking at her.

"Yes," he answered, staring up at the portrait. "She died."

"I'm sorry."

"Don't be." He turned, facing her. "It was nearly eight years ago."

"That long? You must have both been very young."

"We met in New York when I was only twenty-two. She was seventeen."

"New York? So, she was American, then? How did you meet?"

"A friend of mine was marrying an American heiress,

and he asked me to attend the wedding as best man. I met Rebecca at the wedding breakfast."

"She's very beautiful."

"Yes," he said simply. "She was."

"What was she like?"

He was silent so long, she thought he wasn't going to reply, but then he laughed a little and said, "I'm not sure what to say. It's not an easy question to answer."

"No? But you were married."

"Only for two years. And we'd only known each other two months when we wed."

"Quite a whirlwind courtship."

"Yes. You see, Rebecca wasn't like any other girl I'd ever met. From the moment I saw her, I wanted her— across a crowded room, just like in some romantic novel, before she said a word, before I even knew her name. And when I heard her laugh..." He paused, turning to look up at the picture. "She looked like an angel, but she had the throatiest, most wicked laugh I'd ever heard in my life. I heard that, and my heart was lost."

"You fell in love that fast?"

"Yes. At least," he amended with a grimace and returned his attention to her, "I thought it was love. God knows, it felt like love."

"But it wasn't?"

"It was passion and desire, infatuation and lust, the sort of thing that makes you feel so gloriously alive and happy that it becomes easy to ignore your own better judgment. Is that love?" He paused to consider. "I suppose it is, but it certainly isn't the kind that lasts." He tilted his head to study her. "I think perhaps you know what I mean?"

"Me?" Evie stared at him. "What makes you say that?"

"The pigeon, of course."

"Oh, Rory." She gave a laugh, shaking her head. "That wasn't the same thing at all. Rory and I had known each other forever. After he went to Germany, we only saw each other once, briefly, when his father died. He came home to settle his father's things. We wrote to each other often while he was away, but there was nothing romantic about it for either of us until he came back."

"What changed?"

"Not much, as it turns out." She saw his puzzled look and hastened to explain. "When he first came back, it was so good to see him again, and I started hoping there could be more than affection and friendship between us, but that was just wishful thinking on my part. You're the one that made me realize it."

"When?"

She made a face. "When you called him a pigeon."

Max laughed, his eyes creasing at the corners in that devastatingly attractive way. "I'd apologize for my bluntness, but I can't, because I'm not sorry. He wasn't worthy of you."

"I know. My father couldn't see it. To the day he died, he always hoped Rory and I would make a match of it."

"In heaven's name, why?"

"He wanted me to be settled. You see, Rory's father owned the confectionery next door, and both our fathers thought it a suitable match. But after Rory's father died, Rory sold the shop to Anna's husband, and returned to Germany, and that was that. My father died not long after that." She paused, considering. "I've always been very fond of Rory, and when he came back, I started to wonder if it could be more than that. You see—"

She broke off and looked down. "It's amazing how easy it is to deceive yourself when you're lonely," she confessed, her voice low. "It's not easy to be alone, day after day. Heavens," she added, laughing a little, pride impelling her to lift her head. "That sounds terribly weak, doesn't it?"

"No, Evie," he said gently, "that doesn't sound weak at all. It sounds human. We all need more than ourselves to be happy."

"Well, either way, what I felt for Rory wasn't anything like what you felt for your wife. I admit, it was rather fun to dream about him and wonder what it would be like to kiss him, but—"

A smothered sound came from his throat, interrupting her. "Sorry," he said, giving a cough and patting his chest. "You were saying?"

"What I felt for him was never a mad passion. In a way, I wish it had been." She paused, then added softly, "I envy you that."

"Envy me?" He stared at her as if she were a candidate for Bedlam. "For God's sake, what I felt was nothing to envy, believe me," he muttered, looking away. "Love like that is torture, if you want the truth."

"Yes, perhaps it is, but to feel that way about someone, to be so carried away by passion that nothing else matters... I've never felt that in my life." She paused, then added softly, "I think it would be wonderful to feel like that."

"Only until reality sets in," he said grimly. He looked at her again, his dark blue eyes hard and opaque. "For Rebecca and me, that happened less than a year after the honeymoon."

"Within a year? Is that all?"

"Maybe less. We came from completely different backgrounds. Her father was wealthy, but she was born in a tent in a mining camp in Denver, Colorado. Whereas I..." He paused, gesturing to their surroundings. "Well, you see for yourself where I come from. Rebecca's father was a widowed, hard-bitten miner who happened to strike it rich. They moved to New York when she was sixteen so that she could enter society, but even New York society was difficult for her. She was very New Money, you see. Marrying me and coming here, as you might guess, was an enormous shock. She had no idea how to navigate my world, and she was painfully ill-suited to being a duchess. She encountered a great deal of opposition and ridicule in society, and she had no idea how to overcome it. My mother was still alive then and tried to assist her, but she, too, disapproved of the match, and she found it hard to hide her feelings, so she was of little help. Rebecca felt everyone's disapproval of her, and it cut deep. It wasn't long before she came to hate the life she was expected to lead here."

"Couldn't you help her?"

"God knows, I tried. I fought hard to gain her acceptance, I called in every favor of every friend and relation, did my best to guide her, but despite my best efforts, society simply would not accept her. The aristocracy can be breathtakingly cruel."

"Yes," she agreed, hearing the tinge of bitterness in her own voice. "Yes, it can."

"Making things worse, she thought everything about being a duchess was shallow and pointless. The longer she was here, the more contempt she had for the world she'd married into and the title she had assumed, and it wasn't long before she found it intolerable."

Those words banished any idle speculations she might have had about what being a duchess would be like for someone from her class of life. It would be hell. "Her feeling was understandable, wasn't it, given society's treatment of her?"

"Of course, but as I said, that's a sword that cuts both ways. My circle of acquaintance sensed her animosity and reacted by reciprocating in kind. The invitations slowly trickled away, then stopped coming altogether, leaving her feeling even more isolated and alone, and I felt the same. Any of the passion we felt in the beginning was gone by our first anniversary, and by our second, we were two strangers living in the same house with nothing in common, not even a shared vision of the future. If we'd had children, that might have made a difference, but—"

He broke off and the hardness in his face faltered, showing pain. "It's difficult to have children when your wife shuts her bedroom door to you. She blamed me, you see, for all of it, and she wasn't wrong."

Evie studied his handsome, pain-ravaged countenance. "I doubt that," she said softly.

He shook his head. "I appreciate your show of faith, but it's true. Rebecca had doubts about marrying me, you see. She refused me twice, saying she didn't want my life. I was so carried away by my ardor that I would not accept her refusal, and I used every scrap of charm I possessed to persuade her to marry me. I spent that summer wearing her down, and I finally succeeded, but it was no victory in the end. A week after our second anniversary, she left me flat and returned to America. The scandal sheets got hold of it straightaway, and they reported her desertion of me with great glee. We tried to say she'd just gone home for a visit, but no one believed it. Everyone knew she'd left me."

"That must have been humiliating."

His mouth tightened. "Yes, it was. Not only for me, but everyone in my family. But I could endure that. The worst part was that the dukedom itself was in jeopardy. I haven't a single male relation who can inherit. If I don't have a son, the title forfeits to the crown."

"You and your wife couldn't reconcile?"

"I had no choice but to try, and I wrote and told her so. Divorce would have required a bill in parliament, which is a messy business and ruinous for all concerned. And because I need an heir, permanent separation was an unacceptable option. But..."

"But what?" she prompted when he paused.

"When I got to New York, I found that Rebecca had been run down by a carriage three days before my arrival. Rebecca's father, you see, had refused to shelter her from her obligation as my wife. I will never know..."

He paused again and swallowed hard, then he went on, his voice so low, she barely heard, "I will never know if the carriage was an accident or if she stepped in front of it on purpose to save herself from coming back to me."

The first dinner gong sounded before Evie could reply, resonating through the gallery with painful finality.

"Half past seven," he said as the notes died away. "I'd best be in the drawing room before the others start arriving. Shall we?"

He offered Evie his arm, and she took it, but neither of them spoke as they walked to the drawing room. That wasn't surprising, of course. What was there to say?

In looking back on the disaster of his marriage, Max had always thought of it, at least in part, as the idiocy of youth. After all, he'd only been twenty-two at the time.

By the age of thirty-two, he felt, a man ought to be sure enough of his ground and strong enough in his character that temptations of the flesh and yearnings of the heart would not derail his plans or compromise his ethics. But Evie Harlow was putting Max's convictions on that score to the test in every way possible.

After his conversation with her at her shop, he'd hoped they were back on friendly, neutral ground. He'd hoped that ten days away from her would put out the fire she roused in his blood, and that returning to his home, where he could be surrounded by all the reminders of his position and his duty, would renew his resolve to set a different course than the one he'd embarked upon ten years ago.

Those hopes, however, had been dashed the moment he'd seen Evie's lithe, slim form standing in his gallery. At once, his heart had leapt in his chest, his pulse had quickened, and his need for her had come roaring back stronger than ever.

If time and distance and sheer will had proven insufficient to deter him from the course his body seemed bent upon, the portraits of his ancestors, so stern and disapproving, ought to have done the trick, but no. Watching her profile as she'd studied the faces of his mother and father had only served to set his mind wondering if he could steal a kiss before anyone else strolled into the gallery.

When she'd asked about Rebecca's portrait, he'd seized on it like a drowning man seizing a lifeline. Telling her that sordid tale, he'd thought, would surely put his priorities back in order. And as he'd relived the pain of those days so long ago, he'd felt his hungry yearning for Evie receding, and his resolve once again coming to the fore. Through dinner, port, and cards afterward, he'd scarcely thought about her, and he was glad to note that his sleep had not been disturbed by any dreams of making love to her. By morning, it seemed his latest effort to obliterate his desire for her had worked splendidly.

As plans for the day's amusements were discussed by the various guests over breakfast, his gaze barely strayed to where she was sitting across the table, until the subject of the ladies' afternoon croquet match came up.

"Do you play croquet, Miss Harlow?" asked Sarah Harbisher, who was sitting beside her.

"I'm afraid not," Evie answered. "I've never been very accomplished at sports."

"Oh, but you must try," cried Sarah. "Croquet is a tradition at Idyll Hour. We play in teams. It's great fun."

"Teams?" Something in Evie's voice caused Max to look up from his plate. "You play croquet in teams?"

"It's always done in teams," Sarah explained. "Teams and rounds. That's the only way with this many people. We draw lots as to who plays with whom."

Because he was looking straight at Evie, he was able to see the shimmer of dismay that crossed her face, the same dismay he'd seen there when he'd told her about the upcoming ball.

He felt impelled to jump in. "You don't have to play, Miss Harlow," he said. "Not if you don't want to."

"Quite right," Edward Harbisher put in, leaning past his sister to look at Evie down the table. "Don't let my sister bully you."

"I'm not doing any such thing," Sarah protested. "If Miss Harlow doesn't want to play, of course she doesn't have to."

"It's not that I don't want to," Evie clarified. "It's just that I don't know how. And I wouldn't want to disappoint my team."

"Oh, don't worry about that," Sarah told her. "No one takes it that seriously. And besides, it's always good to try new things, isn't it? Sometimes they turn out to be much more fun than we thought."

"Yes," Evie murmured, looking at Max across the table. "So I'm discovering."

That made him smile. "Croquet's a bit like dancing," he remarked. "It's usually best to relax and not think about it too much."

"What excellent advice." She smiled back, the extraordinary smile that always sent him topsy-turvy. "I'll remember it this afternoon."

"Does that mean you'll play?" asked Sarah eagerly.

"Yes, yes," Evie said, laughing. "I'll play. Though I won't guarantee the results."

Watching her laughing face, Max could feel his wits skidding sideways and all his hard-won fortitude slipping away again, and when Lord Ashvale spoke beside him, it was all he could do to tear his gaze away.

"Sorry, Desmond, what did you say?"

Desmond laughed. "I was hoping your silence was inspired by a feeling of dread. I was challenging you to a game of tennis this afternoon."

A hard, sweaty game of tennis was just what he needed. "You're on. Tennis sounds like a smashing idea."

But like everything else in his life these days, tennis didn't go according to plan. Instead of keeping his eye on his own game, his attention kept straying from the tennis court to the croquet lawn. Every time Evie made a shot, he watched her, silently cheering her on. When she got into the weeds, he crossed his fingers for her. And when she managed to hit the wicket on a nearly impossible shot, winning the game for her team, he almost tossed his racquet in the air with a whoop of jubilation.

Needless to say, Desmond trounced him in straight sets.

# 16

Max's tennis game was a fitting prelude to the remainder of his weekend. At dinner, he could see Evie plainly from where he sat, and though he tried to keep his attention properly fixed on the guests to his left and right, it proved impossible. The Countess of Portlebury was dull as paint, and the Bishop of Avonlea insisted upon quoting from various sermons about sins of the flesh, a topic that did nothing to prevent his gaze from sliding down the long dining table to Evie's place.

Unlike him, she seemed to be enjoying her dinner companions, both of whom, he was aggravated to note, were men. Every time Max glanced in her direction, she was either leaning closer to Doctor Brandon for an intimate tête-à-tête or bestowing that amazing smile of hers on Edward Harbisher. And both of them, he noted grimly, seemed every bit as delighted with her company as she was with theirs.

None of this was a surprise, of course. He'd known all along that if Evie could be brought out of her shell, she'd have men dancing attendance, but being right about her attractions was now proving to be no satisfaction at all, especially since he had no right to claim her attention for himself.

Over the port, he arranged a game of cards with three of the other gentlemen, but whist required a level of concentration he simply could not muster, and much like his tennis game, he got shredded and lost a packet.

On Sunday morning, Whitsun church services found her seated right across the aisle from him. The scent of bergamot that kept wafting to his nose during the service was imaginary, he knew, but it seemed real enough to bring memories of that scorching kiss in his London ballroom roaring back, making church a painful and hypocritical ordeal.

As the interminable hours of the weekend went by, memories of the touch of her lips, the taste of her mouth, and the scent of her skin became impossible to push away, transforming into a sweet addiction that he knew he would be unable to break as long as she was so tantalizingly close.

In consequence, he avoided her as much as possible, but nonetheless, he got no peace of mind and very little sleep, and by the time guests started leaving on Monday morning, it was all he could do to hide his happy relief as he paid his farewells to everyone.

Unfortunately, Delia was one to oversleep as a matter of course, and because of that, she had booked the later train for her and Evie to return to London. With all other distractions now gone, Max had no choice but to take refuge in his library—a decision that proved beyond doubt he'd lost his wits, because only an idiot would think to avoid a bibliophile by going to his library.

"Max?"

As the sound of her voice floated from the library into the muniment room where he was sorting estate papers, Max nearly groaned aloud.

"Max? Are you in here?"

Taking a deep breath, he set aside the papers in his hand and stepped into the doorway.

She was standing near the entrance to the library, and though she wore no hat, she was already dressed for the train in a brown linen traveling suit. At the sight of him, she came all the way into the room, smiling a greeting. "Good morning."

He bowed. "Good morning."

Something in his voice must have given an inkling of his feelings, for her steps faltered and her smile faded to an uncertain expression.

"Am I disturbing you?" she asked, taking another step forward.

"Not at all," he lied, crossing the room to her side. "Can I help you with something?"

"Delia mentioned to me during the train journey up that your library was splendid, and I thought I'd have a look at it before we go back to London."

Despite how he was feeling, her words made him smile a little. "I'm surprised it took you this long."

"So am I, rather," she confessed, glancing around. "But it's been a busy weekend."

"Yes, I heard you were the terror of the other teams on the croquet field on Saturday."

She laughed. "I was, wasn't I?" she agreed, sounding surprised. "Beginner's luck."

"Or a newly discovered talent."

"I doubt that. I've never been particularly good at athletic endeavors."

"And yet your team won twice, thanks to you."

"And you, since it was only due to your advice not to overthink things that I did so well. Although," she added with a wink, "the glass of champagne I gulped down just beforehand probably helped, too."

He couldn't help a chuckle at that. "No doubt," he said and made an expansive gesture. "Now that you're here, would you like a tour?"

The moment the words were out of his mouth, he wanted to kick himself in the head.

"Oh, yes, please."

The damage done, he mustered his fortitude and gestured to the nearest shelves. "Here we have history and geography. And over here," he added, stepping a safer distance away from her as he began circling the room, "are books on world politics."

He led her around the room, ticking off the subjects of each collection as quickly as he could without seeming rude, until they were nearly back where they started. "And lastly," he said, glad this tour was almost over, "we have novels and poetry. Well," he finished, pausing by the door, "now you've seen it all."

"All?" she echoed, glancing around, tilting her head back, her gaze traveling the floor-to-ceiling shelves lined with volumes. "You could store all the books in my shop here and it wouldn't take up a third of the space."

"Ah, but most of your books are far rarer than most of mine," he reminded her. "Nearly all of what you see here was acquired by ancestors of mine who cared less about the books themselves than they did about simply filling the shelves with leather-bound volumes appropriate for a duke's library. Very little in this room is rare, or even particularly noteworthy."

"So, their concerns have traditionally been aesthetic rather than literary?"

"For the most part, yes."

"And which view do you share?"

"Both," he said at once. "And neither."

"A curious answer."

"Not really." He gestured to the shelf beside her. "Most of the novels, the modern ones anyway, are my acquisitions. You see, I don't acquire books to impress others, nor am I an avid collector. I simply buy books I think I would enjoy reading."

"There's nothing wrong with that."

"I doubt my father would agree. He, like many of the dukes before him, had little interest in books with popular appeal. He found such things frivolous."

"From his portrait in the gallery, I'm not surprised," she said, laughing.

Staring into her laughing, upturned face, he appreciated how close they were standing, and arousal flickered dangerously inside him.

She turned toward the books, tilting her head as she began scanning the titles. "Is it all right if I take a book with me to read on the train?" she asked, pulling out a volume partway, then shoving it back into place. "I forgot to bring one to read when we came up on Friday."

"Of course. Take anything you like."

"Thank you." She continued reading titles, moving closer to him as she did so, but as the soft, delicate scent of talcum and flowers floated to him, he did not step back.

Instead, he closed his eyes, breathing deep, his heartbeat quickening. She moved again, and without opening his eyes, he could discern precisely how close she was just from the warmth of her body. Another inch, he judged, maybe two, and she'd be touching him. The arousal in him deepened at the thought, spreading through his limbs.

She moved, her shoulder brushing his arm as she reached for a volume overhead, and he jerked back, coming to his senses.

"While you look for a book, I'd best carry on with what I was doing," he said, jerking a thumb over his shoulder. "If you need anything, I'll be back there, in the muniment room."

Her face lit up like a candle, and he knew he was doomed. "You have a muniment room?"

"I do, yes." Resigned to more torture, he turned, gesturing to the doorway at the other end of the library. "Care to have a look?"

Without waiting for an answer, he turned, beckoning her to follow, and he led her into the small, dim cubbyhole of a room attached to the library, where all the estate papers and records were kept.

"Heavens," she said, glancing around at the stacks of papers, photographs, diaries, and rolled-up maps that crammed the shelves, littered the writing desk, and spilled from the drawers of the ceiling-high filing cabinets. "How do you ever find anything in here?"

"It is rather a mess, I know."

"More than that." She reached out and delicately touched a bundle of yellowed letters on the shelf beside her. "Some of these papers are so old, they're crumbling."

Along with his sanity.

"If you want to preserve them," she went on, "they ought to be properly packed and stored in archival boxes."

Sadly, he could not preserve himself in a similar fashion until she was safely out of reach. "I did make a bit of a start on things last year, but as you might guess, it's hard to know where to even begin something like this. No one's ever bothered, as you can see."

"I'd soon have it sorted for you, if I were staying longer."

If that happened, he'd be forced to jump off a cliff.

"I'm sure," he agreed. "But as you said, you're going back to town, worse luck."

"Are you staying here, then?"

"For another week or two, yes. But I'll be back in time for the ball."

"A pity we won't be able to put our practice to use there. Dancing together," she prompted at his blank stare. "At the ball."

"Oh, that, yes," he said, hauling his imagination back from the dangerous imaginary place where they practiced things much naughtier than dancing. "A great pity."

"We dance so well together. I still fear any other partners I may dance with will rue having asked me."

"Nonsense. You had similar apprehensions about dancing with me, and about croquet, and look how both of those turned out."

"True," she agreed, laughing. "You may win that bet, after all."

"That's the spirit," he approved. "Now," he added, donning the brisk air of a busy man, "I'd best get on with this. Feel free to take any books you like. Just be sure to jot the titles in the record book on your way out. Have a good journey back, and I will see you at the ball."

He bowed, and when he straightened, she had already turned to leave, but then she stopped, showing he wasn't out of the woods. "Max?"

*Christ, have mercy.*

"Yes?"

"Are you—" She broke off and bit her lip, staring

at him in uncertainty. "Are you angry with me for some reason?"

He blinked. "Angry? With you? Far from it." His gaze lowered, sweeping with hot longing over her figure, envisioning the naked image that had been tormenting him for weeks, and he could feel himself splintering apart. He lifted his gaze again, stopping at her chin, not quite meeting her eyes, afraid of what she'd see in his. "Of course not," he answered. "I can't imagine why you'd think such a thing."

But he knew the answer, even before her lips twisted into a wry smile. "Perhaps because you've hardly spoken to me all weekend?"

"Forgive me," he said at once. "But with so many guests and so much to do, there hasn't been much time, and now—"

He broke off as something shimmered in her face, a hint of hurt that made it clear he hadn't sounded the least bit convincing.

"I'm sure you're very busy," she said and took a step back. "I won't trespass on your time any longer."

She turned away, and he couldn't bear it. Like a dam breaking, his resolve cracked and broke apart, and he reached for her, turning her around and pulling her into his arms before he could stop himself.

At once, the feel of her body against his sent the desire he'd been holding back flooding through him. "Evie, for God's sake," he muttered, lifting one hand to cup her face as his other arm wrapped around her waist. "You're killing me. Don't you see? All I want is to kiss you and touch you. All I can think about is what you look like under your clothes and what it would be like to have your body naked under mine. And I know that I can never find out because nothing good can come of it. You said it yourself, that being a duchess is the last thing in the world you'd ever want, but that doesn't seem to stop me from wanting you, and trying to keep that in check is driving me a bit mad."

She was blushing as he offered this torrid speech, soft pink flooding her face and neck. "Oh," she breathed. "I didn't know you were thinking..." She paused, pulling back in his hold. "I didn't realize—"

He cut her off with a kiss, pressing his lips to hers before she could withdraw, the temptation to have her, if only for a few more agonizing moments, far stronger than any sense of self-preservation he'd ever possessed.

Her mouth was warm and soft, and she melted against him, her lips parting beneath his.

His body responded at once, desire flaring higher, blazing into outright lust. He deepened the kiss, sliding his tongue into her mouth, and she responded, meeting his tongue with her own, every bit as sweetly willing as she'd been during their first kiss, making him want her even more.

As he kissed her and tasted her, he slid his hand down, his fingertips tracing her cheek, her jaw, the slender column of her throat, and the hard ridge of her clavicle, then he took his exploration one step further still, his palm opening over her breast.

Despite the stiff barrier of her corset, the contact was exquisite, but it wasn't nearly enough, and he tore his lips from hers with a groan of agony.

"You haunt my dreams at night," he murmured, fanning the flames with erotic words as he shaped her breast against his palm. "About bedding you, and taking your virtue, and making you completely mine."

He kissed her ear, flicking it with his tongue, and she gasped, her knees buckling beneath her. Tightening his arm around her waist, he recaptured her mouth with his and eased her backward, moving them both out of view of anyone who might pass the library doorway. Wedging her between the filing cabinet and the desk, the tiny room's only scrap of space, he pressed her body to the wall with his own.

Rock-hard now, aching from days of suppressed sexual need, he dipped at the knees, pressing his hips to hers, sliding his cock against her closed thighs.

The pleasure of that tiny move was so luscious that he groaned, and he had to bury his face against the side of her neck to smother it. She must have felt the same, for she jerked her hips, instinctively demanding more. He gave it, flexing his hips against hers again, and then again, torturing himself until his body was screaming for release.

He couldn't give in to that demand, but what he could do was pleasure her. Still caressing her breast with one hand, he grasped a fistful of linen and silk with the other and began drawing her skirts upward as he pressed kisses to the side of her throat.

When he succeeded in working his hand beneath her skirts, he slid it upward along her thigh, the callus on his palm catching on the delicate muslin of her drawers as he caressed her, savoring the scorching heat of her skin through the thin fabric. When he reached her hip bone, he glided his fingertips back and forth across her belly, feeling her quiver in response.

She was panting now, and when he moved his hand between her thighs, she stirred in his hold, making a soft sound of agitation even as she wrapped her arms around his neck. Deeming the time was right, he turned his hand, cupping her mound.

Her reaction was immediate, a startled cry of pleasure

loud enough that he immediately captured her lips in another kiss. They didn't dare be overheard, and yet, despite the risks, there was nothing, no power on earth, above in heaven, or below in hell, that could have stopped him from sliding his hand inside the slit of her drawers to touch her.

She was warm, wet, insanely inviting, and he groaned against her mouth. He caressed her, gliding his finger between her folds, and she shivered in response, making soft sounds of agitation and pleasure against his mouth as her hips jerked instinctively against his fingertips, driving her toward orgasm.

"Evie?"

Both of them went still at the sound of Delia's voice calling her name. He tore his mouth from hers, but he had no intention of stopping this glorious interlude. "Wait here," he whispered. "I'll get rid of her."

With that, he stepped back, pulling his hand from beneath her skirts as he raked his other hand through his hair, working to tamp down his raging need for her, but it was useless. The sight of her, flushed and breathless, loosened tendrils of her hair falling around her face, her lips puffy from his kisses and her tawny eyes wide with astonished pleasure at what was happening to her, was so delectable that even the holiest saint couldn't have curtailed lust. And when Delia's voice called her name again, he knew he had no time to waste on pointless endeavors like that anyway. "I'll be right back," he whispered. Pressing a quick kiss to her lips, he left the muniment room to put an end to this interruption and return to Evie before either of them had time to think too much. Heading for the library door, grabbing a book along the way that might provide a measure of camouflage over the evidence of his raging desire, he crossed the library and stuck his head through the doorway just as Delia turned the corner.

"Looking for Evie?" he called, striving for the most natural voice he could muster as his cousin started toward him.

"I am. She said she was coming to see the library."

"She was here, but she's gone again."

"Already?" Halfway down the corridor, Delia halted. "I'm shocked. I'd have thought to find her rooting happily amid the shelves like a nesting bird."

"She said something about wanting to be sure her things were packed."

"Well, I should hope she's packed by now. We're leaving for the station in half an hour."

Half an hour, he calculated, gave him enough time for about fifteen more minutes of pleasure for her and exquisite torture for him before he'd have to let her go. "You might just go upstairs and see if she's ready," he suggested. "You won't want to miss the train."

"Good idea." Delia turned away, and he breathed a sigh of relief as she turned the corner and disappeared, but as he turned to rejoin Evie in the muniment room and continue where they'd been forced to leave off, he found his hopes dashed.

The door to the terrace had been closed, but now it was wide open, the soft spring breeze fluttering the draperies.

She was gone.

"Damn," he breathed, rubbing his hands over his face, his body still afire with unrequited lust. "Damn, damn, damn."

Lifting his head, he stared at the open doorway, striving to cool his blood, regain his sanity, and return everything to how it had been before, but it wasn't long before he realized his efforts were in vain.

Nothing could be as it had been before. Helen, he knew now, was not destined to be his duchess. His sensible plan for a marriage of fondness, affection, and nothing more was gone—had been gone, he realized, from the moment he'd stood with Evie Harlow on the ballroom floor at Westbourne House and kissed her for the first time.

Now he was choosing a different future, and he could only pray that this time, his choice wouldn't find him in shreds with an absent duchess and a broken heart. Again.

# 17

For Evie, the fortnight following the house party was even more frenetic than the one prior to it had been. Peers, parties, and dance practices filled nearly every waking hour, and though Delia assured her such a pace was typical of the season, it wasn't anything she was accustomed to, and she was forced to insist on time away from it all every now and then, just to catch her breath. But if she thought a few occasional hours away from society would offer the chance for some much-needed peace and quiet, she was mistaken. Any scraps of free time she managed to carve out for herself were taken up with supervising the final renovations to the shop, and as a result, she fell into bed exhausted every night. Sleep, however, proved aggravatingly elusive.

*All I want is to kiss you and touch you.*

As she had every night since the house party, Evie lay in bed wide awake, staring up at the ceiling over her bed, her body burning as she remembered those extraordinary moments with Max in the muniment room.

His caress, so hot and tender, so wickedly luscious, had ignited a longing within her that she'd never felt before. She tried to suppress it with reminders that he was not hers to dream about and that he still intended to marry someone else, someone beautiful and elegant, who suited him far more than she ever could. However, those cold facts were not enough to banish the erotic confessions that made her ache.

*All I can think about is what it would be like to have your body naked under mine.*

She'd never had anyone explain the facts of life to her, but thanks to texts on biology and medicine, and a few stealthy peeks at pornographic literature during her adolescence, she knew what Max's confession meant.

He wanted to lie with her. To invade her body with his own and have carnal knowledge of her.

Not even in her wildest romantic daydreams could she have imagined herself to be the recipient of such erotic masculine desires, and every time she thought of Max wanting her in such a way, euphoric joy rose up inside her, making her feel so vibrantly alive that sleep was impossible. Sometimes she even imagined his hand caressing her again in that shocking, intimate way, evoking the same rising tension, the same desperate hunger she'd felt then.

At the time it had happened, she'd run, yanking down her skirts and ducking out of the library when his back was turned, but now, two weeks later, in the quiet darkness of her room, there was no such escape. She could only lie awake, her body afire with this strange, aching need, her mind wondering what more she could have experienced with him had they not been interrupted.

Whatever might have happened, by the time the ball was twenty-four hours away and the end of this fantastical romantic holiday was in sight, Evie feared she'd spend all the remaining days of her life wondering just what wondrous things she'd run away from on that glorious spring afternoon.

"Wait, miss, wait," Liza implored. "Don't move until I've got this last hook done up."

"But I want to see," Evie cried, in an agony of suspense, her back to the dressing mirror. "Oh, do hurry, Liza, please."

Delia, fully dressed and watching from the doorway, laughed. "Really, Evie, darling, when are you going to give a nod to etiquette and address Moore here in the proper way?"

"But it seems so unfriendly to call someone by only their surname," she protested, trying not to fidget as the maid fastened the last hook beneath her armpit. "Blame it on my middle-class upbringing."

"There, I've finally got it," Liza said and stepped back. "You can look now."

"No, she can't," Delia cried before Evie could turn around. "We have to wait for Chapman."

Evie groaned at the additional delay, but before she could ask why on earth they had to wait for Delia's maid, Chapman herself came bustling in. "Here at last, my lady."

"Finally!" Delia cried, turning as her maid crossed to her side. "I began to fear the hotel had lost them somehow."

"Sorry, my lady. There was a long line of ladies' maids at the concierge. Lots of balls tonight, it seems."

"What is that?" Evie asked, leaning closer.

"Something of mine for you to wear, darling. I had Chapman fetch it from the hotel vault."

The maid opened the box, and Evie gasped at the stunning necklace of emeralds set in gold that was nestled inside. "I'm to wear that? Are those real emeralds?"

Delia laughed. "Have you wear paste jewels to your first ball? Never! Of course they're real."

"Goodness," Evie breathed, feeling giddy as Chapman slipped the necklace around her neck. "The only jewel I've ever worn is my mother's carnelian ring, and that's only at Christmas. Can I look now?" she asked, the question ending on a plaintive note. "If you say no," she added at once, "I'm looking anyway."

Delia smiled and placed her hands on her shoulders. "Yes, darling, you can look now."

Evie turned to face the mirror and stared, completely stupefied by what she saw.

The gown, pale jade silk shot with threads of gold, shimmered in the light, giving her skin an almost ethereal glow and sparking the amber and gold glints in her hazel eyes. Vivienne's design had eschewed the enormous leg-o'mutton sleeves that were so ubiquitous now in favor of absurdly small scraps of silk that skimmed the very edge of each shoulder in a way that was modern and fresh and scandalously daring.

Her hair, a riot of curls piled high on her head with a few loose tendrils framing her face, was secured with gold-studded hairpins, each stud shaped like a rose. She'd always thought of her hair as boring, but now, with the gold of the roses to enhance the mink-brown strands, she realized her hair didn't have to be boring at all. She could only hope Liza had used enough of those pins to keep it all from tumbling down in the middle of the ball.

Emeralds glittered at her throat, falling in cascades to the plunging neckline of her gown, so dazzling that she blinked. "Heavens!" she cried, laughing in amazement, feeling a bit dizzy as she stared at her reflection. "Maybe I really am Cinderella."

"Just as long as you remember you don't have to dash off at midnight," Delia replied. "In fact, you won't be leaving until at least four o'clock. You have to stay all the way to the last waltz."

"Only if I've danced every other dance until then," Evie reminded, nervously fingering the blank dance card and tiny pencil attached to her wrist.

"You'll have every man in that room clamoring for a dance," Delia told her with a breezy assurance she could not share. "What do you think, Moore? Will the gentlemen think she's the prettiest girl at the ball or not?"

"Well, I'm not the one to ask about gentlemen's opinions, ma'am, really, since I've never had a suitor in my life until a few weeks ago. But," she added, turning to Evie, "you do look ever so lovely."

"Thank you, Liza. Tell me about your young man. Is he handsome?"

"Oh, yes, miss." Liza's round, currant-bun face lit up. "Hair like gold, he's got, and the bluest eyes."

"Ooh," Delia and Evie said together, laughing when Liza blushed.

"As for your dance card, Evie, dear," Delia said, "I'll make a wager of my own tonight that it'll be full before we're even past the reception line. Speaking of which," she added with a glance at the clock on the wall, "we'd best go down. The dancing starts in half an hour."

With those words, a jolt of sudden panic twisted Evie's insides, but she knew she couldn't run away from this. It was time to face the slights and injuries of the past that had been hampering her for so long. Time to face them, conquer them, and lay them to rest. She'd known that from the moment she'd seen Arlena and Lenore smirking at her in Vivienne's showroom.

Taking a deep breath, she turned from the mirror. "I'm ready," she said and meant it. "No matter what happens."

But a few minutes later, she was proved a liar, for when she stepped through the doors of the Savoy's glittering Lancaster Ballroom, she was not the least bit ready for the mob of young men who surrounded her. And though Delia's prediction didn't quite come to pass, they weren't in the reception line more than a few minutes before Evie had already penciled the names of Lord Ashvale, Edward Harbisher, Ronald Anstruther, and five other men she'd met during the past few weeks onto her dance card.

"Was I right?" Delia asked, leaning closer to peer at the list of names as they approached the front of the line where Max was greeting the arriving guests.

"Only half right," Evie told her, laughing. "Eight dances so far. Heavens, what a relief to know I won't be a wallflower."

"You, a wallflower? What nonsense! As I told you before, Max knows a beautiful woman when he sees one."

"I certainly do."

Both she and Delia looked up to find Max standing in front of them, and at her first sight of him since that extraordinary afternoon at the house party, Evie's heart skipped at least three beats.

He looked splendid, of course, in his white tie and tails, but that wasn't what quickened her heartbeat. He was smiling, a knowing little smile that tipped the edges of his mouth and creased the corners of his eyes, but still, that wasn't what made her throat go dry and her knees go wobbly. No, it was his eyes. When she looked into them, the tenderness and passion she saw in their midnight-blue depths sent the room spinning, as if she were in his arms and they were waltzing again at Westbourne House.

*All I want is to kiss you and touch you.*

His ardent words of two weeks ago came roaring back, so real that it was almost as if he'd said them again, here, just now.

"But then," he went on, stepping closer to her as Delia moved past him, "I'm not sure beautiful is the way I'd describe you."

"No?" She gave a shaky laugh. "What word would you use then?"

His lashes lowered as he looked down, then lifted as he met her gaze. "Incomparable."

Joy rose up inside her, an exhilarating, dizzying wave of joy, and she laughed again. "Let's hope at least eight more men share your view and ask me to dance. I dearly want to win that bet."

"Do you, now?" he drawled. "And to think, two months ago, you laughed at me and told me I was—How did you put it? Blind as a bat?"

She had said that, she realized, remembering it. She'd scoffed at Max's contention that she could be transformed into a beauty, but now, looking into his eyes full of longing, hearing his passionate words of two weeks ago echo in her head, her lips tingling as she remembered his kiss and his touch, she knew it didn't matter if anyone else in this room thought she was a beauty or as homely as a mud fence. For the first time in her life, she *felt* beautiful, and that wasn't because of clothes or jewels or a dance card full of names. No, she felt beautiful because of the yearning she saw in one man's eyes.

The ball was nearly over. Many guests had already departed, and the last waltz was minutes away. Evie had danced every dance, and though the shock of Freddie and the Banforth brothers was satisfying indeed, it was nothing compared to the satisfaction Max felt knowing that Evie could put the designation of wallflower behind her for good. Even the fact that she was currently bestowing that dizzying smile of hers on Edward Harbisher rather than on him could not dampen his pleasure at her success.

"Well, Duke," Timothy Banforth said beside him as he watched Evie on the ballroom floor with Harbisher, "only one more dance, and you'll have won."

That wasn't going to be the outcome, but Max didn't say so. He merely smiled.

"We never thought you'd do it," Thomas Banforth said from his other side.

"I did nothing," Max said, without taking his eyes from Evie. "Like a jewel, all she needed was the proper setting in order to shine. I tried to tell you that."

"And you were right," Timothy said. "The girl's far prettier than any of us gave her credit for, and I think we can all admit the fact—even Freddie, here."

"I will admit it," Freddie said, moving in front of him, and forcing Max to lean around him to keep watching Evie as the music ended and Harbisher escorted her back to Delia's side. "Of all the girls in London, I'd never have thought her to have a partner for every single dance tonight. Never."

"And," Thomas said, "since I see Ronald Anstruther headed in her direction, looking very purposeful, I think it's time to admit defeat."

"Don't concede yet, gentlemen," Max told them and set aside his glass of tepid rum punch. "For if I have my way, I'm about to lose."

He didn't wait for a reply. Instead, he stepped around Freddie and walked away, making for Evie. Thankfully, he reached her before Anstruther. Bowing in front of her, he said, "May I have this dance?"

Evie stared at him, her eyes wide, her lips parting in shock.

Beside her, Delia laughed. "You never cease to surprise me, Cousin."

"Evie?" He held out his hand. "Will you?"

She stirred, glancing past his shoulder. "I can't," she said, a regret in her voice he found immensely gratifying. "I've promised the last waltz to Ronald Anstruther. He's headed this way right now to claim me."

"Is that the only reason you refuse?"

"Of course," she whispered. "How could you think otherwise?"

Ronald joined them before he could reply, but Max had no intention of being gainsaid now.

"Then it's a problem easily solved," he told her, and turned to Ronald. "Sorry, old chap," he said and took Evie's hand in his. "Ducal privilege."

He pulled her with him onto the dance floor. "See how easy that was?" he said, smiling into her astonished face as he bowed.

"Max, you just lost the bet."

"So I did," he replied and straightened. "You have to curtsy to me. It's expected, and everyone's watching us."

She dipped at the knees, the barest courtesy required. "But why?"

He took her hand in his and slid his other hand to the

small of her back. "Evie," he said tenderly. "After what happened between us at Idyll Hour, did you really think I could pass up the chance to hold you in my arms again?"

She had no chance to reply, for at that moment, the music began, and he started off, pulling her with him, and it wasn't until they had made several turns around the ballroom floor that she spoke.

"Why are you doing this? Why dance with me? Why talk of holding me in your arms when you're going to marry Lady Helen? Why aren't you dancing with her?"

"Well, for one thing, she's not here. She's at the embassy ball in honor of Prince Olaf. She's dancing with him at this very moment, I daresay."

"Don't tease me, Max. Don't make jokes."

"I'm not joking. I mean what I say. And I'm not going to marry Helen."

"You're not?"

He shook his head. "I can't. Not now. You see, Evie, you've revealed me to myself. You've made me realize that no matter how I've tried to believe otherwise, I can't marry just because it's suitable."

"Like Rory and me." She sighed. "I ought to be sorry, I suppose, that I ruined your plans."

He had a new plan now, one he'd made that fateful afternoon in the library at Idyll Hour, one that was his only choice if he didn't want to go mad. But he couldn't tell it to Evie, for if he did, she'd probably bolt for the nearest door.

"Are you really sorry, Evie?" he said instead. "Because I'm not."

She bit her lip, and she took so long to answer that he thought she wasn't going to. "No," she said at last. "I should be, but I'm not. You see..."

She paused, lowering her gaze. "You see, I've been wanting it, too," she said, her voice so low that over the music, he barely heard.

"Wanting what?"

"You know," she whispered, staring at his chin, blushing as she spoke. "What you said."

Oh, God. He was coming undone right here on the dance floor. He wanted, so badly, to kiss her. To stop dancing and haul her into his arms right now and wrap his arms around her and taste her mouth as he had at Westbourne House. To touch her and caress her as he had at Idyll Hour, and so much more. He wanted all of it, tonight, tomorrow night, and every night beyond. He wanted to see that smile of hers a dozen times a day, every day, until his eyes closed forever and they put him in the ground.

But he wasn't the same man he'd been a decade ago, ready to believe that passion, however strong, made for love that lasted forever. He also knew that what he really wanted with Evie could not be forced into being. True love, the kind that lasted a lifetime, could not be rushed. It had to be earned. And so, when the music stopped, he didn't pull her into his arms. He escorted her back to her place in the proper manner, bowed, and walked away. It was the hardest thing he'd ever done in his life.

Two hours later, as dawn was breaking, he lay in bed, staring at the ceiling, making plans for the future, even as he still ached with longing. He thought of how it would have to be: two years of walks accompanied by chaperones, dinner parties where they sat miles apart, only two dances together at balls, and all the other wretched customs of a proper courtship, and it was almost more than he could bear. He turned onto his belly with a groan and wondered if perhaps he could persuade Delia to look the other way once in a while and let him pull Evie into a darkened corner for some passionate kissing.

But what if, after a proper courtship, she still wouldn't marry him? What if, after two years of showing her what life with him would be like, he couldn't convince her to become his duchess? What then?

Even as he asked himself that question, his heart rejected the possibility. Failure was simply not an option. He'd persuade her, somehow.

Suddenly, he heard a soft knock at the door of his suite. At this hour? Frowning, he lifted his head, wondering if he'd imagined it, but then, it came again, and Max got out of bed.

Wrapping his naked body in a dressing gown, he left the bedroom and walked to the door, knowing it had to be Stowell, though why his valet would presume to awaken him at six o'clock in the morning, he couldn't imagine.

But when he opened the door, he found that it wasn't Stowell waiting on the other side. It was, in fact, the last person in the world he'd have expected.

"Evie?" He blinked twice, but she was still there. "What the devil?"

She'd changed out of her ballroom finery into a loose-fitting tea gown, and her hair was down, caught in a braid down her back, as if she'd been getting ready for bed and had then changed her mind.

"Evie, what are you doing here at this hour?"

She grimaced at the raised note of his voice and pressed a finger to his lips. "Shh, not so loud," she admonished in a whisper.

The touch of her fingers was almost more than he could bear, and he took a long step back.

She seemed to take that as an invitation, and she followed him, closing the distance. "I needed to talk to you."

With that one touch from her, desire had already started spreading through his body, and the last thing he wanted was a conversation. When she moved as if to take another step into his room, he didn't fall back, forcing her to remain on the threshold. "You can't be here," he said. "What if someone catches you standing here outside my room? Where's Delia?"

"Sound asleep, of course, and so is everyone else in the hotel, most likely."

"Except you," he pointed out tersely. "And me."

As if to prove them both wrong, murmured voices floated down the corridor, and with a muttered oath, he grabbed her arm, hauled her completely inside before whoever was talking could come around the corner and see them, and closed the door.

"Evie, listen. Whatever it is you want to talk to me about, it has to wait until morning."

For some reason, that made her smile. "Max, it is morning. It's after six."

He couldn't share her amusement. "All the more reason for you to go back to your own room." He moved to lean around her and reopen the door, but she stopped him, flattening a hand against his chest, and as her fingertips touched the bare skin in the vee of his dressing gown, he remembered that he was wearing nothing else. "Evie, for God's sake," he muttered and grabbed her wrists, but she replied before he could push her away.

"Max, please. This is important. In fact," she added, giving a decidedly shaky laugh, "this may be the most important thing I ever do in my life."

With a sigh of long-suffering, Max let her go, switched

on the nearest electric light, and prayed for fortitude. "I'm listening."

"Ever since the house party, I haven't been able to stop thinking about you."

Any other time, Max might have found those words quite gratifying, but just now, they weren't helpful. "Evie," he began.

"Over and over, I thought about what you said. About what you wanted..." She paused, her cheeks flushing a delicate pink, and she ducked her head. "And I told you earlier tonight that I want it, too. The...the kissing and...well...you know."

How could he not know? The very same desires that had inspired his torrid words at Idyll Hour were raging in him now, and if he didn't get her out of here soon, what he had been imagining would become reality, and not in the honorable way he'd intended. He had a plan, damn it, and this wasn't it. Courtship was the goal. Not fornication.

But even as he reminded himself of all that, she moved closer, and he felt his control slipping. Desperate, he worked to shore it up again. "No, you don't want that. You can't. Hell, I doubt you even know what I really meant by what I said."

"Of course I know what you meant," she said, sounding a little indignant. "I'm not a child. You want to lie with me. Well," she added before he could even express shock at such blunt speaking from an innocent like her. "Well, I want that, too. Max, I'm leaving soon. Tomorrow, or perhaps the day after, I have to return to my old life."

"No, you don't. You have connections now, and Delia said she'd chaperone you—"

"Oh, Max," she cut him off, smiling, shaking her head. "This holiday has been wonderful, the most romantic, beautiful two months of my life, but that's all it is, and we both know it."

He didn't know anything of the kind. But how could he argue the point in a way that didn't show his hand too plainly? If she had any inkling his intention was to make her his duchess, she'd panic and bolt, or laugh in his face, or—worst of all—she'd harden her resolve against the idea so completely, he might never convince her. No, this had to be done gradually, easing her into the idea of becoming a duchess.

Before he could decide what to say, she closed the distance between them and cupped his face in her hands. "That's why I'm here," she said softly. "I've never had a romance before, and given the circumstances of my life, I doubt I ever will again. And we have one night left. So, I'm here to give both of us what we've been yearning for before it's too late."

She rose on her toes and kissed his mouth, and with that, all of Max's resistance crumbled to dust. Honorable courtship, he decided as his arms wrapped around her, could start tomorrow.

# 18

He might be weak as water where she was concerned, but that didn't mean he was about to abandon the patient tenderness of courtship. In fact, making love with Evie was going to require every bit of patience he could muster, so that he could make it as tender and gentle as he'd intended his courtship of her to be. He forced himself to pull back.

"If we do this, there's no going back," he said, impelled one last time to caution her. "Once it's done, it can't be undone."

She nodded. "I know."

"All right, then." Banking his lust as best he could, he took her hand in his. "Come with me."

He led her into his bedroom, pausing at the foot of the bed. "Wait here," he said and pressed a quick kiss to her mouth. "I'll be right back."

He walked to the dressing table and opened his toiletry case, rummaging amid the contents, hoping Stowell had packed the one little thing he really hadn't thought he'd be needing this season. When his fingers closed around the slim velvet box at the bottom, he let out a sigh of relief, decided his valet deserved a raise, and pulled the box out of his case.

"What's that?" she asked as he returned to stand in front of her.

He opened it, revealing the flattened wisp of vulcanized rubber and silk ribbon nestled within a crimson velvet lining. "It's called a French letter."

"Oh, a condom?"

He gave a shout of laughter. "Evie, you never stop surprising me."

"I don't know why you're surprised. I'm quite well-read, you know."

"Yes, but this isn't the sort of thing innocent women usually read about." He pulled it out, enabling her to have a better look at it before he put it back in the box. "Given your extensive literary knowledge, I'm sure I don't even have to ask, but is there anything you'd like me to explain before we start?"

She shook her head and looked up. "I don't think so."

He nodded, then he moved to the side of the bed, where he placed the box under his pillow.

"There is one thing I ought to tell you," he said as he returned to stand opposite her and took her hands in his. "It might hurt, Evie. Sometimes it does, for women. But if so, it's only the first time," he rushed on. "After that, it doesn't. And if there's anything I do that you don't like or don't want, or if you want me to stop at any point, just tell me so. And I'll stop." He drew a profound, shaky breath. "I'll stop."

"I won't ask you to." She smiled. "Not now, not after coming here and flinging myself at you so shamelessly."

"Just so you know, you can."

"Remember what you told me you wanted to do to me that afternoon at Idyll Hour?"

He had only the vaguest recollection of the actual words in his frenzied, passionate declaration that day, but the essence of it he could hardly forget, especially since he was aching with it right now. "Yes."

"Good." She lifted their joined hands, pulling his to her breasts. "Because it's time for you to do it. All of it."

He opened his palms over her breasts, making a sound of appreciation as he realized that this time there was no confining corset to get in the way, but as he cupped and shaped them against his palms, he knew it wasn't enough. He had to see them.

He slid his hands out from beneath hers and looked down, but though the light spilling through the doorway from the sitting room enabled him to see well enough, the flounces of lace that trimmed her gown made it impossible for him to find any hooks or buttons. "Help me, Evie. How do I unfasten this thing?"

"I thought you knew all about women's clothes," she said, laughing a little.

"I thought I did, but as I said, you continually surprise me."

She pulled the ends of a bow at her waist, drawing apart what he saw now was a pelisse of sorts that covered a separate gown beneath. "Ah," he said when she turned around and let the pelisse fall to the floor, revealing a row of pearl buttons down her back. "Now I see."

She laughed softly as he unfastened the first button, making him smile.

"Why are you laughing?" he asked.

"When you insisted I get a maid to undress me, I never thought it would be you."

He grinned. "Neither did I, though I spent many agonizing hours imagining that scenario." As he slid the pearl buttons free of their holes, he caught a glimpse of her bare skin and caught his breath, realizing that not only was she not wearing a corset under the gown, she wasn't wearing anything at all.

*Evie, you clever, naughty girl,* he thought, leaning closer as he pulled the gown off her shoulders, inhaling bergamot scent as he pressed his lips to the side of her throat, relishing the shiver she gave in response.

More of the same pretty golden freckles that dusted her face were scattered over her shoulders and he wanted to kiss them all, but he knew they didn't have time for that, not now. Within a couple of hours, people would begin waking, and though Delia's suite was only a few doors down the corridor, he didn't want anyone to see her slipping out of his room and back to her own. Reluctantly, he pulled back.

Reaching for the plait of her hair, he untied the ribbon and unraveled the braid, spreading the long, silken strands apart, then he turned her around. As he did, her arms immediately went up between them, folding across her breasts to hide them.

"No, Evie, no," he chided softly, his hands clasping her wrists. "Don't hide your breasts from me. I want to see them."

She was blushing, a rosy wash of color across her face and neck, and when he pulled to spread her arms apart, he could feel the resistance in her, and he stopped.

"Evie," he murmured, "I've been imagining this for weeks. Don't deprive me of the chance to see the reality."

"I don't..." She paused, licking her dry lips nervously even as she slackened in his hold. "They're just so small. I don't want you to be disappointed."

"That," he said gently as he spread her arms apart, "would be impossible."

Only one glance proved that his imagination had not played him false at all, and he had to swallow hard before he could say so. "This just goes to show women are hopeless about judging these things," he said, his voice unsteady. "They are small, yet round and sweet, with the prettiest pink nipples—" His voice utterly failed him at that point, but the words he'd managed to utter proved to be enough.

"Pretty?" She looked up, a hint of wonder in her voice. "Really?"

"Don't sound so surprised," he said and drew her closer, sliding his arm around her waist. "As Delia told you, I know a beautiful woman when I see one."

She laughed, but then, he bent his head, and her laughter ended in a gasp as he kissed her breast, her head tilting back, the ends of her hair tickling his wrist.

He savored the moment, then drew back, his hands grasping handfuls of her gown to pull it down her hips, wanting to see the rest of her, but Evie, of course, confounded him again. Taking his wrists, she pulled his hands down, stopping him. "Wait."

He froze, agonized. "Evie?" he murmured and pulled back to look at her, praying she wasn't losing her nerve.

She hesitated, biting her lip, driving him mad. "Don't I get the same chance?" she whispered at last.

By the time his lust-drugged senses figured out she was not calling a halt, she had already reached for the sash of his dressing gown, and as she untied it, his worry dissolved and he laughed.

"Want a peek, do you?" he asked, and when she nodded, he spread his arms wide, allowing her to pull the edges of his dressing gown apart. "Look your fill."

"Oh." The pink in her cheeks deepened to scarlet, and her eyes went round as she stared at his flagrant arousal. "Ohhhh."

Fearing she might be losing her nerve, he opened his mouth to offer a reassuring word, but then she lifted her gaze to his and said in an aggrieved voice, "Statues don't look at all like you."

He laughed. He couldn't help it. She was the most unexpected woman he'd ever known.

She laughed, too, showing him that smile as she leaned closer, spreading her hands across his bare chest, and his laughter ended in a groan of pleasure. "Go on," he urged when she stilled, looking at him in sudden uncertainty. "Go on. Touch me."

She complied, running her hands across his shoulders, along his arms, and over his ribs, then she stilled, her hands curling at his waist as she leaned in and pressed a kiss to his chest.

"I think you're beautiful, too," she whispered.

His heart twisted, constricting with powerful emotions—fear because he knew he'd fall off that pedestal one day, and hope that when he did, the reality would be enough to make her happy.

Her hands slid down, her fingertips grazing his belly and moving even lower. That he couldn't allow, for if he did, her first time would be far too quick and far less romantic than she deserved.

"That's enough," he said and grasped her wrists, drawing her hands away and sinking to his knees. "Stop teasing me."

He grasped her foot in his hands. "I almost wish you had stockings on," he said and slid off her slipper.

"Why?" she asked, giving a shaky laugh. "So you could take them off?"

"Yes. The day I came to your shop to inquire about the dinner party," he went on as he tossed aside her shoe and began removing the other one, "I watched you step up on a ladder, and I caught a glimpse of a very pretty little red garter."

"You saw my garter?"

"I did, and to me, it proved beyond doubt that despite what Freddie and his friends believed, you weren't the least bit prim. In fact, it led me to think perhaps there was a very naughty girl under that shirtwaist and necktie."

"I'm not the least bit naughty!" she protested.

"No?" He chuckled, tossing her second shoe to join the first one as he looked up at her. "My darling Evie," he said tenderly, "if you weren't at least a little bit naughty, you wouldn't be here."

Having established that irrefutable point, he slowly began gliding his hands up the backs of her legs. "It was that red garter, by the way, that started my imagination thinking how it would be to make love with you."

As he spoke, his fingertips skimmed over the backs of her knees, and she wobbled a little on her feet, making him pause. "Ah," he murmured, tickling her there, "like that, do you?" He grinned as she gave a shivering gasp.

"If we had time," he murmured, "I'd kiss you there, and every inch of your gorgeous legs, all the way from your pretty feet to your shapely bum. But that, my sweet, will have to wait for another day. Right now, I have something else in mind."

He straightened on his knees. Cupping one of her breasts in his hand, he leaned in, opening his mouth over the other, flicking his tongue over her turgid nipple. She gasped, her head tilting back, her hands raking through his hair to cradle his head.

He caressed her and toyed with her, shaping her breasts, suckling her nipples until she was moaning low in her throat and her body was quivering. Pulling back, he yanked her gown down the rest of the way and slid an arm around the backs of her thighs, pressing a kiss to her stomach.

She stirred in agitation, but his arm tightened around her hips, anchoring her in place as he kissed her again a little lower, then lower still.

Her fingers worked convulsively in his hair, and she began to whimper, stirring in his hold, her hips instinctively trying to move, but he wouldn't let her, tightening his hold to increase the tension.

"Max," she wailed softly in protest. "Oh, oh, oh."

He moved an inch lower, and kissed her again, his lips grazing the apex of her thighs.

She jerked, crying out in shock. "Max, oh, don't!"

He stilled, his breath tickling her curls. "Evie," he said, his voice a bit unsteady, "I've dreamed of kissing you here, touching you here. Let me do this."

She hesitated, then her hold slackened, her body relented. "All right," she whispered, and he lowered his arm, easing her back an inch or two until she was up against the bed.

"Grab the footboard behind you," he said, and when she did, he leaned in, nuzzling her. "Part your thighs."

She complied, and he slid his hand between her legs, his finger probing the crease of her sex. She was soft and wet, and the scent of her made him dizzy. He caressed her again, and again, until her hips were moving in frantic jerks and soft, primitive cries were coming from her throat. Then, at last, he drew his hand back, nuzzled between her thighs, and ever so gently grazed her clitoris with his tongue.

She came almost at once, long, sweet sobs of feminine release, her body shuddering, her hips jerking against his mouth, but he didn't stop. He lashed her with his tongue until she came again, and then again, until at last she collapsed, letting go of the brass footboard as her knees gave way.

He caught her as he stood up, lifting her into his arms. She wrapped her arms around his neck, her breath coming in gasps hot and quick against his throat as he carried her to the bed and laid her on the sheets.

She stared up at him, stunned. No biology text, no erotic poetry, nor any other words she'd ever read had prepared her for what had just happened. That sweet, hot tension, a bit like what she'd felt every time she'd thought of his impassioned words at Idyll Hour, only so much stronger, building and building until her entire body was on fire, and then...explosions of sensation, one after another, again and again. Even now, she still felt it, tiny convulsions deep inside.

But there was more to come. Even if she hadn't known it, Max's hot, intense gaze would have told her so as he slid his dressing gown off his shoulders.

The mattress dipped with his weight as he lay down beside her. Reaching under his pillow, he pulled out the box, removed the condom, and tossed the box on the floor beside the bed. Her gaze slid down his naked body to his groin, and as he slid the condom over his hard arousal, she remembered his words about pain, and for the first time, she felt a jolt of nervousness. "Max?"

He seemed to sense it, for he rolled to his side and reached out to caress her cheek. "If you want to stop, Evie, please tell me now," he said, his eyes hungry with need, his voice surprisingly gentle. "If you tell me later," he added, smiling a little, "I fear it'll rip me in half."

The admission and the smile disarmed her, and her

nervousness passed as quickly as it had come. She smiled back at him, curling her hand behind his neck. "I don't want to back out," she whispered as she pulled him close and kissed him.

He groaned against her mouth, rolling his body against hers, pushing her onto her back, then he eased on top of her, the hard shape of his penis pushing against her. She opened her legs, and he slid between them.

He rested his weight on one arm, and as he looked down at her, that wayward lock of his hair fell over his forehead. She reached up, smiling a little as she drew it between her fingers. "Your valet's despair," she murmured.

His brows drew together in a puzzled little frown, but he didn't give her time to explain. Sliding his hand between their bodies, he touched her where he had before, a brief caress, and then he lowered his weight onto her, moving his hips against hers. As the hard ridge of his penis rubbed against the place he'd kissed her so erotically a few minutes ago, the friction sent renewed pleasure washing through her, and she moaned his name.

"Evie, my darling," he whispered, his voice harsher now, his breathing heavier as the tip of his penis pressed against her, then into her.

She wriggled beneath him, uncomfortable, trying to adjust her body to this invasion. The movement seemed to ignite something in him, for he made a rough sound deep in his throat and came down fully onto her, capturing her mouth in a hard kiss as he thrust his hips against hers, bringing him fully into her.

He'd warned her, but nonetheless, the pain hit her like a stinging slap deep inside, and she gave a squeal against his mouth, her eyes opening in shock, the heels of her hands pressing instinctively against his shoulders.

Then he was pulling back, pressing kisses to her face. "Evie, Evie, it'll be all right," he said. "It'll be all right. I swear it will."

"I think this is going to be a bit like dancing for me, Max," she whispered, forcing a laugh, but it was shaky to her ears.

He heard it, too, for he kissed her. A long, slow, deep kiss. "Are you all right?"

She took a deep breath and nodded. "I think so."

He kissed her again, then lowered himself onto her and rocked his hips, sliding his shaft into her, then pulling back, again and again, and as he did, the pain began to ease, giving way to a rising, thickening pleasure.

She started to move, trying to match his rhythm, and as she did, he groaned, making her smile, for she knew she was pleasing him, as he had pleased her, and she liked that. She worked her hips, trying to enhance his pleasure.

It must have worked, for he slid his arms beneath her as if he wanted to bring her even closer, and he quickened the pace, his thrusts becoming harder and deeper, his breathing ragged against her hair. With each thrust, her own pleasure rose higher, too, and then, suddenly, she felt it—that white-hot, convulsive explosion—and she cried out, holding him tight, all her muscles tightening around his shaft.

He cried out as well and thrust against her several more times, then he went still, his body settling on hers. Breathing hard, he buried his face against her neck.

She stroked him, relishing the hard, smooth muscles of his back beneath her palms, feeling a sweet, tender bliss she'd never felt in her life before. It was heavenly.

But, of course, it couldn't last.

Stirring, he rose up on his arms. "We need to get you

back to your room before anyone sees you. If Delia wakes up and finds you gone..."

She nodded. "Of course."

He rolled off the bed, held out his hand, and pulled her up. As he helped her dress, the blissful euphoria began to fade, and by the time he had fastened the last button, Evie felt an absurd desire to cry, not out of regret for the choice she had made to come here and be with him, but because she knew that this was the end.

It had been wonderful and magical, all of it, from the moment he'd first told her she could be a beauty, through the champagne and the dancing, and this sweet, wondrous thing with him called lovemaking. But now, it was midnight, metaphorically speaking, and Cinderella was about to leave the fairy tale and go back to reality.

At the door, he drew her into his arms, and his kiss was so tender that the moment it was over, she had to turn away so he wouldn't see the pain in her face.

"Good night, Evie," he said behind her as she opened the door, but she didn't reply, not until she was walking down the corridor and she heard his door close behind her.

Then, only then, did she stop, turn, and look back.

"Goodbye, Max," she said, and with those words, something inside her cracked, threatening to break her apart.

Immediately, she stiffened, reminding herself that she'd known all along this day would come, that she would have to go back to her old life. What she hadn't known, what she could never have foreseen, was that leaving his life and going back to her own would feel as if she were tearing herself in half.

# 19

⁂

$\mathcal{M}$ ax woke from a heavy, blissful sleep, hauled into consciousness by a knock on his door. Unlike the soft tap Evie had made a few hours earlier, however, this was an absolute pounding, loud enough to disturb not only his rest but that of everyone else in the corridor.

"What the devil?" he muttered, tossing back the counterpane and once again reaching for his dressing gown.

"Max!" Delia's voice, muffled but holding a decidedly frantic note, came to him through the door as he crossed the sitting room, tying the sash of his robe and trying to come out of the delicious dream he'd been having about feeding peaches to a naked Evie on an Arabian carpet.

"Max?" More pounding ensued. "Max, are you in there?"

Deprived of both his dream and his much-needed sleep, he yanked open the door, feeling both sluggish and cross. "Delia, for God's sake," he muttered, rubbing his eyes, "are you trying to wake the dead?"

"So it would seem, since I've been standing out here

pounding away for ages." She didn't wait to be invited in but shoved her way past him. "I was beginning to fear you'd already heard and the shock caused you to keel over. And given what's happened, that's quite a reasonable assumption on my part, although—"

"What are you talking about?" he interrupted, wide awake now. "What's happened?"

"Evie's gone. She must have left early this morning."

Max's gaze slid to the bedroom door, thinking of last night. "She's probably just gone out," he said, looking again at his cousin. "To the shop, or something."

Delia shook her head. "I woke to find a note of farewell from her on the mantel. And her clothes are gone—her old ones. She left her new ones behind. Not that I blame her for that after what's happened."

Max frowned, realizing this was the second time Delia had referred to some catastrophic event. "Damn it, Delia, what are you rattling on about?"

"This." She pulled a newspaper from under her arm, one he'd been too somnolent to notice until now, and thrust it at him. "Today's edition of *Talk of the Town*."

"That gossip rag?" he muttered, taking it from her fingers. "What could possibly be so important about—"

He stopped, his half-formed question answered as he read the headline splashed across the front page.

*DUKE OF WESTBOURNE? OR DUKE OF SEDUCTION?*

He scanned the words below the headline, trying to assimilate their meaning, but his wits felt thick like tar. Something about torrid letters and clandestine meetings and Evie Harlow.

He let out the foulest oath he knew.

"My sentiments, exactly." Delia leaned forward, her

finger tapping the paper. "They know you bought Evie's clothes—"

"What? How?"

"I don't know, but it's there. If she read that, it would explain why she left the clothes behind, although I don't think Evie's really the sort to read the scandal sheets. Either way, the accusation in the paper seems to be that while courting Lady Helen, you've also seduced dear Evie, making her your mistress. And that you did it all behind Helen's back, making a fool of her, and me, and all of society."

"Helen has no claim on me, nor I on her," he cut in, feeling the need to say something, and deciding it was best to start with the one thing he could absolutely refute. "There is no romantic understanding between Helen and me. Things never got far enough for that, and Helen would be the first to say so. She's angling for a far better catch than me anyway, trust me on that."

"And Evie?" She gestured to the paper. "There is mention of secret meetings at your house, arranged between the pair of you. You and Evie? It's absurd. I can't think of two people less likely to engage in such a tawdry arrangement. Where do they get such ridiculous ideas?"

Guilt lashed him like a whip. Those arrangements had all been his, and his alone. She'd said it was wrong, that she couldn't meet him alone, that it wasn't proper, but he'd waved aside such pesky, inconvenient notions of morality, persuading her to come anyway.

"It says," Delia went on in the wake of his silence, "that you deliberately introduced the girl into society to cover the affair you two were conducting. And they're not sure, they say, if you ruined an innocent girl and made her a strumpet, or if she was a strumpet already, with an eye for the main chance, but they are determined to find out the truth. Truth?" she added with a sound of contempt. "They wouldn't know truth if it bit them. Evie is as innocent as a lamb. As for you, I know you would never, ever ruin a girl—"

She broke off, and he knew something in his countenance must have given him away. "My God," she whispered, staring at him in horror, a slow, dawning awareness coming into her expression. "You mean, some of this dross is actually *true*?"

"Of course not. At least—"

He broke off, appreciating that there was no way to explain or justify. It had all seemed such a lark at first, but from the moment he'd kissed Evie on the ballroom floor at Westbourne House, everything had changed, and though she was too much of an innocent to appreciate that fact, he had no such excuse. He ought to have put a stop to the whole thing then and there, but God help him, he just hadn't had the will. From that moment on, he'd wanted her too much for common sense, too much for caution, too much even for chivalry. And Evie was now paying the price.

In the silence, Delia stared at him, appalled, grasping the gist of what he had not said. "Oh, Max," she said with a sigh, "what have you done?"

He tore his gaze away, looking at the scandal sheet in his hand, knowing that by tomorrow, it wouldn't be the only one speculating about Evie's character and smearing her reputation. So much for a lengthy, proper courtship. In light of this story, there was no time for such a thing.

She'd already lost her virginity to him. Now, if he could not persuade her to marry him, she would also lose her good name. She'd be ruined because of him, probably for life. He could not, he would not, allow that to happen to her.

"Max, what are you going to do?"

He looked up, meeting the concern and disappointment in her eyes with a hard, determined look of his own. "Isn't it obvious?"

Without waiting for an answer, he dropped the paper onto the table by the door. "Where is Evie now?"

"I don't know. As I told you, when I got up a few hours ago, she was already gone. She's at her shop, I suppose. She may know about this by now. But she may not."

He nodded. "I'll go see her straightaway. You'd better get busy, too, Delia," he added as he turned away and started for his room. "You've got a wedding to plan."

Everything seemed just the same.

Evie leaned back against the counter of the shop, hands curled around her afternoon cup of tea, studying her surroundings with a vague sense of surprise.

She'd barely bothered to glance around on her arrival in the dim light of dawn. Instead, she'd gone straight upstairs to her flat, dropped her suitcase to the floor, and fallen into her new bed for some much-needed sleep. But now, in the mellow light of late afternoon, refreshed from her long nap, with a cup of strong tea in her hand, she was able to get a good look at her surroundings, and as she did, her first impression was that nothing much had really changed—an odd feeling to have, considering that the renovations had been extensive, and all the furnishings rearranged.

Not that she wasn't pleased by what she saw. Quite the contrary. The old, peeling cabbage-rose wallpaper had been replaced with a lighter, less stodgy pattern of blue-and-white toile that went beautifully with the bookshelves, which were now polished and gleaming. The ceiling had received a fresh coat of plaster, the worn oak floor had been sanded, waxed, and buffed to a soft glow, and the paintings on the walls, though never great works of art, were at least clean and bright. Her flat upstairs was no longer painted a drab and boring beige, but a fresh, crisp white, and all her damaged furnishings had been replaced, including her mattress, which was now every bit as thick and luxurious as anything at the Savoy.

Her fingers tightened around her cup. Best not to think of the Savoy and of what had happened there. It was over. And life went on.

A better life than before, she decided, looking around. A life where she stepped out of her shell sometimes and tried new things. Maybe, she thought, she could add a rack of newspapers and magazines to the shop. Papa would have hated that, but Papa wasn't here, and periodicals would bring in some additional income. And perhaps she'd start selling some of the newest novels as well. Harlow's had gained its reputation as a purveyor of rare books, but that didn't have to be all the shop was known for. Perhaps she and Anna could hold some events together—have authors in to autograph their novels for the customers, with tea and confections served next door.

Reminded of the tea in her hand, Evie took a sip, made a face, and decided there was another thing in her life that needed to change. She was no longer going to save a few pennies a week by sacrificing sugar. Feeling oddly defiant, she marched into the pantry and added three lumps to her cup, along with an extra dollop of milk.

*Have a sweet tooth, do you?*

She paused, staring down at the clouds of milk swirling in her cup as Max's words and bittersweet memories of that wonderful night at Westbourne House swirled through her mind. That was the night they had feasted on Escoffier's fantastical versions of Middle Eastern cuisine, when Max had shown her that she really wasn't such a bad dancer, when he had held her in his arms and kissed her for the first time—

With an abrupt move, she jerked the spoon out of her teacup, tapped it on the side, and set it in the dry sink. She could not think about any of that now. She had work to do.

She took her tea upstairs and unpacked, noting sadly that even the fresh coat of blue paint on her armoire could not make her old clothes look anything but drab and boring. She'd gotten spoiled, she realized, wearing those lovely, lovely clothes from Vivienne.

She paused, wondering if it had been a mistake to leave the clothes behind. But she couldn't see the point in keeping them. Her life here had no place for such elegant finery. But perhaps, she thought wistfully as she laid her folded white blouses in the armoire, she could at least buy a few new things that weren't too expensive. Anna might help her, for Anna still had some connections from her days in a dressmaker's showroom.

Her things back in the armoire and her suitcase back in the attic, Evie returned downstairs. The books, she noted as she walked between the shelves, were in good order. Clarence was responsible for that, and for keeping the workmen up to snuff during the renovations, and he'd done an excellent job of both, while still helping his mother in the confectionery. In addition to his pay, he deserved a reward for all his hard work. She could spare the money for that, given that she wasn't making mortgage payments anymore.

She stopped, her practiced eye spotting a book out of place. Chaucer didn't belong here. She pulled the volume out, moved it up a shelf, and slid it into its proper place, then continued perusing shelves. Satisfied at last that the shop would be ready to open tomorrow, she moved to the storage room, which she saw at once Clarence hadn't had time to put in the same apple-pie order as the front. Crates of books delivered during the past few weeks were stacked unopened against the wall and a large bin overflowing with rubbish left behind by the workmen stood by the back door. Unopened letters, circulars, and tradesmen's bills lay in an enormous pile atop her desk.

The work, she appreciated with a sigh, never stopped.

She sat down, but she'd barely picked up her letter opener before she set it down again, frowning as she remembered that Max's letter to her suggesting the picnic dinner at his house had not been with the other things in her dressing table when she'd packed this morning.

How could she have misplaced it?

Feeling a sudden panic that her one and only letter from a lover was missing, Evie jumped up, tossing aside the letter opener, and ran upstairs, but the letter, she soon discovered, was not in her handbag. Nor, she realized when she went up to the attic, was it tucked in her suitcase. She must have missed it somehow when she was packing this morning.

Groaning, she sank down on the edge of her bed. Now she'd have to go back and look for it, and she didn't want to do that. Just the thought of going back brought a knot to her stomach, for she knew walking away a second time would be even harder than the first time had been.

Evie closed her eyes, memories assailing her of her extraordinary night with him. Incomparable, he'd called her at the ball, and for the first time, she'd truly believed it, that she wasn't a plain-faced wallflower who couldn't dance. And later, when he'd described how her body looked to him, it had been the most beautiful thing anyone had ever done.

*Perfect*, he'd said.

That was how he saw her. And how he'd made love to her, worshipping her with his body, the scorching tenderness of his kiss and his caress transforming her into the desirable woman he thought her to be.

She would never forget that night. Never. It was the most beautiful, wonderful thing that had ever happened to her.

But then, dawn had come. Leaving him had been the hardest, most wrenching thing she'd ever done, and the only way she'd been able to endure it was to push it away. As she'd packed her clothes into her little suitcase, she'd shoved all the wonder of the night deep down inside, reminding herself over and over of the harsh realities that separated her class from his, realities they'd both learned the hard way.

When she'd finally stepped out of the Savoy and walked home in the cool light of dawn, she had fought tears the whole way, striving to accept that her extraordinary holiday with him was over.

Now, eight hours later, she was all right. She wasn't a quivering jelly of held-back tears. But if she had to go back, she feared all her efforts to put it behind her would be for naught. And yet, if anyone found that letter, read it—

A sound lifted her head, a tapping downstairs that diverted her from contemplations of the missing letter. It came again, a knock on the front door, and she stood up with a sigh. The shop was closed, the sign saying so was in the window, but customers, she knew, were sometimes a tenacious lot. She'd go down and tell whoever it was to come back tomorrow when she was open again.

But when she emerged into the front of the shop and saw who was standing on the other side of the plate glass, she knew it was not a customer.

She stopped, staring with hunger and renewed pain at Max's tall frame by the door. She couldn't let him in, for with just one glimpse of him, the composure she'd drawn around herself this morning like a protective shield was already slipping. She moved to step back, thinking to retreat upstairs again, but then he leaned forward, cupping his hands to the glass, and saw her.

Straightening, he gestured to the door, indicating she should let him in, making it too late for her to run away.

Taking a deep breath, she walked to the door. Her hands shook as she slid back the bolt and opened the door.

"Good afternoon," she said, trying to smile as if she didn't have a care in the world.

He didn't smile back. His face was grave, his eyes dark and opaque in the afternoon sunlight. "We need to talk."

Her mask faltered. "What is it?" she asked, stepping back, pulling the door wide to admit him. "Has something happened?"

He came in, closing the door behind him, taking off his hat. "I can see you haven't heard."

"Heard what?"

His lips pressed tight together, and a knot of fear twisted in her stomach. Something was very wrong. "Max?" she prompted when he didn't answer. "What am I supposed to have heard?"

He reached into his breast pocket and pulled out a newspaper. He handed it to her without a word.

Evie stared at the printed words, trying to take them in. Compromising letters, secret meetings, smears on her character that blackened her reputation with callous disregard. "Oh, my God," she whispered, looking up. "The note you sent me, where you told me not to eat first because you were bringing a picnic dinner for us. They got hold of it?"

"It appears so, yes."

"I noticed it was gone when I got back and unpacked," she murmured, a strange numbness coming over her. "I thought I'd left it behind, but I must not have done. But how could anyone get hold of it?"

"Your maid would be my guess. She may have taken it for money, or been an innocent dupe, it's hard to say."

Evie's numbness shattered, and her knees gave way.

He caught her, dropping his hat to pull her hard against him. "It's all right," he told her, pressing a kiss to her hair. "It's all right."

His words, such a palliative, tore a laugh from her throat, a caustic sound of disbelief rather than humor, for she knew nothing could be made right after this. A woman's good name, once lost, was almost impossible to regain. She pulled away, stepping out of his hold, taking a wild glance around, wondering what would happen to her now. No one would come to a shop owned by a fallen woman. "Oh, God," she choked, and suddenly, she felt as if she were suffocating. "Oh, God."

"Evie, listen to me." Max closed the distance between them, putting his hands on her arms. "You will be all right. I will take care of you."

She laughed again, a wild laugh with an edge of hysteria. "The scandalmongers seem to think you've been taking very good care of me already."

"That isn't what I mean. Evie..." He took a deep breath. "Marry me."

"What?" she whispered, unable to completely take it in. "What did you say?"

"I want you to marry me."

This was becoming more unreal with every moment. "You don't want to marry me. You're only proposing out of obligation."

"Of course I feel an obligation. How could I not, given that I am to blame for all of this? But if you think the idea of marrying you was not already on my mind, you would be wrong."

She was stupefied. "What?"

"Why do you think I abandoned the idea of marrying Helen? I told you at the ball I can't marry simply for suitability. What did you think I meant?"

"Not marrying me," she countered at once. "Given your history and my background, I can't imagine why you'd even consider such a thing."

He smiled a little. "And I can't imagine how you think I wouldn't consider it, especially after you seduced me so shamelessly last night."

She stared at him, diverted by an appalling new thought. "Max, you don't believe I came to your room to gain a marriage proposal, do you? Because I didn't. I would never attempt to trap a man with something like that. I'm sure there are some women who'd happily try such a low trick, especially with a man like you. You're a duke, after all, and terribly rich, but you know I don't care about any of that, so I hope you don't believe I—"

"Evie," he cut in gently, "I was teasing."

"Oh." The wind out of her sails, she couldn't think of what to say next. And when he took her hands in both of his, she began to think he was in earnest, deadly earnest, and deep inside, she started to shake, feeling a fear that had nothing to do with her reputation.

"The truth is," he said, "ever since we danced for the first time—maybe even before that, if I'm honest—I've had a passionate desire for you. I tried to deny it, I tried to snuff it out, but the more I tried to fight it, the deeper and more ardent it became. And that afternoon at Idyll Hour made me realize I was fighting a losing battle."

She couldn't help thinking of another moment at Idyll Hour, one not nearly as romantic. Their conversation about his late wife.

*It was passion and desire, infatuation and lust. Is that love?*

"What are you saying?" she asked, pulling her hands from his. "Are you...are you saying you're in love with me?"

Even as she said it, she told herself it was absurd.

But then, to her amazement, he nodded. "Yes."

Her fear, instead of dissipating, only deepened, squeezing her heart like a fist, twisting her stomach into knots. She didn't believe him. How could she? "You don't mean it," she said, shaking her head in violent denial. "You can't possibly be in love with me. You've only known me two months."

*We'd only known each other two months when we wed.*

"Yes, well," he said, his voice barely discernible past the roar in her ears, "I have come to accept I'm the sort that falls in love fast."

"In two months?" she countered, her words hard and brittle to her own ears as she gave a voice to the fear within her. "About the same amount of time you knew your wife before you married her, so you told me."

He frowned, looking suddenly wary. "Yes, but it's not the same."

To her, it sounded just the same. "How is this different?"

"Because it is. I'm ten years older, for one thing."

"And the fact that you are older has made you wiser?"

"God, I hope so. And not only me. You're not a seventeen-year-old girl. We both know what we feel."

She did know. Like him, she felt passion, a passion he'd ignited, one she hoped would fade once she returned to the world where she belonged. But now, looking at him, facing a proposal of marriage, something she'd never even considered, she suddenly dared to wonder what it would be like to have not just his passion, but his love.

The moment that thought went through her head, another followed, one born of her innate caution and common sense. She'd not only be his love, she'd also be his wife, his duchess.

Evie tried to imagine it—tried to see herself mistress of his enormous estates, wearing a tiara on her head as she blundered her way through balls and parties and banquets like a moth in lamplight, crashing at every turn into the ton's hostility for daring to marry above her station. She'd endure their disapproval of her low birth, while trying to comply with their rigid rules of conduct. She'd feel like a fraud, and she'd certainly be a joke.

And he'd realize it, too, soon enough. The tittering ridicule and the veiled insults—she could probably handle them, for it was nothing she hadn't endured before. But what she could not endure was watching the passion he felt for her slowly wither away and die in the face of her obvious inadequacies. He would be embarrassed by her, ashamed of her. That, she could not bear.

Rebecca, she appreciated, had probably felt the same.

"What *we* feel?" she echoed, forcing a cool acidity into her voice. "You presume a great deal about my feelings."

Hurt shimmered across his face, hurting her, too. But when he spoke, his voice was as cool as hers had been. "Do I?" he countered. "You came to my room last night, if you recall. You gave yourself to me. Are you saying you don't feel what I feel?"

*Deny it*, she told herself. *Lie. Tell him what you felt was sated by a single night. You wanted him, you had him, and that's the end of the story. Drive him away, now, before you start to believe in fairy tales.*

"You said that what you felt for your first wife was passion and desire," she said instead. "Infatuation and lust. That rather sums up what brought us together last night, doesn't it? You said," she went on as he opened his mouth to reply, "marrying Rebecca was a mistake that ruined both your lives. Yet, here you are, ready to make that mistake again?"

"Damn it, Evie, stop throwing my first marriage in my face."

He was angry now, just as she'd intended, but she took no satisfaction in her success, for spurning him was already becoming agony. "Why not?" she cried. "Because it isn't relevant?"

"Well, it isn't," he shot back. "Not now. Given what's being said, we have to marry, and the sooner the better."

She sucked in her breath, drawing back at the reminder of the stark choice he was laying before her. "So, you want to rush me, push me into marriage, just as you did your first wife?"

"No, damn it, that isn't what I wanted! I'd have preferred a proper courtship, where we spend time together and allow the passionate ardor we feel to deepen into the kind of love that will last a lifetime, where I show you what being a duchess would mean before ever asking you to take it on.

The very thing I had vowed not to do was rush you or push you into something you weren't ready for. But with the printing of this scurrilous story, that choice has been taken away from me, and from you."

She stiffened, everything in her rebelling against the implication that she had no choice. "What does it matter what people in the gutter press say about me?"

"It isn't those scandalmongers that concern me. But the people I know are a different matter. Perhaps you don't care if my acquaintances smear you and call you a strumpet, but funnily enough, I do. And," he added before she could reply, "do you think I am absolved from blame because of my sex or my position? Do you really want the world to think I am such a cad that I would not do right by you? Because they will, Evie. You are not the only one who will be condemned."

She bit her lip, for she hadn't thought of the consequences to him. "I am happy to tell any journalist who'll listen that you did the honorable thing and I refused you."

"And you think that discharges my obligation?"

"Doesn't it?"

"To the world, perhaps, but not to you. Would you have me spend my life knowing I ruined you, living with that on my conscience?"

Inside, she began to shake, and she feared if he stayed much longer, she would break into tears. "I accepted the clothes, the hotel room. I willingly came to your house and danced alone with you. I came to your room last night. You owe me nothing."

"Evie, Evie," he said, his voice soft, chiding; so tender, she almost splintered apart. "You surely don't believe that."

He lifted his hands as if to pull her to him, and she jerked free, taking another step back. She couldn't let him hold her. If she did, she'd be lost.

She swallowed hard, striving for the words that would drive him away. "I don't deny that I feel a passion for you, but passion is not love. And despite your declaration, I have no reason to believe what either of us feels is anything more than transient desire that will fade with time. I don't see it deepening into love when we have so little in common." She shook her head. "I will not make a lifetime commitment—one that cannot be undone—because of what scandal sheets say about me, or out of a sense of obligation, or even to assuage your conscience. No, Max. My answer is no."

He muttered an oath, raking his hands through his hair. "You know my position demands that I marry. I must have an heir, and if you refuse me, I will eventually have to find someone else to wed."

"I hope you do!" she cried, anguished. "I want all the best in life for you. I want you to be happy, with a wife who comes from your world, who suits your life. We both know, have known from the start, that's not me."

Her voice was shaking, and she knew she could not tolerate much more of this. Another minute, and she would break into tears. Or worse, she would soften, relent, agree to marry him to be safe, craving his touch, hoping love would last, dying inside as it all fell apart.

He didn't reply. Instead, he tilted his head back, giving a laugh that sounded in no way amused. "We are back where we started, it seems," he muttered.

She frowned. "What are you talking about?"

"You, Evie." He lowered his chin and met her gaze. "You, playing safe and being afraid to aspire to more than you have. You, settling for less than you deserve and telling yourself it's enough. You, always believing you're not worthy of anything more."

Having the same words he'd said to her two months ago flung at her again now made her feel as if she'd just been slapped. "You have my answer," she said. "Now, I would like you to leave."

He didn't move.

"Go, Max," she cried, her voice cracking on the word. "Please, just go. Go, find someone else to love, and be happy."

He looked at her steadily, still unmoving, and only by sheer force of will was she able to hold his gaze.

At last, after what seemed an eternity, he bent and picked up his hat. "This isn't over, Evie," he said as he put it on. "Not by a long chalk."

With that, he turned and departed, and though she'd driven him off with deliberate intent, she couldn't help running to the window after the door had closed behind him, hungry for one last glimpse of him before he vanished from view.

She'd done the right thing, she knew, but as she watched him walk away down the pavement, his elegant clothes such a contrast to dingy little Wellington Street, she couldn't help thinking of what lay ahead of her, of the interminable days and lonely nights of her bookshop spinster's life, with nothing but memories of a fleeting romance to sustain her and not even her good name to protect her. She pressed a hand over her mouth, catching back a sob.

He turned the corner, and as he disappeared from view without a backward glance, the shell of brisk efficiency and practical good sense that had been enveloping Evie all day finally cracked into pieces and fell apart. Now that he was truly gone for good, the pain she'd been holding back since she'd left his room at dawn could no longer be suppressed. A tear spilled over, and then another, and she leaned forward, pressing her wet cheek against the glass, staring, anguished, at the corner where he'd vanished from her life. The words she had refused to say to him, words she had refused to admit even to herself, suddenly came spilling out of her.

"I love you," she cried. "Oh, Max, I love you so."

Her confession echoed through the shop, meaningless and hollow, because no matter how much lovers wanted to believe otherwise, love was not enough, especially for a duke of the realm and a girl from Wellington Street.

# 20

The five days that followed were some of the hardest Evie had ever endured.

She felt no regrets for the choices that had brought her to this point, though whenever she remembered the beautiful moments she'd spent with Max, she felt a bittersweet pain that only deepened with each day that passed.

She was sure she'd done the right thing in refusing him, but during the five nights afterward, alone in bed, remembering the extraordinary way he'd made love to her, the rightness of her position didn't help her fall asleep.

She became the favorite topic of the gutter press, not just *Talk of the Town*, but all the other scandal sheets as well, and though she had resolved to avoid reading them, it had been impossible not to give in to the morbid impulse to read what they were saying. Every time her curiosity got the better of her, she'd regretted it, of course. The things they said about her both enraged and sickened her.

Even harder to avoid than the papers were the so-called journalists themselves, for in their efforts to dig up more dirt on the duke's mistress, they came into the bookshop, hounding her with questions, ignoring her prim refusals to comment. They grilled Anna in the confectionery, and they cornered poor Clarence in the alley when he took out the rubbish. They even hounded members of her family.

"'The reporters torment us daily,'" she read aloud from Margery's latest letter as she and Anna had tea together in the sitting room of her flat. "'It has become such a trial for us that I fear Harold and I will have to take the children and go to the seaside to get away from them.'"

She broke off, rolling her eyes with a sound of exasperation. "Poor Margery, to be forced to take a holiday by the sea. How will she stand the suffering?"

Anna smiled and held up the plate of chocolates she'd brought to share. "Your cousin is nothing if not self-absorbed."

"To say the least." Evie took a violet cream from the plate and popped it into her mouth as she resumed reading. "'Lord Merrivale is beside himself at the shame brought upon our family,'" she continued around a mouthful of chocolate. "'He talks of confronting the duke directly and demanding he do right by you.'"

Evie stopped reading and looked up in horror. "Oh, God, I hope she's not serious."

"Would—" Anna broke off, biting her lip, her cornflower-blue eyes meeting Evie's. "Would that be such a bad thing?" she asked after a moment. "It might at least force Merrivale to stand by you."

"Or just the opposite," Evie muttered, making a face. "Max would have to tell him he already proposed to me, and that I refused him, and then Merrivale would come here, blustering and shouting and trying to bully me into accepting him. Or worse, he'll send Aunt Minnie, who will sob and wail about my shame and how I've disgraced us all. And when I remain adamant, they'll probably write me off as a lost cause and abandon me altogether. Not that I'd notice, given the amount of attention they've paid me in the past."

Anna said nothing, merely looking at her with those placid, angelic blue eyes, and yet Evie felt immediately defensive. "Don't you start," she begged. "I couldn't bear a lecture. Not from you. I've had enough recriminations from Margery the past few days."

"I would never presume to lecture you, dearest."

"But you think I was wrong to refuse him?"

Anna shook her head. "That's not for me to say."

"I don't want to be a duchess."

"An understandable point of view. It would be a tremendous responsibility."

"Exactly," she said, relieved that Anna understood. "Running charities and committees, organizing fetes and church bazaars and flower shows—I've no experience with any of that. I'd be lost."

"Quite so," Anna replied. "Running your own business has been so much easier."

Suspecting sarcasm, Evie shot her a sharp glance, but Anna wasn't even looking at her. She was occupied with surveying the sandwiches on the tea tray.

"You can't seriously think to compare the two," she cried, her defensiveness growing. "My little bookshop is nothing compared to what I'd be doing. I'd have to play hostess to kings and diplomats. I'd be in the public eye every moment, with journalists waiting to pounce on the jumped-up slut from the trades the moment I make the slightest mistake. And if all that's not enough," she went on in the wake of her friend's silence, "I don't know a thing about country life. Tenant farming, and cricket matches, and point-to-points? I don't know how to play cricket and I've never even ridden a horse!"

"I think only the men play cricket, dearest."

"That's not the point! You should have seen his house, Anna. It's like a palace. Miles long in every direction. I got lost more than once navigating my way through it. And he's got half a dozen more houses scattered all over England. How could I ever run all that?"

"It would be intimidating," Anna agreed, selecting a sandwich. "His first wife was completely overwhelmed, from what you told me."

"And who could blame her? I'd be the same—supervising hundreds of servants whose backgrounds probably aren't much different from mine. They wouldn't respect me. I doubt they'd do a thing I say."

"You'd have to earn their respect, certainly. Very few women of our circle could manage it."

"Damn it, Anna," she muttered, growing irritated, "stop agreeing with me. The more you agree with me, the more unsettled I feel."

Anna smiled. "I don't mean to be the cause of your doubts. That is," she added, shooting Evie a pointed glance, "if you're having doubts."

"I'm not."

"That's good." Anna leaned back and began to eat her sandwich. "After all," she said between bites, "it hardly matters, since it's all over and done with."

*This isn't over, Evie. Not by a long chalk.*

"Quite over," she agreed firmly. "He's hosting some

big dinner party at the Savoy tonight, so he clearly isn't pining away for me," she went on, a fact that demonstrated Max's vow not to give up had been nothing but empty words. "He hasn't tried to see me. He hasn't even written me a note."

"Well, that's a relief."

It ought to have been, of course, but sadly, it wasn't. The only effect his absence from her life was having on her was to make her depressed, and she reached for another chocolate.

"The papers are speculating that he may begin paying his addresses to Lady Helen again soon," she said, pouring salt in her own wounds. "'But will the auburn-haired beauty forgive his transgressions?'" she quoted gloomily. "'Will she take him back?'"

As she spoke, a shaft of raw jealousy pierced her heart like an arrow, and she shoved the chocolate into her mouth, reminding herself as she ate it that she had no right to be jealous. She meant what she'd said to him. She wanted him to be happy. She wanted him to find someone else, someone perfect for him.

*If you refuse me, I will eventually have to find someone else to wed.*

"How do you know what the papers are saying?" Anna asked, forcing Max's voice out of Evie's head. "I thought you weren't reading them."

Caught, she wriggled guiltily beneath her friend's mild stare. "It's impossible not to see the headlines as I go shopping," she muttered, refusing to admit she'd done far more than glance at the headlines during the past five days. "The newsstand is right there, you know, between the grocer and the bakery."

"Of course," Anna said gravely.

"The point is," Evie said, giving her friend a look of reproof, "it would be a suitable match."

"Most suitable."

A loud knock sounded from the shop below before Evie could list any more reasons why there was no possibility of reconsidering her decision. "His family and friends would certainly approve," she went on, ignoring it, "which they'd never do if he married me—"

The knock came again, louder this time, and Anna gestured to the open doorway of the flat. "Shouldn't you go down and see who it is?"

"No need. I closed for the day and put the sign up."

"Yes, but..." She paused, then added gently, "It could be the duke."

Hope leapt in her chest and dread knotted her stomach, but she shook her head. "Don't be silly. It's probably a reporter."

This time, the knock was an absolute pounding, and Anna ate the last bite of her sandwich, brushed the crumbs from her fingers, and rose from the settee. "Whoever it is, I'll send them away. You stay here and have your tea."

"Thank you, Anna."

"What are friends for?" she asked as she left the sitting room and started down the stairs to the bookshop. Evie waited, listening, and when she heard the low murmur of a masculine voice, her hope and her dread both rose in equal measure.

What if it was him? What if, despite what the papers said, he was here to try again? She'd have to refuse him a second time, and after five agonizing days she wasn't at all sure she could remain steadfast.

She'd done the right thing. Hadn't she?

Evie closed her eyes. *Go away, Max*, she prayed. *Please, go away.*

Anna's steps sounded on the stairs, and Evie opened her eyes, reaching for Margery's letter, pretending to read it as her friend reentered the flat.

"It's not the duke," Anna told her.

Hope and dread both died. "So, I was right then?" she said flatly. "A reporter."

But to her surprise, Anna shook her head. "It's Rory. He wants to see you, insists upon it. He's waiting below."

"Rory?" She felt a pang of conscience, remembering that he had come to the shop asking about her more than once, and though she'd meant to dash off a letter to his lodging house, what with the house party and everything that had happened since, she'd forgotten all about him. "I'll go down at once."

"I'll come with you," Anna said, following her as she started for the door. "I ought to be going back to the shop anyway. We're open until eight tonight, and I've left Clarence on his own. He's probably eaten all the caramels in the shop by now."

Rory was lounging against one of the bookshelves by the front as she and Anna entered the shop. He straightened at once, giving Anna a nod as she passed him on her way out.

"Rory, this is a nice surprise," Evie said, moving to stand opposite him as Anna closed the door behind her. "I heard you called a few times. But I've been—"

She stopped, appreciating that he, along with everyone else in London, probably knew the reason she'd been busy. "I've been away," she said instead.

"Yes, so I heard." Beneath his cap, his sky-blue eyes met hers. "Evie, I know all about what's happened. I'm so sorry."

At the compassion in the eyes of her childhood friend,

she almost wanted to burst into tears, an emotional reaction that she'd become nauseatingly familiar with during the past week. She blinked, holding the tears back. "Yes, well, I appreciate that," she mumbled, not knowing what else to say.

"Evie," he began, then stopped. Jerking off his cap, he held it to his chest, and then, to her utter astonishment, he sank to one knee and grabbed her hand. "Evie, will you marry me?"

The question was so unexpected, so astonishing, she almost laughed, but laughter at a man's proposal, even if it was born of surprise, would be cruel, and she stifled the impulse. "Rory, I'm...stunned."

"Are you? Surely after all these years, you know how I feel?"

Clearly, she didn't, since she was utterly surprised he was down on one knee in front of her. With all the time they'd known each other, all their many letters back and forth, she'd always known they were friends, but despite the silly girlish hopes she'd harbored about him upon his return a couple of months ago, she'd never really believed he felt anything for her that was in the least romantic. And her own romantic hopes about him seemed puerile now, shallow and silly. She swallowed, struggling for something to say. "Rory, do get up," she said, pulling her hand from his and gesturing him to his feet. "It feels so strange staring down at you this way."

He got to his feet, laughing, clearly relieved. "Since you've told me to stand up, does this mean you're saying yes?"

Dismayed, she hastened into speech. "Rory, I know we've always been friends, and I have a great deal of affection for you, but—"

"Yes, exactly," he cut in before she could finish, taking her hand again. "Affection and friendship are what I feel, too. And you can't say our marriage wouldn't be suitable. We understand each other, we come from the same class."

"Well, yes," she murmured, "but that's hardly enough for two people to commit their lives together."

She winced as she said it, appreciating that she'd sent Max off to find exactly that sort of marriage for himself.

"Evie, I can't stand by and see your name dragged through the mud this way, especially when it's clear what happened."

"Is it?" She frowned, not sure what he meant.

"Of course! But I don't hold it against you."

Evie stiffened, pulling her hand free again. "Indeed?"

"Rich toff turns your head, buys you some pretty things, squires you around for a bit of fun. You think there's no harm in it, and then, before you know it, he's taken advantage of you in the worst way a man can. He's made you his plaything, then left you flat. That's how they are, men like him. Think they can just take what they want. And now he's gone. The papers say he's off with some other girl already, one of his own class, one he thinks is good enough to marry, and here you are. Soiled goods, your reputation ruined."

At that painful reminder, she grimaced.

He saw it. "Don't worry, Evie. Marry me and you'll be all right."

That was probably true. If she married Rory, the damage from her fling with the duke would be mitigated, if not completely forgotten, by those who knew her. But nonetheless, she wasn't the least bit tempted.

"You're right, of course," she murmured, striving to find a polite way to refuse that wouldn't hurt his feelings. "And

I'm touched, Rory, deeply touched, that you would come riding to my rescue this way. But..." She paused and took a deep breath. "I can't marry you to save myself. What about your political career? Marrying a woman tainted by scandal won't help you there."

"I'll give it up," he said. "I'll come and take over the shop."

"You'll run my shop? What about me?"

He laughed. "You'll be having babies, silly girl. That'll be taking up most of your time. Don't worry," he added. "I'll take good care of things here. We'll live upstairs. It's just what our fathers wanted, remember, all those years ago? They were sure all along we'd suit, that we'd be happy together."

That was true enough. With their shared backgrounds, affection, and fondness, she and Rory were a suitable match, the sort that everyone, no matter what class they moved in, believed would deepen into love and make a happy marriage. Her father and his, were they alive, would be dancing a jig about it. She herself, two months ago, would probably have silenced any misgivings rattling around in the back of her mind and accepted him.

But she wasn't the same girl now that she'd been then.

"You're right, I'm sure. But I can't help feeling that there has to be something more to marriage than safety or suitability, or affection. There has to be love."

"Well, of course," he said, laughing, and for the third time, he grabbed her hand. "But I do love you. I do," he insisted as she made no reply. "I admit, I didn't really know just how I felt about you until recently. But since I've come back, I've come to see that my affection for you is far deeper than I ever realized."

It must be, she supposed, since he knew what had

happened to her and was proposing marriage anyway. Only a man who cared deeply would marry a girl who had already given herself to another man. And yet, his declaration of love had a strange, unreal quality to it. She couldn't really believe it. Not that it mattered. Even if he loved her madly, she couldn't accept.

"Rory, I am flattered and...and honored, but..." She paused to pull her hand away, yanking it free as his grip tightened. "But, with regret, I must refuse. I can't marry you."

He stared in obvious astonishment. She couldn't blame him, really, given her situation. Most women would jump at the chance to be saved from ruin. But safety, as she was discovering to her surprise, was not nearly as important to her as she used to believe.

"Evie, you haven't thought this through. You don't know what you're saying."

"Yes, I do. As I said, I've always had a great deal of fondness for you. But that's all. I don't love you."

"But you love him? Is that it?" He made an exasperated sound through his teeth. "You love your fancy man, is that it?"

She stiffened at the insult. "Please don't say things to taint my fondness for you."

Rory ignored that. "He won't marry you, you know, if that's what you're hoping for. Oh, he'll put you up in a hotel and come to you at night. He'll buy you pretty clothes and hire a hotel maid to dress you in 'em, but that's all."

She frowned. "How would you know he—"

She broke off as Max's words from five days ago about the missing note passed through her mind.

*Your maid would be my guess. She may have taken it for money, or been an innocent dupe...*

"How would I know?" Rory echoed, scowling. "A toff like that, marry you? Why would he when he got all he wanted from you already?" He raked a hand through his blonde hair, his sky-blue eyes flashing with anger.

*Hair like gold, he's got, and the bluest eyes...I've never had a suitor in my life until a few weeks ago.*

"Oh, my God!" she burst out. "It was you!"

His anger faltered. Uncertainty flickered across his face, then vanished. "What are you rattling on about?" he asked, assuming an air of bafflement that didn't fool her for a second.

"You're Liza's suitor. That's how my letter from the duke went missing. You got Liza to let you into my room. Or," she added as he shook his head with a scoffing sound, "you somehow persuaded Liza to take it for you and you gave it to the papers. There's no other way you could know the duke hired a maid from the Savoy to attend me."

"Don't be stupid. I read it in the papers."

A plausible explanation, and one she couldn't refute, since she hadn't read all the stories, and yet, she felt certain he was lying. "Poor Liza. You seduced her, pumped her for information. She saw the coronet on the duke's note to me—she probably told you about it, you got it and gave it to *Talk of the Town*. Don't try to deny it, Rory. I know you did it. But what I don't know is, why? Why would you do that to me?"

"You ask me why?" he countered and made a sound of disdain. "Men like him only want one thing from girls like you. I had to get you away from him."

She gave a laugh. "You ruined me to save me, is that it?"

"He ruined you, not me. And I only did what I did to bring you back here, where you belong."

Having her very own reasoning about her place in the

world thrown at her gave Evie the odd desire to argue against it. "Oh, really? Who are you to decide where I belong?"

"It's not me who decides these things! It's the way things are. He might bed you, but to him, you're dirt under his feet."

"You have no idea what he thinks of me," she said coldly.

"At least I'm prepared to marry you. He's not."

"If you're so sure of that, then why didn't you just wait, bide your time until he grew tired of me and set me aside, then come and propose? You didn't want to wait, is that it? After all, you might have had to wait years. Or," she added, another explanation coming to her, "you weren't absolutely sure I would marry you after he hypothetically left me, so you hedged your bets. By ruining me so publicly, you thought I'd have no choice but to demand he marry me, and when he inevitably refused, you'd come riding to the rescue like my white knight and save me?"

He didn't answer. He didn't have to. She watched his chin jut out, making him look just as he had when he was a little boy and got caught doing something naughty.

"Well, it didn't work," she said in the wake of his silence. "Ruined or not, I'd never marry you. Not in a thousand years."

"Still holding out, waiting for him, are you? Well, you'll wait in vain, my girl. He'll never marry you."

She smiled, wondering what he'd say if she told him how wrong he was about Max. "You think not?"

"Why would he? He's a duke. And you're skinny and freckled and plain as mud."

That was a brutal assessment, but not, she realized suddenly, all that much harsher than her own view of herself had always been. Until Max had come along.

*I know a beautiful woman when I see one.*

She laughed, causing Rory to blink in disconcerted surprise.

"What the hell's so funny?" he demanded.

"I think," she said, "we can dispense with any illusion that you have ever had any love at all for me."

Thankfully, he seemed to agree that marrying her was a lost cause. "You, a duchess?" he jeered. "What a joke. You'd never pull it off. You'd be the laughingstock of society."

At having her own opinion quoted back to her almost verbatim, Evie's amusement vanished and she stared, stunned, because she was seeing for the very first time just how awful, how cruel, she had been to herself all these years with her low opinion of herself. How much and how often she'd sold herself short.

That, she decided, was going to stop. No more self-disparagement. No more—how had Max put it?—hiding her light under a bushel. No more thinking she'd fail at something just because she'd never tried it before.

Could she be a duchess? She'd thought, as Rory thought, that the answer was no. But was that true?

Nothing would please her more than proving herself and Rory and anyone else who dared to doubt her wrong on that score. After all, she'd tried so many new things in the past two months; she'd shoved aside all her insecurities, risen to every challenge, and she'd enjoyed every minute of it. Even with Max by her side to support and guide her, being a duchess would be the most work and the biggest challenge she'd ever taken on. There'd be daily opportunities to make a complete fool of herself. She'd be in the public eye all the time, the subject of gossip, open to ridicule. There'd be no running away. Nowhere to hide.

Even as she reminded herself of all the pitfalls, all the risks, she could feel excitement rising within her. Even as she told herself everything that could go wrong, she felt more and more that it was right. Even as she felt fear knot her stomach, she felt exhilaration, too.

She did want it, she realized. She wanted to be Max's duchess, and she wanted all the challenges and inevitable faux pas that came along with that role. She wanted the house that was too grand for words, and the servants who didn't respect her, and all the rules and duties she didn't know—yet. She wanted to learn everything there was to know about committees and charities and flower shows. Maybe she'd even learn to ride a horse. Most of all, she wanted Max. She wanted to be his and make him hers.

This, she knew, was the elusive *something more* she'd been yearning for when he had come along two months ago with that silly bet. The adventure, the challenge. The love of one amazing man.

She took a deep breath. "I think you and I have said all there is to say, Rory. I'd like you to leave. Good luck to you. I doubt we'll see each other again."

He stared at her for a moment as if unable to believe she really meant it. Then, with a muttered curse, he turned and walked out.

Evie waited long enough to be sure he was truly gone, then she raced next door to Anna's confectionery.

"Evie?" Anna said, looking up from a tray of petit fours she was decorating. "Did you come to buy something?"

She shook her head. "No, I want to borrow something. A dress. Something good enough for a dinner party at the Savoy. Do you have anything from your dressmaking days that might do?"

Anna's face, usually so calm and placid, broke into a grin. "I suppose I can find something in one of the trunks upstairs that isn't too out of fashion. I take it Lady Helen's out of luck?"

Evie nodded, feeling giddy and terrified and gloriously happy. "Only if I'm not too late."

# 21

*M*ax was in no mood for a party.

Not that he didn't appreciate the sentiment that had brought it about. The moment his sisters had heard about the scandal, they'd come rushing down from all parts of England to support him, their titled husbands in tow, and though it wasn't much help to his low mood, he loved them all the more for it. They'd put out the call to aunts, uncles, cousins, and friends as well, and the result had been an all-out family campaign to show solidarity and lift his spirits, including this lavish dinner party at the Savoy. The only problem was that the guest of honor heartily wished he could be anywhere else.

He looked around the glittering reception room, filled with so many beloved faces, and all he could think was that this ought to have been an engagement party. Had Evie said yes, they'd be here now, together. He'd be on top of the world, and all his relations would be relieved that the crisis had passed, happy the duke was getting married at last, and Evie would be saved. As it was, Evie was ruined and disgraced, his family was pretending to be in a partying mood, and all he wanted was to get roaring drunk.

Nan walked by, giving him a rallying pat on the arm. His sister Idina followed, offering a sympathetic look. Penelope, in her turn, murmured something hopeful about a picnic in Hyde Park tomorrow if the weather was fine, and Audrey wondered if perhaps a trip abroad might be just what he needed.

Delia, being more practical than any of his four sisters, brought him a cocktail.

"This," he said, taking the glass, "is why you are my favorite cousin."

She smiled, moving to stand beside him, gazing at the milling crowd of family and friends. "Idina says that Westbourne House will be ready by tomorrow."

"Good. That means my poor brothers-in-law won't have all their wives' relations crammed into their London townhouses."

"And what about poor Ritz? You should have seen his face when Idina told him she wanted this dinner party and he and Escoffier had two days to help me prepare. I thought the poor man would have a heart attack."

"He loves it. And besides," Max added, nodding to the massive flower arrangements, trays of elaborate hors d'oeuvres, and elegant footmen in Savoy livery, "the results speak for themselves. I just don't know what good it'll do."

"Yes, you do. The papers must know we stand behind you, whatever has happened or will happen."

His hand tightened around his glass. "I'm not the one who needs that sort of bolstering."

"Look at it this way. A lavish party like this gives the scandal sheets something to talk about besides Evie."

"Except they'll all be wondering why she's not here. Every day that passes with no engagement announcement only further cements the idea that she's been nothing more to me than a mistress, and that in light of the scandal, I've set her aside."

"I do wish you'd let me see her, talk to her—"

"No." He took a swallow of his drink.

"What about your sisters? If they went with me, if we assured her we would welcome her into the family with open arms, that we'd do all we could to help her, it might allay her fears about the whole thing and persuade her to change her mind."

"No. You'll do nothing, Delia." He turned his head, giving her a hard stare. "Don't interfere."

She sighed. "Oh, very well. But what are you going to do?"

He shrugged, accepting the inevitable. "Nothing."

"What?"

"What would you have me do, Delia? I won't push her to marry me. And I won't have you or my lovely, interfering sisters pushing her either. I did that to Rebecca, and we all know the result. I won't do it to Evie."

"Evie's not Rebecca."

"No," he agreed and gave a humorless laugh. "Instead of allowing herself to be charmed, cajoled, and strongly persuaded to change her mind about marrying me, she's more likely to just dig in her heels and harden herself further against the idea."

"I expect you're right. She is very stubborn and proud. But there must be something you can do. You're not giving up, surely?"

"God, no. I thought I'd wait a bit longer, then go see her."

"You realize time is not on her side?"

"Of course, but I see no other course that has a prayer of working. This way, I'm hoping she'll relax her defenses and perhaps soften. I can only hope it also gives her the chance to miss me."

"If you call on her with no engagement in place, you give the papers the chance to say she's resumed being your mistress."

"I can't help what they say. All I can do is work to slowly, gently persuade her to marry me. Show her, if she'll let me, what being a duchess would be like, and hope she'll see her way to taking it on. That isn't something that's going to be done in a week. For this to work, it has to be a long, slow courtship, and that might take a year, or two, or even more. If..."

He paused and took a deep breath, saying a silent prayer. "If it works at all."

"It will," Delia said, holding up her own drink and clinking it against his. "It will. I have no doubt."

Max wished he could be that sure. But when it came to Evie, he knew it was best not to take anything for granted.

There wasn't a cab in sight. Evie leaned out from the cab stand at the corner of Wellington Street and Russell Street, the train of Anna's burgundy-red crushed velvet gown over her arm to keep it off the dirty sidewalk. She peered up and down, left and right, but among all the vehicles clogging traffic, she couldn't see a single hansom or growler in any direction.

It was, she judged, about a quarter to eight, and if she didn't hurry, she wouldn't be able to see Max before he went in to dinner. If that happened, what with all the inevitable courses, followed by port, coffee, cards, and who knew what else, it could be hours before she had another chance to talk with him.

Nothing for it, she decided, turning to start up Wellington Street toward the Savoy. She'd have to walk. A bit ridiculous in this ensemble, but she had no choice.

She hurried as fast as her tight corset would allow, but after a few minutes, she realized walking wasn't going to work. She had just crossed York Street when, suddenly, a roaring crack of thunder sounded, followed by the flash of lightning, and then the heavens opened and rain began to pour down, torrents of it.

With a cry of dismay, she hiked the train higher and broke into a run, thanking God she was wearing flat slippers instead of court heels. Pelted by the downpour, she ran as fast as she could, round the corner onto the Strand, pausing for traffic at Savoy Street, where the hem of Anna's gown was splashed by a hansom as it went by. Then, across the Savoy courtyard, past the liveried doorman, and into the hotel. By the time she reached the concierge desk, she was soaked to the skin.

"The Duke of Westbourne's dinner party?" she panted as the concierge looked up.

"Miss Harlow?" His eyes widened, telling her she must look a fright, but true to the Savoy's reputation for unflappable conduct on the part of its staff, the man merely pointed toward the far end of the foyer. "Penzance Room," he told her. "To the right, at the end of the corridor."

"Of course it would be the dining room at the end of the corridor," she muttered, gasping for breath as she ran, oblivious to the stares she received from guests and staff as she went.

By the time she reached the end of the long corridor, she had a hitch in her side, her thighs were chafed from her heavy, wet clothes, and her lungs were burning. Ducking past a pair of footmen carrying trays, she shoved open the door to the dining room and went inside.

"Miss, wait," one of them said. "It's a private party. You can't go in there."

She didn't reply but let the door swing shut behind her in the footman's face.

The Penzance Room, like most other private dining rooms at the Savoy, was actually two, a reception room and a dining room, and she was in the dining room, meaning she'd passed the proper entrance right by. But there was an open connecting door to the reception room at the other end where she could see guests milling about, and she raced toward it as the door behind her opened and the footman gave chase. She entered the reception room, the servant a few dozen steps behind her, and there, she came to an abrupt halt, her gaze searching for one dark head amid the crowd.

Thankfully, Max's exceptional height enabled her to find him almost at once. A cocktail in his hand, he was standing near the center of the room beside a woman with rich, flaming auburn hair, a woman of such stunning beauty, Evie knew she could only be Lady Helen Maybridge.

The scandal sheets had gotten the story right, then. Evie's stomach plummeted at the thought, for she really hadn't believed—or perhaps she just hadn't wanted to believe—he'd go back to Helen, and her hope began to falter as the crowd quieted, and one by one, faces turned to see who had dared to invade a duke's dinner party uninvited.

Max seemed to notice the quiet. He looked up, turning toward the door, and when their eyes met, she knew the only sensible thing to do was flee, run straight back out of his life.

She didn't move.

Panting, dripping, a lock of wet hair tumbling over her face, she could only stare at him as footsteps halted behind her and a panting footman said, "I'm so sorry, Your Grace. She just ran past us. We couldn't stop her."

A flicker of something showed in Max's face—shock, amusement, and something else, something that might have been...pleasure? He smiled, his eyes creasing at the corners, and her heart tumbled in her breast.

"Evie?" He started toward her, the crowd parting like the Red Sea to let him through. "Evie, what are you doing here?"

She opened her mouth, realizing only now that she had no idea what to say. She wanted to say something worthy of the position she was hoping to assume, and she ought, she supposed, to have given that some thought on the way here, but it was too late now. No time to come up with anything eloquent and duchess-like.

"I've been thinking about everything you said," she burst out, hurling herself over the cliff, hoping he'd catch her and she wouldn't crash to the ground. "In fact, I've been thinking about it for five days. It's all I've been thinking about, truth be told."

He halted in front of her, glancing down, making her appreciate that she was leaving a puddle of water on the carpet of the Savoy's elegant Penzance Room, that at least twenty of London's fashionables were now staring at her as if appalled, including his former (hopefully) love interest, and that she was probably making an utter fool of herself.

None of that, however, was going to stop her, not now,

not if that smile in his eyes meant something, not if there was the slightest chance he still wanted her. She sucked in a deep breath and plunged ahead. "And coming here now, I'm sure I'm too late," she said, speaking quickly as she caught sight of the beautiful redhead approaching them. "After all, when I turned down your marriage proposal, you told me you'd have to marry someone else someday—"

She broke off as the other woman resumed her place by his side, staring as if Evie had two heads, her eyes wide with shock, her rose-pink lips parted in astonishment.

"I'm so sorry," Evie said, turning to her, feeling a sudden pang of conscience—if not regret—for what she was doing. "I hope you won't hate me for this, because you look like a very nice person, and God knows you're every bit as beautiful as everyone says, and I'm sure you would be the perfect wife for Max—"

The woman laughed, a choked, ladylike giggle that was echoed at once by several others in the room, but even that wasn't enough to deter Evie. Let them laugh. Let every single person in the world laugh at her, ridicule her, shun her, despise her—for the first time in her life, she didn't care a jot.

"But the thing is," she went on, overriding all the laughter, "you don't love him. And he doesn't love you."

"Evie," Max cut in, but if he was going to toss her out for this unbelievable impertinence, she didn't want him to do it until she'd said everything she had to say.

"You're probably considering the possibility of marrying him because it's so suitable," she went on doggedly, still looking at the woman by his side, "but without love, it would be awful, wouldn't it? No woman ought to marry a man if she's not wildly in love with him. Even if he is a duke and is rich as Croesus, it wouldn't be worth it.

Especially if he isn't in love with you either. That's why I turned him down, you see, when he asked me to marry him, because I didn't think he really loved me—not real love, true love, the kind that lasts. I thought he was just infatuated with me and that he was, perhaps, being noble. Hate me if you want—"

"I don't hate you," the other woman interrupted, smiling so warmly that Evie, nonplussed, could only stare at her. "In fact, though we've only just met, I think I already like you quite a lot."

"Evie," Max cut in again, speaking before she could think how to reply, "please allow me to introduce my sister Idina."

"Sister?" Evie blinked, not taking her eyes off the beautiful redhead by his side. "You're his sister?"

"One of the four," she answered lightly. "I'm the oldest. And you," she added, still smiling as she held out her hand, "must be Miss Harlow."

Evie dropped her train and the sodden velvet hit the floor with a thud as she took the other woman's hand. She couldn't seem to think straight. Any reply was beyond her.

The woman turned to Max and murmured, "I think I shall have to tell the Savoy to set another place at the table. If you two will pardon me?"

With a nod to both of them, she glided away.

"Your sister?" Evie returned her attention to Max, trying to find her wits, fearing they were irretrievably lost. "Why didn't you tell me straightaway?"

He gave her an apologetic look, but it was clearly bogus, for his smile was widening as he spoke. "I did try. But you wouldn't let me get a word in."

A valid point, but that didn't stop her from a huff of vexation. "Still," she muttered, glancing around at all the amused faces, "you never seem averse to speaking up when you really want to."

"Neither do you," he countered, making her grimace, for she still didn't know just what nonsense had come spilling out of her mouth a few moments ago.

"So, you just let me go rattling away?"

"I decided it was best, at least until you revealed exactly why you're here."

She gave a wild laugh. "I thought it was obvious."

"Not quite." His smile faded, his blue eyes turned grave, and her poor heart began skipping beats like a rock skipping across a pond.

"I thought—" She broke off and sucked in air, still trying to catch her breath. "The papers said you might resume paying your addresses to Helen Maybridge. Are you?"

"Would it matter to you if I were?"

Words, something she had seemed to have no trouble with a few moments ago, now seemed stuck in her throat, and she could only stare at him.

"I told you," he went on in the wake of her silence, "I'd have to marry someone."

"I know, but..." She paused, but she knew there was no going back now. "But I'm hoping maybe that someone might be me," she whispered.

"I see." No change in his face. "So," he said, turning casually to hand his drink to the footman, "are you proposing marriage to me, then?"

She stared at him, dismayed, fully aware that every person in the room had heard the question and was waiting for her answer. "What, here? In front of all these people?"

A stupid response if ever there was one, given that she'd paid no heed to discretion from the moment she'd burst through the door.

"Yes," he said, seeming of no mind to make things easier.

He was serious. The room was dead quiet. Evie licked her suddenly dry lips. "Proposing marriage to a man is not a ladylike thing to do," she mumbled, stalling for time, taking refuge in primness.

"No, it's not. But—" He broke off and looked down, taking her hand in his. As he looked up again and met her gaze, she saw something in his eyes she'd never seen there before. She saw fear, and she realized even before he spoke again why he was putting her through this.

"If you're going to take this on," he said quietly, as if reading her mind, "we both have to know you'll be able to see it through no matter how hard it gets."

Never, she decided, could she possibly love him more than she did right now. Evie squared her shoulders, lifted her chin, and shoved back the lock of wet hair that had fallen over her face. "Well, then, yes," she said, trying to assume some semblance of duchess-like dignity. "I suppose I am proposing marriage. Just don't expect me to go down on one knee," she added at once, glancing down over her gown as another round of laughter rippled through the room. "Not in this ensemble." She looked at him again. "I'd never get back up."

He didn't laugh with them, but the fear left his eyes, and a smile twitched at the corners of his mouth. "Well, then," he said, "now that I know you're serious, perhaps we should discuss the details in private? That way," he added in a murmur, leaning closer, "when you go down on one knee and can't get up, I can lift you without shocking everyone."

"I think it's too late for that," she muttered with a sigh. "I fear I've already shocked them all out of countenance. They'll remember this for years."

"No doubt," he agreed. "You do have a way of making even the dullest evening memorable, Evie." Turning, he went on in a louder voice, "Ladies and gentlemen, it appears dinner shall be a bit late, for Miss Harlow and I have something urgent to discuss in private. If you will excuse us for a few minutes?"

Taking her arm, he led Evie into the adjacent dining room, and having made an utter fool of herself already, she was glad to follow. He waved away the footmen making final adjustments to the table, and they departed the way she'd originally come in.

As the doors closed behind them, leaving her alone with Max, Evie felt her courage faltering. During the mad rush here, she'd given herself no time to think beyond getting to him and telling him how she felt. As he had taught her when they'd practiced dancing together, it was usually best not to think too much. But now, given her admission that she was proposing marriage, she couldn't help wondering what she'd do if he refused.

Her heart gave a tremble of fear.

"You aren't really going to make me go down on one knee to do this, are you?" she asked at last, giving a decidedly shaky laugh. "Because I meant what I said. This dress is laced so tight, I can barely breathe, and if you——"

His hands came up, cupping her cheeks, cutting her off midsentence. "My darling." He kissed her. "Do you mean it? You'll marry me?"

"I thought I was the one doing the proposing."

"You take too long." He pressed another kiss to her lips, then her cheek, then her forehead, then her nose. "My dearest, sweetest Evie. You really will marry me and be my duchess?"

"Yes, I will." She nodded. "Yes."

She nodded again, emphasizing the point just to show him she was in complete earnest, and then he was kissing her again, a long, deep kiss that made her dizzy—though whether that was due to his amazing prowess at kissing or her oxygen-deprived lungs, she couldn't have said.

But at last, he drew back. "If you want more time to think it over—"

She shook her head, cutting him off. "Thinking is overrated."

He didn't laugh with her. Remembering his fear of a few minutes before, she hastened on, "I've had five days to think, and I don't need any more time than that. I love you, you know. I realized it—or at least, I finally admitted it to myself—after you proposed and I turned you down. I stood at the window, watching you walk away, out of my life, and I knew I loved you with all my heart and soul."

"And you knew this five days ago? Woman, why didn't you come running after me straightaway and tell me?"

"Well, for one thing, as I said, I wasn't completely sure you loved me, not in a lasting way."

"And what changed your mind?"

She smiled a little. "Nothing. I'm being a bit of a gambler on this, Max. I'm taking the depth of your love on faith. After all, nothing in life is sure."

"That's where you're wrong, Evie. My love is the one thing in this world you can be sure of. I love you more than you can ever know, more than words can express."

His eyes, the beautiful midnight blue of a starless sky, were so tender, so filled with love, she had to catch back a sob of joy.

"But I'll try just the same." His hand lifted, his fingertip tracing a light caress back and forth across her lips. "When I think of how it would be to see your wonderful, funny smile every single day, of having daughters with your tawny eyes and pretty freckles, of watching you slay your opponents at croquet at all the Whitsuntide house parties to come—when I think of all of that, it makes me glad to be alive, so, so glad that it hurts." His hand fell to cover his heart. "Right here."

Tears pricked her eyes and clogged her throat, and it took her a moment to reply. "Goodness," she managed at last, "for a man who didn't think there were any words to describe the love he feels, you were pretty damned eloquent just now."

"But does it convince you, my darling?"

She considered. "Yes, Max," she said with a sureness she'd never felt before. "I do believe it does."

"And being my duchess? You're sure you want the job? You were dead set against it," he reminded before she could answer. "And even now, you don't know what's involved."

"It doesn't matter. Whatever it is, I'm going to tackle it and conquer it and make it my own. I'll make mistakes, I expect, but that can't be helped. You'll just have to help me along a bit, and I'll muddle through."

"Are you saying that because you love me, and you hope to make the best of it?"

"No, I'm saying it because I want to do it. I know," she said, laughing as he raised an eyebrow. "Quite an about-face from five days ago, isn't it?"

"To say the least," he murmured. "If it's not your love for me that changed your mind, then what was it that did the trick?"

"You have the pigeon to thank."

"Him?" Max frowned, not seeming too pleased by that. "Why him?"

"He proposed marriage to me, not two hours ago."

"What?" Max's frown deepened. "That scoundrel."

She laughed. "How can you say that?" she teased. "It was a genuine proposal of marriage."

"Yes, well, perhaps it was," he said grudgingly. "Perhaps I've been wrong about him."

"You weren't, believe me. You had him pegged accurately from the start."

She explained, and as she did, his displeasure became a look of hard, cold implacability she'd never seen in his face before, and she realized just how intimidating the duke could be when he tried.

"I'll have his head on a pike, Evie. By God, I will."

"It isn't the Middle Ages, Max. You can't hang him, quarter him, and cut him into pieces."

"You think not?"

"I appreciate the sentiment, but really, you should be grateful to him. He was so angry at being refused that he insulted me, calling me plain and skinny—"

"I'll kill him."

"No, you won't. He said I'd never be a real duchess. I'd be a joke, the laughingstock of society, and when I heard all that, I got angry, because he was saying the very same things I'd been saying to myself, some of which I had said to you as well."

"Yes, I remember."

"As Rory said those things to me, it was like looking into a mirror but seeing myself in a whole new way. You were quite right to say I was afraid, but at that moment, I realized the only way one can tackle fear is to face it. You showed me that, these past two months. I also realized something else: that none of the disparaging things I'd been thinking about myself were facts. They were simply opinions, and opinions varied. They could also be changed. I might be plain to some and pretty to others. I might not be the most accomplished dancer, but I'm not the worst either. And I might not have been born to be a duchess, but I realized there was no reason I couldn't be one if I wanted to."

"I don't doubt it one bit." He smiled, lifting his hand to tenderly tuck back another tendril of her wet hair. "And you do want it?" he asked. "Truly?"

She nodded. "I do. I want all of it—house parties and fetes and charities and horses and committees and sales of work, and plenty of sons. And," she added as he laughed, "whatever else it is duchesses do."

He cupped her face. "You haven't mentioned the most important duty a duchess has, my darling."

"What's that?"

"Loving the duke."

She smiled, sliding her arms up to wrap them around his neck. "That will be the easiest duty of all," she said, rose on her toes, and kissed him.

# ABOUT THE AUTHOR

*New York Times* bestselling author **Laura Lee Guhrke** spent seven years in advertising, had a successful catering business, and managed a construction company before she decided writing novels was more fun. The author of twenty-seven historical romances and a two-time winner of the Romance Writers of America Rita Award, Laura lives in the Northwest US with her husband and two diva cats. Laura loves hearing from readers, and you can contact her at:

LauraLeeGuhrke.com
Facebook/LauraLeeGuhrkeAuthor
Instagram @Laura_Lee_Guhrke
Twitter @LauraLeeGuhrke

*Get swept off your feet by charming dukes and sharp-witted ladies in Forever's historical romances!*

### *A SPINSTER'S GUIDE TO DANGER AND DUKES*
by **Manda Collins**

Miss Poppy Delamare left her family to escape an odious betrothal, but when her sister is accused of murder, she cannot stay away. Even if she must travel with the arrogant Duke of Langham. To her surprise, he offers a mutually beneficial arrangement: a fake betrothal will both protect Poppy and her sister and deter Society misses from Langham. But as real feelings begin to grow, can they find truth and turn their engagement into reality—before Poppy becomes the next victim?

### *ALWAYS BE MY DUCHESS*
by **Amalie Howard**

Because ballerina Geneviève Valery refused a patron's advances, she is hopelessly out of work. But then Lord Lysander Blackstone, the heartless Duke of Montcroix, makes Nève an offer she would be a fool to refuse. Montcroix's ruthlessness has jeopardized a new business deal, so if Nève acts as his fake fiancée and salvages his reputation, he'll give her fortune enough to start over. Only neither is prepared when very *real* feelings begin to grow between them...

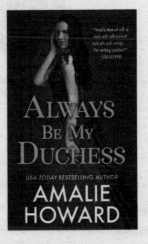

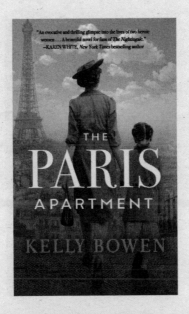

**THE PARIS APARTMENT**
**by Kelly Bowen**

*2017, London:* When Aurelia Leclaire inherits an opulent Paris apartment, she is shocked to discover her grandmother's secrets—including a treasure trove of famous art and couture gowns.

*Paris, 1942:* Glamorous Estelle Allard flourishes in a world separate from the hardships of war. But when the Nazis come for her friends, Estelle doesn't hesitate to help those she holds dear, no matter the cost.

Both Estelle and Lia must summon hidden courage as they alter history—and the future of their families—forever.

### WAKE ME MOST WICKEDLY
#### by Felicia Grossman

To repay his half-brother, Solomon Weiss gladly pursues money and influence—until outcast Hannah Moses saves his life. He's irresistibly drawn to her beauty and wit, but Hannah tells him she's no savior. To care for her sister, she heartlessly hunts criminals for London's underbelly. Which makes Sol far too respectable for her. Only neither can resist their desires—until Hannah discovers a betrayal that will break Sol's heart. Can she convince Sol to trust her? Or will fear and doubt poison their love?